# ALTER EGO

# ALTER EGO

## A JONATHAN STRIDE NOVEL

## BRIAN FREEMAN

Quercus

New York • London

# Quercus

New York • London

© 2018 by Brian Freeman
First published in the United States by Quercus in 2018

ISBN 978-1-68144-129-0

Library of Congress Control Number: 2018931639

Distributed in the United States and Canada by
Hachette Book Group
1290 Avenue of the Americas
New York, NY 10104

This book is a work of fiction. Names, characters, institutions, places, and events are either the product of the author's imagination or are used fictitiously. Any resemblance to actual persons—living or dead—events, or locales is entirely coincidental.

Manufactured in the United States

10 9 8 7 6 5 4 3 2 1

www.quercus.com

*For Marcia*

*Know you? I wonder do I know you? Before I could answer that, I should have to see your soul.*

—OSCAR WILDE, *THE PICTURE OF DORIAN GRAY*

# 1

The man in the Australian oilskin coat and black cowboy hat didn't realize it yet, but fate already had dealt him the thirteenth tarot card. A skeleton on a white horse rode his way, bringing death. He had ninety seconds to live.

He struggled through knee-deep snow past skeletal birches and evergreens that shook their hunched shoulders at him. The bitter, driving wind in his face was so cold, it actually burned. Under the clouds, the night was black, with no moon or stars. He used a flashlight to make his way back to the lonely highway. When he looked behind him, he saw wind and snow filling in his footsteps. Soon there would be no evidence that he'd been here at all.

An owl hooted above him. The bird was close by, but then it lifted invisibly over the high trees as if alarmed by his arrival. Its mournful calls got farther away. Owls were another harbinger of coming death, but he didn't think about that.

He was a summer man in a winter place. It was January in the empty lands northwest of Duluth. The coat he wore would have been fine for a Florida cold front but not for the subzero temperatures here. His leather gloves were unlined. His feet inside his boots were wet from the deep snow. The cowboy hat left his ears exposed, and he wore no scarf over his face.

He'd been outside for half an hour. Skin froze in ten minutes.

The trail back to the road felt endless. He didn't recall traveling so far on his way in, but if you were hiding something you didn't want anyone to find, you had to look for the most remote section of the forest. Adrenaline had propelled him at first, but now he was simply numb. He was ready to get away and go back home to the South. In his imagination, warm sunshine glowed on a long stretch of sand by the still waters of the Gulf.

Sixty seconds remained.

The light of his flashlight finally glinted on his rented Chevy Impala on the shoulder of Highway 48. Its windshield was already dusted over with fresh snow. He trudged the last few steps and climbed inside. He switched on the engine and waited for warm air to blast through the vents. In the mirror, he saw his face, which was mottled white. He left his hat on. He peeled off his gloves, threw them on the seat, and struggled to bend his fingers. He kicked off his boots and rolled off his wet socks. He'd drive barefoot.

The windshield wipers pushed away the snow that had gathered while he was gone. He glanced at the woods from where he'd come and couldn't see his trail in the darkness. A few more minutes, another inch of snow, and the white bed would look virginal again. He drove away fast, kicking up a white cloud behind him. His speed was reckless. The pavement was almost invisible in the blizzard, and the plows wouldn't be out until morning. Even so, he wanted to put as much distance as he could between himself and the place where he'd stopped.

He grabbed his phone from the inside pocket of his coat. The signal was weak here, but he punched a single speed-dial number with his thumb. He'd used the phone only to call that one number. When he got to Minneapolis, he'd find a place to ditch the phone for good. No one would ever find it.

He heard a ringing on the other end. It was the middle of the night, but his contact was waiting for the call.

"It's me," he said. His numb lips slurred the words.

"Any problems?" the person on the other end asked.

"No."

"Where are you?"

"I'm leaving town."

"Okay. Good luck."

That was all. He hung up the phone.

If he'd glanced out the window next to him, he might have seen the skeleton keeping pace with his car and counting off the last few seconds with the bones of its hand. Ten, nine, eight—

Headlights shone in the opposite lane. There were only two vehicles out on the snow-swept road: his Impala and a truck roaring northward toward him.

He leaned forward, squinting.

Something strange was happening. The truck's lights blinked at him. A shadow came and went in front of them. He heard a bass horn, a thud, and a quick screech of tires. His heart pounded, but the truck passed him safely with a shudder of wind. For a millisecond, the deserted highway stretched out in front of him, just wilderness on both sides and snow swirling in his lights like thousands of flies.

He remembered that he was going home.

That was the last conscious thought of his life. In the next instant, his neck snapped and he was dead.

*

Maggie Bei of the Duluth Police zipped her down coat to her chin as she hopped from the driver's seat of her beat-up yellow Avalanche. The jacket draped to her knees. It was bright red, making her body look like a tube of lipstick. She pulled the fleece hood over her head, but the wind chill hit her like a shovel to the face. The air temperature was twelve degrees below zero. In the wind, it felt like forty below.

"Why the hell do we live here?" she asked Sergeant Max Guppo, not hiding her crabbiness.

"Oh, it's not so bad," Guppo replied cheerfully. "A little nippy maybe."

Guppo was as round as he was short, and he had the advantage of 250 pounds of padding on his frame. He seemed blissfully unaware of the cold, although the bulbs on his cheeks looked extra rosy tonight.

The highway around them was closed. Clouds of snow blew past the lights of the emergency vehicles. A trailer truck was parked safely on the shoulder a hundred yards to the north. The Impala, which had spun when the driver lost control, was lodged tail first in the drifts at the base of the highway shoulder. Its windshield was completely shattered.

Maggie could see the forlorn brown carcass of the deer where the first responders had dumped it in the snow after prying it from the front seat of the Impala.

"Tell me again what happened here," she said.

"Freak accident," Guppo replied. "The truck back there hit a deer, and the thing went airborne. Must have been like a missile. The deer landed on the Impala, went through the windshield, and took out the driver. Broke his neck, practically decapitated him. Talk about your bad luck."

Maggie shook her head. "Yikes. Killed by a flying deer two weeks after Christmas. What do you think? Dancer? Prancer? Vixen?"

Guppo choked back a laugh. "I heard the EMTs saying they should stick a red nose on the deer before you got here."

Maggie grinned. She had a well-earned reputation for sarcasm. When you're a forty-year-old detective small enough to buy your clothes in the teen section—and you have to boss around twenty-something Minnesota cops who look like Paul Bunyan—you learn pretty fast to develop a smart mouth.

"Who called in the accident?" she asked.

"The truck driver. He saw the car go off the road in his mirror."

"Is he okay?"

"Fine. The deer barely dented his truck."

"Was he drunk?"

"The deer? I don't think so." Guppo laughed as Maggie's blood-shot eyes narrowed into annoyed little slits. "No, the truck driver was sober."

"Okay, you want to tell me why we're here?" Maggie asked. "This looks like nothing more than a weird traffic accident. I'm guessing there must be some other reason the highway cops called us in."

Guppo nodded. He hoisted a hard-shell plastic case in his gloved hand and set it on the hood of Maggie's Avalanche. "The cops found this case in the snow a few feet from the wreck of the Impala. It must have been ejected through the window when the car went off the shoulder. As soon as they saw what was inside, they called me."

Guppo popped the lid of the case. Inside, nestled in foam cushioning, was a black Glock and a spare ammunition clip.

Maggie leaned forward and gave it a whiff. "This thing's been fired recently."

"Yeah. And it gets more interesting. I checked the guy's pockets after they pulled him out. He had ten thousand dollars in cash wrapped up in a tight roll. His wallet had nothing in it except a Florida driver's license under the name James Lyons at an address in Miami. No credit cards. No other ID. I made a call to the Miami PD to check him out for me. They're supposed to call me back."

"Anything else?"

"He was barefoot. His boots were soaking wet and covered with pine needles. So were the legs of his pants. He'd been walking through the woods not long before the accident."

"In the middle of the night? In a blizzard like this? I don't like that. Have we checked the trunk of the car?"

"No, it's buried in the snow. We won't be able to get to it until we get a tow truck out here."

"What about a cell phone?" Maggie asked.

"The EMTs found it on the floor of the car. The call log shows half a dozen calls to the same Duluth number. That was it, nothing else. I dialed the number. No answer."

"And the car?"

"It was rented ten days ago at the Minneapolis airport. He also had a receipt in his pocket from a cheap place that rents efficiency apartments up on the hill in Hermantown. Paid cash. He's been in town since he rented the car."

Maggie shoved the hood back from her head. The wind made a mess of her black hair. She'd worn bowl-cut bangs for most of her life, but she'd been growing her hair out for six months. Her stylist had added some spiral curls. Now she looked like Lucy Liu if Lucy wore no makeup and hadn't gotten any sleep in days.

She wandered over to the ambulance and gestured for the EMTs to open the rear doors. She clambered inside, where the body of the Impala driver lay under a sheet on a metal gurney. She drew the sheet back to study his face, which was difficult to distinguish because of the dried blood. She could make out scars and a dimpled square jaw. His blondish hair was short and shot through with gray, and it had a ridge where he'd worn a hat. He wasn't old but probably was north of fifty.

"What were you shooting at?" she murmured. Then she stared through the back of the ambulance at the empty forest land that went on for miles. "And what were you doing out here?"

Maggie pulled the sheet back over the body and climbed out of the ambulance. She slid down the slick slope from the highway to the wreck of the Impala, which jutted into the air at a forty-five-degree angle. The front doors were cracked open; the back doors were entombed in drifts. All the windows were shattered and empty. She peered inside and saw that the front seats were covered in glass and blood. Through the back windows, she saw a cowboy hat upside down against the rear window. On the rear floor, she noticed a crumpled piece of newspaper. She reached in through the broken window to grab the paper with her gloved hand. Blood had soaked the pages. When she smoothed out the four-page sheet, she recognized an entertainment tabloid called the *National Gazette*. The newspaper was at least a week old.

"That's what you were reading?" she murmured. "Really?"

She turned over the sheet and saw an article outlined with black marker. The headline read:

NEW DEAN CASPERSON THRILLER
DOGGED BY WINTER WEATHER

The rest of the article was illegible, but Maggie didn't need to read it. She knew all about the film that was being shot on location around Duluth. It was called *The Caged Girl*, and it was based on a series of murders that had taken place in the city more than a decade earlier.

She'd lived the case; she'd been part of it. Of course, in typical Hollywood fashion, the role of the Chinese cop was now a bit part given to a redheaded bombshell. Life was unfair.

She heard the labored breathing of Max Guppo as he slipped down the snowy slope to join her beside the car. She pointed at the article in the tabloid.

Guppo read the headline, too. "You think this is about the movie?"

"Could be."

"You going to call Stride?"

"Sure," she replied. "Why should he get to sleep when we're awake?"

"I've got something else," Guppo added. "I just got a call back from the police in Miami."

"And?"

"The driver's license is for someone named James Lyons, but the real James Lyons died five years ago. Our corpse is a John Doe with a stolen identity. He's some kind of ghost."

# 2

In what felt like an out-of-body experience, Jonathan Stride watched himself sprint toward the hunting lodge on the shore of the small lake. He could see himself from the side, where silver sprays of snow washed across his face. His black-and-gray hair was pushed back by the wind. He could see himself from above, running along the narrow dirt road through ruts of ice. He could see his face screwed up with intensity as he neared the tiny cabin.

There, inside an eight-foot by eight-foot cage, a young woman was near death and running out of time.

It wasn't real, of course.

None of it was real except the Duluth snow. The detective on the road was actually a Hollywood star named Dean Casperson. A camera followed Casperson on railroad tracks built beside the road. A drone filmed him from overhead as he ran. Microphones picked up the sound of his breath and the whistle of the wind. As Stride watched, Casperson reached the wooden door of the shed and ripped it open.

Cut.

End of scene.

The actor, the director, the camera operators, the sound engineers, the gaffers, the grips, the production designers, and the location manager all began to reset for the next take. The crew worked quickly. It was already midafternoon, and the natural light wouldn't last long. Days were short in January, and time was money on a movie set.

*The Caged Girl.*

Inspired by actual events.

Eleven years earlier, Stride had rescued a young woman named Lori Fulkerson from a cage that was almost identical to the one on the set. It had been built by a serial killer named Art Leipold. Lori had been his fourth victim. Stride had been too late to save the three earlier women who had died while Art played his game of cat and mouse with the police.

The movie script took liberties with what had really happened when Stride rescued Lori. He hadn't been alone. Maggie Bei and half a dozen other police officers had stormed the remote hunting lodge with him. The real cabin wasn't anywhere near a lake; it was hidden inside a few acres of forested hunting land. But this was the movies, where reality didn't mean a thing. The only thing that mattered was what looked good on the big screen.

Even so, the Hollywood version made Stride think about the past again.

He hadn't even been forty years old back then. His first wife, Cindy, was still alive. It would be three more years before she died of cancer. He'd just been made the lieutenant in charge of the city's detective bureau that summer. The audio CD that had arrived at his desk on a sticky July day was like a grim welcome to the responsibilities of his new position.

The tape was of a woman breathing raggedly, crying, and banging on the walls for freedom. She said the same four words over and over.

*"Save me, Jonathan Stride."*

That was what made the case so personal. Every victim used his name.

The voice on the tape belonged to a St. Scholastica journalism student named Kristal Beech. She'd gone missing after the evening shift of her job at Maurice's at Miller Hill Mall. Stride and his detectives had analyzed the sound recording for clues to her location. They'd done chemical analyses of the envelope, handwriting, and postage stamp. They'd delved into Kristal's life to find out who could have taken her.

But they failed.

Kristal died of dehydration before they could find her. Stride received a photograph of her body with a message scrawled across the back:

## BETTER LUCK NEXT TIME.

Next time came two months later. Tanya Carter was a twenty-five-year-old waitress at Bellisio's in Canal Park. Stride had received another CD with a message from Tanya: *Save me, Jonathan Stride*. As before, he and his team had no idea where she was being held and no clues about the killer's identity. And as before, they didn't find her.

Better luck next time.

It happened all over again just before Thanksgiving with a thirty-one-year-old publicist for a nonprofit organization named Sally Wills. The third victim.

After that, for six weeks the killer went silent, but they knew he wasn't done. In January, during one of the city's most bitter stretches of cold weather, the next audio CD arrived. This time the woman was Lori Fulkerson, a twenty-two-year-old bookkeeper.

The message was the same: *Save me, Jonathan Stride*.

The only thing that was different was that the killer finally had made a mistake. They found a small broken shard of plastic from a pen in Lori Fulkerson's apartment. The killer must have dropped it, stepped on it, and then tried to pick up the pieces. Maybe he was hurrying because of the cold, but he missed a piece. The fragment of plastic had a partial fingerprint on it, and the fingerprint led them to Art Leipold.

From there, they'd located Art's hunting cabin in the remote woods. That was where they found Lori Fulkerson.

"Brings it all back, doesn't it?" said a voice at his shoulder.

Stride turned and found Chris Leipold standing next to him.

"It does," Stride agreed.

"Is it strange to see yourself in the movies?"

Stride shrugged. "It's not me."

"You know what I mean," Chris said.

"I do, but it must be worse for you."

"Well, the movie's not about Art. It's about you and Lori and the other women. Definitely not Art."

Chris was the screenwriter and executive producer behind *The Caged Girl*. He was also the son of the man behind the crimes, Art Leipold. Chris had been a creative writing student in Duluth during his father's killing spree. He'd sat in court every day as a trove of DNA, fingerprint, and soil evidence made the case against Art. He'd left Minnesota for Los Angeles soon after his father was convicted to get away from the notoriety of being the son of a serial killer. On the West Coast, he'd gotten lucky. He'd written back-to-back screenplays that became indie award winners at Sundance. From that point forward, he'd been in demand.

"I wasn't trying to make peace with my father by making the movie," Chris went on. "I was trying to get inside the heads of people whose lives are affected by someone like him."

"I'm not a fan of people getting inside my head," Stride said.

"That's not exactly news, Lieutenant."

Stride's lips twitched into a smile. He'd resisted Chris's invitation to talk about the case as Chris did the research for the screenplay. He had no interest in having his life dramatized for the world to see. After nine months of playing hard to get, he'd finally relented. Stride's new wife, Serena, had encouraged him to do it. So had Cat Mateo, the teenage girl who lived with them. When Serena and Cat teamed up, Stride found it hard to say no.

So he and Chris had spent a weekend talking about what Stride had gone through as each victim died. Along the way, they'd become friends.

Chris wasn't a big man. He was slight, five foot six, with a narrow face and thinning sandy blond hair. He wore tiny wire-rimmed glasses over his brown eyes that made him look like a scientist rather than a writer. A decade of L.A. weather had thinned his blood. He looked cold even in a heavy down coat and a *Fargo*-style hat with ear flaps.

Stride, by contrast, wore only his decades-old leather jacket and a dark green wool cap that bore the word NORTH in red stitching. Fifty-one years in Duluth had made him oblivious to the frigid temperature.

"I'm glad you decided to check out the filming," Chris went on. "I wasn't sure we were ever going to see you out here."

"Actually, it's not a social call," Stride said.

"Oh? How so?"

Stride peeled off his gloves and took a phone from his pocket. "This is hard to look at," he warned Chris. He found a photograph and enlarged it to show the face on the screen.

Chris took a look, then winced and turned away. "Oh, man. Is that guy dead?"

"Very."

"Who is he?"

"I was hoping you could tell me," Stride said. "It's tough to make out the details of his face in this condition, but I was wondering if you knew him or if he was connected to the film in any way."

Chris steeled himself and took another glance at the photo. "I don't think so. I've never seen him before. Why would you think he's part of the movie?"

"He had an article about the film from the *National Gazette* in his car when we found him."

Chris couldn't hide the distaste on his face. "That rag? Well, we've had one of their reporters nosing around the set to drum up gossip, but the reporter's a woman, not a man. What happened to this guy, anyway? Was he murdered?"

"We're simply trying to identify him."

"Well, I can ask around if you text me the photo. Maybe someone else knows him. You get a lot of hangers-on at every film set, particularly when you've got big-name stars."

"Thanks. I appreciate it."

"Meanwhile, as long as you're here, would you like to meet your alter ego?" Chris asked.

Stride spotted Dean Casperson on the other side of the field, surrounded by an entourage. The actor was drinking from a bottle of Fiji water, and like Stride, he seemed unaffected by the cold. Their eyes met. Casperson knew who he was. The actor lifted the water bottle in a toast. He pushed his cowlick away from his eyes and gave Stride the boyish grin that every moviegoer in the world recognized.

"Sure," Stride said. "Why not?"

*

Dean Casperson.

He'd been one of the biggest box-office draws in the world for almost forty years, ever since his scene-stealing turn in a Robert Altman film as a teenage concert violinist blinded by a blow to the head. He'd left the audience in tears. From that moment forward, he was a star who grew quickly into a legend. Over the years, Casperson had made a specialty of accepting wildly different roles with every new film. It didn't matter whether he was a hero or a villain or whether the film was a thriller or a comedy. He was simply one of those charismatic players who made you not want to look away from the screen.

He was also one of those rare Hollywood actors who was as popular offscreen as he was in his movies. He steered clear of politics. He had an easy laugh and a humble way about him when he appeared on the nighttime talk shows. He'd been married to his high-school sweetheart, Mo, for decades. Casperson had survived three decades in the world's most backstabbing business with a reputation as a nice guy, but that was partly because few people really knew him. He and Mo rarely ventured outside their bubble. They kept a small, tight circle of friends. They lived in Florida, not Malibu. They were careful never to let their public masks slip.

Chris Leipold waved Casperson over, and the seas parted for the actor as he crossed the field toward Stride. He carried an aura that made other people defer to him. Casperson extended his hand as the two men met.

"Lieutenant, it's a pleasure."

Stride shook his hand. "Thank you, Mr. Casperson. I'm sure you hear this all the time, but I'm a fan."

In fact, Stride couldn't remember the last time he'd seen a Dean Casperson movie, but he knew that the expected thing to do with famous people was to stroke their egos. He'd met dozens of actors and singers at Duluth events over the years, and most of them were insecure about their fame.

But not Casperson.

The gleam in the actor's eyes let Stride know that Casperson was well aware that he was being flattered. Obviously, Casperson didn't need anyone pretending to be starstruck around him.

"That's kind of you to say, Lieutenant, but all I do is go out and read lines that other people give me. It's people like you that are the heroes. Police officers. Firefighters. Soldiers. You do the real work."

Stride smiled, because he knew he was being flattered right back. He was cynical enough to wonder whether Casperson was sincere or simply practiced at saying the right things to strangers.

He sized up the man who was playing him in the movies. Casperson was smaller in real life than he appeared on the big screen. Stride was over six feet tall, and Casperson was at least four inches shorter. The actor was several years older than Stride, but he had the Hollywood ability to appear years younger than he was. At fifty-five, he could have passed for forty. Casperson's hair was whatever color and style the movie needed it to be. In this case, it was much like Stride's: wavy, unkempt, and laced with gray. Otherwise, the two men looked nothing like each other. Stride had a weathered face that was like a map of every winter he'd experienced. Casperson's face featured a strong chin, a sharp nose with a bulb at the end, and arresting sky-blue eyes.

"Are you enjoying Duluth?" Stride asked.

"I am, thanks. You have some of the friendliest people around here that I've ever met. I guess that makes up for my balls feeling like ice cubes."

Stride laughed. "Yeah, welcome to January. Where are you staying while you're in town?"

"I rented a little place from one of your docs. It's an area called Congdon Park, I think. Nice. Feels like going back in time. Several of the cast members found places over there."

Stride doubted that any home Casperson had found in Congdon Park was a little place. More likely, it was a sprawling brick estate from the city's glamour days in the previous century.

"We should have a drink sometime," Casperson went on, flashing his grin again. "In fact, we're having a party for the cast and crew this evening at one of the lakefront restaurants. You should come."

"Thanks, but we're in the middle of an investigation right now."

Casperson squeezed Stride's arm in a solid grip. "Sure, of course. The job comes first. Enough small talk; you're a busy man. I appreciate your coming over here so quickly. We're all worried about Haley."

Stride cocked his head in confusion. "Who?"

"Haley. Our intern. Aren't you here about her?"

"Sorry, I'm not."

When Casperson realized that Stride didn't know what he was talking about, the actor's blue eyes shot to Chris Leipold. In that instant, Stride could see an angry flash of the man's power. It was like watching a tiger and realizing that he could eat you whenever he wanted.

"Didn't you call him, Chris?" Casperson asked.

Chris wilted in front of the star. "No. We're still checking around. We didn't want to push the panic button prematurely."

"What's going on?" Stride asked. "Who's Haley?"

Casperson turned his attention back to Stride, and there was concern in his eyes. "Haley Adams. She's a local film student who's been interning with us. She was supposed to be working with my costar, Aimee Bowe, but Haley hasn't shown up at the set for the last two days. That's not like her. We've had people looking for her ever since, but we haven't had any luck. She's missing."

# 3

"I checked the apartment in Hermantown where John Doe was stay-ing," Maggie told Stride as she climbed into the passenger seat of his Ford Expedition. "He was paid up for the rest of the month, but it looks like he decided to leave early. The room was empty, and we found a suitcase in the trunk when we dug the Impala out of the snowbank."

"What was in the suitcase?" Stride asked.

"Clothes. That's all. No personal effects."

"Was there anything else in the trunk?"

"Like a body?" Maggie asked. "No, he didn't make it that easy for us. No body, no blood. But I don't think he was out in the woods doing target practice with his Glock in the middle of a winter storm."

"Did he leave anything behind at the apartment?" Stride asked.

"Nothing. I mean *nothing*. We didn't find so much as a strand of hair in the room. He bleached everything. He even cleaned the drain traps in the sink and shower. This guy was a pro. If that deer hadn't clocked him, he would have disappeared without a trace."

Stride frowned. They had an unidentified dead man with a gun who'd taken pains to leave no evidence behind of who he was or why he was in Duluth. John Doe had all the hallmarks of a paid assassin.

And now they had a missing girl, too.

He was parked on Third Avenue in the Central Hillside area, across the street from the apartment of Haley Adams. He wanted to know whether Haley had any connections to John Doe.

"So who was this guy?" Stride asked.

Maggie shook her head. "We still have no clue about his real identity. I had one of the uniforms drive the DNA and fingerprint samples down to the FBI office in the Cities, along with the Glock. I sweet-talked the Gherkin to see if she could expedite a search through their databases."

Stride's eyebrows arched. "Sweet talk? You and Gayle?"

"Hey, we're friends now."

He suspected that was an exaggeration. Gayle Durkin was an FBI agent and Duluth native who'd worked with his team during the marathon bombing the previous summer. Maggie, who wasn't known for her love of the feds, had nicknamed her the Gherkin, and the name had followed Gayle ever since. Maggie thought it was funny. Gayle didn't.

Maggie was an acquired taste for most people. She was full of sharp edges, and she had almost no life outside work. Stride had hired her nearly twenty years earlier, when she was a young, way-too-formal Chinese immigrant with a criminology degree from the University of Minnesota. She'd loosened up and developed a tart tongue over the years. She'd also nursed a romantic crush on Stride for most of their time together. They'd had a short-lived affair a few years earlier, and Stride still regretted the damage it had caused, like a Lake Superior storm tearing up the boardwalk. The affair had driven Serena out of his life for months, and the inevitable breakup had wounded Maggie much more than she'd let on. Her bravado hid a fragile soul, which Stride knew better than anyone.

In the aftermath, Maggie finally had moved past her feelings for him, but she was still a disaster when it came to relationships. She'd been dating Troy Grange, the head of security at the Duluth Port, for the past eighteen months, but at Christmastime, Troy and Maggie had crashed and burned. She still hadn't told anyone the details of what had happened.

"What about the woods on Lavaque Road near the crash site?" Stride asked. "Any luck searching there?"

Maggie shook her head. "Guppo's been leading teams all day. If John Doe hid a body up there before the accident, we haven't found it. But that's like finding a needle in a haystack. We're using dogs, but the snow's not helping."

"Okay. Let's see if Haley's apartment tells us anything."

Stride got out of the Expedition. It was already night. Darkness fell like a stone during Duluth winters. So did the temperature as soon as the sun went down. The snow had stopped, but the wind lanced his face like the slash of a knife. Maggie grumbled and cursed under her breath. They tucked their chins into their coats as they crossed the street.

They were only a few blocks from Lake Superior, at the intersection of Third Avenue and Fifth Street. During the day, the blue water would have been visible at the bottom of the hill. For a small city, Duluth had numerous distinct neighborhoods, and the Central Hillside area was a low-rent district that drew a lot of police attention during the warmer months. Haley Adams lived in a two-story tan brick building with room for one apartment upstairs and one downstairs. There were two mailboxes hanging on the wall out front. Both were empty. The apartment doorbells had no names, just labels for units 1 and 2.

"Take your pick," Stride said.

Maggie pushed the button for the second-floor apartment. A few seconds later, a male voice crackled through the intercom. "Yeah?"

"Police," Maggie replied. "We're looking for Haley Adams."

"Downstairs."

"Can you let us in?"

The front door buzzed, and the lock clicked open. Stride and Maggie went inside, where it wasn't much warmer than it was outside. A set of wooden stairs led to the second floor in front of them, and a song by Imagine Dragons boomed from an upstairs radio. On their right was a white door that needed paint. Stride knocked sharply.

He called out, "Haley Adams?"

There was no answer. He turned the knob. The door was open.

They went inside carefully. Stride found a light switch that turned on a small overhead dome fixture. There wasn't much to see and no sign of a disturbance. The furniture looked as if it had come with the apartment and had been there for years. The apartment consisted of a living room, a kitchen, and a doorway that led to a small bedroom and bathroom. It was impersonal. No artwork. No books. No pictures. Nothing that said anything about the girl who had been living here.

There was a beat-up oak desk near the window overlooking the street. Maggie began pulling open drawers. Stride checked the kitchen.

"So you met Dean Casperson, huh?" Maggie called to him as they searched.

"I did."

"You know, I always figured Russell Crowe would play you in a movie. Tough. Emotionally sensitive."

"Ha," Stride retorted.

"So what's he like?" Maggie asked.

"Casperson? You'd expect him to be charming, and he is."

"Did you watch them filming?"

"Yeah. Ten seconds of Casperson running across a field. That probably cost a few hundred thousand dollars."

Maggie was quiet for a while as she rifled through the desk drawers, and then she said, "Is this whole thing as hard on you as it is on me?"

Stride closed the refrigerator, which was virtually empty, and turned around. Maggie was staring at him from the other side of the apartment.

"I mean, watching that case come to life again," she went on.

"I know what you mean. Sure it is."

She shook her head. "Art Leipold. It still blows my mind all these years later. We *knew* him."

"We thought we did," Stride said. "We were wrong."

He'd known Art Leipold long before the killings began. When Stride was a young cop in his late twenties, Art was a television reporter and a friend of Stride's partner, Ray Wallace. Art got inside tips from

Ray, so he was in and out of police headquarters all the time. To Stride, the relationship between Art and Ray was always too cozy. They were both cocky bastards who manipulated stories to put pressure on suspects and get TV ratings. But Stride was a junior cop back then, and Ray was the boss. He'd never complained.

Art climbed the media ladder to a gig as one of the anchors on the local morning show. In a town like Duluth, that made him famous. He'd always been arrogant, but he began to get drunk on his celebrity.

That was when women began dying.

"Anything in the desk?" Stride asked, joining Maggie on the other side of Haley's apartment.

"No; it's been cleaned out," Maggie said. "This looks like John Doe's place. Either Haley skipped town or someone else got here first."

Stride wandered into the girl's bedroom. Without light, he almost reached for his gun as he found himself staring at a human figure hidden behind the bedroom door. Then he realized it was a mannequin. When he switched on a lamp, he saw the white statue clearly. She was sculpted in a provocative pose and dressed in a negligee, with a blond wig hanging down to the small breasts.

He opened the closet door. Inside, on hangers and shelves, he found a wild array of clothes and wigs that would have suited everyone from a schoolteacher to a stripper.

Maggie joined him and whistled as she assessed the wardrobe. "That's quite the collection. Haley liked to play dress-up?"

"Apparently."

"Was she an extra on the movie?"

"Chris didn't mention it. These clothes don't look like anything they'd use in the film."

Stride used his phone to take pictures of the clothes and the mannequin. "I'll text this to Serena and see if she can get some answers for us. I asked her to go to the cast party tonight and find out more about Haley."

Maggie mocked the sexy pose of the mannequin. "So you're sending your happily married wife to a Hollywood party, and meanwhile, your unattached partner gets to play with dolls?"

Stride grinned. "None of those actors would be safe around you, Mags."

"That's what I was counting on."

The two of them quickly checked the rest of the bedroom. Stride opened each drawer in a heavy oak dresser against the wall and found nothing but jeans, sweaters, and a few button-down shirts. The clothes were ordinary compared with what Haley kept in the closet. In the bathroom, he found shampoo, conditioner, toothpaste, makeup, and some over-the-counter pain relievers, but there were no prescription medications and nothing for birth control.

Haley was a mystery. There was nothing in the apartment to tell them where she was, who she was, or whether she was alive or dead.

He was about to leave when he noticed a metal wastebasket shoved against the tall oak dresser. The plastic bag inside the wastebasket was empty. Looking back to the living room, he noticed that Haley's desk was in a direct line ten feet away. There was no other garbage can near the desk. The only other trash container he'd seen was in the kitchen, and that one was empty, too.

"How good a shot do you think she was?" Stride asked.

"What?"

He grabbed a blank piece of paper from the notebook in his jacket, crinkled it into a ball, and shot it across the room like a free throw. He deliberately aimed high. The paper rolled across the varnished surface of the dresser and disappeared in the narrow gap between the dresser and the wall.

Maggie knew what he was thinking. She dragged the dresser away from the corner, and they found a collection of garbage on the carpet behind it. Tissues. Wadded-up paper from yellow pads. Restaurant receipts. Stride bent down with a gloved hand and began sifting through the trash. Most of it told him nothing. Then he picked up a crumpled delivery receipt from China Cafe. When he smoothed it out, he glanced at the details and stopped.

"Hang on."

"What's up?" Maggie asked.

Stride pointed at the receipt. "It's Thursday now. This order was from five days ago. Saturday night. The name says Haley Adams, but the delivery address isn't her apartment. She had the food sent somewhere else."

Maggie checked the address. "That's over near Congdon Park. Isn't that where some of the cast members rented houses?"

Stride nodded. "Maybe Haley Adams has been sleeping somewhere else while the film crew is in town."

# 4

Serena Stride parked on the shoulder of the scenic highway between Duluth and the town of Two Harbors. The black water of Lake Superior loomed only steps away, where a snow-covered trail led down to the beach. They were a dozen miles north of the city. The highway was dark and empty through the long stretch of forest, but the Lakeside Café glowed with light across the street. Serena could hear the chatter of voices floating from inside. The cast and crew of *The Caged Girl* were at the party.

Beside her, Cat Mateo could barely contain her excitement.

"You are the best!" Cat exclaimed. "I can't believe I get to meet these people!"

Serena smiled at the girl's enthusiasm. She remembered what it was like to be a teenage girl meeting celebrities. She'd felt the same way when she moved to Las Vegas, where every party had someone famous on the guest list. She also remembered, as a cop, how easily those parties could get out of control.

"Do I need to review the list of noes?" she asked Cat.

The seventeen-year-old rolled her eyes and chanted the list like a mantra. "No drinking, no swearing, no drugs, no sex."

"And you stay inside the restaurant, and you don't leave with anyone except me," Serena added.

"Yes, Mom," Cat groaned.

The girl no longer called her that ironically; she meant it. Jonny was always Stride to Cat, but over the last year Serena had become Mom to her. She liked it that way. Serena was unable to have kids of her own, and she'd made peace with that long ago. But it also made her grateful that Cat had become a part of their lives. She and Jonny both loved this girl as much as if she were their own daughter.

That didn't mean it was easy. Two years earlier, when they'd rescued her, Cat had been a pregnant girl on the streets, dabbling in drugs and prostitution. Since then, two steps forward with her had always been followed by one step back. But Cat was a different person now. She visited with the parents who'd adopted her son every week. She was razor-sharp in school and was thinking about college. She still hung out with people Serena didn't trust—particularly a slick young con artist named Curt Dickes—but Cat had matured into a serious, determined young woman.

Even so, a party like this was, well, catnip to a teenager. And Cat had tumbling chestnut hair and a sculpted, angular beauty that Hollywood types were bound to notice. Her Hispanic roots gave her golden skin, and her face was an alluring combination of innocent sweetness in her smile and mature sophistication in her dark eyes. When she wanted to, she could easily look ten years older than she was.

The two women got out of Serena's Mustang. They were dressed to impress, and the long walk in heels to the restaurant door was icy and cold. They held on to each other to avoid stumbling. A security guard was at the door, and Serena showed him her badge and gave him both of their names. Stride had called ahead to clear them, and the security guard held the door as they breezed inside.

The room was packed shoulder to shoulder. Serena saw a dozen faces she recognized from television and movies. Even among the strangers, the men and women all looked too beautiful to be ordinary human beings. They were dressed as if they'd stepped off a runway. She had to remind herself that this wasn't Los Angeles. It was still Duluth.

Cat grabbed Serena's bare arm as her eyes soaked in the ambience. "Oh. My. God."

"It is pretty cool," Serena admitted.

"I suppose they wouldn't like it if I streamed this on Facebook Live, huh?"

"Probably not."

"Can I mingle?"

"Sure. Go mingle. Remember the rules."

Serena watched Cat put on her game face. The teenager squared her shoulders, threw her hair back, and melted into the crowd as if she belonged there. Serena felt a twinge of anxiety, thinking about her own teen years in Las Vegas. Back then, she'd run away from the abuse she'd suffered at home. She'd been pregnant, like Cat, but she'd chosen an abortion, which had gone badly. Those were dark days for her. She wanted a different life for this girl.

"Hello, Serena."

She hunted through the faces in front of her and saw Chris Leipold smiling from behind a can of Bent Paddle Kanu. He was one of the only men in the crowd in a suit and tie. His wispy hair was greased down. In her heels, Serena towered over him. He approached her and kissed her cheek.

"Chris, it's good to see you again," Serena said. "How's the filming going?"

"It's fine when the weather cooperates. No one on the crew appreciates my interest in location shooting at this time of year. They'd rather be in Vancouver."

"Well, so would I right now," Serena admitted.

"Is Stride coming?"

"No, sorry; he asked me to fill in."

"Thanks again for getting him to agree to work with me. I know that wasn't easy."

"Jonny's a private guy," Serena said. "But the money you're paying will put Cat through college, so how could we say no?"

"Have you found out anything more about our missing intern, Haley Adams?" Chris asked.

Serena shook her head. "That's why I'm here."

"Aimee Bowe may be able to tell you more."

"Aimee is costarring with Dean Casperson?"

"Yes, she's 'the caged girl.' In a lot of ways, it's her film. Aimee worked with Haley a lot. She probably knows her better than anyone else on the set."

"I'll talk to her. When did you last see Haley?"

"I've asked around, and it looks like no one has seen her since some-time Tuesday morning. Oh, and I ran the photo of that other man past several people here. I haven't found anyone who knew who he was."

"I appreciate your help."

"Of course. Enjoy the party."

Chris disappeared with a little wave.

Serena worked her way down the long, narrow restaurant. The dining room was paneled in light oak and had been cleared of tables. Despite the frigid outside air, the crowded bodies made it warm inside. She wore a knee-length navy blue dress that she hadn't put on in years, and she was pleased that it still fit. It showed off her statuesque body. Her long black hair caressed her white shoulders. If anyone looked closely at her legs, they would see the mottled scars she'd suffered in a fire several years earlier. But time had taken away her self-consciousness about how she looked and who she was. She still had her Vegas attitude.

Several men hit on her. The badge on her belt didn't dissuade them. She laughed at the idea of any of these men coming face to face with Jonny. In each group, she asked about Haley Adams, but no one had anything helpful to say. They didn't know anything about Haley's background. They didn't know if she'd grown up in Duluth or where she had gone to school. They didn't seem to know who'd hired her for the film crew. It was as if Haley had shown up out of nowhere and started working.

So many people said the exact same thing that Serena began to wonder if a script had been passed around the party: *When the police ask you about Haley Adams, this is what you say.*

The only answer that varied from person to person was the one thing that should have stayed the same. When Serena asked them to provide a physical description of Haley, their replies varied. Some said her hair was short; some said long. Some said blond. Some said redhead. Some said her eyes were blue; some said green. Some said freckles; some said clear skin. It was as if they'd all met a different girl each day.

Serena didn't understand it.

After an hour asking questions and getting nowhere, she finally spotted the woman she'd been trying to find all evening. Aimee Bowe stood off by herself near the windows that looked out on the dark forest. She held a glass of white wine. Serena recognized her because she'd seen the actress in a comedy the previous year in which she'd done a memorably drunk, half-dressed version of the Macarena. Her role in Duluth was 180 degrees from that. She was playing a character inspired by Lori Fulkerson, the last of Art Leipold's victims.

Lori was the woman Stride had rescued from inside the box.

Aimee wasn't tall, but she had presence, the way every actor did. In a profession in which beauty was commonplace, she had a unique look that made her stand out. Her nose was a little long, her forehead a little high, and her chin a little pronounced. She had penetrating and intelligent blue eyes, and one looked slightly larger than the other. The cascading blond hair she'd worn in other roles had been cut into short spikes and dyed to a squirrel brown for this role.

As Serena approached her, Aimee's eyes made a quick assessment, the way one beautiful woman typically did to another. Her eyes stopped when she saw Serena's badge. The actress's face immediately turned cautious.

"Ms. Bowe? My name is Serena Stride. I'm a detective with the Duluth Police. I was hoping to talk to you about Haley Adams."

Aimee didn't look surprised. "Have you found her?"

"No, we haven't. Not yet."

The actress took a sip of wine and then said, "I don't think you will."

Serena gave her a curious look. "Why do you say that?"

"You'll think this is very Los Angeles of me," Aimee replied, "but sometimes I sense things."

"Sense things? What do you mean?"

"I guess some people would call it psychic," Aimee said. "That's not the word I use, but it's close enough."

"I see."

"No, you don't. That's okay. Anyway, I sense something about Haley."

"Which is?"

"She's dead," Aimee said.

Serena tried to keep the skepticism off her face. "Can you think of a reason why something would have happened to her?"

"Maybe because she was a spy," Aimee replied.

Serena blinked. "I'm sorry?"

"She was here to spy on us. I don't know why or who sent her. Don't misunderstand; I liked her a lot. She was sweet and very smart. Too smart to be an intern. But she was always watching. She never missed a thing. And then there were the disguises, too."

"Disguises?"

"She looked different every time she came on the set. Different hair, different type of clothes, even different eye color and skin makeup. Half the time, I didn't know it was her until she introduced herself. She said she did it because she was only comfortable talking to people when she was pretending to be someone else. I can relate to that as an actor. But I think Haley didn't want anyone around here to know who she really was."

"I heard she was a film student at UMD," Serena said.

Aimee's lips bent into a smile, but without showing her teeth. "I doubt that's true."

"If you thought she wasn't who she claimed to be, why didn't you blow the whistle on her?" Serena asked.

"I told you, I liked her. And it wasn't my problem. She wasn't spying on me."

"Then who?"

Aimee took a moment to reply. "I have no idea."

Serena could see that the actress knew more than she was saying. Psychic or not, Aimee was obviously an intelligent and intuitive woman.

"I feel you're not being completely candid," Serena said.

"I'm sorry, but I just met you."

"Yes, but you also said you liked Haley Adams a lot. If you know something that might help us find her, I wish you'd tell me. You may not know me, but you can trust me."

This time Aimee's smile showed her perfect teeth, as if Serena had said something very funny. "I don't think you understand the people who have invaded your city. We play by West Coast rules. Don't ever trust us and don't ever ask us to trust you."

Serena rarely felt naive, but she found herself oddly outclassed by this woman, as if she were foundering in deep water because of a twenty-seven-year-old actress. She didn't know what to say.

"It's okay if you think I'm a condescending little bitch," Aimee went on more playfully. "You wouldn't be the first."

"That's not what I was thinking," Serena replied.

"Well, I deserve it. Anyway, I did like Haley, but I really don't know what happened to her. And I'd rather not speculate about why she was here. Shooting off your mouth in this business gets you into trouble, and I had to work hard to get this role."

"Why is that?" Serena asked. "You're very good."

"Have you seen my other roles?"

"I saw—"

"The Macarena bit. Yeah, I know; everybody did. You do what you do to pay the bills, but good luck convincing anyone you're serious after you jiggle your tits in a Judd Apatow flick."

"I have no trouble realizing you're serious," Serena told her.

"That's sweet of you to say."

Serena smiled. "It's called Minnesota nice."

"Yes, I've heard about that. I'm afraid there's no Hollywood equivalent."

"I just mean you really can trust me."

"I'll do my best," Aimee said, "even if it goes against my nature. You know, if you're interested, I'm filming tomorrow. We've rented a warehouse down near the port. You should come watch."

"I'd like that."

"I'll make sure you're cleared," Aimee told her.

"Thanks. I'll be there."

"May I ask a favor in return?" she said.

"What is it?"

"You're married to Lieutenant Stride, right? The man Dean's role is based on?"

"Yes."

"I wonder if you could ask him to talk to Lori Fulkerson for me. My role is based on her experience, and I want to know more about what she went through when she was in the cage. She won't take my calls. I get it, she doesn't want to go through the pain again, but I need her. I was hoping your husband might be able to persuade her to talk to me."

"I'll mention it to him, but honestly, I don't think he'll do it. I wasn't around for what happened back then, but I know it was emotional for everyone. I can't imagine he'd put any pressure on Lori. If I was a victim, I wouldn't want to talk about it."

"I understand. I appreciate your trying. And listen, for what it's worth, there's one more thing I can tell you about Haley Adams."

"Is it something you know or something you sense?" Serena asked.

"It's something I sense, but it's important."

"Okay. What is it?"

"I'm pretty sure her name wasn't Haley," Aimee said.

# 5

In less than an hour at the party, Cat had twelve offers of drinks, seven offers of drugs, two hands on her ass, and one marriage proposal from a drunk fifty-nine-year-old who said he was something called a key grip. She decided it was one of the best evenings of her life.

Then it got even better.

As she tried to decide which actor's clique to crash next, a man bumped into her near the restaurant entrance. He was in the process of slipping on his heavy coat. She heard an apology from a familiar voice and found herself staring up into the electric eyes of Dean Casperson.

Her studied maturity went right out the window, and she was nothing more than a teenager with a crush. "Oh! It's you! I can't even—wow! Mr. Casperson!"

She knew he had been approached like this a million times in his life, but she still went weak in the knees when he said, "Call me Dean."

"You are so amazing. I just love you."

"That's very sweet of you. I'm lucky to have good people around me when I make movies. And who are you? Are you with the film? I can't believe that, because I'm sure I'd remember your face."

"Really? Oh, no, no, no, I'm not. Just a civilian. I mean, a Duluthian. I'm sorry, I sound like an idiot."

"You don't. I promise. What's your name?"

"Cat."

He unleashed his smile on her like a nuclear weapon. "Cat as in meow?"

She couldn't seem to stop giggling. "Yes, as in meow."

"Well, meow, Cat. It was a pleasure meeting you. Maybe we'll run into each other again. You know, I meet a lot of pretty young people in this business, but I can honestly tell you that you're one of the most beautiful women I've met in a long time. You are a rare prize; remember that."

Cat could feel her cheeks burning red. She tried to say something, anything, but her tongue was tied. Casperson winked at her, and then he was gone. He swept through the restaurant door as two people held it open and two others followed him outside. The cold air blew inside to diffuse the heat she felt. She watched him go and put both hands over her face.

"He's smooth, isn't he?"

Cat turned around. A man stood near her with a lowball drink in his hand and a grin that was much like Dean Casperson's, only more cynical. He actually looked a lot like Casperson, but he was at least fifteen years younger and far less polished. Even so, he was cute. He had black hair and a muscular body, with hawkish pale eyes and a square chin. He wore an untucked Tommy Bahama shirt decorated with blue palm trees and glistening black slacks.

Cat stared at him. "I'm sorry, what?"

"Dean. He's smooth as peanut butter. You can't help but love him. Of course, I take the punches, not him."

"What do you mean?"

The man put his hand out, and Cat shook it. His hands were rougher and more callused than the others she'd shaken this night. "My name is Jack Jensen. Jungle Jack is what people call me. I'm Dean's stunt double. You see him take a header from a window? That's me."

"That's very cool," Cat said.

"Mind you, I'm just the muscle. Acting is in the face, and Dean works his face like he's some kind of concert pianist. I'm in awe of what he can do."

"Me, too. I think he's great."

"He brought me into this business. He's my best friend in the world." Jungle Jack snaked closer, and Cat felt herself flushing again under his high-wattage smile. "He has an eye for women, too. He was absolutely right about you, you know. You are stunning."

"Really?"

"Really. I don't see you with a drink in your hand. Do you want one?"

Cat had been good all evening. She remembered the list of noes, and *no drinking* was one of them, but this was a party. She was in a crowd of people. She really didn't see the harm in it. She looked around to make sure Serena wasn't watching, and then she said, "Um, yeah, why not?"

"Champagne?"

"Oh, definitely, yeah."

Jack didn't leave her side. He simply snapped his fingers, and a waiter appeared by magic with a silver tray, and Jack grabbed one of the crystal glasses that was nearly fizzing over with champagne. He put it in her hand and then clinked his lowball glass against hers.

"To the prettiest girl here," he said.

"What? No way." Cat blushed. She took a sip, and it was really, really good champagne.

"So what brings you to the party, Cat?" Jack asked.

"I came with my—I came with a friend. A woman."

"Yeah? A friend? Are you party models? Because if you're getting paid to dress up the place, believe me, you're doing your job."

"Oh, no, nothing like that. I've done that, though. I mean, not at parties like this, but you can make some real money." She was saying way too much and talking way too fast. She realized that she'd already finished the first bubbling glass of champagne in a couple of swallows and that Jack had put another one in her hand. It went down as easily as Sprite.

"I bet you can," Jack told her. "Make money, that is. You wouldn't believe what the girls make in L.A."

"Really? How much?"

"Oh, thousands. Easy."

"No kidding? For one party?"

"The stunners like you? Absolutely. And that can lead to magazine gigs, too. I can pass your name along to the right people if you want. You know, if you ever want to visit the Coast."

"I do!"

"Just give me your number. Maybe we can hook up while I'm in town and talk about it some more."

"Wow, okay. Sure, it's—" Cat was so excited that she was having a hard time remembering her phone number.

Then a voice interrupted them. A subzero, furious voice.

"Let me help you out," Serena said, clamping Jungle Jack's shoulder like a vise and digging in her long nails. "Her number is 218-F-U-C-K-O-F-F. And she is *seventeen years old.*"

Jack looked at Serena, saw her badge, and paled. The blood disappeared from his face. Cat knew men well enough to know that the blood had probably vanished from other places, too.

"Hey, I'm sorry," he murmured. Then he tried to recover smoothly. He brushed back his hair and used his charm on Serena. Cat could have told him it was a losing effort. "Really, officer, I apologize. I had no idea about this young woman's age. It was an honest mistake."

Serena measured out her words one by one. "*Did—you—put —anything—in—her—drink?*"

"No, no way. Absolutely not." His composure faltered again.

"I'm going to have her tested. If I find any date rape drugs, I will be back to put you in a cell. Do you understand me?"

"Completely," Jack said.

"I don't want you ever speaking to her again. Not one word. Got it?"

"Got it."

Cat didn't have time to say anything before Serena grabbed her by the wrist and dragged her out the front door of the restaurant into the frigid air. The steam coming from Serena's mouth as she breathed could well have been smoke. She yanked Cat through the parking lot toward the Mustang and didn't say a word. Cat knew she'd screwed up. It always happened this way. She got carried away in the moment and went back to being a stupid girl from the street.

"Serena," she said.

"Don't talk."

"Serena."

"I said don't talk. Don't say anything."

"*Mom*, please. All I want to say is you really kick ass."

Serena stopped dead in the middle of the highway and looked up at the stars. Cat could see her breathing in and out and shaking her head. For all the bad things she'd done in the past, she wasn't sure she'd ever seen Serena so mad. Then, out of nowhere, Serena reached out with her long arms and pulled her into a fierce hug. She whispered in Cat's ear. She was still angry, but her voice was soft.

"I need you to listen to me, Catalina."

Cat was shocked. Serena almost never called her that.

"Hey, I know I blew it," Cat said.

Serena was still whispering. "Yes, you did, but that's not what I want you to hear. Somebody told me something important tonight, and now I'm telling you the same thing. These people from the movies are so outside our world, they might as well be from another solar system. *Don't trust anything they tell you.*"

\*

Stride found the house in the Congdon Park neighborhood where Haley Adams had ordered a delivery of Chinese food. It wasn't what he'd been expecting.

The house was on the sharp slope of a wooded neighborhood along Hawthorne Road just north of Fourth Street. The winter trees were bare, making it easy to see the upscale homes built on huge lots. The house was made of red brick, and all the lights were off. The sidewalk and driveway hadn't been plowed from the overnight storm, and the snow throughout the yard showed nothing but rabbit tracks. The house looked unoccupied.

"This doesn't look right," Stride said. "No one's staying here."

He checked the number on the address he'd written down, but this was the place listed on the receipt. Even so, it obviously wasn't being used by anyone from the movie.

"I think I know this place," Maggie said. "Gorgonzola lives here."

Stride chuckled. "Mags, you really need to dial it back on the nicknames."

"Hey, Troy came up with that, not me. The guy's name is George N. Zola. He used to be an exec at the port, but he retired last spring. Troy and I went to a going-away party here at the house."

There was a long pause between them after Maggie mentioned Troy Grange. The name slipped easily from her mouth, but then he could see her face twitch unhappily as she thought about a relationship that had turned sour. It was a shame. Stride liked Troy. He'd thought Maggie had finally found someone for the long haul.

Stride squinted at the house through the darkness. He realized his eyes were becoming a casualty of his age. His night vision wasn't what it once had been. "Does Zola still live here?"

"I think he winters in Scottsdale," Maggie said.

"Well, if the place is empty, what was Haley Adams doing here?"

They both got out of the Expedition into the street. The air was cold, and the night was quiet. Stride trudged up the long sidewalk through the deep snow with Maggie following him. Tall trees rose around them, sheltering the house. They flushed a rabbit from the bushes, and it scampered away. At the front door, Stride rang the bell, but he knew that no one would answer. The house was clearly empty.

"Let's check around back," he said.

"Yeah, because my feet aren't wet enough," Maggie replied.

They went down into the snow, which was deeper in the yard, where it had been gathering with every storm since November. Stride followed the brick walls of the house to the other side, which butted up against a dense patch of woodland. Near the line of trees, he saw pockmarks in the snow that the latest storm hadn't filled completely.

Footsteps.

Someone had made their way toward the Zola yard via the forest and then crossed to the rear wall. The back of the house was lined with windows. As they got closer, Stride saw that one of the windows on the four-season porch had been shattered and then covered with plywood and duct tape on the outside.

He shone his flashlight through the other windows.

"Someone broke in here," he said. "I can see glass on the floor."

"Do we check it out?"

Stride nodded. "Haley could be inside."

Carefully, he peeled away the strand of tape and removed the piece of wood covering the window. The lock was already undone. He pushed open the window and helped Maggie squeeze through the frame onto the porch. When she was inside, she unlocked the rear door for him, and he joined her. They listened for noise, but the house was dead quiet. The interior smelled musty from being shut up for months.

"Haley?" he called.

There was no answer.

Slowly, they made their way deeper into the house. Other than the broken glass at the rear window, there were no signs of trespassers or vandals. Everything looked undisturbed. Stride passed through a formal dining room and noticed a bureau stocked with expensive crystal. The artwork and sculpture decorating the house were expensive.

"If Haley broke in here, she wasn't trying to rip them off," Stride said.

"And I wouldn't order chow mein while I was doing it," Maggie added.

They reached a dark wooden staircase that led to the upper floors of the house. Stride called out again. "Haley Adams? Haley, are you up there?"

No one replied. He climbed the steps, which creaked under his boots, and began examining the upstairs bedrooms. They hadn't been used recently. The beds were made, and a thin layer of dust had settled on the furniture. He and Maggie took the rooms one by one, and then they found a last set of stairs that led to a finished attic below the sharp peak of the roof.

That was obviously where Haley Adams had been hiding. She'd spent a lot of time there.

Stride's flashlight revealed a sleeping bag unrolled on the hardwood floor. The overflowing plastic garbage can included empty containers of pop and Chinese food. There were movie magazines on the floor.

He saw a MacBook charging cable plugged into the wall, but the computer was nowhere to be found.

"What the hell was she up to?" Maggie asked.

He directed his flashlight at the tall, narrow windows overlooking the dense woods to the south. There the beam illuminated a tripod and a sleek high-powered telescope pushed close to the glass. A stool was placed in front of it where the viewer could sit and examine the stars.

"That looks like a hell of a telescope," Maggie said. "Pretty fancy equipment for a college girl living on pizza and moo shu."

Stride walked over to the window. The telescope wasn't pointed up at the stars. It peered through the naked winter tree branches at the next house down on Hawthorne Road.

"She wasn't interested in astronomy," he said.

He bent down and brought his face close to the eyepiece. A bright world shot into focus. He was staring through the narrow gap of heavy curtains at the bedroom window of a house fifty yards away. The lights were on. He could see ornate, expensive furniture.

"I wouldn't figure this girl for a Peeping Tom," Maggie said.

Stride shrugged. "The question is what she was looking at."

As he asked the question, the telescope answered it for him.

A man walked into the bedroom in perfect view. He had his lips clamped around a cigar, and as Stride watched, the man tilted his head back and blew a smoke ring into the air.

It was Dean Casperson.

# 6

"Thanks for meeting me on short notice, Chris," Stride said.

Chris Leipold shrugged and drank from the bottle of beer in front of him. He gave Stride a mellow smile. His tie was loose, and his suit coat was draped over the chair next to him. "Why not? No one in L.A. ever says, 'One more drink? Oh, no, really, I couldn't.'"

They were in the upstairs bar at Grandma's restaurant in Canal Park. In January, the midevening drinkers were mostly locals, not tourists. Frost clouded the windows of the glassed-in patio, giving a hazy glow to the lights of the hotels outside. Lake Superior was a vast dark stain beyond the city's boardwalk.

While Chris drank beer, Stride drank coffee. He could see that Chris was a different man when he was away from the set and the movie stars. More of his Duluth roots came out. His Minnesota accent slipped back into his voice. You could take the boy out of the Midwest, but you couldn't take the Midwest out of the boy.

"It freaks me out when I come back to Duluth," Chris reflected in a slightly drunken monologue. "Seeing the old places. Seeing old school buddies from Denfeld. Of course, no one knows what to say to me anymore. Some of them think I'm a stuck-up alien because I live on the Coast. Some think I must be homicidal because I'm Art's son.

One of these days I'm going to wise up and remember that I just don't belong here anymore. It's all in my past."

Except it wasn't in the past. Not by a long shot. Stride knew that, but he let Chris get his frustrations out.

"And yeah, I know, it's my fault," Chris went on. "I did it to myself. I wrote the movie. I pushed to get the filming done here. Maybe you're right, Lieutenant. Maybe this really is all about Art. I told myself all along that it wasn't, but here I am. I'm right back where the son of a bitch wanted me to be."

"No matter what he did, Art was still your father," Stride said.

Chris took off his wire-rimmed glasses and cleaned them and positioned them on his face again. His brown eyes glistened. "I know. I'm stuck with that. When my mom called to say that he'd hanged himself, I actually cried. Not for long. One burst of tears and I was done. Mom didn't cry at all. She knew he was a bastard long before the rest of us did. She was smart enough to get out of that marriage years ago."

Stride kept silent. He hadn't liked Art, not from the very beginning, but he didn't need to say so.

"It goes without saying," he told Chris, "but I'll say it anyway. You're not your father."

"Maybe so, but it's hard living with bad genes."

"Art was careless about people's lives long before he became a killer," Stride said. "I saw him report stories that were reckless and wrong, but he never seemed to have any regrets about the collateral damage. That's the kind of man he was. He didn't have a conscience. But it's *not* the kind of man you are. Anyone can see that in your movies."

Chris picked up his beer bottle and then put it back down without drinking. "Well, thank you for that."

"It's true."

"I know. You're right. Sorry for pissing and moaning about my family tree. Generally, I don't do that. I think it's because I'm back home. You know, I did something last week that I haven't done in years. I went out to see the cabin in the woods where Art brought all the victims. I guess I wanted to see it before we started filming."

"There's not much left out there," Stride said. "Somebody torched the cabin years ago."

"Yeah. Good riddance. People still go out to see it, though. Did you know that? There were footprints in the snow everywhere. It must be some kind of morbid tourist attraction."

"The movie's been in the news," Stride replied. "There have been a lot of stories about the murders. People are curious."

"So it's my fault again," Chris said with a wry smile. He put both hands flat on the table and shook himself to clear his head. He made the knot of his tie a little tighter as if it were time for business. "Well, anyway. I'm sure you didn't call to listen to me go on about Art. I saw Serena at the party tonight."

"I know."

"I heard about Jack hitting on that teenage girl who lives with you guys. Sorry about that. I'm glad Serena intervened. You get something of an entitlement culture with celebrities. I'm not defending it or defending Jack. I'm just saying it is what it is. You might want to keep your girl away."

"Oh, believe me. We will."

Chris stared at his beer bottle again as if it were calling to him. He tilted it to his lips and finished it and wiped his mouth. Then he waved at the waitress to order another. "Do you know anything more about what happened to Haley Adams?" he asked.

"That's why I wanted to talk to you. The more we learn about Haley, the more questions we have."

"There are rumors flying around the set, you know," Chris said.

"Like what?"

"People are saying she's dead. Is that true?"

"I hope not," Stride replied.

"Do you have any reason to think she might be?"

"For now, we just want to find her."

"You guys seem awfully interested in an intern who simply stopped showing up for work," Chris pointed out. "That makes me think there's something more going on here."

"Nothing that I can talk about," Stride said.

Chris pursed his lips and nodded. "Okay. I get it. What do you want to know?"

"Who hired Haley to work on the crew? How did she get the job?"

"The production manager hires local film students as interns. It's pretty common. They're usually cheap and enthusiastic. Haley was the best of the bunch. Mature. Reliable. It was strange, though. For a UMD student, she didn't know much about Duluth."

"What do you mean?" Stride asked.

"Being from Duluth myself, I made it a point to be friendly with the local kids. I talked to them when I could. Last week I was talking to Haley, and I made some offhanded joke about lefse. She didn't know what it was. I laughed. I said, 'How can you grow up in Minnesota and not know what lefse is?'"

"What did she say?"

"She said she's from Florida, not Minnesota. She came to Duluth to go to college. Apparently, one of her high school teachers grew up here and was telling her what a great area it is."

Stride frowned. "Okay. Maybe."

"Yeah, maybe. The thing is, the next day I took some of the crew across the bridge to get burgers at the Anchor Bar. Haley went along and made a comment about never having been there. I mean, really? A UMD senior who has never been to the Anchor Bar? Hell, I was thrown out of there twice before the end of my freshman fall semester."

"So you think she's not who she said she was?"

"It raises some red flags," Chris said. "It makes me wonder whether she was telling us the truth about her background."

Stride eased back in the chair and drank his coffee, which was getting cold. "Odd question, but can you think of any reason Haley would have been spying on Dean Casperson?"

Chris stared at him. "Was she?"

Stride waited a moment and then said, "It looks that way."

"What kind of spying do you mean?"

"Focusing a high-powered telescope on his bedroom window," Stride said.

Chris's brown eyes widened. "Wow. That's disappointing. I thought better of the girl than that. But yeah, that kind of stuff happens all the time. It's a real problem during location shooting, when celebrities don't have the same privacy protections they do at the studio."

"What would someone be looking for?" Stride asked.

"Anything. Sometimes it's paparazzi trying to get candid photos they can sell. There's big money in that. Sometimes it's tabloid reporters looking for gossip and dirt. They'll spy, bribe, hunt through garbage, whatever it takes. You already mentioned something about the *National Gazette* today, didn't you? Believe me, this kind of crap is their specialty."

Stride thought about the possible motives. Photos. Gossip. Dirt. Scandal. That would explain Haley Adams peering through the bedroom window at Dean Casperson. It didn't explain why she was missing. It also didn't explain John Doe and the recently fired Glock.

"Have there been any leaks about the film or the cast?" he asked.

"There are always leaks."

"Anything serious or embarrassing?"

Chris shook his head. "Nothing out of the ordinary. The weather has put us behind schedule and hurt our budget, but that's par for the course. I don't get too worried if something like that shows up in *Variety*."

"What about other problems? Things that you wouldn't want to see in a tabloid headline."

Chris hesitated. "I'm sure I don't know half the crap that goes on when the cameras are off. And I don't ask."

"That seems like a cautious response, Chris."

"Well, filming a movie is like a nonstop high school dance. There are rumors, fights, hookups, romances, parties, breakups. Most of the time, you simply try to drag the project across the finish line before complete chaos ensues. By that standard, things have gone pretty smoothly so far."

Stride heard something in Chris's voice that hadn't been there before. It was an airy lightness that sounded forced and insincere. He wasn't talking like a Minnesotan anymore. He was keeping secrets.

"There's something you're not telling me," Stride said.

Chris took a long time to answer. "Okay, you're right, but it has nothing to do with Haley."

"Tell me anyway."

Chris sighed. His mouth squeezed into an unhappy frown. He played with the beer bottle between his fingers. "One of the other interns quit the crew after two days. There was an incident."

"What kind of incident?" Stride asked.

"She went out drinking with a cast member. Things got out of hand. At first she claimed she was sexually assaulted. Then she changed her story and said it was simply a misunderstanding."

"Rape's not a misunderstanding."

"I'm only telling you what she said. She didn't want to pursue it and didn't want the police involved. She quit. That was the end of that."

"What was her name?" Stride asked.

"I'd rather not say. She won't talk to you anyway."

"Why not? Was she paid off? Is that why she changed her story?"

"I can't say anything more," Chris said. "Our lawyers would freak. I'm sorry, Lieutenant."

Stride shook his head in disgust. He hated seeing people played like pawns. "Which cast member? Who assaulted her?"

"There was no assault," Chris insisted. "Please don't characterize it like that."

"Who?"

Chris looked over his shoulder as if to make sure they weren't being watched. Spies were everywhere. His voice sank to a whisper.

"Jungle Jack," he said.

# 7

Stride was restless. He didn't go home.

Instead, he drove north out of the city on Jean Duluth Road until the buildings, traffic, and people disappeared around him. It didn't take long to leave civilization behind in Duluth. There was nothing but small towns and dense forest all the way to the Canadian border. Sometimes he felt as if the city were the last pioneer outpost, holding back the encroaching wilderness. It was grayer up there. More primitive. And more ominous.

His headlights guided him. He had to be cautious about deer at night, as John Doe had learned too late. This far north, he had to think about wolves, too. Stride stayed on the road until it ended, and then he turned onto Highway 44 and continued into the middle of nowhere. There was nothing on either side of him but evergreens crowding the pavement. He passed no homes and no crossroads. A few snow flurries kept him company by skittering across his windshield.

He knew where he was going, but he didn't really know why. He hadn't been to this place in years. He hadn't even thought about going back until Chris had mentioned it. This was the part of the Northland where Art Leipold had owned hunting ground. This was where three women had died.

Instinct guided him. He remembered what he was looking for and knew when to slow down. Ahead of him, through his headlights, he saw a spur road snaking off the left side of the highway. It was a dead-end road that didn't get much attention from the plows. Stride turned onto the road, and the tires of his Expedition chewed through the packed snow. He went slowly. Every so often, a rusted mailbox leaned into the road. A couple of recluses lived up here, but not many.

He drove until the road ended at a yellow gate marked with "private property" and "no trespassing" signs. On the other side of the gate was an old bridge over the Cloquet River that wasn't likely to support the weight of anything other than foot traffic. That was the border of Art Leipold's land.

Stride pulled to the gate and stopped. He wasn't alone.

A red Toyota Yaris was parked in the tall weeds. Chris was right. The killing ground from years earlier had become a tourist attraction for beer parties, ghost stories, and teenage make-out sessions. Beyond the gate, he could see that the deep snow was riddled with footprints.

Stride got out of the truck and walked around the gate. The ribbon of river water was frozen solid under the bridge. He listened for the noise of whoever had come there in the Yaris, but the only sound was the creepy rattling of tree branches in the wind. He remembered where he was going. Even if he hadn't, the overlapping footprints in his flashlight beam showed him the way. The trail went north into the pines, and it was so narrow that he had to turn sideways in places and duck to avoid the low-hanging branches. Snow dusted his hair and melted down his back like cold fingers.

He didn't have far to go. The cabin was built only a hundred yards into the forest, but the cold and night made it feel like a long trek. He still didn't know why he had come back after so many years. Maybe, like Chris, the movie made him want to confront old demons.

Ahead of him, the trail widened. A tiny clearing had been hacked out of the woods. The cabin was in front of him, or what was left of it. His flashlight lit up beams scarred into black charcoal by fire. One wall had fallen, and so had most of the roof. Snow and dead brush pushed up to the door. Much of the forest had burned, too, but nature had begun to bring it back to life. Saplings had squeezed in on the ground, and the branches of the surviving pines spread overhead like the open arms of a priest.

He remembered.

*Here, in here!*

*Mags, get a lock cutter out here now.*

*Is the ambulance on the way?*

*Water, we need water.*

*She's alive, she's alive!*

His voice echoed down to him over the years. He remembered ripping open the cabin door much the way Dean Casperson had done it in the movie. Every second counted. He remembered the cage itself, built of steel mesh and covered with sound-resistant foam. You could stand next to it and barely hear someone screaming inside. He remembered the microphone wire that had been used in recording the messages to him.

*Save me, Jonathan Stride.*

He remembered dragging Lori Fulkerson from the cage, her muscles atrophied, her hair dirty and brittle, her lips desiccated. Later, the doctors said she would have died if they'd reached the cabin even two hours later. It was that close.

They'd found the bodies of the other three victims buried in the woods behind the cabin. Kristal Beech. Tanya Carter. Sally Wills. He'd been too late for them. They'd died in the box. Along the way, terrible things had happened as they dealt with hunger, thirst, and desperation. Stride had never shared the graphic details with anyone else. Not even Serena.

Stride directed his flashlight beam into the open, burned interior of the cabin. He was startled to find a bone-white face staring back at him like one of the walking dead. He wondered for an instant if he was dreaming, but he wasn't. It was Lori Fulkerson. She was the one who'd driven here in the Toyota Yaris. She stood in darkness in the same place where she'd been held prisoner eleven years earlier.

Lori was pointing a gun at him.

"Who are you?" she screamed. "Get out of here!"

Stride turned the flashlight toward his own face. "Ms. Fulkerson, it's Jonathan Stride with the police. You're safe. Put the gun down."

He didn't hear an answer.

"Ms. Fulkerson? There's no reason to be alarmed."

He waited again, and finally her voice murmured out of the black night, barely audible. "Okay. I'm okay."

He pointed his flashlight toward the ground. He stepped closer, through the missing wall, inside what would have been the entrance of the cabin. Lori was six feet away. The cage would have been right there where she was standing. He watched her slip the gun into her pocket.

"Why are you here?" he asked.

She said nothing. He didn't like what he saw in her face. Her skin had no color. Her lips were pushed tightly together and blue with cold. She wasn't dressed warmly enough for the night. Her dark eyes had the fury and fear of someone who'd never gotten over what was done to her, and she trembled like a deer that was ready to run. She was tall and stocky with tight brown curls on her head. She'd been twenty-two years old when she was imprisoned, so she was only in her early thirties now. She looked much older.

"Ms. Fulkerson?" he said again.

The trance she was in seemed to break. She slumped and could barely hold herself up. He went to grab her, and she was ice cold.

"Come on, let's get out of here," he said.

Stride coaxed her arm around his shoulder and helped her toward the forest trail with an arm around her waist. Her trembling turned into out-and-out shivering. Her knees were weak, and she stumbled as they inched through the snow. He bent her down when the branches were low. She didn't say a word. When they finally broke from the trees near the river, he took her to his Expedition and guided her into the passenger seat. He got in and made the truck's heater roar. He grabbed blankets from the rear seat and draped them over her shoulders and lap.

"Let's get you to the hospital," he said.

"No."

"You may have hypothermia."

"I'm just cold. I wasn't out there long."

Stride didn't like it, but he left the truck in park. He noted that the heat had begun to revive her. Her voice was stronger and clearer. She stretched out her fingers. Color came back to her face.

"Do you have any water?" she asked.

He didn't comment on his sense of déjà vu. He found a plastic bottle of water that was mostly frozen and unscrewed the cap. He made sure she dribbled only a little between her lips.

"What were you doing out here?" he asked.

"I come out here sometimes. This place draws me back."

He slipped a hand inside the pocket of her coat and found the revolver and made sure it was secure. Without asking her permission, he unloaded the bullets and put them away in his jacket. "Why the gun?"

"Protection. You meet strange people out here."

Stride didn't doubt that was true, but he wondered if the gun was really for protection or was for something else. He wondered how many times she'd brought it with her. He wondered how many times she'd stared into the barrel with her finger on the trigger. The past didn't give up its grip easily. Horror had a way of coming back like a virus.

She looked at him unhappily and then looked away, as if she could see what he was thinking.

"How are things going for you, Lori?" he asked pointedly.

"You don't have to worry about me."

"Of course. I'm just expressing my concern."

"Well, don't."

Lori had never been a warm person, even after he'd rescued her. She was prickly and hard to like. He didn't know how much of that was her natural personality and how much was a reaction to the time she'd spent in the cage. She was a loner. As far as he knew, she'd never been married. He didn't know much about her family background.

"Are you getting help when you need it?" he asked. "I'm not asking for details; I just want to make sure you know about resources—"

"Trust me, I've burned through most of the shrinks in Duluth," Lori interrupted. "My head should be the size of a walnut by now. Same with antidepressants. Nothing makes it go away."

He didn't say anything more, because anything he said would make things worse. He'd had to remind himself years ago that not every victim was a saint.

"So they're making a movie about you," Lori went on with acid in her voice. "You must be pretty impressed with that."

"Not in the least."

"Oh, come on. It's got to be a big ego thing."

"There's nothing about what happened back then that I want to remember. Three women died. You nearly died, too."

Lori shrugged. "Well, Art Leipold hung himself. So at least one good thing came out of it."

Stride didn't know how to respond to such raw pain. Eleven years had gone by, but it might as well have happened yesterday.

"The actress who's playing me keeps calling," Lori continued. "She wants to meet me. She says she wants to know what it felt like to be in the cage. She invited me to visit her on the set tomorrow."

"Is that why you came back here tonight?"

"I don't know. Maybe. It's not like I need a reminder."

"You don't have to talk to Aimee Bowe," Stride said. "On the other hand, maybe it would help to have someone else try to understand what you went through."

"It's not like some Hollywood blonde can spend ten minutes with me and get inside my head."

"You're right," Stride said. "Nobody will ever know the truth except you."

"Yeah. Me and the ones who died. Sad little club, huh?"

"You're alive," Stride pointed out softly.

Lori didn't look at him like being alive was any prize. "My mother thinks I should talk to Aimee Bowe. She says it would be good for me. She says I'm still in the box and maybe it would help me get out. She told me to be *brave*. Like she has any idea what that's like. At the first whiff of trouble, she runs away. Did you know my mom walked out on my father when I was ten years old?"

Stride shook his head. "I didn't. I'm sorry."

"She took me away from him. Moved us across the country. I never saw my father again. When he died, she didn't even tell me about it for six months. Six months! She got married again, and she and my step-father pretended I had brand-new parents. Like the past was nothing, you know. Like I should just forget it. Well, that's not me. First chance I had, I got out of there and got the hell away from them. I went to business school when I was eighteen, and when I was done with that, I moved back to Duluth. I figured I'd be happy coming home. You want to guess how well that turned out?"

The venom in her voice filled Stride with sadness. He hated to see a young life destroyed, and he hated that there was nothing he could do about it. He was a fixer, but some things couldn't be fixed.

Lori opened the truck door. "I'm leaving now."

"I wish you'd let me take you to the hospital, Ms. Fulkerson."

"You can't make me, can you?" she asked.

"No."

"Then good-bye, Lieutenant," she retorted. She climbed down into the snow, but before she closed the door, she leaned back inside. Her eyes were bloodshot. Her voice cracked with despair. "Two hours, right?"

Stride cocked his head in puzzlement. "I'm sorry, what?"

"Two hours. The docs said I would have been dead in two hours."

He nodded. "That's right."

"I wish you'd been late," she said.

*

It was after midnight by the time Stride made it back to the matchbox cottage on Park Point where he lived with Serena and Cat. The house was on the other side of the sand dunes from Lake Superior, and the lake was oddly quiet. Most of the year he heard the thunder of waves twenty-four hours a day, but sometimes the long cold of January built enough ice beyond the beach to dull the noise.

He let himself into the dark house. The first thing he did was check on Cat, who was asleep in the corner bedroom facing the street. She didn't wake up. Her breathing was soft and regular. He stared down at her pretty face, which was lost in a tangle of chestnut hair. It was hard to be mad at her even when she did foolish things. He closed the door softly and let her sleep.

Stride took a shower and then tried to get into bed without disturbing Serena. It was impossible, because the old timbers in the floor always groaned. She murmured a drowsy greeting at him. He slipped into bed behind her, slid an arm around her waist, and kissed her neck. Those were the moments that reminded him how good it was to be married again.

"You're late," she said. "You want to talk?"

Normally, he would have pretended to be tired and let her go back to sleep, but not tonight. He'd told her about Art Leipold before, but he found himself talking about the case all over again. How personal it was. How the voices of the women got inside his soul. How much it made him question whether he was really ready to be in charge of the detective bureau.

Eventually he fell silent, but he kept thinking about what the women had gone through inside the cage. He remembered the bodies of the other victims and the details of the autopsies. He knew what they'd done to themselves. Unspeakable things. Desperation drove people to dark places.

"We never released the details publicly," he murmured. "Some of the things the women did in the box were—disturbing. No one else needed to know."

Serena turned around to face him. "But you know."

"Yeah. I wish I didn't."

They couldn't see each other in the darkness. All he could feel was her warmth. She put her hands on his face and kissed him softly, over and over, until he kissed her back. Then, in silence, she wrapped herself up in his body and made him forget for a while.

# 8

Stride found Maggie with her feet up on his desk when he arrived at police headquarters at seven in the morning. She was drinking a jumbo-size Coke through a straw and eating a Sausage McMuffin.

"Hash browns?" she asked as he sat down. She dug inside a bag on the floor and waved a little oval patty of fried potatoes at him.

"No, thanks."

Maggie shrugged and took a large bite. Stride found it amazing that Maggie could consume McDonald's nearly every day of her life and never put an ounce on her tiny frame. Her metabolism, even in her forties, was like the growling engine of a sports car.

He eyed the darkness outside his office window. Dawn was still almost an hour away thanks to the short winter days. The rest of the building was mostly quiet. He was halfway through his coffee and slowly starting to wake up.

"How early did you get here, Mags?" he asked.

"Not early at all," she replied.

"How do you figure that?"

"If you never leave, it's not early," she explained with her mouth full.

"You were here all night again?"

"Yup."

Stride shook his head. "This is extreme even for you, Mags. You really need to get some rest."

Maggie shrugged without replying. Her cheeks made dimples as she sucked on the Coke. He leaned back in his chair and studied his partner's face, which couldn't hide her exhaustion. After so many years together, there were very few secrets between them.

"Is this about you and Troy?" he asked.

"Troy and I are done. Over. Kaput."

"I know. And you never told me what happened between you two. You just walked in after Christmas and announced between bites of a Big Mac that the longest relationship of your life was over."

"What's to tell?" Maggie said. She dropped her feet back on the floor. She crushed the empty bag in her hands and shot it across the room, where it landed in Stride's wastebasket. "I guess I'm a better shot than Haley Adams."

"Come on, Mags. Was it an argument?"

"Nope."

"Was there a problem with Troy's kids?"

"Nah. I love the girls."

"Then what?"

Maggie rolled her tongue around her teeth as if there might be a bite of McMuffin that she'd missed. "Oh, let's not make a big deal of it, okay? On Christmas Eve, Troy asked me to marry him."

Stride froze with his coffee cup at his lips. Then he blinked and put the cup down. He'd talked with Serena about a lot of possible reasons Maggie and Troy had broken up, but that wasn't one of them. "He did what?"

"Yeah, it was pretty romantic for a big teddy bear like Troy. He waited until the kids went to bed. Then he opened champagne. He put on Michael Bublé, and of course I immediately turned *off* Michael Bublé. And the next thing I know, he had a ring in his hand and was on his knees popping the question."

"That must have been quite a surprise."

"It was."

"And you said—"

"No."

Stride sat in his chair in silence. He didn't know how to respond.

"Needless to say, that killed the mood," Maggie went on. "About five minutes later, I was back in my truck heading home. And that was that."

"That was that?"

"Right."

"Have the two of you talked?" he asked.

"No."

"Come on, Mags. You guys really need to talk."

"About what? I don't want to get married, boss. Period. Remember the one time I tried it? Dead husband, me accused of murder, the damn sex club that screwed up my head?"

"I'm not sure it's fair to generalize about marriage from your particular experience," Stride said drily.

"Well, being married made me rich. Otherwise, there isn't much I want to remember about it. Marriage isn't for me. Never again. I was happy with the status quo with Troy. I wasn't asking for anything more. But that's not what he wanted. So it's over, and I'm moving on."

"And by moving on you mean not getting any sleep?" Stride asked.

"There's no connection. I'm not obsessing about it."

"Are you sure? It's a big deal."

"Look, I appreciate your concern, but I'm okay, boss. Really."

Stride sighed and didn't push her any further. "If you say so."

He knew she wasn't okay, but with Maggie you had to settle for information in dribs and drabs. She wore a suit of armor around herself and didn't like to take it off. Plus, the two of them were still wary about getting too personal with each other. They'd been burned that way in the past.

"So did your all-nighter here result in any new information?" Stride asked.

"Actually, quite a lot," Maggie replied. "Remember the phone we recovered from John Doe's car? He used it to call the same Duluth number about a dozen times while he was in the city. We figured he was talking to his handler, getting instructions. The number he called is dead now, but I pulled the call logs for that phone. Every call went back to John Doe's phone—except one."

"What was the other call?" Stride asked.

"You'll enjoy this. It went to Sammy's Pizza downtown."

Stride chuckled. "Seriously?"

"Yeah, I'm betting whoever it was made a mistake and used the wrong phone to order his pizza."

"Can we trace the order?"

Maggie shook her head. "No, we know the date and time of the call, but the orders are written up on one-part paper receipts that go out with the pizza. Guppo's going to be talking to their delivery drivers."

"Okay, anything else on John Doe?" Stride asked. "Are we any closer to identifying him?"

"No, he's still a mystery. But the Gherkin says she expects a ballistics report back on the Glock later today. See, my charm really does pay off."

"How about Haley Adams? What have you found out about her?"

"She's a mystery, too. Apparently Haley is a pretty little liar. She's *not* a UMD student. Nobody in admissions or in the film studies department ever heard of her. And the apartment we searched? She rented it last month. It looks like she came to town when the film crew did and conned her way inside. Her whole identity is a fraud."

"Chris Leipold thought she might have been spying for one of the tabloids," Stride said.

"Maybe, but if she was, I doubt the *National Gazette* would admit it. Not when she left a telescope pointed at Dean Casperson's bedroom. That's an invitation to a lawsuit. And speaking of the telescope, the model she had is called a Moonraker. It costs like five thousand dollars. This girl didn't just walk away and leave it behind. Something happened to her."

"Aimee Bowe told Serena that she thinks Haley is dead," Stride said.

"Based on what?"

"She sensed it. Like some kind of psychic vision, I guess."

Maggie rolled her eyes. "California."

"Well, vision or not, Aimee may be right. We've still got John Doe and his Glock to think about."

Stride took his phone out of his pocket and opened up the photographs he'd taken inside Haley's apartment. He scrolled through them again, hoping to see a clue that he'd missed the previous night.

"So who *is* this girl?" he asked.

"I don't have any leads on her, either," Maggie replied. "It doesn't help that we can't even get a read on what she looks like. Everyone describes her differently. Hair color, hair length, eye color, skin tone, it's different with every witness. She wore disguises like day-of-the-week underwear."

"She told Chris Leipold that she grew up in Florida."

"Right, which may or may not be another lie," Maggie replied. "Even if it's true, we don't know whether her name is really Haley Adams. However, just to be sure, I got Florida driver's license records on every Haley Adams in the state."

"What did you find?" Stride asked.

"There are about two dozen people with that name in Florida. I culled it to six women who seemed to be about the right age, weight, and look. I printed out copies and figured we could run them by the people on the crew. We can see if anyone recognizes her among the photos."

She handed Stride a sheet of paper with enlarged copies of multiple Florida licenses. He took a quick look at the faces and realized that Maggie was right. Any one of these women could have been the Haley Adams they were looking for. Or none of them.

"Didn't you say you culled it to six?" he asked. "There are seven licenses on this page."

Maggie nodded. "Yeah. See the one on the bottom? Haley Adams from Fort Myers? She can't be our girl, but I included her anyway."

"Why?"

"She had something in common with our fake John Doe identity," Maggie said. "She's dead."

Stride stared at the face of the pretty young girl from Fort Myers. Strawberry blond hair and green eyes. Sweet smile. A Florida beauty,

102 pounds. According to her birth date, she would have been twenty-four years old the next month if she were still alive.

"Interesting coincidence," he said. "Maybe we have two ghosts."

"Maybe so. There was something else that made me curious about this particular Haley Adams, too."

"What's that?" he asked.

"She was murdered."

# 9

Serena sat across from Cat at a wobbly wooden table in the basement bakery in Canal Park called Amazing Grace. She ate a scrambled egg skillet with Yukon potatoes while Cat picked at a sugar-sprinkled blueberry muffin with her slim fingers. The girl didn't look at her. The two of them hadn't said much since they'd left the cottage. For Cat, the worst punishment was not knowing what her punishment was going to be.

"Drew and Krista asked me to baby-sit today," Cat murmured after a long stretch of silence. "Can I still do that?"

"Of course."

"They're counting on me," the girl went on as if Serena hadn't said anything. "And I haven't seen Michael in like a week."

"Cat, I said it's fine," Serena told her.

"Well, I wasn't sure if I was grounded or something."

"You're not. And regardless, I would never tell you not to see your son."

Michael was now a fifteen-month-old toddler. His adoptive parents, Drew and Krista Olson, had encouraged Cat to play a role in his life. After months of reluctance, Cat finally had stepped up. Drew and Krista were busy rebuilding their camping shop, which had been destroyed in the marathon bombing, so they called on Cat regularly for baby-sitting duties.

"I'm sorry about last night," Cat said finally, biting her lip.

"I know you are."

"Is Stride mad?"

"He's mad at Jungle Jack. Not you."

"Yeah, but I was drinking," Cat said.

"Well, you're right, we're not happy about that. I know it doesn't seem like a big deal to you, but you have no idea what someone might put in your drink at a party like that. Plus, it's easy to go too far before you even realize it. Look at that poor girl in Proctor this weekend."

Cat nodded. "Rochelle Wahl."

"Yes, her. She figured it would be fun to have a drink while her parents were out of town. And one drink led to a few more. She went outside to throw up, she fell down, she hit her head. She froze to death, Cat. Imagine her parents coming home to that."

"I know."

"So yes, you made a mistake," Serena said, "but actually, last night was mostly my fault."

"Your fault? How?"

"I brought you to the party. You weren't ready for it. I shouldn't have left you alone with those people. That's on me, and I apologize."

Cat looked up from the table and stared at her with wide eyes. "You can't blame yourself."

"Yes, I can." Serena reached across the table to stroke Cat's hair. "Sometimes I look at you and see a young woman, and I'm really proud of how far you've come. It's easy for me to forget that you're still a teenager. When I was your age, I wouldn't have been able to handle last night, either. It was wrong of me to put you in that position."

Cat pulled off a chunk of blueberry muffin and ate it. Her forehead crinkled. "I'm not a kid. I don't like that you guys have to keep bailing me out when I do stupid stuff."

"Give yourself a little credit," Serena said. "Look at Michael. Look at all the right choices you've made with him. You made sure he had parents who could take good care of him. You've stayed in his life."

The girl's mouth pressed into a little frown. "Yeah, but I should be doing more to help *you*."

"You do. Believe me."

Cat went back to her breakfast, but she looked unhappy with herself. That was fine. Serena knew that Cat couldn't recognize how much she'd grown in the last year. In the early days of living with them, Cat had acted out constantly. She'd tried to get Serena and Stride to throw her out, as if that would justify her belief that her life wasn't worth anything. Now she was angry with herself for not living up to her own standards. That was progress.

Serena bit into another forkful of her Yukon scramble, but she almost choked as a hand slapped her sharply on the back. Her nose was filled by a sickly strong cologne, and a voice boomed in her ears. The noise was way too loud for the morning quiet of the bakery.

"Good morning, pretty ladies!"

Cat looked up, and her anxious face smoothed into a smile. "Curt!"

Curt Dickes pulled over an empty chair from a nearby table and straddled it backward as he sat down between them. His long wool coat was unbuttoned, and he wore oversized boots studded with rivets and chains. He grabbed Serena's fork out of her hand and snagged a bite from her skillet. As he chewed the eggs, he nodded his head happily and shouted at her. "Hey, that's good. Nice choice, Detective. I'll have to get that next time."

"Inside voice, Curt," Serena said.

Curt cocked his head. "What?"

Then he realized that he was still wearing his AirPods, and he popped them out of his ears and buried them in his pockets. "Oops, sorry about that. I love me some Halsey."

He stole more of her eggs, and Serena pushed the plate over to him. "Here, be my guest."

"Thanks!" Curt replied, diving into her breakfast. "How's the hubster?"

"Lieutenant Stride is fine."

"Excellent, excellent." Curt winked at Cat. "How about you, kitty cat? What's with the sad kitty eyes?"

Cat shrugged. "Nothing. I'm fine."

"Oh, yeah? Word is some hotshot was putting the moves on you last night. Everything okay?"

Serena leaned across the table. "How the hell did you hear about that?"

"Aw, give me some credit, Mrs. Stride. Nothing gets past me."

That was true.

Curt Dickes had his fingers in everything in Duluth. He knew everyone, and everyone knew him. He popped up at every city event, usually with something to sell. He blended in like a chameleon all along the social scale, from the rich party crowd to the homeless hanging out in Lake Place Park. He always had money, but it never lasted long. Then he was on to the next scam to earn more.

Curt had been a part of Cat's life since her days on the street. No matter how far behind she left that world, she always seemed to drift back into Curt's orbit. It had taken Serena a long time to realize that Cat simply had a perpetual, inexplicable crush on Curt. The girl liked him.

The crazy thing was that Serena liked him, too. She didn't want him anywhere near Cat, but she also knew that Curt didn't have a mean bone in his body. Or an honest one.

He was twenty-seven years old but acted like a teenager. His musky cologne usually lingered in the room long after he left. He wore baggy clothes over a beanpole frame, and he sported shoulder-length stringy black hair. Today he had a purple fedora positioned low on his forehead, with multiple gaudy rings on his fingers. His teeth were stark white, and he flashed them as he grinned.

"So what's the latest scam, Curt?" Serena asked.

Curt slapped an open hand dramatically against his chest. "Scam? Me?"

"There's always a scam with you."

"No, no, *this* is different," he assured her. "What I'm offering locals and tourists today is a once-in-a-lifetime opportunity to be part of history! I mean, we are having a big-budget Hollywood movie filmed in our very own backyard. When's that likely to happen again? *Iron Will* was all the way back in 1994. *You'll Like My Mother* was in 1972, for heaven's sake. Plus, given that our beloved Lieutenant Stride is practically the *star*, I knew I needed to commemorate the event."

Cat giggled.

"Commemorate it how?" Serena asked suspiciously.

"With this!" Curt dug into his pocket and produced a Rubik's Cube and put it on the table in front of them. Instead of the usual solid colors, this version of the game had photographs on each side of the cube, broken up into small squares. Serena picked it up and saw two pictures of Dean Casperson on opposite sides, two pictures of Aimee Bowe, and a photo of the Duluth lift bridge with the caged girl and the month and year of filming printed across the sky.

When she turned it over, she saw a photo of Jonny—her Jonny—on the bottom.

"Are you kidding, Curt?"

"What? It's professionally done and a *bargain* at $39.95. Do you want one? I use Square, so if you've got a chip card, we're all set."

"It's also completely illegal. Did you license any of these photos? And where did you get a picture of Stride?"

"I took it myself. He's a handsome man. You're very, very lucky."

Serena sighed in exasperation. Cat picked up the game and spun the segments repeatedly until all the photographs were fragmented around the cube. Then she started trying to put it together again. Having snippets of photos rather than solid colors made the puzzle ten times as hard.

"I think it's supercool," Cat said. "Can I have one?"

Curt spotted the look on Serena's face and grinned. "For you, kitty cat, it's free. A promotional sample."

"Neat!"

Serena felt a headache coming on, which usually happened when she was around Curt. "Listen, I didn't ask you to meet us here for a marketing pitch on your latest product line. I need information."

"You want free merchandise *and* free information?" Curt replied. "Wow, you are an expensive date, Detective."

"It will get even more expensive if I make a call to the film's lawyers and you have to destroy all of your little pirated cubes."

Curt nodded. "Excellent point. Proceed."

"Obviously, you've got a pipeline into the film crew."

"Sure I do. When strangers in our city have needs, I am a one-man tourist bureau."

"What kind of needs are we talking about?" she asked. "Girls? Drugs?"

"My inventory and contacts are wide-ranging, Serena; you know that. Visitors from Los Angeles do not always appreciate the recreational opportunities that Duluth offers when it's ten degrees below zero. So they look for alternative sources of entertainment to pass those long, cold evenings."

"Girls. Drugs."

Curt groaned and lowered his voice. "Sure. Yeah."

"Do you supply?"

"No way! I'm just a go-between. People who need people come to me." Curt glanced at Cat, who'd already solved the puzzle. It had taken her less than a minute. "Holy crap, kitty cat, how do you do that?"

Cat grinned and looked pleased with herself. She scrambled the cube and started solving it again. Serena was routinely amazed by the girl's brain. It was the emotional side that still had some catching up to do.

"Has anyone approached you for information about the movie?" Serena asked. "I'm thinking about reporters. Tabloid writers. Paparazzi."

"Yeah, there are a few of them scavenging around and looking for dirt."

"What about a girl named Haley Adams?" Serena asked.

"Names really aren't my thing. What does she look like?"

"Honestly, I don't know. We think she changes her appearance a lot. But she had a spy setup with an expensive telescope next door to Dean Casperson's rental house."

Curt drummed his fingers on the table as he thought about it. "Well, I know one girl who was really, really interested in Dean Casperson. Midtwenties. Long, bombshell blond hair that was obviously a wig."

Serena slid out her phone and found the photograph of the mannequin that Stride had texted her from Haley's apartment. "Hair like this, you mean?"

"Yeah, just like that," Curt replied, nodding.

"What did she want?"

"She knew people came to me to round out the guest list at crew parties, if you know what I mean. She wanted a tip-off when there was going to be a big party at Casperson's place."

"And did you give her what she wanted?" Serena asked.

"Sure, why not? She paid well."

"Did she say why she wanted the information?"

"No."

"When was the last party?"

"Saturday night," Curt said. "Lots of people."

"Were you there?"

"I may have put in an appearance, yeah. It's good to keep up the contacts, you know?"

"Was Haley there?"

Curt shook his head. "I didn't see her. Although you said she liked to wear different looks, so who knows? But if she had a spy setup, she was probably watching from the neighbor's house."

"And would she have seen anything interesting?" Serena asked. "Did anything happen at the party?"

"It was a little wild, but I didn't see anything that was way over the line."

Serena frowned. Then she thought of something else, and she picked up her phone again.

"What about this guy?" she asked, hunting down the photograph of John Doe from the traffic accident. "Have you ever seen him before?"

Curt glanced at the phone. He seemed unfazed by the blood or by the fact that the man in the photograph was dead. "Yeah, he was there."

His response was so casual that Serena took a second to catch up. She pointed at the phone again. "Hold on; you're saying you saw *this man* at a party at Dean Casperson's house last Saturday night? Are you sure?"

Curt shrugged. "Yeah, I'm sure."

"Who is he?"

"No idea. When I saw him, I was grabbing a smoke outside. He was loading a girl into his car."

"Could the girl have been Haley Adams?"

"I don't think so. Haley was short. This girl was pretty tall."

"What did she look like?"

"Sorry, no idea. Her back was to me. She couldn't even walk by herself, so I figured she was drunk. He was taking her out the back, like he didn't want anyone to see her."

"Then what happened?"

"He drove off."

Serena tried to put the pieces of the story together just as Cat was doing with the Rubik's Cube.

There was a party on Saturday night at the house Dean Casperson was renting in Congdon Park. Something went wrong, and a girl had to be taken away. Serena didn't know who she was or what had happened to her. But the girl wound up in a car driven by John Doe, who bore all the signs of a hired killer.

And through the trees, Haley Adams was watching.

# 10

Dean Casperson's rental house in Congdon Park felt austere and Gothic, full of chimneys, gables, and Tudor crossbeams. It was hidden among two acres of forested land, secure behind a brick wall that ringed the property. In winter, the trees gave up some of their secrets. Stride could see outbuildings and a tennis court beyond the main house, which was built in two perpendicular wings. The estate was a hand-me-down from Duluth's early days, when the riches from timber, mining, and shipping had created an upper class of Northland millionaires.

A gate blocked the driveway, and a private guard stood watch in the cold. Stride handed him his identification, and the guard used a remote control to swing open the gate and let Stride drive his Expedition inside. As he parked and got out, he stared northward through the web of trees. From there, he could just barely see the windows of the attic room where Haley Adams had zeroed in on the estate through the lens of her telescope.

He rang the bell and was surprised when Dean Casperson answered the door personally.

"Lieutenant, it's a pleasure to see you again." Casperson waved him inside. "Would you like some breakfast? I just finished myself, but I can have something made up for you. And we have coffee, of course."

"No, I'm fine, thanks," Stride replied. "Are you filming today?"

"No, Aimee Bowe is on set, not me. She's doing her scenes in the box. She's constantly improvising, so we'll see how long that takes. Getting inside the emotional state of those women is no small task."

"I'm sure."

Casperson beckoned him toward the back of the house. "I know you're busy, but come with me. There's somebody I want you to meet."

The actor led him through a maze of rooms. Everything was built in stone and dark wood and was furnished as if time had stood still for a century. The heat had been cranked to warm the house, but the high ceilings and old windows couldn't keep winter out entirely. Casperson was dressed in pastels, including emerald green slacks and a yellow golf shirt. He looked out of place here. Or maybe, Stride thought, the house looked out of place around Casperson.

The maze led them to a large den with no windows. A chandelier hung over an elm-wood billiard table that probably cost as much as Stride's truck. Built-in bookshelves lined one wall. Another wall featured oil paintings from Duluth's early history. Casperson went to a marble bar and poured a mug of coffee and held up the pot in Stride's direction. Stride shook his head again.

The room was empty, but Casperson took a remote control and pointed it at a seventy-inch television nestled among the bookshelves. He turned on the television, and Stride found himself staring at an outdoor patio that looked out on a private boat dock and an inland waterway. A woman sat at a glass-and-marble table in a floral bikini, with a white lace jacket over her shoulders. She was drinking coffee, too, and soaking up the sunshine.

"Mo and I like to have breakfast together every day," Casperson explained. "It doesn't matter if she's home in Captiva and I'm a thousand miles away. Mo, this is Lieutenant Stride. Lieutenant, meet my wife."

"It's a pleasure, Mrs. Casperson," Stride said.

She was practically life-size on the screen, and Stride felt an odd impulse to reach out to shake her hand.

"Oh, I'm Mo, please," she replied with studied politeness. "Everyone calls me Mo. I feel as if I know you, Lieutenant. I did my research on you before I suggested to Dean that he accept the role. You're an interesting man."

Stride didn't know what to say to that.

He knew that Mo had to be about his own age or even older, because she'd been married to Dean Casperson since the two of them were teenagers. Their relationship was legendary in Hollywood. Even so, the bikini and the 4K screen hid nothing, and Mo didn't look a day over forty. She had thick honey-colored hair with a trace of dampness. Her brown eyes shot through the screen like arrows. She had a hooked nose and a sharp chin. Her skin had an all-over golden tan, and she showed no discomfort at all in displaying her toned body in front of a stranger. Like her husband, she conveyed absolute self-assurance and control.

"I was especially impressed with your handling of the terrible marathon incident last summer," Mo went on.

"That was the work of a lot of good people," he replied. "Not me."

Mo narrowed one eye as she smiled at him. It made him feel as if he'd fallen into a trap. "See, that's what impressed me, Lieutenant. You never took any credit. I always tell Dean that if he forgets to be humble about what he's accomplished, that's the day I'll divorce him. None of us walk our path alone."

"I agree."

Casperson broke in with a laugh as if the conversation had gotten too serious. "See what I live with, Lieutenant? Now make him jealous, my dear, and tell him what the temperature is in Captiva."

"Eight-five degrees," Mo announced with a wink. She squared her shoulders as if emphasizing her swimsuit and everything beneath it.

"Well, that's about ninety degrees warmer than here in Duluth," Stride replied. "You made the right call not coming along on this particular film shoot."

Mo shrugged. "Oh, please, I never bother with filming. That's Dean's life. There's plenty in our business and charitable interests to keep me busy when he's away. Which reminds me, my dear, I have bad news. Tiffany Ford called. I'm afraid Tommy passed away yesterday. She wanted to be sure you knew."

Stride watched grief darken Dean Casperson's face.

"Poor kid," he said. "Thanks for telling me."

"Of course. I'm very sorry, I have to run. We'll talk later."

Casperson nodded without saying anything more to his wife.

"Oh, one thing, Lieutenant," Mo called to Stride. "If you don't mind my asking, how is your daughter? Or rather, the teenage girl who lives with you. Chris Leipold told me there was a regrettable incident at the party with Jungle Jack. I believe Dean had already left at that point. I want you to know I'll speak with Jack myself and express how disappointed I am in his behavior. He's a dear longtime family friend, but sometimes he's less than careful about where he plies his charms."

"She's fine," Stride replied evenly, "but I appreciate your concern."

"Good. I'm glad."

"What happened?" Dean asked his wife. "I didn't hear about this."

"Nothing to concern yourself with, my dear. It's just Jack being Jack in the usual way. My regards to you, Lieutenant. I hope I'll have a chance to meet you in person someday. Although, to be honest, I'd rather it be down here than up there."

She smiled, waved at both of them, and then cut off the connection.

Stride found himself feeling oddly intimidated by Mo Casperson. She was beautiful. She'd said all the right things. Yet he stared at the blank screen and felt as if he'd been threatened. It wasn't simply that she knew about Jungle Jack's behavior with Cat or that she'd made sure that Stride knew Jack was a close family friend. It was the other, throwaway line that he remembered.

*Or rather, the teenage girl who lives with you.*

She'd made a point of making it clear that she knew Cat wasn't his daughter. It made him wonder what else she knew about Cat. And he suspected that was precisely why she'd said it.

Stride turned away from the blank screen and realized that Dean Casperson hadn't said anything more since the call. He was distracted, holding the coffee mug near his lips but not drinking from it. The actor's blue eyes had a faraway look of loss that Stride knew very well.

"Your wife mentioned someone who passed away?" he said.

Casperson looked at him as if he'd forgotten that Stride was there. "What? Oh, yes, I often do things for Make-A-Wish. This eight-year-old boy with cancer, Tommy Ford, wanted to be in a movie. So I arranged for him to have a little role in the last film I did. A scene with me. It's not out yet, but I managed to get an early copy to his parents so they could all watch it together. I've tried to FaceTime with Tommy every month to see how he is."

"That's a very gracious thing to do," Stride said.

"Oh, how could I not? If you don't give back on the things you get in life, what's the point?"

Stride could see that Casperson was genuinely affected by the boy's death. He watched as Casperson idly rolled balls across the billiard table and then grabbed a cue and began shooting them one by one into the various pockets. His mouth was grim. His aim was perfect, and the crack of the cue with each shot was angry. He acted, again, as if he were alone.

"I don't mean to bother you at a difficult moment," Stride said, "but I do have a few questions."

Casperson looked up blankly. "Questions?" Then he put down the cue and focused. "Of course, sorry. Please, go ahead."

"Did you have some kind of party here at the house last Saturday?" Stride asked.

"Saturday? Yes, probably. I don't pay a lot of attention to individual days on location, but I try to get the cast and crew together as often as I can. It brings everyone closer, which makes the process go more smoothly."

"Who was here?"

"Honestly, I have no idea. Most of the film people and probably some locals. I don't get involved in any of that. Usually I put in an appearance, have a drink, and then go upstairs to read."

"Did anything unusual happen at the party?" Stride asked.

"Not that I'm aware of. Why?"

Stride pulled his phone from his pocket and made his way to the photograph of John Doe. "Does this man look familiar to you? Do you know him?"

Casperson peered at the screen. "No. Chris showed me the same photo, but I've never seen him before. Pretty gruesome, whoever it is."

"Someone saw him here at the party on Saturday," Stride said.

"Here? That man? Well, I didn't see him myself, but that doesn't mean anything. Who is he?"

"We don't know."

"Then why are you interested in him?"

"We believe he was using a stolen identity," Stride said without giving more details.

"Well, I'm sorry I can't help. Is that all, Lieutenant?"

"There's one other thing," Stride told him. "This may be unpleasant, but the woman who calls herself Haley Adams also doesn't appear to be who she said she was. And we believe she's been spying on you."

Casperson leaned on the pool cue. "Spying?"

"She had a telescope focused on the master bedroom upstairs."

Casperson took a step backward in surprise. He twirled the cue in his fingers and then chalked it. He didn't say anything for a while. "Well, just when you think people can't stoop any lower," he murmured.

"Did you have any idea what she was doing?" Stride asked.

"None. She seemed like a nice young woman."

"Forgive the question, Mr. Casperson, but in looking into your bedroom, would she have seen anything?"

Casperson shrugged. "Me reading Tippi Hedren's autobiography? Tippi and Hitchcock. Wow."

"Nothing else?"

"That's as exciting as it gets around here, Lieutenant."

"Have there been any problems on the set? Any issues with the tabloids or the paparazzi?"

"No more than usual. The tabloids don't bother me and Mo too much. If you don't want a dog to bite you, you keep it fed. We give them interviews. Exclusives. Candid photos. In return, they don't run stories about transgender Venusian mermaids swimming in our Captiva pool."

"Well, that sounds smart," Stride said.

"It's self-protection. Anything else?"

Stride removed the page of Florida driver's license photos from his pocket. "I wonder if you could take a look at these pictures and let me know if any of these women look familiar to you."

Casperson found reading glasses in his back pocket and positioned them at the end of his nose. He eyed the pictures one by one. He noticed the names, too. "These are all Florida women named Haley Adams?"

"Yes. Are any of them the Haley Adams you knew on the set?"

Casperson took a look at them again and shook his head. "No. At least I don't think so. Oddly, I was never entirely sure what Haley really looked like. She looked different to me whenever I saw her."

"What about the last picture on the page? It's a woman named Haley Adams who lived in Fort Myers. Do you recognize her? Even if it wasn't from the set."

Casperson's eyes flitted to the page, but his review looked perfunctory this time. There was no reaction on his face. For a chameleon like Casperson, the lack of expression looked out of character. "No. Sorry."

"Are you sure about that?" Stride asked.

"I am."

Stride took the paper back and filed it in his pocket again. "Well, thank you for your time, Mr. Casperson."

"Of course. I'll walk you out. You might get lost in this place."

Stride followed Casperson on the twisting route back through the house, and when they reached the foyer, the actor pulled open the front door, letting in a frigid blast of winter air. Neither of the men shivered.

"Oh, one quick question," Stride said as he stepped onto the porch. "I'm not very good with my Florida geography. Where is Fort Myers in relation to Captiva?"

Casperson smiled, but his eyes looked as cold as the Duluth morning.

That was the moment Stride realized they were going to be enemies, not friends.

"It's close, Lieutenant," Casperson told him. "Very close indeed."

# 11

Aimee Bowe was in the box.

There was dead silence on the set. Serena watched from the rear wall of the warehouse, where it was dark and cold. They were nowhere near the rural lands where Art Leipold had his hunting cabin. Instead, they were inside a giant empty building steps from the frozen water of the Duluth-Superior harbor. Shipping had closed for the winter, and a film company renting warehouse space was a welcome source of off-season cash.

The movie version of the cage where Art kept his victims was built with one side open for filming, but otherwise the interior details were shockingly real. Jonny had shown her crime scene pictures, which were enough to make her shiver at the thought of being trapped there. The straw floor. The filth. The steel mesh. The tiny claustrophobic space that made you feel as if the walls were closing in on you.

Aimee didn't look like Aimee today. There was nothing sexy or glamorous about her appearance. Her skin was made up to look pale and drawn, to emphasize the bones in her face. Her fingers were covered in fake blood, as if she'd tried to claw free of the box, the way all the victims had. Her clothes were dirty and frayed, and she huddled in one corner, shivering. She yanked at her hair.

The cameras rolled.

The look that took over Aimee's eyes alarmed Serena. She knew the woman was acting, but she felt terror emanating from her anyway. Aimee mumbled in hushed, disjointed words, too low for Serena to hear. Then Aimee screamed out a wail of frustration and fear and threw herself against the wall. She beat on it with her fists and tore at it with all the futility of a moth beating against glass. She fell back and kicked the wall with her bare feet. More fake blood—Serena hoped it was fake—seeped between her toes.

Aimee collapsed. Tears leaked down her face.

She murmured again, louder now. "Save me."

She shouted it. "Save me, Evan Grave."

Evan Grave was the character name of the detective in the movie. It sounded strange to Serena's ears to hear it that way. The movie was fiction, but she still expected to hear Aimee say it the way all the other women had.

*Save me, Jonathan Stride.*

Aimee emerged from the box, and the crew swarmed around the set like insects. They touched up her makeup. They fixed her hair and clothes. Someone handed her water, but she shook her head.

"Those women didn't have water," Aimee said.

Serena waved from the back of the set, and Aimee came over to her. The two of them stood in the shadows at the back of the warehouse, and frozen air from outside blew in from a crack under the metal door. Serena wore a coat, but Aimee wore only a dirty white T-shirt with a knot tied at the base and frayed red jeans. She could see the actress was bitterly cold, but Aimee didn't seek any help.

"That was amazing," Serena told her.

Aimee shrugged. "That was crap."

"What? I thought you were great."

"No, I was completely outside the character. I was me, not her. That's the problem. As a human being, you just naturally block out that kind of torment. I don't know how to let it all in. I can't find my voice."

Serena didn't understand the actor's craft or what Aimee was looking for in her performance. However, she could see the frustration in

Aimee's face, and she hesitated to intrude on her mind-set. "Look, I wanted to ask you a few more questions, but I can see it's a bad time."

"It won't make any difference. I just don't have it right now. What do you want to know?"

"I'm trying to find out more about a party at Dean Casperson's house on Saturday night. Were you there?"

Aimee shook her head. "No, I wasn't feeling well. I popped a couple vitamin C pills and spent the evening in a hot bath."

"Did you hear any stories about the party?"

"What kind of stories?"

"Anything that people might not want to see in a newspaper."

"Sorry, Serena. I wasn't there."

Serena noticed that Aimee had dodged her question. "I'm curious. How well do you know Dean Casperson?"

"Dean? We're not in the same circles. Dean Casperson is an A-lister. He's a household name. I don't exactly jet off to Dean and Mo's house for brunch."

"You've worked with him before, though, right? I looked up your profile on IMDb. Your first role six years ago was in a Dean Casperson film."

"Yes. That was a huge break for me. Dean picked me himself."

"Did he help you get this part, too?" Serena asked.

"In fact, he did. Why are you asking about this?"

"Because you were right that Haley Adams was a spy," Serena said. "She was spying on Dean. I was wondering if you had any idea what she might have been looking for."

Aimee hesitated. "Honestly, these questions are making me uncomfortable."

"Why is that?"

The actress looked over her shoulder to make sure that none of the crew was within earshot. She lowered her voice. "You have no idea how much power someone like Dean Casperson has. If he thought I was gossiping about him, he could ruin me."

"This isn't gossip. Haley Adams is missing."

"I know, and I feel bad about that, but I'm sorry, Serena. I'm not saying anything about Dean."

"Okay. What about Jungle Jack? I heard there was something going on between him and one of the interns."

"Interns. Extras. Crew. Jack keeps plenty busy."

"Did he get busy with Haley Adams?" Serena asked.

"He tried."

"Did Haley tell you that?"

"She did. She also asked me how tight Jack was with Dean. I figured Jack was giving her a line. He was probably hinting that he could get her a role in the movie if she slept with him."

"What did you tell her?"

"I told her to stay away from Jungle Jack," Aimee said.

Before Serena could ask anything more, she heard a loud voice on the set. "Ms. Bowe, we're ready for you."

"I have to go," Aimee told her. "Time for take two."

Serena watched the actress walk away, and she noticed Aimee get in character as she neared the box. Her shoulders slumped. Her legs wobbled as if they would cave under her. Aimee crawled inside, and when she turned around to face the cameras, she was already a different person.

As the crew finalized the cameras and sound for the scene, Serena saw a triangle of light stream across the floor near her, and a blast of outside air roared through the rear of the warehouse. Someone slipped inside. A woman. Serena struggled to see through the shadows, but then she realized that the new visitor on the set was Lori Fulkerson. They'd never met, but Serena had seen her photo in the papers and seen her interviewed on television. Lori lingered near the door ten feet away as if leaving herself the option for a quick exit. They were nearly the same height, but Lori was heavier. Her curly hair crept from under a wool cap.

Before Serena could go over and introduce herself, take two began.

Serena watched Aimee in the box, but she also studied Lori Fulkerson out of the corner of her eye to see how the woman reacted. Lori's expression never changed or showed any emotion. The woman's eyes were lifeless. She kept her hands buried in her pockets. To Serena, Aimee's performance was as gut-wrenching as it had been before, but it seemed to have no impact at all on Lori Fulkerson.

They did another take and then another before Aimee broke free again. She walked toward Serena, but as she did, she saw Lori Fulkerson hovering by the door. Aimee walked past Serena and up to Lori and hugged her. It was a mistake. Lori reacted stiffly, obviously uncomfortable. Serena also noticed the physical differences between them. Aimee was the small, slim, Hollywood version of the victim, whereas Lori was the reality.

"I'm very glad you came," Aimee said.

"Well, my mother wouldn't get off my back about it," Lori replied.

"I really could use your help," Aimee told her. "Did you see the last couple of takes? I'm not getting it."

"No, you're not," Lori replied without any subtlety.

"What am I doing wrong? What am I missing?"

"Everything."

Aimee didn't react defensively, but she looked at a loss for words. She beckoned Serena over as if searching for another way to make a connection with Lori. "This is Serena Stride. She's Lieutenant Stride's wife."

Lori's eyes expressed no warmth or curiosity. "I suppose Stride told you about finding me last night?"

Serena nodded.

"He keeps rescuing me," Lori said, but she didn't make it sound like a good thing.

The silence that followed was awkward, and Serena thought that Lori looked ready to bolt. Aimee saw members of the crew eyeing them with sideways stares. The warehouse felt crowded. The actress took Lori's hand and pulled her toward the exit door, and Serena followed behind them. They went out into the subzero cold beside the gray warehouse wall. They were no more than fifty yards from the water. The sky was crisp and blue, but the sun gave no warmth. No one else was outside. Aimee did a jittery frozen dance, and Serena slipped off her heavy coat and put it over her shoulders. Lori unwrapped a stick of gum and chewed it as she stared across the ice of the harbor.

"I know this is hard for you," Aimee said, "and I appreciate your being here at all. Is there anything you can tell me?"

Lori shrugged. "Like what?"

"Anything about the emotional experience you went through. Or the physical experience. Something to help me understand. Something I can grab on to."

Lori said nothing for a long time. The wind lifted a cyclone of snow from the ground and threw it in their faces. Serena shivered, but Lori was like a statue made of white stone.

"I don't know what to say," she told her finally. "You can't fake it."

"I'm not trying to fake it," Aimee replied.

"Are you afraid to die?" Lori asked her.

"Yes. Sure."

"What if I told you that your plane going back to Los Angeles was going to crash? What do you think would go through your head in those last seconds?"

Aimee hesitated. "I don't know. Terror. Regret. Anger, I guess."

"You have *thirty seconds*. The last thirty seconds of your life."

Aimee groped for a response that wouldn't sound foolish. "Hope maybe. Up to the last second. Physically, maybe dizziness. Nausea."

Lori spit out a wad of gum. "This is a waste of time. I don't know why I bothered. I'm out of here."

Aimee grabbed the woman's shoulder and wouldn't let her leave. "No, please. You're the only one who knows what it was like. The others died."

"You need to let go of her, Aimee," Serena murmured.

The actress ignored her. She held on to Lori Fulkerson and turned her around. "I can't answer your question. About the plane. I've never been in that situation. And I was never in the box. You were. That's why I need your help."

Lori ripped away Aimee's hands and shoved the actress against the wall of the warehouse. Aimee lost her balance in the snow, and Lori physically picked her up and pinned her where she was. Serena moved closer to intervene, but Aimee shook her head and waved her away.

"You want to know what you do in the box?" Lori spit back at her. Her voice was barely louder than the wind. "After seven days in pitch blackness? Cold, no food, no water? You really want to know what happens to you?"

"Yes," Aimee whispered.

Lori shoved her face to within an inch of Aimee's. "You're not human anymore. You're an animal. A beast. Everything that made you a person falls away like dead leaves."

"What does that mean?"

"You're thirsty. You're so dry you can't swallow. You can't think about anything except water. Nothing. If you have any piss left, you start peeing into your hands so you can drink it. Does that paint the picture?"

"Oh, my God."

"God? There is no God. You bargain with the Devil, not God. Jesus isn't in the box. You say *Save me, Jonathan Stride*, because that's what the voice tells you to say, but you don't believe it. You know no one is going to save you. After a while, you don't *want* them to save you. You want to die, because if you get saved, you know you'll be in the box for the rest of your life. You'll never get out. It will be there every time you close your eyes. At least if you die, it's over. It's almost euphoric when you feel it getting close."

"What else?"

"You want more? You hallucinate. You hear voices. You see dead people. You can't breathe. You shiver so hard in the cold that your bones break. You get so weak, you lie on your back and can't move."

"What else?"

"What else? What else? Are you kidding me? Here's what else. The other women had a *bird* inside the box with them. Did they tell you about that? A chickadee. You can't see it, but it flies around in the darkness, and it sings to you. It's like this one beautiful thing that keeps you alive and reminds you of the outside world. But the whole point really is to drive you crazy. To see how long it takes before you decide to catch it and kill it and eat it raw and drink its blood."

Aimee put her hands over her mouth. She began to cry.

"Is that enough?" Lori asked. "Are we done here?"

Aimee nodded mutely, with tears ruining her makeup. Lori let go of her, but the actress stumbled as if she couldn't stand on her own. Serena leaped forward and grabbed her. Lori Fulkerson stalked off across the slushy street to the curb where her Toyota was parked. She never looked back.

"Are you okay?" Serena asked Aimee.

The actress watched Lori drive away, her tires spinning on ice. Aimee separated herself and slipped Serena's coat off her shoulders. She didn't look cold anymore, and she seemed to have her strength back. Her face was pink and windburned, but Serena was surprised to see a grim smile of determination bend upward on her lips.

"I'm fine," Aimee said.

"Is that really what you wanted?" Serena asked.

"That's exactly what I wanted," Aimee replied as she headed back toward the warehouse door. "I'm in the box now."

# 12

At noon, Stride got the call. They'd found a body.

He stood on the shoulder of Lavaque Road, surrounded by a posse of ambulances and police cars. Up and down the road in both directions, he saw nothing but evergreens, naked birches, and a few ash trees whose dried yellow leaves had clung to their branches deep into the winter. They were less than a mile north of the accident site where they'd found the Impala in the ditch.

A narrow break in the trees led east into the woods. The deep snow was littered with the boot marks of cops and the paw prints of search dogs. Stride skidded down the slope and followed Guppo on the trail.

"We got lucky," the oversize cop called over his shoulder as he wheezed his way through the snow. "We were two hundred yards in and about to turn back when one of the dogs picked up the scent and dived into the trees."

"John Doe was smart," Stride said.

The remoteness of this location didn't feel random. Without the car accident and the Glock to prompt a search, it was unlikely that a body ever would have been discovered up here even after the spring snowmelt. Hikers simply didn't wander through these woods. Haley's disappearance never would have been solved. Without evidence of foul play, they would have had no reason to consider it a murder. She just would have been one more unexplained lost soul.

Stride continued behind Guppo into the teeth of the wind. He wore sunglasses against the bright sun, had put on earmuffs, and his green cap was low on his forehead. Ahead of them, the footsteps veered into the thick of the forest. Guppo turned, and so did Stride. There was no path; they slogged through dense, sharp branches and low weeds. The shadows from the crowns of pines overhead made it hard to see more than a few feet in front of them.

Guppo stopped abruptly. Stride stopped, too, nearly running into the man's back. He saw crime scene tape awkwardly looped around tree trunks. There was no clearing. Looking down, he saw only a pink athletic shoe jutting out of the brush to let him know that they'd reached the body.

"End of the line," Guppo said. "This is where he dumped her."

Stride bent down under the tape and took two steps forward, careful to stay in the footprints that had been left by the police officers who'd already been there. The young woman was at his feet, practically invisible until he was looking directly down at her. John Doe had covered her in feathery snow, but the wind had brushed it aside in patches, like a terrible treasure being revealed. She was frozen solid. Where he could see her limbs, she looked bony to the point of anorexia. Her milky white face stared at the sky, blue eyes wide open, mouth parted in surprise between colorless lips. She had blond hair in a short, boyish cut. There were a few freckles across her forehead, but mostly he saw the burned bullet hole in the center that had killed her.

"Is that Haley Adams?" Guppo asked.

Stride studied the body and realized he had no idea. He hadn't seen a single photograph of the girl from the movie crew, and none of the descriptions they'd gotten matched one another. He bent down to get closer to the girl's face. Her features weren't familiar. She wasn't a match for any of the Florida driver's license photos that Maggie had pulled. So far, she was as much a mystery as John Doe.

They had two dead strangers in town. One killer. One victim.

"The age and physical appearance are consistent," Stride replied, "but that's all I can say right now. We'll have to get people on the movie set to see if they can identify her."

Guppo shook his head. "She looks like a sweet kid. I don't think she knew what hit her."

"I guess that's a good thing," Stride said.

Some faces of the dead were hard to get out of his brain. This girl was going to be one of them. Guppo was right. She looked innocent and lost, not like a spy. She had a loneliness about her, as if it were somehow inevitable that she would end up in a lonely place. One small body among the miles of wilderness.

He'd suspected all along that she was dead, but there was a terrible finality about finding her here. Every missing persons case held out faint hope until they located a body.

"I assume this isn't where he did it," Stride said.

"No, she wasn't killed here," Guppo told him. "We widened the search area and found a Flexible Flyer and some bloody plastic sheeting about fifty feet away. That was how he dragged the body in. He weighted it all down with heavy branches and covered it up with snow."

"John Doe must have scouted the area in advance to figure out where he was going to dump the body. The guy was definitely a pro."

"If he was so smart, what was he doing in Duluth in January without a decent coat?" Guppo asked with a chuckle.

Stride laughed, too. Not many people were prepared for the reality of a Minnesota winter. It had been six days since the air temperature had climbed above zero.

"I guess he figured, why buy a coat if you're heading home to Florida?"

"Do you think he really was from Florida?" Guppo asked. "The ID was a fake. He could have been from anywhere."

"Maybe, but the Sunshine State keeps coming up everywhere we look. John Doe had a Florida license. Haley Adams told Chris she grew up in Florida. And Dean Casperson has a mansion on an island down there. That's a lot of connections."

"So why did Haley get killed up here?" Guppo asked.

Stride frowned. "Good question. It's a long way to go to commit murder. It might help if we knew who the hell she really was."

*

By the time Stride made it back to the highway, Maggie had arrived at the crime scene. She had Aerosmith booming on the radio, but she clicked it off as he climbed inside her Avalanche and warmed his hands in front of the vents. When he'd thawed out, he showed her the photo of the girl in the woods.

"Damn," she murmured with regret in her voice. "I hate it when we find snow angels."

"Yeah."

They didn't talk for a while. For all of the prickliness about Maggie, she had a soft spot for victims. A death like this always got to her. He also could see in her face that the weight of everything was catching up with her. Her lack of sleep. Her breakup with Troy. And it was hard not to feel depressed here in the dead of winter, when the days were short, bitter, and gray. If the sun shone at all, it wasn't around for long.

"I called Serena," she said eventually. "I told her about the body."

"Thanks," Stride said. "Was she able to get any more information out of Aimee Bowe?"

Maggie nodded. "One little tidbit. It sounds like there might have been something going on between Haley and Jungle Jack."

"Well, I've been looking for an excuse to have a little chat with him," Stride said.

"Try not to break his face, boss. He's a jerk, but he's pretty."

"No guarantees," Stride replied. "What have you been able to find out about Jack?"

Maggie didn't bother consulting her notes. She could recite everything from memory. "Where Dean Casperson goes, Jack goes, too. They're thick as thieves. Jack has worked every Casperson movie for more than fifteen years. He's a stunt double, but the relationship goes much deeper than that. When they're not filming, Jack lives with Dean and Mo."

"At their estate on Captiva?"

Maggie nodded. "That's what his ID shows. Like I said, they're close."

"Does Jack have a record?"

"Not that I could find. It sounds like he's the bad boy on every set, but being a pig isn't a crime. From what I could find out, Jack gets away with a lot because he's tight with Casperson. Nobody wants to cross him, and Casperson has the money and influence to make bad things go away."

"Speaking of bad things, did you track down the other intern Chris Leipold mentioned? The one who quit after saying she'd been assaulted."

"I did," Maggie said. "She stuck to the party line. It was all a misunderstanding. She also had a brand-new Subaru BRZ parked outside her apartment. These people know how to cover their asses, boss."

Stride shook his head. He stared through the window at the police activity in the woods. They'd be bringing out the body soon. His first thought about the murder was that something had happened between Haley Adams and Jungle Jack. Another assault. And maybe, unlike the other intern, Haley wouldn't take a payoff and slip quietly away.

But that didn't explain the telescope. It didn't explain why Haley Adams had no identity of her own.

"Do we know how Jack originally hooked up with Casperson?" Stride asked. "They seem like an odd match. Was it a Hollywood thing? Did they get together on one of Casperson's movies?"

"No, Jack doesn't have any acting or movie background," Maggie replied. "He's got a degree in security management from the University of Central Florida. He specialized in celebrity security and worked with some of the rich and famous down on the Gulf Coast. That's how he met the Caspersons."

"Florida again," Stride murmured.

"Yeah. The trail leads down there."

"You sound pretty sure about that."

"Oh, yeah. I'm sure."

He heard something in Maggie's voice, and his eyes narrowed curiously. She had information that she hadn't shared with him yet, and based on the look on her face, it was something big. "Okay, what did you find out?"

"I have no idea how to explain it, but here's the thing. John Doe killed Haley Adams."

"Yeah, that seems like the obvious conclusion. What's your point?"

"No, that's not what I mean," Maggie went on. "I'm not talking about the girl here in the woods. I'm talking about Haley Adams *in Florida*. The girl from Fort Myers who was murdered, the one I put on the lineup of driver's license photos. John Doe shot her."

"*What?* Are you sure?"

"The ballistics report on the Glock came back from the Gherkin at the FBI. The gun was used in one other unsolved crime. Two years ago, a twenty-two-year-old Florida woman named Haley Adams was found shot to death in the parking lot of a shopping and restaurant complex called Tin City in Naples, Florida. One bullet in the middle of the forehead. It's a match for the gun we found in John Doe's rental car."

"And now we have another girl using the name Haley Adams, killed in the same way, probably with the same gun," Stride said. "Only the two crime scenes are a couple thousand miles apart."

"Exactly."

"What did you find out about the Florida murder?" he asked.

"Not much. The investigation went nowhere. The girl was a waitress at one of the seafood joints in the area. The police never found a motive. There were no witnesses. Her wallet was missing, so it got written off as a street crime. Except clearly it was something else."

Stride didn't have any trouble reading her mind. "I'm guessing there's somewhere you want to go, Mags."

"Naples," she said. "We need to get some answers down there."

"I don't suppose this has anything to do with the fact that it's about ninety degrees warmer down there right now?"

A grin crept across Maggie's face. "That thought never occurred to me."

Stride didn't protest. "Okay. Fine. It would do you good to get away from here for a couple days, anyway. I'll talk to K-2 about finding a way to pay for it. Get some sunblock and go."

"Way ahead of you," Maggie replied cheerfully. "The chief said there's not a hope in hell of him paying for it, but don't worry, I bought the ticket myself. I have a flight out of Minneapolis in three hours, so I need to crank down the freeway."

Stride glanced in the backseat of Maggie's Avalanche. He wasn't surprised at all to see that she already had a suitcase there, and he laughed. "It may be warmer, but it's pretty sticky down there with all the humidity. You'll hate it."

"We'll see about that."

"What's your plan?" Stride asked.

"I'll talk to the Naples police when I get there and fill them in on what we've found. I also want to track down the detective who originally worked on the Haley Adams murder. He left the force and went private a while back. The guy's name is Cab Bolton."

# 13

Stride found the apartment complex in the flatlands that led from Duluth toward the Iron Range. They were individual one-room cottages dotted among soaring evergreens, and it was a good place to stay for people who didn't want anyone to see them coming and going. The rentals were month to month and not expensive. They were across the street from empty fields and at a crossroads that led north toward the intersection with Lavaque Road.

This was where John Doe had stayed for ten days.

It was also where Jungle Jack Jensen was renting an apartment.

Stride turned off the highway into the dirt parking lot, which was a slippery mess of matted-down snow and ice. Daylight already was waning in the late afternoon, and the evergreens cast long shadows. John Doe had rented a unit tucked back among the trees and invisible from the road, but Jack's unit was closer to the street. There was a rental Lexus parked outside that looked out of place in the downscale surroundings. The boxy cottages all needed a coat of paint

He knocked on the apartment door. No one answered, so he knocked again and called Jack's name. Finally, the door opened. Jungle Jack stood in the doorway with nothing but a motel towel wrapped around his waist. He grimaced as subzero air whipped against his bare skin and brought up goose bumps.

"Jack Jensen? I'm Lieutenant Stride with the Duluth Police."

"It's not a great time to talk right now," Jack replied.

Stride could see over Jungle Jack's shoulder into the one-room apartment. There wasn't much to see: just a bed and some modest furnishings, a kitchenette, and a doorway to the bathroom. There was a dark-haired young woman in the bed with a sheet pulled up to her bare shoulders.

"See what I mean?" Jack went on, letting a grin creep onto his face. "Can this wait?"

"I'm investigating a murder, so no, it really can't."

The word "murder" didn't affect the uninterested look on Jack's chiseled face. He shrugged and called over his shoulder. "Why don't you hop in the shower, sweetie. I'll join you in a couple minutes."

Modesty didn't trouble the woman in the bed. She scooted naked from under the sheet and ran across the carpet to the bathroom, where she shut the door behind her. Jack waved Stride inside and then went to the wardrobe and put on a dark blue terry-cloth robe. He took a cigarette from a pack, lit it, and inhaled deeply. He extended the pack to Stride, who shook his head.

Jungle Jack sat on the edge of the bed. Stride pulled over a wooden chair and sat across from him. Jack continued to smile as if his face didn't do anything else. He was in his midthirties and Hollywood handsome, with a jutting jaw and pronounced cheekbones. His jet black hair was swept back like a lion's mane. He had a muscular physique, and he looked relaxed and confident as he smoked. There was no way Jack didn't realize that he'd accidentally hit on the teenage girl who lived in Stride's house, but if it worried him, he didn't show it.

"So what can I do for you, Lieutenant?"

"I'd like to talk about Haley Adams," Stride said.

"Who?"

"She was an intern on the movie set."

"Oh, the missing girl, sure. That's too bad. I hope you find her."

"We did," Stride said. "She's dead."

He showed Jack a photo of the girl they'd found in the woods. Jack's grin vanished. He seemed genuinely upset, but Stride had to remind himself that Jungle Jack, even if he was only Dean Casperson's stunt double, was an actor. You couldn't trust anything on an actor's face.

"Well, that's horrible. Dean is going to be crushed to learn about this."

"Can you confirm that this is the girl you knew as Haley Adams?" Stride asked.

Jack took another look as he examined the picture. "I think so. The face looks right, although I thought her hair was longer."

"Did you have a relationship with Haley?"

Jack eyed the bathroom door, where Stride could hear the shower water running. "You mean that kind of relationship?"

"I mean any kind of relationship."

"Well, did I try to get between her legs? Sure. The big secret of movie sets is that it's usually boring as hell. Hours of downtime while the crew gets everything ready for a couple minutes in front of the cameras. You're always looking for ways to pass the time. And somebody to pass the time with."

"I'm aware," Stride replied coldly. His meaning was clear.

Jack took a drag on his cigarette. Their eyes met with the controlled antagonism of two chess players on opposite sides of the board. "Yeah, I know I screwed up about that girl at the restaurant. Apologies. Mo read me the riot act."

Stride let it go. "So you made a pass at Haley Adams. Did anything happen between the two of you?"

"No."

"She rejected you?"

"I guess she didn't know what she was missing," Jack said.

"I've heard you don't always take no for an answer."

"I don't know where you heard that, but you heard wrong."

"One of the other interns on the movie said you assaulted her," Stride said.

"That was a misunderstanding. It was resolved amicably."

"You mean it was resolved with Dean Casperson buying her a Subaru BRZ?"

"I have no idea what you're talking about," Jack replied. "Look, the fact is I don't have any trouble finding companionship when I'm on the road. The girl in the shower? She was my waitress at lunch. Tomorrow I'll find somebody else. It's the way things are in my world. I suppose that sounds disgusting to you, but most men would trade places with me in a heartbeat."

Stride didn't want to hear about the notches on Jack's bedpost. He took the page of Florida driver's license photos out of his pocket. "Speaking of waitresses. See the last girl on this page? She was a waitress at a restaurant in Naples, Florida. Do you recognize her?"

Jack leaned forward to study the thumbnail. "She doesn't look familiar."

"Her name was Haley Adams, too."

"Well, it's a small world, as we say in Florida," Jack replied. "But I told you. I don't remember her."

"Do you spend a lot of time in Naples?" Stride asked.

"Whenever I can. It's a nice area."

"It's not too far from where you live, right?"

"Right."

"Actually, I understand you live with Dean and Mo Casperson," Stride said.

"Now and then. Off and on. We're good friends."

Stride cast an eye dubiously around the small apartment. "So why are you staying here and not in the mansion downtown with Dean?"

"I am staying with Dean, but I like to have my own place as a backup, too. I entertain a lot. If I did that at Dean's place, people might get the wrong idea."

"Why this place? You're pretty far out of town."

"I like my privacy," Jack said. "There are spies everywhere when you're in this business. Everybody wants to know your secrets. You can't be too careful."

"Speaking of spies, did you know that Haley Adams was spying on Dean Casperson? She had a telescope trained on his bedroom window."

"I didn't know that," Jack replied, "but I can't say I'm surprised."

"Why is that?"

"Haley was a nosy little bitch. Always asking questions. I should have guessed she was working for the tabloids."

"Is that what you think she was doing?" Stride asked.

"I can't imagine any other reason she would have been spying on Dean."

"Why do you think someone killed her?"

"I have no idea," Jack replied. "Maybe she was selling drugs. Maybe she had a jealous boyfriend. Isn't it your job to figure out who killed her, Lieutenant? We play cops and robbers in the movies, but you do it in real life."

"Actually, we're pretty sure we know who killed Haley," Stride replied, finding the next photograph on his phone. "It was this man. Do you know him?"

Jack took a long look at the photograph of John Doe and then an even longer drag on his cigarette. He blew smoke toward the ceiling and seemed to be stalling as he figured out the best answer. "Yeah, I'm pretty sure this man was staying at one of the apartments here. I've seen him around."

"Was he connected to the movie?" Stride asked.

"I don't think so."

"Did you talk to him?"

"I might have said hello in passing. That's all."

"We have a witness who saw this man at a party at Dean Casperson's house last Saturday night," Stride said.

"This guy? I don't recall seeing him there. Then again, I was having a pretty intense conversation that night with a bottle of Glenmorangie, so my memory may have some amber-colored gaps."

Stride shook his head. Jungle Jack was smooth at providing non-denial denials.

"Have you seen this man anywhere else?" Stride asked.

"Like around Duluth?"

"Like in Florida," Stride said. "We think he spent time in Naples, too."

"Really? No, I don't recall ever seeing him before. But like I said, it's definitely a small world down there." Jack glanced impatiently at the bathroom door again. "Are we done here, Lieutenant? Not that I don't enjoy your company, but I have other things to be doing."

"We're done," Stride told him, getting out of the chair.

"Again, sorry about the thing with your girl," Jack said.

"You should be careful when you're looking for companions," Stride replied. "You wouldn't want to make a mistake that would leave you in legal jeopardy."

"Oh, I'll be careful. Count on it." As Stride turned toward the apartment door, Jack added in an oddly congenial voice, "You know, you should probably be a little careful, too, Lieutenant."

Stride stopped. He turned back and tried to assess the meaning behind Jack's warning. "I'm sorry. Careful about what?"

"You're in the movies now. That means you're playing in a whole different league. You're fair game for the tabloids, just like Dean."

"I'm not in the movies," Stride said.

Jack shook his head. He slapped Stride on the shoulder as if they were old friends. He grinned again, but his smile felt nasty. "Oh, not true, Lieutenant. Not true at all. When someone makes a movie about you, believe me, you are instantly a celebrity. And the thing about celebrities is, someone out there is always trying to take them down."

# 14

Serena knew she was in the right place because of the red Toyota Yaris parked in the grass. It was night, and the nearest streetlight was a block away, so she had trouble seeing as she got out of her Mustang. She was at the southern end of Sixty-Second Avenue in West Duluth. Through the bare trees, she heard the whine of traffic on the elevated lanes of I-35 only fifty yards away.

Lori Fulkerson's house was built of brick, but it looked unsteady, as if the wolf could huff and puff and blow this one down. It had been dropped onto a tiny, snowy crescent of grass. A narrow path had been shoveled between the street and the half dozen wooden beams that counted as steps. Serena made her way up to the storm door and rapped her knuckles on the glass.

She heard the buzz of a television inside.

Then she heard a scream that startled her and made her reach for her gun. She relaxed when Aimee Bowe's familiar voice followed the scream, shouting out words that Serena had heard her say earlier in the day on the movie set.

*"Save me, Evan Grave. Save me."*

Serena's heart was still racing, but she smiled at her nervousness. With the movie people in town, it was hard to separate fiction from reality.

Inside, the noise of the television stopped, and Lori Fulkerson came to the door. Her brown curls were a thick bird's nest. She wore a roomy Vikings sweatshirt over her stocky torso and shorts despite the cold. She held a cheap can of beer in one hand and a tiny Yorkshire terrier in the other. The dog barked wildly. Lori opened the door a crack and said, "What do you want?"

"I wanted to see how you're doing, Ms. Fulkerson," Serena said.

"I'm fine."

"Do you mind if we talk for a minute?"

Lori opened the door wider, and Serena squeezed inside. The living room was small, barely twelve feet square. The house was a mess, literally buried in clothes, blankets, music CDs, newspapers, and old magazines. Lori never threw out anything. On the far wall, Serena saw a flat-screen television. Aimee Bowe's face was frozen on the screen, paused in the middle of her scream.

"Sit down if you can find a place," Lori said. She put the dog down, and it ran in circles and yipped at Serena. Lori slumped into a recliner, and her knee bounced nervously. Her feet had been pushed into leather moccasins.

Serena sat on a sofa on top of a six-inch pile of back issues of the *News Tribune*. She pointed at the television.

"Is that from the filming today? How did you get it?"

"Aimee Bowe sent me a web link," Lori explained. "She wanted me to see it."

"That must be hard to watch."

Lori shrugged. Her jaw worked as she chewed gum. The house smelled of burned toast. The dog continued to bark at Serena with its little legs quivering, and Lori threw a rawhide chew toy into the small kitchen to distract it.

"I was impressed that you were able to talk about it," Serena went on. "I'd never heard some of the worst details before. It was horrifying."

"Didn't Stride tell you about it?" Lori asked.

"Not the things you told Aimee. He never released any of that information publicly, out of respect for the victims."

"So what are you saying? I should have shut up about it?"

"Not at all. You were a victim. That's your call."

Lori pointed a remote control at the television. She pushed a button, and the screen went black. "I hate the whole idea of the movie. I took the money because I wanted to move out of this place, but I wish I hadn't. Maybe if I'd said no, it would have tanked the whole project."

"Probably not," Serena told her. "Chris would have just written it differently."

"Yeah. Maybe he would have figured out a way to turn his father into the hero."

"Actually, I think Chris Leipold hates Art as much as you do," Serena said.

As the words left her mouth, Serena knew she'd said the wrong thing. Lori's eyes turned to flame. *"Not. Even. Close."*

Serena nodded. "Of course. I'm so sorry."

The woman was silent, breathing hard and fast.

"Why did you help Aimee if you're so opposed to the film?" Serena asked, trying to recover from her mistake.

"If they're going to do it, they should do it right. And my mom bugged me about it forever. She thinks it will make me famous. Like I want to be famous for that."

Serena looked around the living room and noticed cracks in the wall among the junk and a few photographs of Lori as a child, standing next to someone who was probably her father. Yellow flowered wallpaper peeled at the ceiling.

"Have you lived here long?" Serena asked.

"Ever since I came back to town. It was all I could afford, and it's close to my job. Plus, I grew up on the other side of the freeway. I wanted to be back in my old neighborhood."

"Does your mother live near here, too?"

Lori snorted. "No. When she left Duluth, she took me as far away from my father as she could. She always said she'd never set foot in this city again. She calls, but I haven't seen her in years."

"Is that your father?" Serena asked, gesturing at the photos on the wall.

Lori glanced at the pictures. "Yeah. Those were taken at the playground near the freeway when I was six. It's not even fifty yards away from here. It still looks exactly the same. Nothing ever changes in Duluth."

"What do you do for a living?"

"I do purchasing and accounting at an auto parts store over on Grand. I can walk to work in the summer."

"Nice."

They were silent for a while. The Yorkie in the kitchen gnawed loudly at his rawhide treat.

"So what are you really doing here?" Lori asked.

"Like I said, I wanted to make sure you were okay. The things you said to Aimee were pretty emotional."

"And I told you, I'm fine."

"The movie brings it all back, though, doesn't it?" Serena asked. "I know it does for Jonny."

"Yeah. It does. So what? Let me guess: Stride told you I have a gun. He's worried I'll blow my brains out. And he sent you over here rather than come himself, because he knows I don't like him."

"You're exactly right," she admitted.

"If you lived in this neighborhood, wouldn't you have a gun?" Lori asked.

"Probably."

"Well, there you go."

"Why don't you like Stride?" Serena asked.

"You mean, because he rescued me and I should feel grateful?"

"I didn't say that."

"I'm sorry, I don't see your husband as some kind of saint," Lori said. "And every time I see his face, I'm right back there on the worst day of my life. So no, I don't like him."

"That's all right. I understand."

"You can tell him I'm not going to kill myself. You don't need to worry about that. Your work is done, okay?"

"Okay."

Serena stood up. There was nothing else to say.

"You can let yourself out," Lori told her.

"Of course. Good night, Ms. Fulkerson."

Serena headed for the storm door and went back out into the cold. She waited for her eyes to adjust to the darkness. As she took the treacherous front steps, she twitched as she heard Aimee Bowe screaming again from the television inside.

The voice sounded way too real.

*"Save me."*

*

Cat did her math homework at the dining room table in Stride's cottage. She played "Hard Times" by Paramore at a volume loud enough to fill the house, and she danced in the chair and sang along to the music. When she heard the faint ping of the doorbell in the other room, she switched off the song and skidded in her socks across the hardwood floor to the front door.

It took her a moment to recognize the woman on their porch. She wore sunglasses at night, as if in disguise, and she had the fur-lined hood of her coat tied snugly around her face.

"Oh, hey, you're—" Cat began. "You're Aimee Bowe, right?"

The actress glanced over her shoulder at the empty street. Her eyes were uncertain. "Yes. I was looking for Serena. Does she live here?"

"Serena and Stride are out right now," Cat said, "but Serena just texted and said she'd be home pretty soon. You want to wait?"

Aimee hesitated. "Sure. If I'm not bothering you."

"Well, Jennifer Lawrence was supposed to come over with Emma Watson, but I guess they blew me off," Cat replied.

Aimee gave her a warm smile. "You really can't count on those two."

Cat let her into the house and squeezed the door shut. It was warped and usually stuck. The great space of the cottage was furnished with two red leather sofas, antiques, and bookshelves. A fireplace took up most of the far wall. Walnut steps led up to a closed door that led to the attic. Aimee followed Cat into the dining room, where Cat's schoolwork was spread across the table. The actress undid her coat and took off her sunglasses.

"Do you want anything?" Cat asked. "Stride thinks I don't know how to get into the liquor cabinet, but he is so wrong."

"No. I'm fine." Aimee glanced down at the open pages of the calculus book on the table. "Math, huh? That was never my subject."

"I'm kind of wired for it," Cat said. "I sort of see it all in my head. Like Sudoku. Serena can't solve one of those puzzles to save her life. She hates it when I give it back to her all done in like thirty seconds."

"Don't let me take you away from your homework," Aimee said.

"I'm almost finished anyway. I'm going to get a Diet Coke. You sure you don't want something?"

"That would be great," Aimee replied.

Cat grabbed two cans, and then she and Aimee returned to the great space and took up places on the sofas. The actress brought her feet casually under herself, and so did Cat. She watched Aimee study the artwork on the living room walls, which included a painting of Cornelius Vanderbilt and a century-old line drawing of Duluth city streets. On the mantle was a wooden plaque that said *believe*.

"It's sort of Addams Family, huh?" Cat said. "Stride likes it that way. Serena keeps trying to slip in some new stuff."

"I like things a little old-fashioned," Aimee replied.

Cat took a sip of Coke. "Just so you know, I'm working really hard not to go all fangirl on you. Part of me wants to sneak out my phone and stream it live so everybody at school can see. But I won't, don't worry."

"I appreciate it. You want a selfie together before I go?"

"That would be great! I mean, really, this is so cool, having you in my house. The whole idea of the movie thing happening in Duluth is just wild. Usually for us, freighters going under the lift bridge is about as exciting as it gets."

"That's sweet. You're Cat, right? Is that short for anything?"

"Catalina."

"What a beautiful name. I like it."

"Thanks."

"Serena shared some of your background with me," Aimee told her. "You've had a rough time. I hope you know she's really, really proud of you."

"Oh, yeah. Serena and Stride are both great. My mom got killed when I was six, so I feel like I got a second chance with Serena. And Stride is Stride. He's more than a dad. To me, he's like the best man in the universe."

"You're lucky."

"I know. I just wish I wasn't such an idiot sometimes."

"For a teenager, I think that's part of the job description," Aimee said. "Believe me, I've done a lot of stuff that I regret. And not just as a kid, either."

Cat never knew what to say when people told her that. She twisted the tab on her can of Diet Coke until it came off and then played with it between her slim fingers. On the coffee table, her phone sang with a snippet of lyrics from Train's "Bulletproof Picasso."

"Hang on, that's Mom's text tone," Cat said. "She got shot a couple years ago; did you know that? But she made it. I always tell her she's bulletproof." Cat read the text and said, "Serena stopped at Beaner's for coffee and now she's at the Zenith Bookstore next door. That means she'll probably be a while. Do you want me to tell her you're here?"

Aimee shook her head. "It's not important. I'll see her tomorrow."

"You sure?"

"Yes, I just wanted to tell her that I felt bad about Haley Adams. I heard the news. Can you pass that along?"

"Oh, definitely."

Aimee got off the sofa. She hadn't touched her Diet Coke. "It was a pleasure to meet you, Cat."

"Same here. Can we do that selfie now?"

"Sure," Aimee said, smiling.

Cat opened up her phone, and the two of them pushed their faces together as Cat snapped several photographs. When they were done, she scrolled through them as if she couldn't believe it. "This is amazing. Hey, before you go, do you mind if I ask you something? It's personal, though."

"Go ahead."

Cat chewed her lower lip and tried to figure out how to say it. "I'm a math person, but I believe in other stuff, too. Spiritual stuff. I never used to buy into any of that, but after everything that's happened to me, now I do. And Serena told me about you—that is, how you said you sense things. I was wondering, is that really true? What is that like?"

Aimee's face had a serious expression. "It's true. At least, I believe it, which is the only thing that matters."

"Is it something anyone can do? Or do you have to be special?"

"I think only a small handful of people are sensitives. Which is why most people don't believe it's real."

"How does it work?" Cat asked.

"Truly, I have no idea. There are moments when I just see things or feel things. I've learned simply to let it happen and not question it."

"I like that. I like thinking it's possible. This will sound weird, but do you sense anything about me?"

Aimee hesitated. "I don't like to talk about those things. It freaks people out."

"Please? That sounds like you do sense something."

"It's just feelings, Cat. It's not specific. Most of the time I have no idea what any of it means."

"Come on, tell me," Cat urged her.

Finally, Aimee sighed. "I sense you doing something very foolish," she said.

"That sounds like me."

"And also very brave," Aimee added.

"Oh."

"That's it. That's all I know."

"Thanks," Cat said. "That's really cool."

Aimee followed Cat back to the front door, and Cat labored to get it open again. When she did, the winter air stormed the house with a cold, blustery slap. Cat clicked on the porch light, illuminating flurries in the wind.

"It's snowing!" she said.

Aimee stared at the silver swirls as if she were hypnotized. "Beautiful."

"I love the snow," Cat said.

"Me, too. You'll give Serena my message?"

"Absolutely."

*"Save me,"* Aimee said.

Cat stared at her in confusion. "What?"

"I said, you'll give Serena my message?"

Cat shivered in the cold and felt little needles spreading across her skin. "I will. I definitely will."

"Thank you, Cat. Good night."

Cat didn't say anything more. She watched Aimee Bowe walk down the steps toward the street and disappear into the darkness and snow. She had no idea what had just happened.

# 15

Maggie sat at an outdoor table with a bowl of conch chowder and a Bloody Mary in front of her. She wore a flowered blouse, pink shorts, and leather sandals, all of which she'd purchased at the hotel gift shop. Through her sunglasses, she eyed the squat palm trees and white sand of the beach. The blue-green waters of the Gulf barely moved in the mild breeze. The sun felt millions of miles closer than it had the day before. When she rubbed a finger on the back of her neck, she felt sweat. It felt wonderful.

"Well, well," she murmured aloud to herself. "So this is how other people spend the winter."

Offshore, young people paddleboarded in bikinis. Treasure hunters, shell collectors, and sandpipers trailed through the wet sand as waves came and went. She saw fishermen with bait buckets. Labradors chasing Frisbees. Sun worshippers baking in the heat. It really was a different world down here.

She was surrounded in the hotel restaurant by rich middle-aged golfers who could afford the upscale prices. The handful of Pilates-trim older women at the other tables looked weighted down by their jewelry. Maggie had indulged in an expensive Versace watch for herself while she was browsing the gift shop. It hung on her wrist like a signal that she belonged here. In Duluth, she never flaunted her money, but she didn't care down here. No one knew her.

The only man who was close to her own age—well, a few years younger—sat at the bar with a mimosa in his hand. He was blond, ridiculously tall, ridiculously handsome, with an I-don't-care smirk on his face. Behind his sunglasses, he eyed her, and she eyed him back with a smirk of her own. There was no Troy in her life anymore. She could flirt if she wanted. He tilted his champagne glass in her direction and smiled at her with teeth that had no business being as white as they were. She smiled back.

Maggie decided that Florida was a very, very nice place.

On the table in front of her, her phone rang. She sighed as she saw the caller ID. She knew it was work, and she wasn't ready to think about work, but she answered the phone anyway.

"Maggie Bei," she said.

"Sergeant, this is Detective Lala Mosqueda with the Naples Police. I got your fax with the ballistics information in the Haley Adams murder. I have to tell you, that was quite the surprise."

"Yes, it looks like we have your killer on ice," Maggie replied. "Literally."

"Well, I wish we could help with the identification of your John Doe, but the Florida ID he was using appears to be straight identity theft. There was nothing suspicious about the death of James Lyons. We'll send the photo around, though, and see if anyone can identify your car accident victim."

"What about the Haley Adams case?" Maggie asked. "What can you tell me?"

"I worked with Detective Bolton on Haley's murder," she replied. "I admit, he and I didn't really see eye to eye on that one. Although that doesn't narrow it down when it comes to me and Cab."

Maggie smiled. "Oh?"

"Let's just say that Cab is not always known for playing nice with others."

"Some folks in Duluth might say the same thing about me," Maggie replied. "So what happened with your investigation?"

"It went cold. Without witnesses, we didn't have much to go on. Haley was a waitress, no record, no evidence of drug use, nothing to suggest a motive. To me it looked random. Wrong place at the wrong time. Her wallet and phone were gone, so it could have been a robbery, but my bet was that Haley interrupted a drug deal or gun sale going on in the parking lot. It happens. We get a lot of strangers passing through town, looking to make a quick buck and then disappearing."

"Detective Bolton disagreed?" Maggie asked.

She heard a little sigh from Mosqueda. "Yes, Cab thought the whole thing was fishy. He was sure Haley was targeted. A hit."

"Why is that?"

"Haley was a party girl," Mosqueda replied. "Friends said she liked to hang out in some fast circles. She knew a lot of celebrities. About three weeks before the murder, she went to a big party, and the other people at the restaurant said she came back pretty upset. She wouldn't talk about what happened, but she had a lot of cash with her. A few thousand bucks."

"No offense, Detective, but that sounds fishy to me, too."

"Well, this is Florida. Rich people throwing cash around at pretty girls isn't exactly front-page news. Neither is girls coming home from a party with morning-after regrets. I didn't think it added up to murder."

"What did you find out about the party?" Maggie asked.

"Nothing much. Haley didn't tell anyone where she was going. She turned off her phone, too, and I'll admit that seemed weird. The only thing we knew was that her SunPass got a toll charge on the Sanibel Causeway."

"Where's that?"

"It's the bridge heading out to Sanibel and Captiva."

Maggie hesitated. She didn't believe in coincidences. "Captiva?"

"Right. Very upscale. Richie Rich territory. Why, does that mean something to you?"

"Someone in our Minnesota case has a place down there," Maggie said.

"Who is it?"

"I'd rather not spread rumors until I know a little more."

She heard coolness enter Detective Mosqueda's voice. "Well, please remember that you're in our sandbox now, Sergeant. We're protective of our wealthy snowbirds. If you want to interview anyone, I'd appreciate it if you let me know so we can send someone with you. And you can tell Cab that I said that goes for him, too. Sometimes he forgets he's not with the police anymore."

"Understood."

"Where are you staying while you're in town?"

"The Ritz-Carlton."

There was a long pause on the phone.

"Well, you'll get along with Cab just fine," Mosqueda said.

"Where do I find him?" Maggie asked.

"In fact, I just got a text from him. He said I should ask you if you'd like a mimosa."

"What?"

Maggie's head snapped up. The blond man from the bar stood over her table now, looking tall enough to block out the sun. He held two champagne glasses in his hands, and he deposited one on a coaster next to her Bloody Mary. He slid into the chair across from her with a charming smile and whipped off his sunglasses to fix her with amazing ocean-blue eyes.

"Welcome to Florida, Sergeant Bei," Cab Bolton said.

*

The mimosa went down smoothly. So did the second one. Cab also insisted that she order the lump crab cake, and it was a superb recommendation.

Maggie had never thought of herself as having a weakness for pretty men, but Cab was pretty in a strangely irresistible way. He wore his blond hair short and used gel that left it in messy spikes. He had baby-smooth skin with a slight sunburn, a Bob Hope nose, and an angled jaw. His dark custom suit was obviously expensive, his purple tie was expertly knotted, and he sported a large diamond stud in one ear. His long neck reminded her of a giraffe. His legs extended all the way to her side of the table, where his shiny leather shoes tapped annoyingly on the sides of her chair.

"The Ritz," Cab said, admiring their surroundings, although it was clear that the servers all knew him. He was obviously a regular. "The police really must have a great union in Minnesota."

"Actually, I'm picking up the tab myself."

"Nice. A cop with independent means. Marriage or family?"

"Marriage. He died."

"I'm sorry."

"I'd be lying if I said it was a great loss," Maggie admitted. "How about you? Marriage or family?"

"Family."

"So neither one of us has to work. Why be a detective? Why not play golf or tennis or something?"

Cab shrugged. "I'm good at being a detective, and I'm not good at golf or tennis. What about you?"

"Same."

Maggie had to admit that it was satisfying to talk to someone who knew what it was like to have money and was so openly comfortable with his wealth. Cab was rich and made no excuses for it. He was also so unlike the men she knew in Minnesota that it was a little like having lunch with a zoo animal.

"I like your earring," she told him.

"Thank you. I like your watch."

"Why the name Cab? Were your parents Cab Calloway fans?"

"Well, my mother was single, and I was unplanned, so I think Cab stands for 'crap, a baby.'"

Maggie laughed. "Is that true?"

"No, if it were true, I'd be named 'Fab.' My mother has quite the mouth on her."

Maggie laughed again. She couldn't help liking him. It was easy to pass the time here with a drink, near the Gulf, in the sunshine, with a charming and handsome man. But when she checked her Versace watch, she saw that it was already past noon.

"So," she said finally, sipping her mimosa. "Haley Adams."

"Yes, Haley Adams. Lala sent me a copy of the FBI report. It was a professional hit, but I knew that all along."

Cab shifted gears smoothly. She could see the intelligence in his eyes, and she suspected that he used his looks and his surface shallowness to his advantage. People probably underestimated him.

"Why were you so sure? Detective Mosquito thought you were wrong."

Cab seemed very amused by the nickname. "Well, Lala and I are oil and water about most things, so that's not surprising. But the fact is, in this case I had a source who insisted on remaining anonymous. Without her, all I had was suspicion and innuendo. That wasn't enough to go after this guy. However, believe me, I didn't forget about Haley Adams. I never stopped investigating what happened to her even after I left the police."

"Really." Maggie didn't say it like a question.

"Yes, I've spent two years trying to piece it together. It goes back long before Haley. She was only the latest victim. The trouble is, all I've got to show for two years of work is smoke and no fire. I don't have any evidence to prove a thing. And as they say, when you shoot at the king, you better not miss."

"The king?"

Cab shrugged. "Most kings don't have as much money or power as this guy."

"You and I have money," Maggie said.

"Not like this."

"So who are you talking about?" she asked.

"Who do you think I'm talking about?" Cab replied.

Maggie leaned back in her chair. She studied Cab over the top of her champagne glass. There was a slight buzz in her head. "I'm going to say a word. You tell me if it's the right word. Okay?"

Cab's blue eyes glittered. He seemed to enjoy the game. "Okay."

"Captiva," Maggie said.

Cab stared at Maggie and said nothing at all, but one of his eyebrows made the slightest upward twitch. That was enough.

"I guess we're on the same page," she went on.

"I guess so," Cab said. He leaned across the table. "Since we're talking about the same thing, I have a question for you."

"What is it?"

His face was suddenly solemn. The lightness was gone from his voice. "I'm missing someone. I haven't heard from her in a few days, and I'm very worried. I'm wondering if you know where she is."

"Why would I know?" Maggie asked.

"Because I sent her to Minnesota to investigate this case."

Maggie closed her eyes. Suddenly it all made sense. The false identity. The second Haley Adams named after the first Haley Adams. "By any chance, did you send her there with a Moonraker telescope?"

"Yes, in fact, I did."

"She was a spy. Your spy. You were trying to get dirt on Dean Casperson?"

"That's right. Trust me, it was the only way I could think of to take him down. I know the surveillance was technically against the law, but if you've got her in one of your cells, I'd really like to get her out."

She realized that he didn't know. He had no idea.

"Cab," she murmured unhappily.

He watched her closely, reading the story in her face. The terrible truth dawned on him like the breaking of a wave. His blue eyes narrowed in disbelief. His clenched fist pushed against his chin. He swung his head to stare out at the Gulf water. She didn't know which emotion held the upper hand in his heart. Grief or rage.

"Who was she?" Maggie asked softly.

Cab took a long time to reply. "Her name was Peach Piper. She worked for me."

"I'm really sorry."

"What happened?" he asked.

"She was shot. We only found her body yesterday."

"Was it this John Doe of yours? The same man who killed the real Haley?"

Maggie nodded. "Yes."

Cab shook his head. "It was Peach's idea to use Haley's name. To see if Casperson reacted. To see if he even remembered. I guess he got the message."

"Are you sure about him?" Maggie asked.

Cab didn't answer. For the moment he was far away. "Peach. I can't believe it. She was this odd, quirky, lovely girl. A total loner. No family left. Lala and I were about the only friends she had in the world. And I sent her to her death."

"That's not fair," Maggie told him. "No, you didn't."

The anger swallowed up his sadness. "We have to *stop* this son of a bitch," Cab insisted, his voice choked with determination. "This has been going on for too long. We have to expose this psychopath for who he is. Casperson is the one who had Haley killed. He's the one who had Peach killed."

Maggie tried to wrap her mind around the idea. "Cab, are you sure? Is that really possible? You said yourself all you have is smoke and no fire. You don't have any evidence."

Cab stood up, which was like watching a flamingo perched atop long, gangly legs. He was at least six foot six.

"I told you I also have an anonymous source. And I want you to meet her."

"Who is it?"

"Someone who has known Dean Casperson for a long time," Cab said. "Someone who knows the truth about him. My mother."

# 16

When Stride saw the blue Hyundai Elantra for the third time that day, he knew he was being followed.

It had shown up the first time as he drove down the Point from his cottage at seven in the morning. He'd noticed it three blocks behind him, but he hadn't paid much attention. Then it had appeared again as he was leaving police headquarters to revisit the apartment used by Haley Adams—who was actually, according to Maggie, a Florida private investigator named Peach Piper. The Elantra had stayed behind him all the way to the Central Hillside neighborhood, where it disappeared when Stride pulled over to the curb. He wasn't close enough to note the license plate or see who was driving the car.

Now the Elantra was back again.

Stride was driving north on I-35 on his way back from the Duluth Grill. He was almost at the Superior Street exit when he spotted the car in his rearview mirror. A blue Elantra wasn't an uncommon vehicle in Duluth, but three times in one day was more than a coincidence. The car hung back, a quarter mile behind him in the left lane. Its headlights were on, and its windshield wipers brushed aside the light snow. He slowed to let the driver get closer, but the Elantra slowed, too, keeping a steady gap between them. He still couldn't see inside the car.

At Superior Street, he left the freeway. The Elantra changed lanes and prepared to exit, too. He stayed on the right-hand fork toward Michigan Street and headed into the downtown streets past the depot and the library. The blue car followed. He eased back on his speed, waiting for the stoplight at Fifth Avenue to change. As the light turned yellow, he accelerated and cruised through the intersection, leaving the Elantra stranded at the red light behind him.

He drove two more long blocks before the light changed and then made a quick turn into the parking lot inside Harbor Center. The covered lot was dark, and he spun the Expedition around so that it was facing the street. Then he switched off his lights, and he waited.

Thirty seconds later, the Elantra slowly passed the driveway. He got a brief glimpse of the driver, long enough to see that it was a woman with short auburn hair. She wasn't familiar to him. He waited until two more cars passed, and then he pulled out of the parking lot and focused on the blue Elantra ahead of him. She drove as if she were trying to figure out where he'd gone, but she wasn't savvy enough to look behind her. She went slowly, and the cars between them got impatient and blared their horns. Eventually, it was obvious that she'd given up on finding him. She sped up and turned off Michigan onto the cobblestoned pavers at First Avenue. Then she turned right onto Superior Street and made another right at Lake Avenue on her way down to the harbor area at Canal Park.

Stride followed.

In Canal Park, the Elantra turned into the parking lot at the Hampton Inn. He parked in one of the diagonal spots across the street in front of Caribou Coffee and watched through his driver's window as the woman got out of the car. She wore a navy-colored bubble coat that looked new and gray dress slacks. She was young, probably no more than thirty years old. She walked swiftly toward the hotel entrance and shook snow from her bobbed red hair, which was highlighted with streaks of royal blue. As he watched, she disappeared inside.

Stride got out of the Expedition and crossed the street into the hotel parking lot. He found the Elantra and made a quick call to Guppo to check the license plate. It was a Thrifty rental car from Minneapolis.

He brushed snow from the side windows and peered inside. A paper map of Duluth was on the passenger seat and, as in John Doe's car, a copy of the *National Gazette*. She'd also printed out a stack of archived articles from the *Duluth News Tribune*. The topmost story was a blurb from the previous winter about Stride's marriage to Serena.

Whoever this woman was, she was definitely watching him.

He headed for the lobby of the hotel. Inside, he showed his badge to the desk clerk and asked about the woman who'd entered the hotel five minutes earlier. Her name, according to the registration, was JoLynn Fields. The address she'd given was in Sarasota, Florida.

Florida again.

Stride got her room number and headed for the elevator. She was on the third floor in a lake-facing room at the far end of the hallway. He walked down the corridor and rapped his knuckles sharply on the door. Someone called cheerfully, "Just a second!"

The hotel door opened. JoLynn Fields saw him, and the smile on her face vanished.

"Oh!" she exclaimed in surprise.

"Hello, Ms. Fields. My name is Jonathan Stride, but I bet you know that."

He could almost see the calculations in her head as she thought about what to say. "Yes, I do, Lieutenant Stride."

"Well, maybe you'd like to tell me why you've been following me. And why you're digging into my personal life."

Her smiled returned. "Okay. Sure. You know, I should have figured you'd spot me. Following someone isn't what they make it look like on TV. And let me guess. When I lost you downtown, you started following *me*, right?"

"You still haven't answered my question," Stride said.

JoLynn opened the door wider. "Do you want to come inside? I don't bite, Lieutenant, I promise."

He squeezed past her into the hotel room, where the heat was cranked high enough to make it uncomfortably warm. There were two queen beds, a desk, and an overstuffed chair near the window. She had a laptop open on the desk, but as she retreated to the far side of the room, she slapped it shut. She gestured for Stride to take the overstuffed chair, and she sat in the desk chair and propped her stocking feet on the bed. From where he was, he could see the lake through the window. Waves beat against the rocks, and snow streaked across the glass. The clouds were like steel. The boardwalk by the lake was empty.

JoLynn looked outside, too. Her eyes were pale and gray. She shivered and tugged on the sleeves of her pink turtleneck, as if she could feel the winter chill simply by looking outside. The blue tints in her red hair looked like twisting snakes. "It's pretty here, but I'm not built for the cold."

"It's a lot warmer in Florida," Stride said.

"You checked me out at the desk, huh? Of course you did. Yes, I'm from Sarasota. Born and raised."

"What brings you to Minnesota, Ms. Fields?" he asked.

"The movie is what brings me here, but I'm sure you already guessed that. I'm a reporter. Entertainment beat."

"Who do you work for?"

"The *National Gazette*. And yes, I know, people roll their eyes when they hear that. Don't worry, I don't cover UFOs or Bigfoot. Although if Bigfoot is hiding anywhere, it would be somewhere like this."

"Why are you investigating me?" Stride asked again.

"I'm doing a story on you."

"What kind of story?"

"Human interest," JoLynn told him. "That's what our readers like. They want to know: Who is Jonathan Stride? Why is Hollywood making a movie about him? What is he like in real life? What kind of a hero is he?"

Stride shook his head. He thought about Jungle Jack's warning the previous day, and he didn't think the timing was a coincidence. Dean Casperson had made a call and put the tabloid on his trail.

"First of all, nobody's making a movie about me. It's an adaptation based on a case I worked on, but Evan Grave is not Jonathan Stride. And second of all, I'm nobody's hero, believe me."

"Even better," JoLynn replied. "People love strong men with flaws."

"The point is, I have no interest in anybody doing a story about me."

She shrugged. "No offense, Lieutenant, but that's not how it works. I'm not asking for permission. I'm *doing* the story. If you won't let me interview you, that's unfortunate, but I'll find other sources. However, I'd prefer to have your voice as part of it. I want to know what you have to say. Readers will want to know, too."

Stride leaned forward in the chair and put his hands on his knees. "Whose idea was this? Yours?"

"Of course. You're the man behind the mask. Dean Casperson is playing you. That's news."

"Following me secretly feels like stalking, not reporting," Stride said.

"I was going to approach you about an interview, but once you know I'm there, you behave differently. Everybody does; it's human nature. I wanted a chance to observe you before you realized you were going to be the subject of a profile. I wanted to see the real you."

"What you see is what you get with me," Stride said.

"Okay. So can I ask you some questions?"

"You can ask. I won't guarantee that I'll answer."

"Do you mind if I tape this?"

"Yes, I do mind," he replied.

"It's only to make sure I get the quotes right."

"I'll speak slowly," Stride said.

JoLynn smiled and leaned way back in the chair. She grabbed a hotel pen and chewed on it thoughtfully. She wiggled her toes on the bed. "You really are interesting. Dean is a good choice to play you."

"How well do you know him?"

"Dean? Pretty well. I've been to their place in Captiva a few times. He and Mo are about as open as celebrities get. They make my job easy."

"He doesn't have any secrets?" Stride asked. "I thought people want strong men with flaws."

JoLynn's pale eyes saw right through him. "Just who's interviewing whom, Lieutenant?"

He shrugged. "What do you want to know?"

"Let's start with your work as a cop. I heard you went off a bridge a few years ago during a fight with a killer. You almost died."

"True."

"That's pretty amazing. Did you think about quitting?"

"I thought about it on the way down," Stride said.

"Funny. Is that how you deflect serious things? With jokes?"

"Going off that bridge nearly destroyed my life in a lot of ways. So no, there's nothing funny about it."

"You've had failures in your career, right? Criminals you haven't caught? Mistakes you've made?"

"Plenty."

"How do you deal with regrets? How do you let your failures go?"

"I never let them go," Stride said. "As soon as you do that, you run the risk of making the same mistake again. The trick is learning to live with them. I'm still working on that."

"Was the Art Leipold case a success or a failure? I mean, you caught him, but three women died before you did."

"Obviously, it was both."

"You'd known Art ever since you were a young detective, right? He reported on some of your earliest cases. And you never once suspected he was the killer?"

"No, I never did."

"How did that change you?" she asked.

"Well, for one thing, I learned not to trust reporters."

"There you go again," JoLynn said. "Making jokes. It's like a defense mechanism, huh? What about your personal life? Your job must take a toll. You've been married three times."

"I don't think I like where this is going," Stride told her.

"Your first wife, Cindy, died. Then you married a Duluth teacher, but that only lasted three years. The people I've interviewed say you don't talk about that marriage much. Is it because it ended when you cheated on her with the detective you're married to now? Serena?"

Stride stood up. "Okay. We're done."

"But then you cheated on Serena, too, right? Before the two of you got married? I heard you slept with your Chinese partner."

He headed for the hotel room door, but JoLynn's legs blocked him where they were propped on the bed. "Let me through," he told her.

"I'm not trying to roast you, Lieutenant. I just want the whole story."

"I told you, the interview's over. Move your legs."

"What's with the girl? Cat? That must have raised some eyebrows, huh? A teenage prostitute moving in with one of the city's top cops."

He knew she was baiting him. And she was good at it. She wanted him to fly off the handle, to say something he'd regret. Or worse, he would do what he really wanted and physically throw her out of his way. He pushed down the anger he felt and kept his voice calm and cold.

*"Move. Your. Legs."*

JoLynn shrugged in resignation. She turned sidewise, and he headed for the door. He threw it open and marched into the hallway. As the door slammed shut, he heard the reporter calling after him in a sunny voice.

"See you in the papers, Lieutenant!"

# 17

In the parking lot outside the Ritz, Maggie found that she and Cab had twin Corvettes. She'd rented a yellow one. His was candy-red with an odd personalized license plate: catcha.

"CATCHA?" she asked. "Is that the guy who gets balls from the pitcha?"

Cab smiled as he held the passenger door open so that she could climb inside. He was elegantly polite. "Actually, my colleagues on the police gave me a nickname that followed me for a while. Catch-a-Cab. I moved around a lot. Never stayed in one place for more than a year or two."

"You've been in Florida for a while, haven't you?"

"Yes, I guess I've settled down. Hence the license plate. I try to embrace the worst things people say about me. And it's not like I can complain about nicknames, because I'm notorious for coming up with them myself."

"You give people nicknames?" Maggie asked.

"I know; it's not my most appealing trait. I get it from my mother. She referred to Lala Mosqueda as Wawa from the moment we started dating. She knew that it drove Lala crazy."

"I'm known for handing out nicknames, too," Maggie admitted, thinking of the Gherkin.

"Well, I guess you're like my twin, Sergeant."

"Call me Maggie," she said.

They drove north. Cab took the I-75 on his way to Clearwater, where his mother lived. It was almost a three-hour drive, but at the speed Cab drove, she figured they would be there in barely over two. She'd always considered herself a fast driver, but Cab left her in the dust.

"So you and Detective Mosquito are an item?" she asked on the highway.

"Off and on. At the moment, off."

"I just got out of a relationship, too."

"Well, I've never been known for my stable romantic attachments," Cab said. "That's another thing I have in common with my mother."

"I was accused of murdering my husband," Maggie said. "Can you top that?"

"Did you actually kill him?" he asked.

"I thought about it, but no."

"Then I can top that," Cab told her. "I shot and killed my girlfriend in Spain. Turns out she was a terrorist."

Maggie's head swiveled to see if he was joking. He wasn't. "Wow."

"I spent a lot of years running away from that, but I'm done running."

Maggie was quiet for the next few miles. She found it disorienting to be speeding along the Florida freeway with this charming and handsome man while the rest of her life was buried in snow 2,000 miles away. It felt like a vacation from reality. She also felt a glimmer, just a glimmer, of what it might be like to be part of a world away from Duluth. That was something she had never considered before.

She and Cab talked easily along the way. She liked him the way someone from the desert finds the mountains foreign and irresistible. He told her stories, and she did the same. She even went so far as to explain her star-crossed crush on Stride and how that particular fever had broken after their short-lived affair. He told her about the case on which he'd met Peach Piper, and it was obvious that he'd thought about the girl as a younger sister.

North of Sarasota, they headed onto the Sunshine Skyway Bridge across Tampa Bay. The blue water seemed endless, sparkling under the bright sun. The high span of the bridge was unsettling even for Maggie, who typically didn't worry about heights. Cab didn't seem bothered by it at all. He weaved in and out of the lanes without slowing down. The barrier between them and the drop to the water whipped by only inches away.

"So Tarla Bolton is your mother?" Maggie asked, peering nervously over the side. "You're a Hollywood baby?"

"Yes. Have you seen any of her movies?"

"If I see one movie a year, that's a lot, but it seems to me I caught one of her films on TNT a while back. An oldie. I think it was called *Society of One.*"

Cab didn't take his eyes off the road. "That was her breakout role. She won a Golden Globe. I was only about six years old then, but I remember a lot of parties."

"If I recall correctly, Dean Casperson was in that movie, too," Maggie said.

"You recall correctly."

He didn't say anything more.

The traffic on the St. Petersburg side of the bridge slowed them down, but they reached Clearwater less than an hour later. Cab navigated them into the underground parking lot of a high-rise condominium building steps from the beach. They took the elevator up. Tarla Bolton lived on a high floor.

As they watched the numbers climb, Cab said, "I should probably warn you about my mother. She isn't subtle."

"In what way?"

"Pretty much every way," Cab said.

When Tarla answered the door, Maggie realized that he was right. She'd obviously just come from the pool. Her golden blond hair was damp. She wore a low-cut blue-and-white dress that left nothing to the imagination. Maggie would have given a kidney for the prospect of a body like that in her midfifties. Tarla pulled her son into a fierce hug.

"Darling, I'm so glad you came to see me. I was devastated to get your call and hear about Peach. That poor, sweet girl. How are you? Are you okay?"

"Not really," Cab admitted.

"No, of course you're not. This is unbelievable. Would you like a drink? Let me get you a drink."

"A drink can wait. Mother, this is the detective I mentioned. Sergeant Maggie Bei from Duluth, Minnesota."

Tarla looked Maggie up and down with a sharp eye. She crossed her arms over her surgically enhanced breasts and cocked her head. "Minnesota? I thought there was nothing but Swedes eating lutefisk up there."

"We do have a lot of those," Maggie said.

"You look like you have money, dear. Do you have money?"

"Yes."

"Money is a wonderful thing. It may not buy you love, but it will buy you plenty of sex, which is just as good. I don't see any ring on that tiny finger of yours, so I assume you've already discovered that."

Maggie blinked and had no idea what to say.

"Mother," Cab said in a pained voice.

Tarla laughed in a throaty, erotic way. She squeezed Maggie's shoulder. "Don't mind me, Sergeant. It's my life's mission to embarrass Cab whenever he visits me."

"And you succeed," Cab replied.

"Oh, look at you, all conservative. I'm afraid Wawa converted you to Catholicism without your telling me. Or worse, turned you into a Rubio voter."

Cab glanced at Maggie and discreetly rolled his eyes. Maggie found it hard not to smile, because she'd never seen a mother-son relationship quite like this one. She followed Tarla and Cab into the living room of the condo, where floor-to-ceiling windows made up the wall overlooking the Gulf and the blue sky. The view looked straight down twenty stories to the beach. The furniture was as white as the sand. She saw a glass sculpture that was probably a Chihuly. The paintings on the walls were mostly squiggles and lines.

"Sit, sit, sit," Tarla ordered them. "Are you sure about that drink? Maggie, what about you?"

"No, thank you."

Maggie and Cab took the leather sofa. Tarla sat in a glider chair, and she rocked back and forth repeatedly, and her fingers had a little twitch about them. Maggie realized that this millionaire actress was actually nervous, and most of her repartee was a way of covering it up. She wondered what could get under the skin of someone who'd conquered one of the toughest businesses in the world, and she knew the answer without Tarla saying a word.

Dean Casperson.

Tarla didn't waste any time getting to the point. Her voice was sober now. Her nails tapped the table next to the Chihuly. "So, Peach. Was it him? Did he do it?"

"Yes," Cab said.

Maggie leaned forward. "We believe we know the man who was responsible for Peach's murder, but it's likely he was a paid assassin. We have no evidence yet about who hired him."

"But Dean's in town?" Tarla asked. "He's filming there?"

Maggie nodded.

"Then Cab is right," Tarla said. "It was him."

Maggie looked at both of their faces. "You need to give me more than that. Cab said you knew something about the murder of Haley Adams from Fort Myers but you didn't want to go public."

Tarla shook her head. "No, I didn't know anything about Haley Adams, not directly. And you're right, I didn't want to go public, and I still don't. But given what's happened, I'm willing to tell you what I know. As of now, Cab is the only other person in the world who knows about this."

"Knows what?" Maggie asked.

"Did you ever see the movie *Society of One*?" Tarla asked.

"I did. Cab and I were talking about it on the drive up here. You were astonishing in that film."

"I was," Tarla agreed without a trace of arrogance. It was simply a fact. "Back then, I was a nobody. A drop-dead-gorgeous nobody, but that doesn't narrow it down in L.A. Dean Casperson was the same age as me, but he was already an international star. He was going to drive the box office for the film, and everyone knew it. Including me. I wanted that part. I knew it was a career maker, and I was right."

She was silent. Maggie said nothing. She noticed that Cab wouldn't look at his mother.

"I got it. Casperson helped me land the role. He made sure I knew that. He said he saw something special in me, and you know what? I truly believe he did. He was being completely honest about that. Whatever else I may think about Dean Casperson's morality, he is a brilliant actor who's utterly devoted to the quality of the art."

She paused again.

"Something happened?" Maggie guessed.

"Oh, yes. It was halfway through filming. I'd done most of my scenes. I was flying. I knew how good I was. Sometimes, on a film, you can feel the chemistry, that everything is coming together. That was true on *Society of One*."

Tarla closed her eyes.

Maggie waited.

"There was a party at the house Dean rented," Tarla went on. "This was in the Hamptons. Very glamorous. I'm the first to say I drank a lot that night. But I know my limit, and I wasn't anywhere near it. I remember Dean offered to show me the house. It was a beautiful place. It probably belonged to some Manhattan hedge fund billionaire. When we were alone upstairs, he poured me another drink."

She stopped. Tears filled her eyes, and she wasn't acting.

"I passed out. When I woke up, he was on top of me. The room was spinning. I can still remember the smell of his breath and the smoothness of his voice, telling me how beautiful I was, how good this was going to be. I was naked. He still had on most of his clothes. I was incapable of fighting back. Literally, I was unable to move my limbs. It didn't last long, thankfully. And then he was zipping up and buttoning his shirt and telling me he was sure I was going to win awards for this film. As if nothing out of the ordinary had just happened."

Maggie shook her head. "Ms. Bolton, I don't know what to say. I'm very sorry."

"But you have doubts, right? I can see it in your face. 'She was a wannabe starlet, she already said she was drinking too much, she owed her role to this man. If he wanted sex, would she really have said no?'

And the funny thing is, you're right. I probably would have said yes if he'd asked me. That's how things are done. But he didn't ask. It wasn't about sex for Dean. It was about power and control. Raping me is what turned him on. And knowing I couldn't do a thing about it afterward."

"Did you tell anyone?" Maggie asked.

"Not a soul. Do you think anyone would have believed me? Or if they had, do you think they would have thanked me for tearing down an icon? No, the only one who would have suffered was me. My career would have been over. I didn't tell anyone until two years ago. That was when I told Cab."

"Believe me, she had to physically restrain me from going out and killing the son of a bitch," Cab interjected.

"Did you tell Cab because of Haley Adams?" Maggie asked her.

"Yes, I was investigating Haley's murder," Cab interjected. "I knew she'd headed across the Sanibel bridge to a party she didn't tell anyone about. I happened to mention it on the phone to Tarla, and she suggested, without giving me any explanation, that I find out whether Haley had been out to Dean's estate on Captiva. I located two different witnesses who saw her there, but neither would go on the record. I didn't tell Lala about it. I wanted to find out first why Tarla knew about this. That was when she told me what Dean had done to her. But she didn't want to make a statement, and without that I didn't have any evidence of anything. I just knew I was going to keep an eye on Dean Casperson. Sooner or later, I was going to bring him down."

Tarla stood up from the glider chair. Her smile had the look of cracked china. "If you'll excuse me for a few minutes, I think I'll shower and change."

Maggie waited until she was gone, and then she spoke to Cab softly. "I know what a terrible experience it was for your mother, but is there really any evidence connecting Haley's murder to Dean Casperson? She was killed several weeks after the party."

"I went through the restaurant receipts at Tin City for the day Haley was murdered," Cab replied. "Guess who had lunch there that day? Jungle Jack Jensen. Do you really think that's a coincidence? If you ask me, Dean assaulted Haley at the party, and then Jack paid her cash to keep her quiet. Either she was planning to go public about it anyway or she was looking for more money. So they had her killed."

Maggie frowned. "And now Peach."

"Right, and now Peach. One murder may be a coincidence. Not two. And definitely not seven."

Her eyes widened. "I'm sorry, what? *Seven?*"

"I've had two years to dig into Dean Casperson, Maggie," Cab went on. "I've researched crime reports in every location where he's done movies over the last thirty years. I found five other unsolved homicides or disappearances involving young women that occurred either during or within days after the filming. And those are just the ones I could find. If you ask me, it's the tip of the iceberg. Dean Casperson is a serial killer by proxy, Maggie. He drugs young women, and he assaults them. If he smells any risk of them talking, he has them murdered."

Maggie thought about Peach and said, "Something doesn't add up."

"What?"

"Peach wasn't at any of the parties. She was spying."

Cab nodded. "Right."

"So if Dean didn't assault her, why is Peach dead?"

"She must have seen something when she was watching the house," Cab said.

"Wouldn't she have told you?"

"Not necessarily. If Peach had one fault, it was that she was secretive. She didn't like to come to me with half information or unproved theories. She wanted everything wrapped up with a bow. This time, she may have waited too long."

"So what did she see?" Maggie asked.

"I don't know, but you better talk to your friends in Duluth," Cab replied. "If she saw something that was worth killing over, you may have another victim up there."

# 18

Serena stared at the photograph of Peach Piper that Maggie had sent her in an e-mail. There was no question that Peach was the girl they'd found in the woods, but in this photo she was fresh and alive. She had blond hair cut in a Mia Farrow pixie style. Freckles dotted her forehead, and her face was small and almost perfectly round. She was tiny, skinny, flat-chested, the kind of girl who could have passed for a teenager if she'd wanted.

What struck Serena most was the loneliness in Peach's blue eyes. The photo showed her smiling, but her smile couldn't completely hide the longing behind those eyes. She looked like someone who was alone in the world and had grown resigned to the fact that it would never change.

It made Serena angry. She had a weakness for lost girls. She'd been one of them herself, which was one of the reasons she'd fought so hard to make sure Cat was not a lost cause. But for Peach, it was too late. That made Serena furious. Particularly if Peach had died because of the whims of someone rich, powerful, and untouchable.

*What did Peach see that got her killed?*

Maggie had called to ask that question. Peach Piper had been spying on Dean Casperson, watching his house night after night from behind the lenses of a Moonraker telescope. What did she see?

Maybe another drugging. Maybe another assault. Maybe she'd seen what Casperson was really capable of. But if she'd witnessed an assault and rape at the house in Congdon Park, where was the evidence to back it up? And was that enough to call in a hit man to kill Peach?

Then Serena remembered: John Doe hadn't come to town to kill Peach. He was already here.

According to Curt Dickes, John Doe was at the party at Casperson's house on Saturday night, helping a drunk girl into his car. Peach must have seen both of them through the telescope.

Who was the girl?

Was she dead? And if so, where was her body?

Serena got up from her desk at police headquarters. She stretched her long arms over her head. It was already early evening. She was tired, but she wasn't ready to go home, because she felt she was close to unraveling something. She went to the vending machine and bought herself a Snickers bar. She unwrapped and ate it as she leaned against the wall. The sugar revived her. She wandered back toward her desk, but then she detoured to Max Guppo's desk, which was just outside Stride's empty office.

Guppo was still at work. Like Maggie, he always seemed to be there. However, Guppo, unlike Maggie, had a life. He'd been married for twenty-five years and had five daughters, a house, a boat, and everything that made a native Minnesota boy happy. He was the most Christian of Christians she'd ever met.

"Hey, Max," Serena said, dropping into the chair in front of the desk.

Guppo took his eyes off his monitor. He typed at a speed that seemed incongruous with his thick fingers. He had an oversized slab of homemade meat loaf on a paper plate in front of him, and he picked off large chunks with a plastic fork. A piece of apple pie waited for him under plastic wrap.

"Hey, Serena," he replied. He held up the plate of meat loaf. "Want a bite?"

"No, thanks."

"What's up?"

She explained what Maggie had told her. "I'm trying to figure out why Peach Piper got killed. This Bolton guy in Florida thinks it must be because Peach found something linking Casperson to another assault. We know John Doe took a girl out of Casperson's party last Saturday, and the girl was either drunk or drugged. That girl has to be our victim. And John Doe was not a chauffeur. If he was there, the girl's dead."

Guppo's round face scrunched into a frown. He leaned back in his wheeled chair, which was a risky maneuver. The chair made noises of protest under his weight. "Except nobody's missing," he said.

"Are we sure about that?" Serena asked.

"Well, there aren't any reports. If a local was missing, we'd know about it. It would have been reported by now."

Serena nodded. Guppo was right. "Yeah, girls don't just go missing around here without somebody noticing. What about someone from the Twin Cities? Maybe she drove up here for the day and got an invitation to the party."

"Alone? And she didn't tell anyone where she was going?"

"It happens. The filming of the movie got a lot of play in the media. Everybody knows about it down there."

Guppo's fingers flew on the keyboard. He spent five minutes loading and scrolling through multiple screens. Then he shook his head. "Good thought, but I can't find a missing person report anywhere in Minnesota that looks even remotely promising. Frankly, a young woman disappearing like that in January would be big news. There would be headlines."

"Well, thanks for checking, Max."

She got up again and went back to her desk. She tried to put herself in the mind of Peach Piper, sitting alone in a cold, empty house in Congdon Park. She was eating Chinese food on a Saturday night and staring through a telescope at Dean Casperson's house. If she saw an assault, then what? There was no missing person. No murder. No report of rape. Yet if it was worth killing Peach to keep her quiet, there had to have been another crime. Another victim.

John Doe was there. He helped a girl into the Impala. He was a hired killer; he didn't just take her home.

What happened to that girl?

Her mind bounced from idea to idea. She thought about the secrets of someone like Dean Casperson. She thought about John Doe and Peach Piper and their lives intersecting. She thought about a single deer crossing the road in the middle of a blizzard and launching the entire investigation.

She was hungry, and that made her think of Chinese food again. And that made her think about Saturday night again.

Saturday night.

*Girls don't just go missing around here without somebody noticing.*

Serena's eyes bolted wide open. She got out of her chair and wove through the cubicles back to Guppo's desk. She sat down and repeated the same thing to him: "Girls don't go missing around here without somebody noticing."

Guppo chewed his meat loaf and stared back at her, confused. "Right, but nobody's missing."

"That's my point. Maybe somebody went missing, and we all noticed, but none of us knew what we were seeing."

"I'm not following," Guppo said.

"Last Saturday night. What happened last Saturday night?"

"Dean Casperson had a party in Congdon Park. Peach Piper was eating moo shu and watching the whole thing."

Serena shook her head. "Not the party. Not Congdon Park. Nowhere near there. What else happened?"

"Um." Guppo scratched his comb-over and searched his memory.

*"Somebody died,"* Serena prompted him.

"Nobody was murdered in the city last Saturday."

"I didn't say murder, but somebody died."

Guppo thought about it, and then he understood what she was saying. "Are you talking about that kid in Proctor? Rochelle Wahl?"

"That's exactly who I'm talking about. Did you see her picture in the paper? Rochelle was a very pretty girl. If she was at the party, she would have gotten Dean Casperson's attention."

"Except she wasn't at the party."

"How do we know? We never looked into it, because we had no reason to think she ever left home. She was found frozen to death in her own backyard."

"The medical examiner said it was an accident."

"Maybe that's what John Doe *wanted* it to look like," Serena suggested. "Call up the police report. What does it say?"

Guppo's fingers flew on the keyboard again. He reviewed the details of the investigation into Rochelle Wahl's death, and then he shook his head. "She was in her pajamas, Serena. Her parents were out of town, and she broke into the liquor cabinet and got drunk as a skunk. She went out into the yard to throw up, and she slipped on the ice and hit her head. She was unconscious in subzero weather for hours. She was dead of exposure and frozen as an ice cube by the time anyone found her. Are you really saying John Doe staged the entire scene?"

"I'm saying John Doe left Dean Casperson's house with a drunk, unidentified girl. The next day, we found a drunk, dead girl in Proctor."

"It seems like a stretch," Guppo said.

"Not for a professional assassin. Curt said the girl he saw at the party was tall. Was Rochelle tall?"

Guppo checked the monitor, and his big lips puckered. "Five foot eleven."

Serena spread her arms. "So?"

"So you think Rochelle crashed the party, got drunk, and had sex with Dean Casperson? And at that point, he panicked and brought in John Doe to get rid of her?"

"That's exactly what I'm saying," Serena replied. "And Peach Piper saw the whole thing. Remember, you're leaving out the single most important fact about Rochelle Wahl. There's a reason she would have been a lethal threat to Dean Casperson if anyone found out about her. She was fifteen years old."

# 19

Stride found Cat on the three-season porch of the cottage when he got home late in the evening. The porch wasn't heated, so the air was freezing, and needles of frost made feathers across the windows. The girl sat on the old sofa he kept out there. She had a wool blanket pulled up around her neck. Her head bobbed slightly; she'd fallen asleep. When he sat down next to her, she stirred, but her voice was tired.

"Oh, hey," Cat said.

"Hey yourself. What are you doing out here? It's way too cold."

"I figured you'd be home soon," Cat said.

"Everything okay?"

"Yeah, I just wanted to talk."

He put an arm around her shoulders and stretched out his legs on the wooden floor of the porch. He pulled off his wool cap; his black-and-gray hair was mussed. Outside, a metal light fixture near the door cast a dim glow into the snowy backyard. He could barely see the woods and dunes that led to the lake. The wind was high.

"What's up?" he asked.

Cat stretched out with her head in the crook of his arm. She brushed her hair out of her face. "Something weird happened last night when Aimee Bowe was over here."

"How so?"

The girl took a long time to say anything. "Do you believe in psychic stuff? I know Serena doesn't. That's why I didn't talk to her. She would just tell me I'm crazy or I imagined it or something."

"Well, what kind of psychic stuff are we talking about?" Stride asked.

"I don't know. Like people who can sense the future. Aimee knew Haley Adams was dead before you found her body, right?"

"I'm not really sure it took psychic abilities to guess that. We were all pretty worried that something had happened to her."

"Yeah. I suppose."

"What happened, Cat?"

"Oh, it was just strange. I was talking to Aimee about what it's like to sense things. And as she was leaving, she asked me to give Serena a message. Then something came over her face, and she said, 'Save me.'"

*Save me.*

Those words had an ugly history for Stride. All of Art Leipold's victims had said the same thing in the audiotapes. *Save me, Jonathan Stride.*

"I didn't understand what she meant," Cat went on, "but when I asked her about it, she acted as if she didn't even know she'd said it. Honestly, it creeped me out."

"Are you sure she wasn't just having fun with you?" Stride asked.

"I don't think so. And I didn't imagine it, either."

"I believe you."

"What do you think it means?" she asked.

He ran one hand back through his hair. "I wish I could tell you, Cat. Years ago I would have laughed it off, but I've realized as I've gotten older that there's a lot I don't know. Remember when Serena got shot in the graffiti graveyard? And you and I held hands and you kept praying?"

"'Do not take her,'" Cat murmured.

"That's right. I was sure she was dying, but she came back to us. The doctors and scientists would all tell me that what you did had nothing to do with that. Me, I'm not so sure."

"So you think what happened with Aimee was real?"

"I don't know. Maybe Aimee didn't realize she'd said it out loud. Keep in mind, she's been going to some dark places in this movie. She has literally been trying to put herself inside the minds of women who died excruciating deaths. That has to take a mental toll on an actor."

"I guess that's true."

"The one thing I know is you're not going crazy," Stride told her.

Cat smiled. "I hope not."

They sat a while longer in the cold. He could tell that Cat still had things on her mind. Getting inside Cat's head was like slowly peeling off the layers of an onion, one by one.

"Maggie left a message for you today," she said finally. "I overheard what it was."

"Oh?"

"I wasn't trying to snoop or anything. I was doing homework when it came in, and I heard it on the machine. She suspects Dean Casperson of doing some really bad things. Rape. Murder. I couldn't believe that. Is it true? A big star like him?"

"You know how it works, Cat. Suspicions aren't facts, and facts are the only things that count in these investigations."

"Except Maggie wouldn't say it unless she believed it," Cat said. "Do you believe it?"

"I can't talk about that. It's also important that you not tell anyone about what you heard. Okay? We're in the midst of a serious investigation, and it's important that we not derail it *and* not smear anyone's reputation without evidence."

"I won't tell anyone," Cat said, "but I just don't get it. He is *so* good. I love him, I love his movies. There was an article about him in *People* a few months ago that talked about him and Mo and how long they've been married. He does all sorts of charitable work, too. I mean, he seems like a good guy. A nice guy. I can't believe someone like that could be mixed up in such awful things."

"I'd like to say it never happens, Cat, but it does. Good people can always disappoint us. And evil people can do some remarkable things in other parts of their lives. We just have to decide for ourselves what tips the scale."

"You've never disappointed me," Cat told him.

Stride chuckled softly. "I disappoint myself all the time. I was talking to a woman today who reminded me about some of the worst things I've done in my life. I didn't like hearing those things used against me, but what really got me angry was knowing many of them were true."

"Who was she?" Cat asked.

"Nobody. Don't worry about it." Then he realized he couldn't make that demand. Cat needed to know the truth. "Actually, I do need to give you a heads-up about something. There may be some stuff coming out in print about me. You probably already know most of it, but there could be surprises. I don't know what they'll dig up and how they'll spin it."

"Who would do something like that to you?" Cat asked. Then her pretty brow furrowed. "Is it Dean Casperson? Does he know you're after him? Is he the one behind this?"

"I have no idea. I just know that I'm a target, and that means my family and friends are targets, too. They may say things about you, Cat. They may talk about your past. I want you to be prepared."

"I don't care what anyone says about me," she replied. "Like you said, it's all true, right?"

"Well, that doesn't mean it's fun having the whole world know about it."

"What are they going to say?" Cat asked. "That you're living with a teen hooker?"

"That may be exactly what they say. And more."

"I don't care," she said, but he knew that some of her toughness was an act.

"Well, I do care. If a tabloid has nothing better to do than make headlines out of my mistakes, fine. But *you* are not one of my mistakes. I'm prouder of you being with me than anything else I've done in my life. Got it?"

"Got it," she said. And then, like any teenager, she found his sore spot and pushed a finger into it. "So what were your worst mistakes?"

"We could be here a long time if you want to hear about those," Stride said.

"I think I know the personal side," Cat said. "You and Maggie, right?"

"Right."

"That was a tough time in your life," she reminded him.

"There are always tough times. That doesn't change a thing."

"Okay, professional, then. Was it my mom? Her dying wasn't your fault."

"I know that, but it doesn't make it any easier to live with. Actually, I've been thinking a lot about my mistakes. One of them was a long time ago—more than twenty years ago, in fact—but Art Leipold was involved. That's why it's been bothering me lately."

"What was it?" Cat asked.

"I was a young cop back then, and a man named Ray Wallace was my partner. Ray did a lot for me when I was growing up. I'll always be grateful to him, but he was one of those men where you had to balance the scale of good and evil. He did some really bad things, too. He was corrupt. He ended up killing himself right in front of me. The bullet wound in my arm? That was Ray. Anyway, I remember this really difficult case he and I were on. Missing kid. An eight-year-old boy disappeared at the zoo. We all took it hard. Ray and I interviewed everyone in the area, and it didn't take us long to zero in on the boy's next-door neighbor. Mort Greeley. Squirrelly type. Aggressive, combative when we talked to him. He was a janitor at the zoo, so we figured he bumped into the kid that day. We were sure he did it, but we couldn't prove it. We got search warrants, but the searches turned up nothing. After six months, the investigation was at a standstill."

"So what happened?" Cat asked.

"Ray and Art happened. Ray got it in his head that we needed to push Mort Greeley. Put pressure on him so he'd confess. So he started leaking stories to Art about the case, and Art ran with it. It led the news night after night. Basically, he told the whole city that the police *knew* Mort was guilty and the only thing we were missing was the boy's body. This went on for weeks. Months. I should have stopped it. I should have said something, but I thought Mort was guilty, too. So you do what you have to do. I was too young to know how wrong it was."

"Was he guilty?"

Stride shook his head. "No. Two years later, police in Santa Fe found the boy, living with the guy who'd kidnapped him. It was too late for Mort. He'd already lost his family and his job. He put a gun in his mouth and shot himself."

"Oh, no! Oh, that's terrible."

"I know. Sometimes you can make up for your mistakes, but not that one."

"I'm really sorry. That is so awful." Cat threw her left arm across his chest and hugged him tightly. She buried her head in his neck, and then, sweetly, she rose up and kissed him on the cheek.

That was when light exploded through the glass, so sudden and bright that he expected a clap of thunder to follow it. The two of them squinted at the windows in shock. Stride was instantly on his feet.

"Get inside," he told Cat.

"What was that?"

"Just get inside."

He took two steps and threw open the porch door. His eyes were still blinded, making the night impenetrable. He blinked, and when he could see, he spotted footprints below the porch windows in the virgin snow. He heard movement from the far side of the cottage. Someone was running away.

Stride jumped off the steps and gave chase. He rounded the corner and saw a man charging through the deep snow toward the street. Something dangled and bounced on a strap from his right hand. A camera. Stride followed, but he was already too late to catch him. The man had a partner waiting. He bolted for a car parked at the curb, and before he'd even closed the door behind him, the car shot off toward the lift bridge.

The driver taunted him with a toot of the horn. Stride ran into the middle of the street, where he could see the red taillights winking at him. The car was too far away to see the license plate, but he didn't need to. He'd already recognized the make and model.

It was a blue Elantra.

JoLynn Fields of the *National Gazette* was still spying on him. And now she had pictures.

# 20

The next morning, Serena found paparazzi footprints in the snow outside Aimee Bowe's house, too.

The actress had rented a modest single-story house on Thirteenth Street high on the hill over the city. It was small and dated, but it had a large lot and a stunning view of the lake through the rear windows. Aimee stood at the front door while Serena investigated the exterior. The footprints made a circle around the house, stopping at every door and window. She could trace them down the hill to Skyline Parkway, where someone had parked and hiked back and forth to Aimee's house through the trees.

"Tell me again what happened," Serena said.

Aimee opened the door wide, and the two of them went inside. The house was full of memorabilia from someone else's life. Serena spotted photos on the wall of a couple with two young children and noticed toys and stuffed animals neatly tucked away in baskets. Families around the area had volunteered to rent their homes to the cast and crew during the filming. Extra money in January was always welcome.

Aimee led them to the back porch, where they sat in wicker chairs near the windows.

"I got back late from the set," she told Serena. "We were working until almost midnight. I saw the footprints, and I knew someone had been here."

"You should have called me right away," Serena said. "Or called 911."

"One of the crew drove me home. I had him check the house to make sure no one was here. I was too tired to do much of anything else. I didn't want to deal with it."

"Stride thinks it was the *National Gazette* at our place. They're probably going after you, too."

Aimee frowned and stared across the treetops at the lake. "Maybe."

"You don't think so?"

"Whoever it was didn't just look through the windows. They came inside, too."

"*Inside.* Are you sure?"

"No, I can't prove it. Nothing was disturbed, nothing was taken. But there was something off about the place when I got back. I can't put my finger on what it was. A different smell. A different feel. I knew someone had been here."

"Is that typical tabloid behavior? To break into a celebrity's place?"

Aimee shook her head. "No. They're usually careful to stay on the razor's edge of what's legal."

"Have you had any problems with fans? Stalkers?"

"Nothing that would worry me."

"How would someone get inside the house?" Serena asked.

"Half the locks here don't work. I didn't really worry about it. Duluth isn't L.A."

"Do you want me to get an officer to stay outside and keep an eye on the place?"

Aimee shrugged. "Honestly, I don't want the attention. I'll be careful. The crew looks out for me, too."

"Well, if you spot anything wrong, don't wait next time. Call 911. And call me, too."

"Thanks."

Serena took a piece of paper out of a manila folder in her satchel purse. "As long as I'm here, do you mind if I ask you a question? I was wondering if you recognize this young woman."

Aimee took the photograph from Serena's hand and studied it. "Her face is a little familiar."

"Did you see her at any of the filming locations? Or at any of the cast and crew parties?"

"Not that I recall. She's pretty; I think I'd remember her. I feel like I've seen this photograph before, but I don't think I've met her in person. Who is she?"

"Her name is Rochelle Wahl. Was. She's dead."

A shadow crossed Aimee's face, and then she remembered. "Is she the local girl who was on the news? That's where I saw her picture."

"Yes, she was found dead in her backyard last weekend."

"That's a terrible thing, but why would you think she had anything to do with the movie?"

"I'm just covering all the bases," Serena said.

Aimee's eyes narrowed as if she knew that Serena wasn't being completely honest with her. "Well, I'm sorry, I didn't see her. Is that all?"

"I do have one more question," Serena went on. "I was wondering if you're aware of any rumors floating around the industry about Dean Casperson."

"What kind of rumors?"

"You tell me."

"I think I already did tell you once before. I won't gossip about Dean."

"Because you're scared of him?" Serena asked.

Aimee didn't answer. Her defenses went up like a wall.

"One of my partners talked to an actress who had a bad experience with him when she was starting out," Serena said.

"What kind of experience?"

"She says Casperson assaulted her," Serena said. "He drugged and raped her."

Aimee flinched sharply, as if she'd been struck. "If that's true, why didn't she go public about it?"

"You said yourself that Casperson has the power to make or break careers. This woman thought it was smarter to stay quiet."

"Maybe it is."

"Casperson gave you your big break a few years ago, didn't he?" Serena continued.

"That's right."

Serena hesitated before going on. "Was there a price for it?"

"What are you talking about?" Aimee asked.

"We both know what I'm talking about."

Aimee got up from the wicker chair. Her face reddened with anger, and she fought back tears. She extended her arm and pointed her index finger at the front door. "Please get out."

"I'm sorry if I upset you."

"Get out, Serena, just get out."

"Whatever you want."

Serena headed for the door, and Aimee stayed where she was. When Serena opened the front door, she looked back, and Aimee was still frozen in the living room. The actress had her face buried in her hands, and Serena watched her body quiver as she sobbed. She thought about going back to comfort her, but instead she slipped out of the house and closed the door softly behind her.

Serena wasn't psychic.

Even so, she knew she was right. Aimee was hiding the truth about Dean Casperson.

*

Half an hour later, Serena met Guppo at Rochelle Wahl's house.

She could feel the devastation in the room as they talked to Rochelle's parents. Her father said nothing and stared down at his lap. Her mother kept a photo album locked in a fierce grip in her hands, as if someone might steal it from her. Condolence flowers filled every table, but they were already starting to wilt, giving a faded look and sour odor to the room.

"I'm not sure what you want to know," Marilyn Wahl said. "Why are you asking questions about Rochelle? I thought the investigation was closed."

Serena tried to figure out what to say. She didn't want to alarm them over nothing. She didn't want to speculate about their daughter's death and find out she was wrong.

Guppo came to her rescue. "When a case involves the death of a minor, even an accidental death, we often have senior personnel review the details to make sure nothing was missed. This won't take long. And trust me, I have five daughters myself. I'm sympathetic to the pain you feel."

Marilyn sniffled but didn't object. She was in her late thirties and attractive. Mark Wahl had the lean look of a runner. Their faces were both drawn with grief, but Serena could see the close resemblance to their daughter. She'd reviewed photographs of Rochelle, who had long reddish-brown hair, turquoise glasses over dark eyes, and a bottle-cap nose that was slightly flattened on the end.

"Can you review the time line on Saturday and Sunday for us again?" she asked. "I know you were away."

"Yes, it was our seventeenth wedding anniversary weekend," Marilyn said with a glance at her husband that suggested they both knew their anniversary would never be the same. "We had tickets to the Guthrie in Minneapolis, and then we stayed overnight at the Hilton. This was the first time we'd left Rochelle on her own. She was adamant about it and said we didn't have anything to worry about. She was going to watch a Harry Potter movie marathon in her room and make microwave pizza."

"What time did you leave on Saturday?" Guppo asked.

"Around one o'clock in the afternoon."

"Were you concerned that Rochelle might have friends over for a party or that she might go out on her own?"

Mark Wahl looked up from his lap. "Rochelle was very reliable and mature. She was fifteen going on twenty-five. She'd never given us any reason not to trust her."

"Plus she didn't have many friends," Marilyn went on. "She painted and wrote and kept to herself. She was very self-contained. We were always encouraging her to find more friends, but she didn't have a lot in common with girls her age."

Serena thought about Cat. And about herself. It was easy to understand the kind of girl that Rochelle Wahl was. She also knew that every fifteen-year-old going on twenty-five was still no older than fifteen.

"Did you talk to Rochelle during the day?" Serena asked.

"Yes, she texted us every hour, exactly as she promised."

"I mean, did you actually talk to her on the phone?"

Marilyn's forehead wrinkled in confusion. "I don't think so. We never really had the chance. Just when I'd think of calling, she would text us again. I was pleased that she was being so thoughtful about it."

Serena couldn't help thinking that Rochelle wasn't being thoughtful. She was being crafty.

"What did she say in her texts?" she asked.

"Nothing much. She was asking about whether we were having fun on our trip. She sent us a picture of the first Harry Potter movie on television that afternoon when she started watching. She was such a huge Dumbledore fan."

"When did you last hear from her?"

"Around eleven-thirty, she texted that she was going to bed," Mark said. "She sent us a picture of herself in her pajamas in bed. She had this big smile, waving at us, with a little 'good night' emoji. Then, in the morning, we couldn't reach her. That's when we began to panic."

Guppo shifted his girth in the chair in which he was sitting, and the wooden legs complained. "I'm sorry to ask this, but did you ever know Rochelle to drink alcohol before that night?"

Mark Wahl shook his head violently. "Never."

"This was just so unlike her," Marilyn added.

Serena gave them a sad smile. "Would you mind showing us her room?"

Mark didn't get up, but Marilyn guided them out of the living room and down a hallway to a large bedroom that overlooked the backyard. Sliding glass doors led outside. The bedsheets were still rumpled and unmade. Dirty clothes made a line from the bed to the closet. There were movie posters hung all over the walls. *Harry Potter. Guardians of the Galaxy*. And a poster from a movie adaption of a popular YA book from the previous year.

The movie starred Dean Casperson.

"Rochelle must have been excited about *The Caged Girl* being filmed in Duluth," Serena said. "It looks like she was a big movie fan."

Marilyn's face lit up. "Oh, you can't imagine. It's all she could talk about. She thought a movie being made here was the greatest thing ever. And as you can probably see, she loved Dean Casperson, too. She got that from me. I've had a crush on him since I was a kid."

"Did the two of you go to see any of the filming?"

"We were planning to. I was just so busy at work. Rochelle wanted to take the bus down to Canal Park one day when they were filming there, but I didn't want her going by herself."

"Of course," Serena said. "Do you mind if we take a look at Rochelle's phone?"

Marilyn looked embarrassed. "Unfortunately, we haven't found it."

"It's missing?"

"Mark and I searched her room. It's not here." Her voice cracked. "It's probably—well, it's probably lost in the snow from when she went outside. We won't find it until the spring."

"I'm sorry."

"Is there anything else?" Marilyn asked them.

"No, we've taken up enough of your time," Serena replied. "We just need to take some photographs of Rochelle's room if that's okay. For our files."

She nodded. "If you like."

Rochelle's mother left the room, and Serena and Guppo were alone. Guppo's round face was as grave as Serena had ever seen it. He'd come to the same conclusions as she had.

"What do you think?" he asked.

"I think this was a very shrewd fifteen-year-old who decided to go on the adventure of her life," Serena said.

She noticed a forty-inch flat-screen television on the wall opposite Rochelle's bed. Below, among the bookshelves, was a Blu-ray player. She walked over and pressed the eject button on the player. When the drawer opened, she spotted a disk still nestled on the shelf inside.

"*Harry Potter and the Sorcerer's Stone,*" Serena said.

"That's the first movie," Guppo said. "She didn't get far."

Serena nodded. "There was no movie marathon. Rochelle took a picture of it to send to her parents. She probably staged the picture of herself in her pajamas, too, so she could send it later. And then I'm betting she ran out to catch the bus and head downtown."

# 21

"So this is how the other half lives," Maggie said as Cab steered his Corvette down the narrow spit of Captiva Island past the mansions that hugged the waterfront. The homes were lavish, but despite their size, they still had a rustic Florida feel, as if a beach bum had found $8 million in a treasure chest to buy a place on the sand.

"I like to come down here now and then to make myself feel poor," Cab replied with a grin. "This is where the Bentleys all have bumper stickers that say 'My other car is a Phantom.'"

"Have you been to Dean Casperson's place before?"

"Inside? No. I've taken a boat down the sound a couple times and sailed in close enough to get their security pretty nervous."

"Haley Adams didn't get in here without an ID and an invitation," Maggie said. "She had to be on a list somewhere."

"Definitely, but those lists disappear once the party's over. Haley was here, but we'll never be able to prove it. I've tried."

Cab slowed on Captiva Drive as he approached the pink stone driveway of the Casperson estate. The sandy walking trail to the Gulf was on their left. He pulled the Corvette into the driveway and drove past thick hanging greenery to the main house, where he parked next to a row of shaggy palm trees. The house was three stories, painted pastel yellow. Most of the upper level was glass. She could see a Roman-style Olympic-size pool attached to the north side of the house, surrounded by travertine tile and covered by a glass-and-stone atrium. The double-wide front doors gave a view straight through to the green waters of the sound.

"So Tarla and Mo are friends?" Maggie asked dubiously. "Even after what happened to her?"

"I wouldn't say friends, but Hollywood is a small community. The players tend to know each other."

"Well, I'm impressed she was willing to get us in here, given her history with Dean. Do you think Mo knows?"

"You mean, what Dean did to Tarla? What kind of man he is? Honestly, I don't know. They've been together for decades. It's hard to believe she could really be unaware, but sometimes you develop a blindness for things when you need to."

A large Filipino man in a white suit met them at the Corvette. He was friendly and polite, but Maggie was sure he was armed and could have snapped both of their necks in seconds if he'd been so inclined. He led them inside the house, which had the airiness of cotton candy and was painted in shades of peach and sea-foam green. Warm, moist air blew through the interior with the fresh Gulf breeze. She saw a grand piano. A vast wet bar. An indoor-outdoor dance floor. It was a mansion built for entertaining, and it was strange to see it completely empty of people.

This home was a shrine. Everywhere Maggie looked, the house showed off memorabilia of Dean Casperson's career. The walls were covered with decades of photographs of Casperson with nearly every mover and shaker in Hollywood, posters from his dozens of movies, awards from nonprofit organizations, pictures of Dean in impoverished areas overseas, and honorary degrees from ten different colleges. In a built-in bookcase, behind locked glass doors, she saw a lineup of his acting trophies. Among them were four Golden Globes, an Emmy, and two Oscars. It was a reminder of who they were dealing with.

A star. A living legend.

The guard led them all the way through the ground floor of the estate without stopping and then to the patio overlooking the water.

The Florida sunshine beat down. The day was perfect, and the water was calm. Maggie could see a sleek fifty-foot speedboat bobbing next to the boat dock on the sound. The name of the boat written on the stern was mo better. She wondered if Mrs. Casperson knew that the phrase was actually urban slang for passionate screwing.

Mo Casperson sat by herself on the patio with a red-and-orange cocktail in a hurricane glass and a laptop open in front of her. Maggie felt a little as if she were approaching the queen for an audience. Mo wore a chic lemonade-colored sun hat over her golden hair. Her flowered knee-length dress would have fit in well at an upscale beach wedding. She had long nails, each individually painted with a different pastel design. The only jewelry she wore was her wedding ring. The square-cut diamond made a statement, and that statement was "I'm one of the richest women on the planet."

She didn't get up, but she removed her sunglasses and greeted them with a smile. "Cab Bolton. I don't believe I've seen you since you were fifteen years old. I'm sure you don't remember it."

"Positano," Cab replied easily. "You were visiting the Amalfi Coast, and you had lunch with my mother during the filming of *Sapphirica*."

Mo's eyebrows arched in surprise. "Well, either you have an amazing memory or I'm very memorable."

"It's all you," Cab assured her.

"And this must be Sergeant Bei?" Mo asked.

Mo held out a hand, and Maggie wasn't sure if she should shake it or kiss it. She decided to shake it. "Mrs. Casperson, thank you for meeting us."

"Anything for Tarla," she replied. "You're from the Duluth police department, is that right? I met your boss, Lieutenant Stride, when I was chatting with Dean yesterday. Stride has quite a presence about him as a man. He's very attractive."

"That's true."

"But of course, I don't need to tell *you* that," Mo went on.

Maggie's eyes squinted in suspicion as she tried to grasp the woman's subtext. Was it an innocent comment? Or was she trying to make it clear that she knew about Maggie and Stride's affair? Mo lived in a world of innuendo where you never said exactly what you meant. Maggie felt an urge to check her back to make sure there wasn't a knife in it.

"Please, both of you, sit down," Mo said. "Sergeant Bei, I can understand why someone would want to get out of Minnesota in January—in fact, I can't understand why anyone would *stay* in Minnesota in January—but I'm curious what you're doing here. And why you and Cab have joined forces."

"We're investigating a murder," Maggie replied.

"Two murders, in fact," Cab added. "One in Florida, one in Minnesota."

"How terrible. But why talk to me about it?"

"We believe the same man killed the two young women with the same gun," Maggie explained. "We only found out about it because of a car accident that killed him in Duluth. He has all the hallmarks of a gun for hire, and we're trying to find out who hired him."

"I still don't see how I can help you."

Again, Maggie tried to read her face, and again she came up short. Mo gave no hint in her expression of whether her confusion was genuine or whether she was simply covering up the truth.

"We're pretty sure the young woman in Florida, Haley Adams, was at a party here not long before she was killed," Cab told her.

"Pretty sure?"

"I can't prove it. Unless you'd be willing to share your guest lists."

Mo smiled. "I'm sorry, Cab, but you of all people understand how important privacy is in our world. Security, too. Do you have a photograph of this young woman?"

"I do." Cab called up a photo of Haley Adams on his phone and held it up for Mo to review. She placed half glasses from a chain around her neck onto her face to examine the photograph. Then she shook her head.

"I don't know her, but that doesn't really mean anything. She certainly could have been here, but if so, I wasn't the one to invite her. I don't know how the party could have been connected to whatever happened to her, though. Unless you think she met someone here. I suppose that's possible, but I wouldn't know how to narrow it down for you."

Mo was poised. She gave nothing away. Or she was simply innocent.

"The woman who was killed in Minnesota has a more direct connection," Maggie said. "She was an intern on the set of *The Caged Girl*, but she was actually there for a different reason. She was spying on your husband."

"Excuse me?" Mo said.

"I sent her there," Cab added. "She worked for me. And now she's dead."

Mo shifted her stare to each of them in turn. She took a sip of her drink. Maggie waited for her to evict them from the mansion, but she didn't. She simply shook her head as if they were misbehaving children. When she spoke, her voice was calm and full of syrupy disappointment.

"Cab, why on earth would you be spying on Dean?"

"May I speak candidly?" he said.

"Please."

"I've been investigating the murders of multiple women over the last two decades, and they all have one thing in common. Your husband."

Mo actually laughed. "Murder? Are you serious?"

"I am."

"Well, then I feel sorry for you. It's ridiculous. Are you actually accusing Dean of murder? I mean, we're used to getting bad reviews, but this is a first."

"I'm not accusing anyone. Not yet."

"Oh, well, now I feel better. Maybe you'd like to explain why you think Dean was somehow involved in the deaths of these women."

"Probably because he sexually assaulted them and he was afraid they'd talk," Cab told her.

This time, Mo's face reacted immediately. Her eyes turned to ice that could have frozen the humidity in the Florida air. "What a grotesque thing to say. If you repeat anything like that in public, I promise you, we will take legal action. This is not a game, Cab. When you are in our position, there are always people who want to invent lies and cut you down to size. You learn to live with it. You learn when to turn the other cheek and when to sue. But honestly, I'm used to dealing with strangers and outsiders about this kind of venomous nonsense. Not people who are part of our world. You should be ashamed of yourself for coming here. You should be ashamed of yourself for manipulating your mother into getting you an invitation on false pretenses. You can both leave now and we'll call this over and done, but I assure you, if I hear even the barest rumor of what you have said coming back to me in the future, I will do whatever is necessary to strip you and your mother of every dollar, every friend, every shred of goodwill and reputation you have in Hollywood. Are we perfectly clear about that, Cab Bolton?"

"Dean raped Tarla," Cab said.

"What?"

"You heard me."

"That is a despicable lie. Tarla would never say something like that."

"It was on the set of *Society of One*. Dean got her the part. She paid for it by being drugged and assaulted. How many other times has he done it, Mo? Don't tell me you don't know."

Mo didn't speak for a long time. She got out of the chair and wandered to the balcony of the porch, where steps led down to the boat dock and the water. She spoke to them without turning around. "At least I understand now, Cab. I don't forgive you, and I don't take back a word of what I said, but I do understand why you would launch yourself on this misguided quest."

"Misguided?" Cab said acidly.

"I really need to speak to Tarla about this."

"Are you saying you had no idea that Dean is a predator when it comes to women?"

Mo spun around with the speed of a snake. She jabbed a finger at Cab. "*Stop it*. You don't know what you're saying. I wish we all lived celibate, virtuous, faithful lives, but we don't. Tarla certainly never has. You think I don't know how many marriages she's broken up over the years with her affairs? You think I don't know that you have no idea who your own father is? Grow up, Cab. Did Dean sleep with Tarla? Of course he did. Did I know about it? Of course I did. I'm very sorry that Tarla feels the need to reinvent herself as an innocent victim in a relationship that *she* instigated. Much as she did over and over again with other married men in the last thirty years."

"You can't possibly believe that Tarla seduced Dean," Cab said.

"A wannabe actress trying to manipulate a huge star by using sex? You're right; that's a story we've never seen in Hollywood."

Cab got up. So did Maggie. She felt shell-shocked, watching the back-and-forth as if it were some kind of battle of gladiators. Tall as he was, Cab loomed over both of them.

"If you're that naive, Mo, I feel sorry for you," Cab told her. "I'm not going to stop. You can't hide from this forever. The truth about Dean is going to come out, and when it does, he'll be in prison, and you'll both be ruined. Count on it."

The guard in the white suit appeared as if by magic to lead them out. Maggie and Cab retreated silently into the house, but as they did, Mo called to them from the balcony.

"Both of you, take a good look at the awards and the honors as you leave," she said in a voice that carried through the empty mansion. "That's forty years of doing good in this world, on-screen and offscreen. That's my husband. That's the truth about Dean."

# 22

Stride looked up as Serena appeared in the doorway of his office. She didn't look happy.

"What did you find out about Rochelle Wahl?" he asked.

Serena sat down on the other side of the desk and glanced over her shoulder before giving him an update. He noticed a strange buzz of conversation in the cubicle farm outside.

"I asked the medical examiner to reexamine the report," she told him, "just in case anything got missed. The body itself was already released and cremated. It's going to be hard to get the manner of death switched at this point."

"Do we have any evidence that the girl was at Casperson's house?"

"Nothing so far. I talked to two of the bus drivers on the Number 3 route out of Proctor. They both knew Rochelle pretty well, but they can't remember whether she took the bus on Saturday afternoon. I've interviewed people on the film crew, but they're tight-lipped. Nobody wants to get in trouble with Casperson. I'm trying to get phone records from Rochelle's cell carrier to see if she called or texted anyone on Saturday about where she was."

"What about Curt Dickes?" Stride asked.

"I showed him a photo, but he couldn't identify her. He only saw the girl from the back as she was getting into John Doe's car."

"So we think we know what happened, but we can't prove it," Stride said.

"Right."

"That seems like the story of this case."

Serena nodded. She glanced over her shoulder again, and the concern in her eyes told him that something was wrong.

"What's going on?" he asked.

"It's out there," she said. "The article about you in the *National Gazette*. It went online a few minutes ago. Guppo found it."

Stride eased back in the chair and exhaled as he ran both hands back through his hair. "How bad is it?"

"Savage."

She held up her phone, so he could read the headline:

COP IN DEAN CASPERSON THRILLER HAS TROUBLED PAST

"Just give me the greatest hits," he said. "Does it talk about you and me?"

"Oh, yeah. You cheated on Andrea with me. I stole you away from her. Then you cheated on me with Maggie. By the way, they imply that your affair with Maggie has been going on for years. Even back when you were with Cindy."

Stride swore under his breath. "Unbelievable."

"They also hint that you cheated on Cindy with Cat's mother, Michaela. Basically, you're just a serial adulterer, Jonny."

"Should I get a lawyer?" he asked.

"They use just enough weasel words to stay out of trouble."

"Plus, some of it's true, right?" Stride said.

Serena stared at him. Her eyes said that this was a road they didn't need to travel again. "Whatever's true is out of context. We both know that."

"Thanks. What else is in there? What about the job?"

"They dredge up the Mort Greeley suicide from years ago. Nothing about Ray. Nothing about Art. They make the whole thing sound like it was your fault. They also suggest that you were friends with Art and that's why you overlooked evidence that implicated him in *The Caged Girl* case. So three women died because you refused to consider Art a suspect."

Stride shook his head. "Dean Casperson wants to make sure I get the message: don't mess with him."

"Right."

"What about Cat? Anything about Cat?"

"No, nothing about her, thank God. And they didn't use the photo of the two of you on the porch. Honestly, I don't know why they left it out."

"This was the shot across the bow," Stride concluded. "If we keep going after Casperson, then they come back and slime Cat. Whatever they do to her will be ten times worse."

"We can't let that happen, Jonny."

"I know."

Dean Casperson had them in a box. Stride didn't care what the tabloids said about him, but attacking Cat was a different story. He would do whatever was necessary to protect her.

Before they could say anything more, another shadow crossed the doorway of Stride's office. His day just kept getting worse.

"Hello, you two," Police Chief Kyle Kinnick said in his distinctive reedy voice that whined like a badly played clarinet. The chief wandered inside, dressed in a light gray business suit that didn't fit him well. He was a small man with a comb-over draped across his head, droopy bloodhound eyes, and ears that jutted out like angel's wings. His feet pointed away from each other when he walked, as if they didn't get along.

K-2, as he was called, had been Stride's boss for years. They were both Duluth lifers. At sixty years old, the chief was stubborn and gruff, but the two of them had carved out a relationship that worked well most of the time. K-2 did the politics and rarely interfered in day-to-day police work. He yanked the leash on Stride only when crime started bubbling over into the newspapers.

Like now.

Serena took the hint and made a quick exit and closed the door behind her, leaving the two of them alone. K-2 leaned over with both hands on Stride's desk. The chief's mouth wrinkled into a scowl.

"You're famous, Jon. And not in a good way."

Stride shrugged. "It's tabloid crap."

"Of course it is, but that's not the point. Now the story becomes the story. You don't think the local media's going to pick this up? Everyone in town is going to be gossiping about you."

"I don't care about that."

"Well, I care. It's not good for you, it's not good for us. Any idea why they came after you?"

"The murder investigation is getting close enough to Dean Casperson to make him uncomfortable. If Casperson picks up the phone, the tabloids do his bidding. He's trying to warn me off."

"Dean Casperson? You sure about that?"

"It's him or the people around him."

"Uh huh. You're poking a beehive with some pretty big bees, Jon. And what the hell is Maggie doing in Florida? I told her I wasn't paying for that."

"She went on her own dime. There was a murder in Naples that's connected to the dead girl up here. She's checking it out. Casperson's name keeps coming up with the police down in Florida, too."

K-2 dropped into the chair and dug in his ear. "I'm not sure you appreciate the kind of people you're dealing with, Jon."

"I think I do," Stride replied. "I'm the one with my personal life all over the papers."

"A tabloid headline is the least of your problems. The mayor was already on the phone with me today to ask why my detectives have been showing up on film sets and harassing the actors and crew."

"If by harassing you mean asking questions about a girl who was murdered, then that's true," Stride replied.

"Oh, hell, I'm not saying your team is doing anything wrong. Thing is, if you push, these people push back. You're dealing with folks who have money, fame, and influence and aren't shy about throwing it around. This film is very important to a lot of people in state and local government who want to put Minnesota on the map for Hollywood projects. If they get complaints, they call me."

"I appreciate your running interference, sir. I always do."

"Well, that's fine. That's my job. I don't care who you go after as long as you find the proof to get them. But this is one where the evidence better be signed, sealed, and delivered. People love Dean Casperson. Hell, my wife loves him, probably a bit more than me on some days. So tread carefully."

"Very."

"If you can make a case, great. If you can't, my strong advice is that you let it go."

"Understood."

K-2 pushed himself out of the chair and shoved his hands in his pockets. "Don't feel too bad about the article, Jon. No one will take it seriously. We've all done stupid things from time to time."

"I'm not concerned for myself. I'm concerned about who they go after next."

"You're thinking about Cat?" the chief asked.

Stride nodded.

K-2 eyed the closed door behind them. No one could hear their conversation, but he lowered his voice anyway. "Every now and then we get a case that's better off unsolved. You might want to think about that."

The chief wandered out of his office.

K-2 was a practical man who saw justice in shades of gray. In his world, some battles weren't worth fighting. It wasn't the first time in Stride's career the chief had suggested that his team consider backing off on a high-profile investigation.

But it was the first time Stride had ever thought about doing it.

*

Cat stood on the snowy beach. She picked up chunks of ice with her cold bare hands and hoisted them into Lake Superior one after another. She did it until she could barely feel her fingers. Her cheeks were pink. The wind tossed around her brown hair. Tears had frozen like tiny glaciers on her face.

"Those bastards," she murmured. "Bastards bastards bastards bastards."

Curt Dickes stood beside her. His wool coat was buttoned from top to bottom, and his scarf blew behind him like a flag. "Hey, I hear you, kitty cat, but you have to let it go. Stride's a big boy. This article isn't going to bother him."

"Well, it bothers *me*," Cat snapped. "How could they say those things about him?"

"It's what those jerkwads do."

She threw another chunk of ice, but she couldn't hear a splash or see where it landed. "Dean Casperson. I can't believe I ever *liked* that man. I'm never going to see one of his movies again."

"Yeah, that'll show him," Curt replied with a sarcastic smirk. "He's really going to miss your ten bucks at the box office."

"Well, what do you suggest?"

"I'm not suggesting anything," Curt said. "I just came over here to stare at that pretty face of yours."

At any other moment, Cat would have blushed to hear Curt say that, but not now. She picked up another sharp, dirty nugget of ice, then threw it back at her feet and kicked at the snow. "I'm just so mad."

"Hey, I'm mad, too. I love the lieutenant no matter how many times he busts me. But if you're talking about a guy like Dean Casperson, Stride has met his match. It's just about impossible to take on a zillionaire, particularly when most of the world thinks he's Saint Dean."

"He's not," Cat snapped.

"Saying it doesn't change anything. You'll never convince people otherwise."

"I know that, but I want to *do* something."

"Yeah, like what?" Curt asked.

Cat shrugged. "I have no idea."

The two of them strolled along the beach with the lake beating and thumping against the high wall of ice beside them. The winter noise always unnerved Cat, because it sounded like an invisible beast pawing at the bars of its cage. She expected to see a huge wave coming over the wall to carry them away.

They got colder and colder. Her lips were numb. The only thing keeping her warm was the anger she felt.

"Men like that think they're invincible," Cat said. "They think they can do whatever they want and no one will stop them."

"Yeah, and they're pretty much right about that," Curt replied. "That girl, Haley Adams, she spied on him, right? And she wound up dead."

"At least she tried. It's better than doing nothing."

"Yeah, well, not for her."

Cat stopped on the beach and grabbed Curt's sleeve. "Hey, we could do that, too."

"Do what?"

"Spy."

Curt waved his hands in protest. "Whoa, whoa, not a good idea, kitty cat. Are you crazy?"

"No, Casperson thinks he's safe. The other girl's dead. He doesn't think anyone's watching him now."

Curt blew out a cloud of steam from his mouth. "Do I need to tell you what Stride and Serena would say about us doing that?"

"I don't care. I'm not going to sit around while they smear Stride. No way."

"And what exactly do you plan to do?" Curt asked.

"Exactly what Haley Adams did. Get dirt on Casperson. That tele-scope she used, do you think it's still in the house?"

Curt shook his head. "Nah, I snuck in and checked. Police took it."

"Well, I'll find another way."

Cat turned around and headed for the dunes as fast as her short legs and the deep snow would allow. The cottage was invisible on the other side of the sand.

"Hey, where are you going?" Curt shouted at her over the wind.

Cat looked back over her shoulder. "To find a pair of binoculars," she called. "You coming with me or not?"

# 23

*"Save me,"* Aimee Bowe murmured.

She was on her back on the dirty floor of Art Leipold's hunting cabin. Her arms and legs lay limply on the ground as if she didn't have the strength to move them. Her blue eyes squinted up at the face of Dean Casperson. She blinked, because the barest light was too much after days of darkness.

"It's okay," Casperson reassured her, sliding his strong arms under her shoulders and pulling her closer. "It's okay, it's over, I've got you."

*"Save me."*

"You're safe now. No one's going to hurt you."

Aimee cried.

The whole scene was nothing but actors playing parts, but Stride's heart was wrenched because it felt so real. No matter how many other people milled around the set, it was as if Aimee and Dean were alone. They were very, very good.

"Who did this—" she began.

"It doesn't matter now. We have him. He's not going to hurt anyone else."

"I can't move. What's wrong with me?"

"Give it time," Casperson said. "You're okay."

"I'm so cold."

"You'll be out of here soon."

"I killed it," she murmured in a fit of grief as Stride struggled to hear her. "I killed it. I killed the little girl."

"Shhh," he hushed her. "Don't talk. You don't have to say a word. You're free."

*Cut.*

The actors relaxed.

Aimee Bowe detached herself quickly from Casperson's arms. She stood up and paced nervously back and forth on the set. Her expression was distressed, as if she had difficulty leaving her character behind. Casperson was the opposite. He immediately began joking with the crew with the casualness of someone who had done this a million times. A green screen glowed behind the small patch of ground on which the interior of the hunting lodge had been built. They were all gathered in the cold rental warehouse near the harbor. It was the fifth take of the rescue scene.

Stride stood next to Chris Leipold at the back of the set. He cocked his head and whispered. "Aimee said she killed the little girl. What does that mean?"

Chris chuckled. "Honestly? I have no idea. Aimee is one of those actors who improvise each take to see how the scenes play out. She's been reworking the monologues for her character to make it more authentic. It's a little different every day. Most of the time I like the spontaneity, but it drives Dean crazy because he doesn't know what's coming next. He's a by-the-book actor."

It was late afternoon, but Chris gulped coffee from a travel mug as if it were early morning. The two of them wandered toward the warehouse door, which was cracked open to let in cold air. The wind felt good to Stride after he'd spent half an hour under the heat of the movie lights.

"The chief says someone called the mayor to complain about police interrupting the filming," Stride said. "'Harassment' is the word she used. Is that true?"

Chris studied him over the top of his coffee. "Yeah. Sorry."

"It was you?"

"I had no choice. I was getting major pushback on the set."

"Let me guess. Casperson."

Chris shrugged and didn't deny it. "Dean's a pro, and he likes things to go a certain way. If he's unhappy, the studio's unhappy, and that means I'm unhappy. I had to formally pass along our displeasure."

"You could have talked to me directly."

"That's not how it works, Lieutenant," Chris replied. "No offense, but these things are over your head. And it's not just Dean who complained. Your people have been talking to everyone. It hurts morale and slows the whole process down. Every day we waste, every hour we fall behind, hits our budget."

"You realize this is a murder investigation, right?" Stride asked.

"I do. And you realize this movie has a budget of more than $100 million, right?"

Stride shook his head in resignation. He and Chris were on opposing sides now, and nothing was going to change that. The investigation of Peach Piper's murder was a threat to Dean Casperson and a threat to the movie. The people putting up the money weren't going to stand idly by and let him derail their investment.

Chris sensed Stride's coolness and tried to repair the schism between them. "Listen, I saw the article in the *Gazette*. That was way over the line. I'm sorry you had to go through that."

"We both know where it came from," Stride said.

Chris didn't try to convince him otherwise. "Yes, you're probably right. Don't let the smiles around here fool you. People in this business play hardball if you get in their way."

"I have a girl with a bullet hole in her forehead who would say the same thing."

Chris recoiled. "Come on, you don't really think that anyone here—?"

Stride didn't answer, and Chris looked shaken by the implication. The writer quickly changed the subject.

"I have a question for you about the article," Chris went on. "It says your friendship with Art blinded you to the idea that he was a suspect. I'm curious. Is there any truth to that?"

Stride wanted to say no. He wanted to tell Chris that Art's name hadn't come up at all until they ran the fingerprint on the shard of a pen they'd found in Lori Fulkerson's apartment. But that wasn't entirely true. In reality, when he looked back, the clues had all been there.

The first victim, Kristal Beech, had been a St. Scholastica journalism student, and she'd interned on the morning news where Art was an anchor.

The second victim, Tanya Carter, had been a waitress at Bellisio's. Art ate there twice a week. Stride had met him for dinner there more than once, and he'd watched Art greet the staff like family. There was no way Art didn't know Tanya.

The third victim, Sally Wills, had worked at a nonprofit organization at which she routinely recruited local celebrities for fund-raising events. She had a signed photograph of herself and Art among the two dozen pictures hung on her office wall.

Each of the victims had a connection to Art Leipold. The truth should have been screaming at Stride, but he'd missed it. Or maybe he hadn't wanted to believe it was possible.

"Deliberately or not, Art left a trail for us to follow," Stride told Chris. "He didn't even hide it well. Later, I wondered if he was taunting me, daring me to figure it out. I didn't, not until it was way too late. But it's not because we were friends. To be honest, Chris, I didn't like Art. I never did."

Chris made a sour little laugh. "Funny, I never did, either."

"He was smooth, I'll give him that," Stride went on. "Right to the end, he was sure he'd beat the charges. I think he could hardly believe it when the jury sent him away. He thought he could talk himself out of anything."

"Yeah. I sat there in court day after day and listened to the evidence. I remember when he got on the stand and used that anchorman voice of his to say that this was a witch hunt and *he* was the real victim. The jury hated him. I hated him, too."

Stride could still hear Art's anchorman voice in his head. He realized that Art had never really been a journalist. He was an actor. He put on one face for the world and another for his real life.

Just like Dean Casperson.

He saw Casperson on the other side of the set. Casperson was dressed like him. Imitating him. Pretending to be him. It made Stride angry, as if his own identity had been stolen. Casperson looked back at him. The actor's composure didn't break, not even for a moment. He was too good. He headed across the warehouse and extended his hand, but Stride didn't shake it. If it was going to be war, let it be out in the open. That was enough to cause the tiniest crack in Casperson's facade. It was also enough to make Stride realize that he couldn't back down in chasing this man no matter what the chief and the mayor wanted.

"Lieutenant, we're certainly seeing a lot of you," Casperson told him. "Don't you have other cases to work on?"

"I'll be here until we solve this murder," Stride replied.

"Well, you better hurry. The clock is ticking."

Stride stared at him. "Oh?"

"Didn't Chris tell you? We only have a couple more days of filming left. Then we'll be out of the city."

"I didn't realize the production was so far along."

Casperson shrugged. "Time is money. Right, Chris?"

Chris nodded, but he didn't look happy. "It is."

"Aimee wrapped up her scenes in the box yesterday," Casperson went on. "Did Chris show you any of the footage? It's amazing. I really think there'll be Oscar buzz for her. And she and I are almost done with our scenes together, assuming I can get her to read the lines the same way for two takes in a row."

"You don't like to improvise?" Stride asked.

"I like to make a plan and execute it one step at a time. Aimee's younger and more free-spirited. She tries different approaches until she finds one that fits. Of course, screenwriters hate it. Writers don't like actors messing with their words, do they, Chris?"

"Most of the time, no."

"Still, I respect her. She's a gifted performer. After this movie, she'll be going places. Count on it."

"I'm sure you're right," Stride replied.

"Anyway, it means we should be wrapping up in the next day or two. I'm sure that will be a relief for everyone around here. I know it's been an intrusion. Especially for you."

"Oh? Why me?"

"I'm aware you had a little trouble with the tabloids," Casperson said. "I saw the article. It was brutal."

"Well, I hope it doesn't hurt your box office draw," Stride said. "You know, doing a movie about a troubled cop."

"Oh, don't worry about that, Lieutenant. By the time the movie comes out, audiences won't care what kind of man you are in real life. They only want three things when they go to the theater. Popcorn. A great story. And me." He smiled with those crazy-white teeth of his.

Stride looked down at the actor, who was oozing arrogance. This was the real Dean Casperson. The man behind the mask. The man who knew he had all the naked power in the world to get what he wanted.

"Well, I'd hate to be the one to derail your career after all these years," Stride said.

Casperson laughed out loud. "Believe me, you couldn't if you tried. My advice is, don't read what the tabloids say. Bad publicity comes with the territory in this business. Just keep your head down for a couple more days. Once the filming is done, the *Gazette* will forget all about you. As soon as I leave town, the tabloids leave with me."

Chris Leipold, standing in the middle of the fencing match, looked as if he wanted the conversation to be over quickly. "I think they're ready for the next take, Dean."

"I have to go," Casperson told Stride. "If I don't see you again, Lieutenant, I want you to know it's been a real pleasure playing you on screen. When you see the movie, I hope you feel I do you justice."

"I'm sure you will."

This time, Stride stuck out his hand. Casperson looked at him with the smallest hesitation and then shook it.

"Enjoy your last few days in Duluth," Stride told him, their hands locked together in a crushing grip. "As far as my team and I are concerned, there's no rush for you to leave. We'd be happy to keep you around for a long time."

Their eyes met. Both of them knew exactly what Stride meant.

"That's a very generous offer, Lieutenant," Casperson replied, "but I never like to overstay my welcome."

# 24

Maggie and Cab shared an open-air dockside table in Tin City.

Boats swayed in the harbor, and moonlight shimmered on the dark water. The restaurant was crowded and noisy, with an acoustic rock band wailing over the laughter of the twenty-something crowd. The two of them picked at a plate of shrimp nachos. Cab had a glass of Chardonnay, and Maggie drank from a bottle of Cigar City Jai Alai IPA. She closed her eyes and savored the damp breeze on her face.

"I think Florida suits you," Cab said with a grin as he watched her.

He was right. This was paradise compared to Duluth.

"In January, definitely. In July, I'm not so sure."

Cab shrugged. "Heat is mostly a state of mind."

"Well, you can always put on more clothes when it's cold. You can only take so many off when it's hot."

"Yes, but which is more fun?" Cab asked pointedly.

His ocean-blue eyes glittered behind his wineglass. She realized with a flush of surprise that he was letting her know that he was attracted to her. Maybe it was the booze or the moonlight, but she was attracted to him, too. She felt a strange romantic urge to reach across the table and run her hands through his gelled hair. And then to kiss him. And then to do other things.

She was flustered. She felt embarrassed and tried to think about what to say next.

"So what happened between you and Detective Mosquito?" she asked before she could stop herself. Looking for details about Cab's ex-girlfriend wasn't a great way to stoke the fire between them, but Cab didn't seem to mind.

"Lala and I only have two choices," he told her. "Everything or nothing. She'll never be happy with something casual in between."

"And casual in between is what you want?"

"I guess so, because here I am. What about you? What do you want out of a relationship?"

"My history would suggest that I'm a casual in-betweener, too."

"Well, what's wrong with two people who simply want to enjoy each other's company while they're together?"

"Absolutely nothing," she said.

The meaning was hard to miss.

She felt the heat of her arousal as they stared at each other. Somewhere deep down, she felt a twinge of guilt, too, like an unwelcome guest at the party. A few weeks earlier, she'd been happy with Troy. His only mistake had been to do what good men are supposed to do, by asking her to marry him. And she'd responded by blowing up their relationship. Like Cab, she'd chosen nothing instead of everything.

Now here she was on a perfect Florida night. She was being romanced by a tall, rich, attractive man who had no intentions other than a one-night stand. Go away, guilt.

"So this is the place where Haley Adams worked?" she asked, looking around the restaurant.

"It is."

The waterside bar looked like every other Florida seafood joint, with nautical ropes and kitschy plastic alligators on the walls, wobbly wooden chairs, and ceiling fans pushing the warm air around. The waiters threaded through the crowd with brightly colored drinks. Haley would have been here on her last night, wearing a navy blue polo shirt and khaki shorts like all the other servers. Somewhere after midnight, she would have wandered alone into the dark parking lot near the water. That was where John Doe had shot her in the head.

"I wonder if anyone remembers her," Maggie said.

"Unlikely. It was a couple years ago. People turn over pretty fast in places like this."

Maggie drank her beer with a frown at the idea that a pretty young girl could disappear so quickly from the world and leave no ripples behind.

"Did you talk to Jungle Jack?" she asked. "Did you ask him about being here the day Haley was killed?"

"I did," Cab said. "I interviewed him when I was still part of the Naples Police."

"What did he say?"

"He told me to try the shrimp nachos." Cab popped a piece of shrimp into his mouth. "And he was right about that."

"Anything else?"

"He hit on Lala right in front of me," Cab said. "As for Haley Adams, he claimed not to remember her."

Maggie shook her head. "We're never going to be able to prove what happened to her, are we?"

"No," Cab replied. "We're not."

"I hate that. I hate these people. I hate that sense of entitlement. They think there are different rules for them because they have money."

Cab shrugged. "There are."

"Not in my book."

"I'm not saying I like it, but if you think the world treats Dean Casperson the same as Haley Adams, you're kidding yourself. Come on, Maggie, you have money, just like me. Don't you get treated differently as soon as people find out?"

"That's why I usually hide it," she said.

"You shouldn't," Cab told her. "I never apologize for being rich. That's my karma this time. For all I know, in my last life I was a street urchin begging on the curb in Pyongyang. And maybe next time around I'll be a crab scuttling along the seabed until I wind up on somebody's plate in a place like this."

"Do you really believe that stuff?" Maggie asked.

He smiled. "If you grow up with Tarla Bolton, you believe it. My mother is a New Age hippy at heart."

"Well, I believe this is my only shot," she told him. "Nothing before, nothing after. One and done."

"Then we really should make the most of it."

Maggie heard the invitation in his voice. She played with her hair. It was still strange having it long after so many years with short bangs that fell across her eyes. "You are a very good-looking man, Cab Bolton."

"I know."

She laughed so hard that she had to cover her mouth to avoid spitting out her beer. "Very few men could get away with that line. I don't know how you do it."

"My charm is not pretending," Cab replied. "I'm equally honest about my faults."

"Which are?"

"I'm not a team player. I'm a loner. I hate bureaucracy, because I like to do things my own way. I get bored easily. I want to give Lala what she wants, but I can't. I'm too selfish for that."

"If you were Chinese and eighteen inches shorter, you could be me," Maggie said.

"And a woman."

"Yeah, that, too," she said.

Cab finished his wine and stared down at her, and she stared back. The music thumped in her ears. Neither one of them needed to say it was time to go. It just was. Cab put a hundred-dollar bill under his wineglass, which was way too much for the bill, and then the two of them made their way out of the restaurant. It was peaceful in the night air, walking beside the docks with the laughter of the crowd behind them. Cab didn't wait long. Just outside the restaurant, he took her face in his hands and kissed her. She had to get on tiptoes, and he had to bend down to reach her like a heron hunting a lizard. It was still great.

Outside Tin City, the neighborhood turned industrial. They walked next to the warehouse wall of a marine manufacturer on their way back to Cab's car. Boat trailers and vans lined the street. There were no lights, making the area dark except for the glow of the restaurants on the other side of the water. Cab had his arm slung around Maggie's shoulder. He hummed a tune under his breath, and she thought it was a Frank Sinatra song, "Ring-A-Ding-Ding."

His Corvette was parked at the end of the street, near a boat lift that hauled speedboats in and out of the water. The night made it hard to see, but she knew something was wrong when glass crunched under her feet. Ten feet from the sports car, they both stopped dead.

Every window in the car was shattered. Some windows had been broken all the way through, scattering sharp fragments in and out of the car; some were simply dotted with starbursts. The candy-red chassis was a sea of dents, as if it had been caught in a massive hailstorm. The mirrors had been knocked off the car and smashed. The tires were slashed and flat. The license plate, catcha, lay at their feet, bent in half.

Cab bent over to pick up the plate. Doing so saved his life.

They were too shocked by the destruction of the car to hear the man sneaking up behind them and swinging a baseball bat at Cab's head. As Cab ducked, the man missed, and the bat sailed by with a hiss of air only inches above Cab's skull.

Maggie screamed a warning. She reached for her gun, but her gun was 2,000 miles away in Minnesota. She dived across the short space and shoved the man's chest with both hands, but she only bumped him a few inches backward. It was like pushing against a horse that didn't want to move. She tried again, but he was ready for her. He swatted her off her feet with a backhand thump of his forearm. She landed hard on her back on the pavement, and the pain was like a cattle prod to her neck.

Cab jabbed a fist at the man's face. The blow jerked the man's head back and bloodied his nose. With a grunt, the man swung the bat again. Cab dodged out of the way, but not quickly enough, and the bat hit him in the meat of his upper arm and knocked him to his knees. The man cocked his arms like a baseball player, but before he could take another swing, Maggie scrambled to her feet and threw herself in his face. She wrapped her arms around his back and sank her teeth into his shoulder. He howled in pain and wrenched free, throwing her to the ground again.

The bat dropped from his hands and rolled.

It rolled right into Cab's hands, and he picked it up and got to his feet.

"Hi," Cab said to the man.

Maggie and Cab closed on him from both directions. The man reached for his back pocket, pulled out a knife with a six-inch blade, and slashed the air. Cab swung the bat, and the man jumped back. Cab swung again, and this time the bat caught the metal tip of the knife and sent it flying. The man heard the clatter of the knife and knew he was done. He turned and ran. They watched him go, disappearing into the Naples streets, and they were in no condition to chase him. Cab let the bat fall to the pavement. He grimaced as he rubbed his arm.

"You okay?" she asked.

"I'll live. How about you?"

"I'll have a headache tomorrow, but I'll be fine."

He came up to her and touched her back, neck, and hair, looking for blood and tender spots. His fingers were surprisingly soft and graceful. She felt along his arm and shoulder but found no breaks. They stayed close to each other. Their skin was bathed in sweat, and they were both breathing hard. The fight had attracted no attention from Tin City. The two of them were still alone near the warehouse.

Eventually, Cab separated himself from her and surveyed the wreckage of his Corvette. He walked through the field of glass.

"Well, it was time for a new car anyway," he said.

Maggie laughed, but that sent spasms through her neck. "I don't suppose this was random."

"Oh, no. This was a message. Stay the hell away from Dean Casperson."

"Except we can't prove it."

"That might be the one advantage we have," Cab said.

"How do you figure that?"

"He's arrogant enough to think there's nothing we can do to him."

"So what do you suggest?" Maggie asked.

Cab didn't answer. He went around to the back of the Corvette and pried at the damaged trunk, which opened with a screech of metal. He dug inside and emerged with a look of triumph on his face. There was a bottle of wine in his hand.

"I always keep a bottle of Stags' Leap in the back for emergencies. Thank heavens it came through unscathed."

"You really are something," Maggie told him. "But you haven't answered my question. What do we do now?"

"First we go to my place and open the wine," Cab said.

"And then?"

"You're not going to like it. Remember, you're still a cop, but I'm not."

"Tell me," Maggie said.

"The rich play by their own rules," Cab replied, "so we need someone who's willing to beat them at their own game. That's why I sent Peach up there in the first place. We need to find someone who doesn't care about the rules. We need someone who's willing to cheat."

# 25

Cat parked her Honda Civic in the parking lot of the Ordean-East Middle School. Her car was the only vehicle in the lot in the middle of the evening. She and Curt slipped out into the cold. There was no snow, but the gusty wind down the hill almost stole the gray trapper hat from her head. A recycling bin had been blown from someone's garage and tumbled down the street; it rattled and rolled around on the asphalt. She shoved her hands into her coat pockets and pointed her face down, and they trudged to the corner.

Through the trees on the other side of Fourth Street, she could barely make out the corner of the red brick wall protecting the estate that Dean Casperson was renting. The wall followed Hawthorne Road up the hill. The intersection of the two roads was empty. They had the neighborhood to themselves.

"So now what?" Curt said.

Cat tapped her foot on the sidewalk as she thought about what to do next. "Do you think we can climb that wall?"

"I could boost you up. You should be able to reach the top."

"Well, let's see if anything's going on over there first," she said.

Cat headed diagonally across the intersection under the glow of a streetlight. She was on the other side of the street from Casperson's mansion. It was dark here, sheltered by tall bushes. She took deep steps through the snow toward the corner house, which was a white Colonial with a green roof. Curt stayed close behind her. They followed the walkway in front of the house, crossed a plowed driveway, and ducked quickly through the snow in the open yard until they reached the next house. They took shelter behind a tall arborvitae.

From there, they had a vantage across the street to the gated driveway at Casperson's estate. Lights glowed on either side of the brick columns. A sedan was parked on the street, and its windows were clouded with steam. Every now and then they could see an arm wipe the front window. A guard was watching the gate.

"I don't think he's going to invite you inside, kitty cat," Curt said.

Cat unzipped her coat and grabbed the binoculars that hung around her neck. She put them to her eyes and focused on Casperson's estate. The angle was wrong to see the house. She could make out the curving driveway and the detached garage, but a stand of evergreens blocked all the windows.

"What can you see?" Curt asked.

"Nothing. This isn't working." Cat tapped her foot impatiently again. "What if we sneak into the house that Haley Adams used? She had a view into Casperson's place. You said you got in there when you were looking for the telescope, right?"

"I barely got out, too. They've got private security checking on the place now."

Cat frowned. She noted the time on her watch and peered through the binoculars again.

"It looks pretty quiet over there," Curt added. "There's no party tonight. I'd know."

"Let's give it a few more minutes."

"Okay, but if we're out here much longer, it's going to take a blowtorch to thaw out my junk."

Cat giggled. "You're on your own with that."

They stayed where they were, shivering in the cold. The night was silent. Across the street, Casperson's place remained peaceful. No cars came and went; no one approached the gate. She began to think that Curt was right and Dean Casperson was spending the evening alone.

At ten o'clock, she decided it was time to go.

They backtracked through the snow, but before they broke out of the bushes, headlights shone from the southern direction on Hawthorne Road. Cat held up a hand to stop Curt where he was. She watched as a white limousine glided up the hill from the lake and stopped in front of Casperson's estate. The security guard got out of the sedan and checked the car and then pushed a button to open the metal gate. The limo backed up, navigated the tight turn, and then drove inside and parked near the front door.

"Hang on," Cat said. "Who is that?"

She scrambled to focus the binoculars. Inside the gate, it was almost impossible to see details. Then, as the rear door of the limousine opened, she saw someone get out. Just one person. The glow from the interior light of the long sedan was enough to make out the face, and Cat recognized her.

It was Aimee Bowe.

Aimee stopped outside the car as if frozen. Her long coat draped to her feet. Her hair blew across her face. Oddly, she looked back toward the gate and the darkness, almost as if she were staring directly at Cat. There was no way she could see her, but Cat felt as if their eyes had met. In her imagination—and it had to be her imagination because she was too far away—she thought she saw Aimee's lips moving. Sending her a message.

*Save me.*

Aimee walked around the car to the front door, which was open for her, and then disappeared inside the house.

"I have to get over there," Cat said.

"What? Are you kidding, kitty cat?"

"There's going to be trouble. I know it."

Cat didn't wait for Curt. She took off running. She bounded downhill through the snowy front yards to the intersection. At the corner, she crossed the street and ducked inside the trees that sheltered the wall surrounding Casperson's estate. The top of the wall was more than a foot over her head.

"What do you think you're doing?" Curt asked, arriving behind her.

"Help me get over the wall."

"You sure about that? This is a bad idea."

"I'll be careful," Cat said, "but I have to make sure Aimee's okay."

"I don't know. I'm already pushing my luck with the cops. If they catch me inside, I'm screwed."

"You stay here," she told him. "I'll go."

Curt heaved a sigh of resignation, and Cat kissed his cheek in gratitude. He squatted in the snow and laced his gloved hands together to form a step. Cat put her boot on his hands, and he hoisted her up until she could grab the top of the wall and swing her other leg over the mortar. She straddled the wall and stared down at the other side, where the ground looked far away.

She was about to jump when headlights swept across her body like a searchlight. Quickly, she flattened her torso along the top of the wall, and Curt took cover among the pines. Looking back, she spotted the white limousine silently disappearing through the intersection and continuing down the hill.

It didn't slow down. No one had seen her.

Cat called to Curt in a hushed voice. "Wait for me. I won't be long."

Before she could lose her nerve, she swung her leg to the other side of the wall and leaped down.

She landed, lost her balance, and fell. When she got up, half her body was white with snow. She shook as much as she could from her clothes and then followed the wall uphill toward the estate. Ahead of her, the gables of the house loomed between the trees. Squares of yellow light dotted the windows. She was approaching from the back, and she veered away from the brick wall to get closer. The trees ended at a landscaped courtyard fifty yards from the house. She saw a stone fountain that was dormant for the winter. A wrought iron table sat in the center of a circular patio with a large pancake of snow on top of it. Deer and rabbit tracks dotted the gardens.

She felt exposed as she crept through the courtyard to the house, whose two wings were connected at a right angle by a rounded turret that looked like something from a castle. A huge bay window in the south wing overlooked the courtyard, and lights were on inside. She stayed low, and when she reached the window, she poked her head above the frame to peer inside. Just as quickly, she ducked back down. Jungle Jack was stretched across a leather sofa, his face only inches from the glass. If he'd glanced left, they would have been staring at each other. Cat shrank down against the rear wall. She could hear the noise of the television inside, but one glance had told her that Jack was alone in the room.

Where was Dean Casperson?

Where was Aimee?

She backed away from the window and made her way around the turret and along the perpendicular wing that was closest to Hawthorne Road. Most of the lights were off. She followed the side of the house until she reached the driveway, where she could see the main gate and the detached garage. She waited, then tiptoed in hushed steps past the double front doors to the far side of the estate. She looked back at the gate. The guard outside wasn't visible on the street.

The wind was in her face, cold and loud. The tall evergreens swayed. Despite the chill, her nervousness made her sweat. She continued around the corner of the house, where she was sheltered by the walls on both wings. The asphalt driveway curved beside her. On the second floor, twelve feet over her head, she saw lights. Behind the sheer curtains, a silhouette moved in and out of view.

It was Aimee Bowe.

Cat needed to see into that room. She spotted a white catering van parked near the back doors of the south wing, and the top of the van was only a few feet below the roofline of the house. She crept down the driveway until she reached the van. The rear door of the house was open. She could hear voices inside and smell the yeasty aroma of bread baking. The front of the van faced her. She put a boot on the bumper and climbed up the hood to the top of the vehicle, wincing as the steel of the chassis shuddered loudly under her feet. The roof was just above her, but the angle was sharp, and the shingles were covered with snow.

She braced her gloved hands against the gutter, hoping it would hold, and slithered awkwardly from the van to the roof. The wind was fierce there, making it hard to keep her balance. She stood up and put one foot in front of the other like a high-wire artist as she marched through the snow along the very edge of the roof. The drop to the ground loomed beside her. Her boots struggled for traction. It was twenty dangerous feet to the corner, but when she got there, she had a perfect view into the second-floor room in the next wing.

The curtains were drawn, but they were sheer, and when she lifted the binoculars to her eyes, she could see clearly. The large room was a study decorated in dark wood and leather, with a fire roaring in a stone fireplace on the far wall. She saw a wet bar glistening with mirrored shelves and crystal. A brass chandelier hung from the ceiling. The heavy walnut door near the fireplace was closed, but another door on the adjoining wall was open, and Cat could see a bedroom beyond the doorway.

There were two people in the room: Aimee Bowe and Dean Casperson.

Aimee sat on one end of the leather sofa. She had a glass of white wine in her hand, but she held it uncomfortably, and her legs were pressed stiffly together. She wore an orange blouse, black slacks, and sky-high heels. Dean sat across from her, on the other side of a Persian rug, in a wing-backed chair. He wore a heavy Nordic-style sweater and khakis. His legs were crossed, and he looked completely at ease. He sipped his drink from a lowball glass. His face had a casual smile, and he seemed to be doing all the talking.

Nothing was happening between them.

It looked innocent.

Where Cat stood, the wind gusted. She squatted and shoved a hand through the snow to the roof tiles to keep her balance. Under her boots, the snow was melting, making it slippery. She couldn't stay up there much longer.

What she saw through the binoculars was two actors talking. Nothing more. Yet Cat didn't like it. It was Aimee's face that bothered her. It seemed almost vacant, as if she weren't tracking on whatever Dean was saying. Her eyes had a strange distance. Minute by minute, as Cat watched, Aimee grew increasingly detached from reality. Her eyes opened and closed in slow, lazy blinks. Her head lolled. Dean talked as if he didn't notice that something was wrong, but to Cat it was obvious.

Then the wineglass tipped and fell from Aimee's hand.

Aimee didn't even seem to notice that it had happened. Wine soaked her slacks; the glass broke into pieces on the hardwood floor. At first she didn't react at all. Then she put both hands on either side of the sofa and tried to get up, but as she did, she fell back. She looked dizzy and confused. Across from her, Dean got up. He didn't jump up in alarm or concern; he simply walked over and sat down next to her. His hand reached to her face and touched her cheek.

For Cat, the whole thing was a slow-motion horror.

She stood on the roof, paralyzed. She had to stop this, but she didn't know how. Before she could decide what to do next, her phone rang, startling her with the loud noise of "Uptown Funk." It was her ring tone for Curt; he was wondering where she was. She reached for her phone, but as her body twisted, she lost her balance. Her feet spilled out from under her, and she toppled backward. She hit the roof, then slid past the gutter with a cloud of snow, and she was airborne.

She couldn't help it. She screamed. She dropped twelve feet and landed in a drift that broke her fall, but the wind couldn't cover the noise. Behind her, near the van, she heard footsteps and shouts. Looking up, overhead, she saw Dean Casperson peering out the window into the darkness and barking into a phone. Cat scrambled to her feet and ran. She tore around the curving driveway toward the front of the house, but when she saw the gate, she also could see the security guard outside. He bellowed at her to stop. The gate was opening; he was heading toward her.

Cat switched direction. She barreled into the woods, bounding through the snow like a frightened deer. She could hear the guard behind her. She didn't dare look back; she just ran. The tree branches ripped at her arms and poured snow into her face. She slipped, got up, slipped, and sprinted again. She zigzagged through the woods until she reached the brick wall on the perimeter of the property, but the wall was keeping her inside now. There was no way to climb. No way to escape.

She ran parallel to the wall with nowhere to hide and nowhere to go. Then, like a miracle, she saw the corner where she'd jumped down into the snow. And there was Curt, on top of the wall, waiting for her.

"Run, run, run!" Curt wailed.

The guard in pursuit was faster than she was. She could almost hear his breath as he got closer. She reached the wall and leaped straight up with her arms outstretched, and Curt grabbed one of her wrists and yanked her up, nearly dislocating her shoulder. She felt herself flying. Below her, the guard's hand grabbed her boot and tore it off, but in the next instant, she and Curt were tumbling free over the wall to the outside. Cat landed in the snow. Curt bounced off the recycling bin he'd grabbed to climb the wall. They didn't hesitate; they were on their feet again, charging across the intersection to the school parking lot and piling into Cat's car.

She fired the engine of the Civic and sped down the hill. Her eyes were glued to the mirror. She turned, turned again, and turned yet again, and when she decided that she'd lost anyone who might be chasing them, she swung to the curb with the engine still running. She hit the speed dial button on her phone and felt a flood of relief when Serena answered on the first ring.

"It's me! Aimee needs help!"

# 26

Dean Casperson answered the door.

He didn't look surprised to see Serena flashing her badge at him. He gave her a friendly smile and cocked an eyebrow as he watched three separate squad cars with flashing lights stream into the driveway in front of the rented estate.

"Mr. Casperson, my name is Serena Stride with the Duluth Police," she said. "Where's Aimee Bowe?"

"Aimee? She came over here to chat, but she wasn't feeling well. I asked Jungle Jack to take her home." He added with a smirk, "Your name is Stride? Are you married to the lieutenant? I have to say, the man has spectacular taste."

Serena ignored the comment. "Please move aside, Mr. Casperson. We need to search this house."

"Search it? What exactly are you looking for? And don't you need a warrant for that?"

"I've got a credible report of an assault in progress in this house," Serena told him.

Casperson shrugged and moved out of the doorway. "Well, come inside, then. I'm afraid you've been misinformed, but do what you have to do. Try not to break anything around here, okay? It's a rental."

Serena swung around and waved to Guppo, who waddled into the house behind her, accompanied by three other police officers. "Check every room," she told him. "Question the staff and see what they know about what's been happening here tonight. Show them photos of Rochelle Wahl and Peach Piper, too."

"Peach Piper?" Casperson asked curiously. "Who's that?"

"You knew her as Haley Adams. Before she was murdered."

"What about this other girl? Rochelle?"

"I don't have time for this right now, Mr. Casperson. Where were you and Aimee Bowe talking?"

"Upstairs, but I told you, she's gone."

Serena saw the staircase leading to the second story, and she took the steps two at a time. Half the doors upstairs were closed, and she went down the hallway, opening each door and looking inside. The rooms were all empty. Then, at the end of the hallway, she twisted a knob and found a door that was locked.

"What's in here?" she called to Casperson as he came up the stairs behind her.

"My bedroom and private study."

"Is this where Aimee was?"

"Yes; it's a good place to talk."

"Why is it locked?"

"I always keep it locked. I keep sensitive materials in here. Scripts, contracts, that kind of thing."

"Please open it," Serena told him.

"If you'd like."

Casperson took a key from his pocket and undid the lock on the study and opened the door. Serena pushed past him. The large room was empty. A log fire burned on the wall beside her, crackling and spitting sparks onto the hearth. The air was warm. Soft jazz played from overhead speakers. She saw an open door leading to a master bedroom, and she went inside and searched it. No one was there.

She returned to the study, where Casperson stood next to the wet bar, refilling a glass of whiskey and adding an ice cube. Her eyes noted the details around the room. She saw the leather sofa and went over to it and put her hand on the end of the cushion. It was wet. She recognized the fruity aroma of wine. She spotted the glint of a tiny shard of glass on the wood floor.

"What happened here this evening?" Serena asked.

"Aimee came over to talk. She had some wine, but she started feeling dizzy, so she made it an early night."

"Where's her wineglass?"

Casperson stared at her with practiced nonchalance. "Like I said, she was dizzy. She dropped it, and it broke. I cleaned it up and threw away the pieces."

"If I tested the glass fragments, what would I find?" Serena asked.

"What would you find? Sad remnants of a Chateau Margaux Bordeaux, I guess."

"Anything else?"

"Like what?" Casperson asked.

"Drugs."

"Oh, please."

"Do you have any drugs here?" Serena asked.

"The strongest thing you'll find in this house is Xanax. I have trouble sleeping."

"Did you spike Aimee's wine with it?"

"I'm sorry, is this a joke, Detective? Of course not. However, what Aimee does is up to her. I have no idea whether she took anything before she got here. And she used my bathroom while I was here, so for all I know, she dipped into my medicine cabinet. The fact is, I don't interfere with how other actors cope with this business."

"What was Aimee doing here?" Serena asked.

"We were talking about box office prospects for the film. I was telling her how impressed I was with her performance. And I was suggesting that she would be perfect for a role in a picture I'll be filming this summer in Switzerland. I wanted to see if she'd be interested."

Serena shook her head. They had nothing to use against Casperson, and he knew it.

She went to the window and pushed aside the curtains. On the roofline of the next wing, she could see the disruption in the snow where Cat had fallen. The girl had been telling the truth, but enough time had passed that Casperson had managed to circle the wagons to protect himself.

She turned around and found that Casperson had crept up silently behind her. He wasn't even six inches away. They were eye to eye.

"What are you really doing here, Detective?" he asked.

"I told you; we had a report of a possible assault in progress," Serena said.

"What kind of report? From who?"

"It was anonymous."

Casperson didn't move or give her any more space. "We had a trespasser tonight."

"Do you know who it was?" Serena asked.

"No, it was too dark to see, but I imagine whoever it was called in this fictitious report. You can't trust spies, you know. They lie."

Serena leaned even closer to prove she wasn't intimidated. She could smell the alcohol on his breath. It was strange, standing here in the presence of someone who was instantly recognizable anywhere in the world. It was strange, knowing he wore two totally different faces. He was Dean Casperson, actor and philanthropist. He was Dean Casperson, serial predator.

"Tell me about Rochelle Wahl," she said.

"You mentioned that name downstairs. Who is she?"

"She was a girl who came to your party last Saturday night. She was found dead outside her house the next morning."

"Who told you she was here?"

Serena was silent. Casperson's lips curled into a small smile of satisfaction.

"So no one did," he said. "You're fishing. Look, Detective, I'm going to do you and your husband a favor. I'm *not* going to call the mayor and have you fired for storming in here tonight, although we both know I could. You can just leave and not come back. But we're done. You and the lieutenant and your whole team are done. I don't want you in this house again. I don't want you talking to me again. I don't want you anywhere near the filming. Do you understand?"

Serena didn't say anything. She just stared at him. After a few seconds passed, he stepped aside and waited. She marched out of the room and headed back downstairs. She heard Casperson closing and locking the upstairs room behind her. On the lower level, she found Guppo and directed him and the team out of the house.

"You didn't find anything?" she said.

Guppo's round head swung back and forth. "No. Sorry."

"Who was in the house?"

"Some people from a catering company. A maid. A chef. They were all deaf, dumb, and blind, and I get the feeling they're well paid to stay that way. I showed them Rochelle's photo. Nobody remembered her."

Serena exhaled steam into the frigid air. "That son of a bitch is going to get away with this. According to Maggie, he's been at it for thirty years. And nobody has breathed a word about it in public."

"So what do we do?"

"Leave someone here to talk to Jungle Jack when he gets back," Serena said. "Let's go find Aimee Bowe and make sure she's okay."

\*

Maggie's phone rang at one in the morning in Florida, waking her up. She could see the screen glowing and hear the phone vibrating on the nightstand. She reached across the bare torso of Cab Bolton in his bed and grabbed it. It was Stride, which meant it was an emergency. As she talked to him, Cab used a remote control to switch on the light and then sat up next to her.

They were both naked.

Cab listened curiously to her end of the conversation, which didn't take long.

"Dean Casperson got interrupted in midassault," Maggie explained when she hung up the phone. "They think he drugged Aimee Bowe and was planning to rape her."

"Can they prove it?" Cab asked.

"No. There was no evidence of anything by the time the police got there. Even if Aimee talks, Casperson laid the groundwork to blame it on her."

Cab shook his head. "The man is Teflon."

He got out of the four-poster bed, and she watched him walk over to the full-length mirror on the back of his bathroom door. It wasn't a large bedroom, and Maggie wasn't a fan of the lime-green paint, but she wasn't here for the decor. The air-conditioning kept it cold, and the overhead ceiling blew a constant breeze over her bare skin.

In the mirror, Cab examined his upper arm, which was mottled with red-and-purple bruises. As he moved it, his face twisted with a stab of pain.

"How's the arm?" she asked.

"Feels like someone hit it with a baseball bat."

"Weird," she said.

"Yeah, I can't figure it out. How about you? How's the neck?"

"Pretty loose now, actually. Intense physical activity must be good for it."

"I hope you mean the sex," Cab said. "Or did you get up while I was sleeping and use my in-home gym?"

"You have an in-home gym?"

"Oh, please. Not a chance."

Cab wandered over to the glass doors that led to the balcony and then went outside. Maggie got out of bed and joined him. They didn't bother with clothes. Cab's house was small, but it was in a secluded location on the sandy peninsula ten miles south of Naples. The balcony looked right out on the Gulf, where moonlight made the calm water glow. Steps led down to the beach. Palm trees guarded the house like soldiers.

"This is one hell of a place," Maggie said.

"I bought it earlier this year. If you're going to live in Florida, you might as well live on the water."

"Any bugs?"

"The size of Cadillacs. If they unionize, I'm doomed."

"So it's not entirely paradise?" Maggie asked.

"Oh, no. It is. It definitely is. Do you want to go for a naked swim? Sex in the water isn't all it's cracked up to be, but you get bragging rights when you tell your friends you did it."

"I wish I could," Maggie said unhappily.

"Ah. All good things come to an end?"

"I need to get back to the Ritz. I have to catch an early-morning flight. Stride wants me back in Duluth."

"Plus, we're at a standstill here," Cab said. "So go."

"I hate to leave you stranded," Maggie said. "You don't have a car."

"Don't worry, my Corvette dealer delivers."

Maggie crooked a finger for a kiss, and Cab bent down to deliver it. Then she went back into the bedroom, leaving him alone on the balcony. She retrieved her clothes, which were strewn across the gray ceramic tiles on the floor, and got dressed. In the bathroom, she studied herself in the mirror. She looked like someone who'd had sex that night. She decided it was a look that worked for her.

She really didn't want to leave.

The balcony doors were still open, letting the sticky air in. She went back to the doorway, and Cab turned around and smiled. The trees and the water framed his tall, skinny body in the moonlight like a portrait. His spiky hair was even messier than usual, which was her doing. He leaned against the balcony, utterly relaxed and utterly naked. He flicked a small lizard off his wrist.

"Come with me," Maggie told him.

"What?"

"You know Dean Casperson and this case better than anyone," she said. "And you know what Peach was doing, so you can help us figure out what happened to her. Come back and work with us. Just for a couple days. You can stay at my place."

Cab tilted his face to the sky as if pondering the idea. He looked back over his shoulder at the perfect water of the Gulf, and then a grin crept across his face. "Duluth in January," he said. "Well, who could resist an invitation like that?"

# 27

Serena recognized the red Toyota Yaris that was parked outside Aimee's rental house on Thirteenth Street. Lori Fulkerson was there.

The woman stood at Aimee's front door, where she'd tramped across the beaten-down snow. She turned around in surprise when she saw Serena and Guppo marching toward her, and her surprise turned to wide-eyed fear when several other police cars arrived at the same time. She looked like a rabbit, ready to run.

"What's going on?" Lori asked.

"We're looking for Aimee Bowe, Ms. Fulkerson. Have you seen her?"

"No, I just knocked on the door. There was no answer."

"Have you been here long?" Serena asked.

"Just a couple of minutes."

Serena checked her watch and studied the empty street around them. "It's pretty late to be paying a visit, Ms. Fulkerson. Why are you here?"

"I couldn't sleep. I needed to talk to her."

"About what?"

"To be honest, Aimee seems like the only person who has ever understood me. It's the strangest sensation, like I can feel her inside my head. Like we're connected." Lori crossed her arms over her chest in the cold. "I don't like it."

"Did you tell her you were coming over?"

Lori shook her head. "No. I just got in my car and drove."

"Did you see anyone coming or going as you arrived?"

"Nobody."

"Okay, why don't you go back home now," Serena told her.

"Is everything all right? Did something happen?"

"It's nothing for you to be concerned about."

Lori looked at the faces of the police officers. Then she wandered into the snow and headed back toward her car. She got into the Yaris, but Serena noticed that she didn't drive away. Lori stayed there, watching the activity outside the house.

Serena pounded on the front door. "Aimee! Aimee, are you there?"

There was no answer.

"She could be unconscious," Guppo said. "If she was drugged, she might not hear us."

Serena was about to put her shoulder to the flimsy door when she remembered Aimee's comment that half the locks in the old house didn't work. She turned the doorknob, and the front door opened with a squeal of its hinges. The interior was dark and cold.

"Aimee," she called again. "It's Serena."

Still no answer.

She walked into the living room with Guppo beside her. A narrow corridor led to the bedrooms, and they checked each one, expecting to find Aimee sprawled on the bed or the floor. The actress wasn't there. Serena checked the two bathrooms, but they were empty.

They did a search of the rest of the house, which didn't take long. It was obvious that Aimee had never made it home. Serena continued to the rear porch, which had a view out onto the dark mass of Lake Superior. Frost coated the windows, and wind whistled through a seam in one of the frames. It sounded like the cry of a witch. She was hoping she'd find Aimee stretched out on a wicker sofa under a blanket, but no one was there.

"Is Jungle Jack back at Casperson's house yet?" she asked Guppo.

"As of two minutes ago, no."

"Where did the son of a bitch take her if it wasn't here? Get a car over to the apartment Jack's renting in Hermantown. I want to make sure he didn't decide to finish what Dean Casperson started."

Guppo nodded. "I'll make the call."

The sergeant turned around and left the house, leaving Serena alone.

Serena stood on the back porch, thinking about Aimee Bowe. There was something odd about her, and she had no idea how to explain it. It wasn't rational, and Serena believed only in rational things. She thought about the story Stride had told her about Aimee and Cat. *Save me.* It was so unbelievable that Cat hadn't even wanted to tell her about it, because she knew Serena would tell her it wasn't real.

And now Lori Fulkerson.

*It's the strangest sensation, like I can feel her inside my head. Like we're connected.*

Not rational.

Serena closed her eyes. She tried to open her mind, as if she could feel a connection with Aimee simply by being there. Aimee's presence was in this house. A hint of her perfume floated over the cold. Serena listened to the wind and thought: *Where are you? Tell me.*

Aimee didn't answer, because things like that weren't possible. Serena felt silly for even having considered it. What mattered was evidence you could feel, touch, taste, hear, and see.

She went back out the front door. Guppo was waiting for her. Lori Fulkerson finally had driven away.

"Have we found Jungle Jack?" Serena asked.

"The uniform at Casperson's place just checked in. Jack's back. That means he didn't have time to go to Hermantown."

"So where is Aimee Bowe?"

"Jack says he dropped her here," Guppo told her.

Temper flared on Serena's face, which wasn't like her. "Well, she is *not here.*"

"I know, Serena," Guppo replied quietly.

She shook her head at her outburst and turned her anger back on herself. She felt like this entire case had a wall around it that they couldn't break through. "I'm sorry, Max. Call the officer back and get Jungle Jack on the phone. I want to talk to him myself."

"You got it."

Serena stamped through the snow into the middle of the yard. She shivered in the wind and studied the house and grounds from a distance. Footprints were everywhere, overlapping. They told her nothing. Some went around the house; some crossed the yard diagonally; some went downhill toward Skyline Parkway. Most probably had been made by kids.

Then she remembered what Aimee had said about someone breaking into the house. *Whoever it was didn't just look through the windows. He came inside, too.*

What if he was waiting for her when she got home?

Who?

There was no sign of a struggle, but in Aimee's condition, she wouldn't have been able to put up a fight. Except there was almost no time between Jungle Jack leaving and Lori Fulkerson arriving for anyone to kidnap Aimee.

She saw Guppo hustling toward her through the snow. He gave her his phone and said simply, "Jack."

"Mr. Jensen," Serena barked into the phone. "This is Serena Stride with the Duluth Police. We're at the house that Aimee Bowe is renting, and she's not here. Where is she?"

There was a long pause on the line. "I don't know what to tell you, Detective. I was there less than twenty minutes ago. I dropped her off."

"Describe the house," Serena said.

"Blue, single story, way up on the hill."

Serena nodded. The description was right. "What exactly happened when you got here with Aimee?"

"She got out of the car. She headed for the front door. I left. End of story."

"What was her physical condition?" Serena asked.

"She said she was fine. I mean, she was wobbly and all, but I figured she'd simply had too much to drink."

"Did you get out of the car yourself? Did you help her?"

"She didn't want any help," Jack replied. "You may find this hard to believe, but Aimee Bowe doesn't exactly like me. She wasn't crazy about the idea of my driving her home. She told me to go."

"Did you wait until she got inside the door?"

"No, I just left."

Serena shook her head in frustration. "Were there any other cars on the street?"

"I don't remember any, but I wasn't paying attention."

She hung up the phone and handed it back to Guppo. "It's freezing out here. We need to find her, Max. If Jack's not lying, Aimee was heading for her front door when he left. At most, we got here fifteen minutes later. And Lori Fulkerson was here before that. In that time, Aimee managed to disappear."

"But she never got inside the house," Guppo said. "The floor mat inside wasn't wet. She didn't carry in any snow."

Serena looked around at the large, sloping expanse of yard and felt a new sense of urgency. "Then she may be outside. Have the men check the perimeter of the property. *Hurry.*"

Guppo whistled with his fingers and shouted at the officers near the house. Serena headed through the snow for the lot line, where the yard was ringed with evergreens whose branches hung to the ground. Even in the moonlight, a body could lay there, unfound. The wind on the hill roared, fast and cold, cutting through her heavy coat and biting at the exposed skin on her face. Anyone outside in this weather didn't have much time.

"Go, go, go!" she shouted. "Spread out!"

The police officers separated on the hillside, one small shadow after another. Serena headed for a sweeping ash tree near the street and had to duck to walk underneath it. The snow was deeper there. She saw nothing, so she pushed her way back into the open yard. Guppo was checking the fir trees near the neighbor's house. Two officers hiked down the steep backside of the slope toward Skyline Parkway. Another was in the wooded land across the street.

Serena thought: *Footprints.*

If Aimee was out here, she had to leave footprints.

She focused on the bed of snow filling the yard and tried to separate out the prints that didn't matter. The tracks of animals. The tracks of kids cutting through the yard from one street to another. The random dimples of ice blown off the trees. The cops who had trampled most of the area near the house. She looked for prints that started near the front door and veered off in a single, lonely track. Just one set, wandering away, getting lost.

She almost missed them.

The ground was higher than she was, making the seam on the hillside almost invisible, like a wrinkle in the snow that the wind was already whisking away. Yet she knew it was footprints. She ran. She took large steps, and when she reached the tracks, she saw an uneven row of small indentations, spread far apart, vanishing toward a stand of blue spruces.

Fifty yards away, where the trees spread their branches and the footprints ended, she saw an almost indistinguishable mound in the snow.

*"Over here!"* Serena called.

She charged downhill, and as she reached the small mound, she dropped to her knees. The wind had mostly covered the body in drifts already, and Serena had to brush aside snow to find the arms, the chest, and finally the face. It was Aimee. Her eyes were closed, the lids white with ice. Her skin was already way too cold. Her mouth was parted and unmoving, the lips slightly open. Serena patted Aimee's cheek and called her name into her ear.

"Aimee, it's me. It's Serena."

There was no answer.

"Get an ambulance!" she shouted over her shoulder.

Serena stripped off a glove and tried to take a pulse, but her fingers were too numb to find it. She put her cheek down next to Aimee's mouth, and as she did, she felt the one thing that made her heart leap. Even in the frigid air, she could feel the steamy puff of a breath as Aimee exhaled.

She was alive.

# 28

In the middle of the night, Stride finally made it back home to the cottage. He went into Cat's room and found the girl still awake, sitting up in the darkness in her T-shirt and sweatpants. One of the front windows was cracked an inch open, letting in icy air. She'd adopted that habit from him.

"Aimee's alive?" Cat asked. "She's okay?"

Stride sat down next to her and turned on a nightstand lamp to give the room a soft glow. "Yes, she's in the hospital now. Serena's with her. It looks like she'll be fine."

"Thank God. I was so scared."

Cat stared at him with wide, vulnerable eyes. She shoved an index finger between her teeth and chewed on a nail, and that made her look younger than she was. He knew part of it was an act. When she was in trouble, when she felt guilty, she tried to look like a little girl.

He didn't know what to say to her this time. He'd seen Cat do bad things in their two years together. She'd stolen. She'd lied. She'd protected people who didn't deserve protection. This was different. It wasn't about herself; it was about someone else. He wanted to ground her for her recklessness, but at the same time he was proud of her.

"That was a brave thing you did tonight," Stride told her.

Cat looked down, embarrassed. "Thanks."

"It was also very, very foolish."

"Well, Aimee said I would do something like that. I guess she was right."

He noticed that she didn't apologize, and he wasn't going to make her do that.

"Tell me why you did it," he said.

"I don't know. I was so angry about that article about you. I wanted to help. I thought if I saw something, if I could spy on Dean Casperson for you, I could help you prove what kind of person he really is."

"Another girl tried to do the same thing, Cat," Stride said, "and she wound up dead. This is dangerous business. You don't belong anywhere near it. Climbing that wall tonight wasn't just trespassing. You were putting yourself at risk. Anything could have happened to you at that house."

"Yeah, I know. I was glad Curt was there to pull me over that wall."

Stride rolled his eyes. "As much as I hate to say it, I'm glad Curt was there, too, but I wish he'd stopped you from going over it in the first place."

"That's not his fault. Nothing was going to stop me."

Stride knew that was true. When Cat set her mind to something, she was as relentless as a runaway train. "Why was it so important to get inside?"

"Because when I saw Aimee getting out of the limousine, I could feel her reaching out to me from across the street. It was just like she said. *Save me.* She needed my help. I knew I had to do something."

"Doing something didn't mean going in there yourself. You could have called me. You could have called Serena."

"And told you what?" Cat protested. "That I saw Aimee going into Dean Casperson's house? There's nothing you could have done about that. That's why I had to find out what was really going on."

Stride hesitated before saying anything, because on one level she was right. If Cat hadn't been there, he didn't know what would have happened to Aimee Bowe. Maybe she would have been fine. Or maybe she would have awakened to find herself being assaulted. Whatever Dean Casperson's plans had been, Cat had interrupted them.

"So what happens next?" Cat asked him.

He hated to tell her the truth. "Nothing."

"Nothing? What do you mean?"

"I mean there was no crime committed, Cat," Stride said.

"Why, just because he didn't get a chance to rape her? That's crazy! I saw what he was going to do to her."

Stride took hold of Cat's hand. "Okay, tell me exactly what you saw."

Cat sniffled and squeezed her eyes shut as she tried to remember. Then she opened them, and her face was serious. "I saw what Aimee looked like. She was drugged; I'm sure of it. She looked completely out of it, like she didn't even know what was going on."

"Did you see Casperson give her anything? Did you see him tamper with her drink?"

Cat shook her head in frustration. "No. They were already drinking by the time I got on the roof."

"So you didn't see anything that couldn't be written off with an innocent explanation."

"This wasn't innocent, Stride."

"How can you be sure?" he asked.

"Because I *saw* his face. It was scary as hell. Aimee got all disoriented and dropped her glass. Casperson didn't do anything. He didn't look surprised or concerned. It was like he was *expecting* it, you know? He got up, calm as anything, and he walked over and sat right down next to her. He didn't get help. He didn't freak out. He just sat there and reached over and started touching her."

"Touching how?"

"Her face. He was caressing her cheek. Real slow, real smooth, like she was some kind of robot. And his eyes? Look, you know some of the things I've done. I know what men look like when they want sex and they're with a girl who can't tell them no. That was Casperson."

Stride's mouth was a thin, angry line. Those were the details that made him crazy.

"And then what?" he asked.

"Then I fell," Cat said. "He heard me and alerted the guards. That's when everybody started chasing me. If that hadn't happened, Casperson would have raped her. I know it. I'm sure of it."

"Between you and me, I think you're right."

"You believe me?" Cat asked.

"Of course I do."

"Then let me tell people what I saw."

He shook his head. "Absolutely not."

"But why not?"

"I'm sorry, Cat. You were there illegally, and as far Serena and I are concerned, you were *never* there. The tip we got was anonymous. Serena didn't use your name, and we're going to keep you out of it. That's it. It's not up for discussion."

Cat leaped out of bed. She paced angrily back and forth across the slanting wooden floor of the old bedroom. "That's just wrong. So Casperson gets away with it? We don't do anything?"

"I'm sorry, Cat."

"Look, I know I was trespassing. Fine. I'll admit it. If I have to get punished for that, I will. But why can't I just tell the truth?"

Stride got off the bed, too. He held on to Cat's shoulders to keep her in place and bent down until they were eye to eye. "Because if you say anything in public—anything—these people will *destroy* you."

"What do you mean?"

"You saw what they did to me. They were just getting started. They didn't leave you out of it to be nice. They left you out to make sure I knew what would happen if we kept going after Dean Casperson. If you stand up and make any kind of accusation, they will rip open your whole life, Cat. They will dredge up every mistake you ever made, every lie you ever told, every law you broke. They'll print every rumor, every innuendo, everything, to humiliate you and obliterate you. They will make sure no one ever believes a word you say."

"Let them try," Cat said, with her forehead crinkled in determination. "I can take it. I'm strong now."

"It's not about being strong. Strong people break, too. I've seen lives ruined this way. Do you remember what I told you about Mort

Greeley? He was an innocent man who lost his whole life to false accusations. You can't imagine what the pressure is like when the media and the public turn on you. I won't let you go through that."

"*You* didn't break," Cat said.

"I'm a cop. It's my job to take the heat. You're a teenager with your whole future ahead of you."

"That doesn't matter."

"It does matter," Stride said. "It's the *only* thing that matters to me and Serena. I know you want to do something. I know your heart is in the right place. But it's up to me to protect you and keep you safe. That means you need to stay out of this. Are you listening to me, Cat? Stay away from Dean Casperson."

Cat folded her arms across her chest. She spoke softly and intensely as she challenged him. It was the first time he'd ever really thought of her as a woman and not a girl. "Even if it means other people get hurt?" she asked.

Stride didn't hesitate.

He stared at Catalina Mateo, who was as close to a daughter as he would ever have, and he didn't hesitate.

"Yes," he told her. "Even if other people get hurt."

# 29

Sitting up in the hospital bed, Aimee Bowe didn't look famous. Her skin was pale, her hair flat and unwashed. She wore a blue plaid hospital gown that even a supermodel couldn't have made fashionable. Her face was turned sideways as she looked out the window toward the gray city and the deep blue waters of the lake.

Serena tapped her fingernails on the door in greeting, and Aimee gave her a thin smile and gestured her inside. Serena closed the door behind her. The hospital room was already crowded with flowers, stuffed animals, and balloons. She couldn't help noticing one particularly large bouquet of roses. The attached card hung open at an angle, so she could read it.

> This will make quite the story for your Oscar speech. Stay strong, and see you back on the set.
>
>                                                              Dean

Stay strong.
Serena could hear the underlying message: *Stay quiet.*
She sat down in the chair next to the bed.

"The nurses are already talking about autographs," Serena said, "so you must be feeling better."

"I am. No permanent damage. I counted fingers and toes. All still there."

"I'm relieved."

"They tell me I could have died out there. Thank you."

"I'm just glad we found you in time," Serena said. "Can we talk about what happened? Are you feeling up to it?"

A shadow passed across Aimee's face. "If you'd like."

"How did you wind up out in the snow?"

"I'm honestly not sure," Aimee replied.

"What's the last thing you remember?"

"I have this image of myself running in the moonlight. I'm not even sure it's really a memory. It's a flash in my head, nothing more."

"Why were you running?" Serena asked.

"I don't know."

Serena knew she was dealing with an actress, and she didn't know what story to trust. She had no idea whether Aimee's memory loss was real or she was just covering up the truth.

"Do you remember where you were earlier in the evening?" she asked.

Aimee's eyes flicked to the roses. "I was at Dean's."

"Why?"

"He wanted to talk about the film. And about new projects. He was offering me another role in his next movie. That's big for me."

Serena waited for Aimee to say more, but she didn't.

"How did you get home from Dean's?" she asked.

"I don't remember."

"Did someone take you?"

"I guess so."

"You don't know who drove you?"

Aimee's face flashed with annoyance. "I said I don't remember. One minute I was at Dean's, the next minute I was outside running in the cold. There's nothing in between."

"That's okay. I understand."

Serena thought about the footprints in the snow outside Aimee's house. They were far apart; she really had been running. But running from what? There was only one set of footprints. No one had been chasing her.

"What happened at Dean's?" Serena asked.

Aimee looked at the roses again. "What do you mean?"

"What did the two of you do?"

"We talked."

"Upstairs or downstairs?"

"I don't know. Both, I guess. Why does it matter?"

"You remember going upstairs?"

"I think so," Aimee replied. Her voice was clipped and impatient.

"Did you have a drink?"

"Maybe. Probably."

"What did you drink?"

"Serena, what difference does it make?"

"Who got you the drink?" Serena asked. "Was it Dean? Was it a butler? Who?"

*"I. Don't. Remember."*

"Okay. But at some point you started not feeling well?"

"Apparently. I have no idea. I told you, everything in between is gone."

Serena nodded. "Do you have a prescription for any sedative drugs like Xanax?"

"What?"

"It's an antianxiety medication. Some people use it for insomnia."

"I know what it is. No, I don't."

"Have you ever taken anything like that?" she asked.

"In my life? Yes."

"When?"

"A few years ago."

"But not recently?"

"No. I don't understand why you're asking me this."

"Xanax was found in your blood," Serena told her. "Do you have any idea how it got there?"

Aimee quickly looked away. "I have no idea."

"The dose was dangerous, particularly when combined with alcohol."

"I can't imagine how it got there," Aimee said.

"Did you take it yourself?"

Aimee was about to say no. Serena could see her mouth forming the word. Then she bit her lip and hesitated. "I told you, I don't remember anything, so I have no idea."

"Did you take anything before going to Dean Casperson's house?" Serena asked.

Aimee frowned. "No."

"Did you eat or drink anything before going over to his place?"

"I had dinner."

"How long was that before you went to Dean's?"

She shrugged. "A couple hours."

"Did you notice any unusual physical effects during that time?"

"No."

"So is it fair to conclude that the Xanax must have gotten into your system while you were at Dean Casperson's house?"

"Maybe. I don't know. Look, Serena, none of this makes any sense. For all I know, the blood test was wrong."

"You blacked out. You don't remember anything. That's consistent with the amount of the drug in your system."

"I'm sorry, but I can't help you."

"Has anything like this ever happened to you before?" Serena asked. "A blackout of this kind?"

Aimee hesitated. "No."

She was an actress, but Serena could see the lie in her face. "Are you sure?"

"Nothing like this has ever happened to me before," Aimee insisted.

"I remember you telling me that your first big break in acting was in a Dean Casperson movie," Serena said.

"So what?"

"I was wondering if you had any similar experiences while you were filming that movie with him."

Serena could see Aimee growing more agitated.

"I told you, no."

"What about other actresses? Have you heard any similar stories about these kinds of blackouts? Any rumors in the industry? Last time I asked you about that, you dodged my question. Why?"

Aimee closed her eyes. She took a deep breath. Then she opened her eyes and grabbed Serena's hand. "Okay, look. I lied about the drugs."

"What do you mean?"

"I took the Xanax myself."

Serena exhaled in frustration. "Aimee," she murmured, shaking her head. "What are you doing?"

"I'm confessing. *I* took it."

"You said you didn't have a prescription."

"I don't. That's why I lied. I got it illegally."

"From who?" Serena asked.

"Someone on the set. There are always people who can get you what you want. You know how it goes."

"What was the person's name?"

"I have no idea. Just some guy."

"There were no pills found on your body. Where did they go?"

"I finished them. I threw the bottle away."

Serena shook her head. Aimee had an answer for everything. "Why take the drugs?"

"Stress. Anxiety. This role has really gotten under my skin. What those women went through in the box? It's horrifying."

"I think you're lying to me about the pills," Serena said.

"I'm not lying. The drugs help. That's the truth."

Serena knew she wasn't going to get Aimee to change her story. Dean Casperson had built a wall around himself, and no one wanted to challenge him. If you were a victim, you kept your mouth shut to protect yourself. If you talked, you risked a Hollywood shunning that ruined your career. There was no upside in coming forward. Only risk.

She leaned closer to the bed. "Jungle Jack says he drove you back to the rental house. You don't remember that?"

Aimee's lip curled with distaste. "Jack? No. If I'd been conscious, I'd have gone home with anyone but Jack."

"He claims he dropped you off, you headed up the walkway, and he left. As far as we can tell, you never made it inside. For some reason, you ran off and collapsed in the snow. The tracks indicate you were alone."

"It must have been the drugs," Aimee said. "I hallucinated something."

"Is there anything else that you remember? Anything else that comes to mind about what happened?"

Aimee closed her eyes. She exhaled, long and slow, until there was no air left in her lungs. She breathed in again, her chest swelling. Her whole body relaxed. She was silent for nearly a minute, not moving, not saying anything. Then Serena watched a spasm ripple through her torso like a seizure, and Aimee's eyes shot open.

"Are you okay?" Serena asked.

"I opened the door to the house," Aimee said, "but I didn't go in."

"Why not?"

"Someone was inside. I didn't see anyone, but I knew someone was there. I could feel it. I *sensed* it. That's why I ran."

"We searched the house," Serena told her. "It was empty."

"Then whoever it was left before you got there."

"It could have been the drugs."

Aimee shook her head. "No. I remember now. Someone was waiting for me. They were going to take me. Kidnap me. Put me in the box."

"In the box?" Serena asked. "Like in the movie?"

"Like in real life. They've been watching me for weeks, getting to know my life, waiting for the right opportunity."

"For weeks?" Serena said. "Aimee, you haven't been in town that long."

Aimee blinked in confusion. She looked as if she wanted to protest, but she knew Serena was right. "Okay, maybe what I was seeing was someone else. Maybe it wasn't me."

"Not you? What are you talking about?"

"Sometimes I channel other people and I don't even know it."

"Channel other people?" Serena asked.

"I see through their eyes. Look, I know you don't understand, I'm just telling you what happens to me sometimes. Was there any kind of crime committed in that house? Even if it was years ago?"

"Not that I know of," Serena replied.

"It wasn't where one of Art Leipold's victims lived?" Aimee asked.

"No. Definitely not."

"Well, I can't explain it, but I felt someone in the house. I knew what they were going to do to me."

"But you didn't actually see anyone? Or hear anything?"

"No, but I knew I was going to end up in the box. And I ran. It's okay if you don't believe me."

"It's not that," Serena said. "You said yourself that this role has taken a toll on you. And you were drugged."

Aimee gave Serena a sad smile. "You're not the first person to think I'm nuts. Premonitions. Mental connections. Half the time I don't really understand what any of it means myself."

"I believe that you're upset," Serena said. "I'll check your house again and see if I can find any evidence that someone was inside. In the meantime, get some rest. When the hospital releases you, I'll take you home myself."

"Thank you, Serena."

Serena squeezed Aimee's shoulder and got out of the hospital chair. She headed for the door, but before she could open it, Aimee called after her. "Could you thank Cat for me, too?"

Serena turned around slowly. "Excuse me?"

"Cat. Tell her I said thanks."

"For what?"

"For saving me."

"I never said Cat did anything at all," Serena replied.

"You didn't have to. I know she was there. Somewhere in my head, I can see her out on the roof. Cat on the roof; that's pretty funny when you think about it."

"Aimee, if you remember something—if you know what really happened—"

"I don't," Aimee insisted. "I already told you, I don't remember a thing. I just know she was there."

# 30

"Jonathan Stride, meet Cab Bolton," Maggie told him.

Stride shook hands with the tall blue-eyed detective, whose linen suit and loud purple tie looked in perfect shape despite a three-hour plane ride and the long drive from the Minneapolis airport. It was hard to imagine this man as a former homicide investigator. Cab's gelled blond hair and diamond earring looked better suited to a Miami night-club than to a grubby police conference room filled with paper coffee cups and pizza boxes. Stride felt as if the entire city had been invaded by aliens, first from Hollywood, now from Florida. Their knowledge of Minnesota probably began and ended with *Fargo*.

"Welcome to Duluth, Cab," Stride told him. "Cold enough for you up here?"

As if Cab could read his mind about *Fargo*, the man replied with a nonchalant smile, "You betcha."

"I appreciate your making the trip. Maggie says you know Dean Casperson a lot better than we do, and right now we could use all the help we can get. Casperson thinks we can't touch him."

"He's probably right," Cab replied. The man didn't hide his direct-ness, and Stride liked that. "Casperson has been at this a long time without a whiff of suspicion. He's not afraid of us."

"Well, maybe you can help us even the odds," Stride said.

"I will if I can, Lieutenant, but the detective you really needed on this case was Peach Piper."

"I know this is personal for you. I'm sorry about Ms. Piper."

Cab tilted his head in thanks without saying anything more. Stride could see that he was open about some things but not about grief.

They all took their seats around the conference table. Stride. Serena. Guppo. Maggie. And Cab Bolton. Maggie and Cab sat next to each other, and Stride sensed an unusual dynamic between them. It was as if Maggie had one foot in Duluth and one foot in Cab's more glamorous Florida world. Serena obviously sensed it, too. She studied them across the table and made an under-her-breath comment that Stride missed.

He grabbed a square of Sammy's pizza from the box on the table and popped the tab on a can of Coke. "So where do we stand?" Stride asked them.

"This won't come as a surprise," Serena began, "but Aimee Bowe has nothing to say about an attempted assault by Dean Casperson. She claims not to remember a thing about what happened at his house. Plus, she says *she* took the drugs herself. So she put Casperson completely in the clear."

"Do you believe her?" Stride asked. "Could our—witness—have misinterpreted what was going on between them?"

Serena shook her head. "I don't think so. Aimee's lying. Whatever she does or doesn't remember, she simply won't implicate Casperson. She thinks it's career suicide."

Cab interjected from across the table: "This has been part of Casperson's playbook for years. He exploits young actresses. He figures they owe him something for helping their careers. According to my mother, it's an open secret in Hollywood but no one wants to say anything on the record."

"And his wife is living in denial about all of it," Maggie added. "Mo wouldn't hear a thing against Dean. To her, he walks on water despite his infidelity. She puts all the blame on the actresses, not on him. They're all just manipulative bitches trying to get ahead."

"Rochelle Wahl wasn't an actress," Stride said. "She was a fifteen-year-old girl. Is that part of his pattern?"

"The underage part?" Cab said. "No. But Haley Adams wasn't an actress, and neither were the other women who were murdered when Casperson was filming in various cities. He just likes young, beautiful women. If Rochelle was attractive, Casperson would have put the moves on her. He also would have been terrified once he found out how old she was. If there's one thing that could destroy his public reputation, it's having sex with an underage girl. Fans don't have a lot of tolerance for that, even with superstars."

"Do we have anything more that could actually tie Rochelle to Casperson? Have we found anybody who saw her at Casperson's place?"

"Nobody will admit it," Serena told him, "but I found circumstantial evidence that she was there. I reviewed the medical examiner's report about the contents of her stomach. She ate sushi the evening before she died. Including uni, which you're not going to find among the California rolls at Super 1."

"Uni?" Stride asked.

"Sea urchin gonads," Cab added helpfully.

Stride repeated that phrase very slowly. "Sea . . . urchin . . . gonads."

"Yes, really quite good if you can get past the texture," Cab said. "It has sort of a custard consistency. Imagine a saltwater flan."

Guppo took a look at Stride's face, which was a mask of disbelief, and smothered a laugh.

"Anyway, nobody flagged it at the time, because the death didn't look suspicious," Serena went on, "but I checked with the catering company that did the party at Casperson's place. They had a whole table of sushi set up. Including sea urchin."

"Which isn't enough on its own to prove anything," Stride said.

"Exactly. For now, the only other evidence we have is what Curt Dickes told me. He saw a girl who matched Rochelle's physical characteristics getting into a car with John Doe outside the party. Unfortunately, he couldn't identify her."

"Plus, it's Curt," Stride added. "Not everyone's favorite witness."

"Yeah, that, too," Serena said.

"So what's your theory about Peach?" Cab asked them. "How did she fit into this? She was only there to keep an eye on Casperson and see if she could get evidence of his sexual assaults."

"Well, she was watching the house on the Saturday night when Rochelle Wahl died," Stride said. "If she saw Rochelle and John Doe together—and then saw the news about Rochelle's death—she may have put it together and started digging into it. If that got back to Casperson, he would know he had a big problem."

Cab nodded. His mouth was a grim line.

"Have we found out anything more about John Doe?" Stride asked.

Maggie pushed a manila folder across the table. "We still have no direct ties to Casperson, but the coincidences keep piling up. We already have John Doe linked to Peach's murder and the murder of Haley Adams in Florida. Cab also identified at least five other murders or disappearances of young women in areas where Casperson was filming. One of those was a woman who vanished in Nashville. The Tennessee police had a witness who saw a man waiting in a car near where the woman was last seen, and they had a police artist draw a description. Guess who it looks like?"

Stride opened the folder. The artist's sketch inside was a perfect likeness of the John Doe who died in the car accident on Lavaque Road. Right down to the black cowboy hat.

"But we can't identify him?" Stride asked. "No actual name? No background?"

"No; he's still a ghost."

"What about John Doe's local contact in Duluth? They were communicating by burner phone."

"The burner phone hasn't come online since the last call from John Doe," Guppo told them. "The only other call in the phone records was that Sammy's Pizza order, but we don't have any records to nail down who made it. We've tracked down most of the store's delivery drivers. The film people have generated a lot of business this month, but nothing we could tie specifically to the phone call."

Stride rocked back in his chair. He wasn't happy. "Anything else?"

There was silence in the room.

"Well, we've got barely two days," he went on. "We better get busy. Once the film crew wraps up and leaves town, the odds of our putting together a case are next to zero. If that's true, Dean Casperson is going to get away with murder again."

\*

As the meeting broke up, Maggie felt Serena tug on her sleeve and pull her away from the others in the room.

"So?" Serena whispered in her ear. "Anything you want to tell me?"

Maggie grinned. "Why, whatever do you mean?"

"You know what I mean."

"Come on, is it that obvious?"

"It is to me."

"Well, I'm going through the breakup blues with Troy, and Cab's doing the same thing with his ex. We figured we might as well enjoy a little physical therapy together."

"I'm sorry about you and Troy," Serena said.

"Yeah, that's on me. As usual."

Serena shot a quick glance across the room at Cab Bolton. "He's easy on the eyes, that's for sure. He doesn't exactly fit in Duluth, though, does he? I can't see him diving into a tater tot hot dish."

"Um, hello," Maggie pointed out. "Does someone remember walking off the airplane from Vegas in her baby blue leather pants?"

Serena winked. "I'm a hot dish, too, baby."

"Go away."

Serena chuckled and strolled out of the conference room. Maggie and Cab were the only two people left inside. The room was warm and still smelled of pizza. Cab sat where he had during the meeting, laying out photographs from a file one by one across the table in front of him. Maggie came around the table and could see that the photographs had been taken in the woods where Peach Piper's frozen body had been found.

Cab, who was as smooth and glamorous a man as she'd ever met, was crying.

"It's probably better not to look at those," Maggie murmured as she sat down next to him.

"I need to see it."

Cab didn't say anything. He picked up one of the photographs, which showed a close-up of Peach's face, still dusted with snow crystals, looking angelic and peaceful. It was easy to imagine her smiling and opening her eyes as if this were just a game, except for the bullet hole in the middle of her forehead. He stared at it and couldn't seem to put it down.

"I'll arrange for the body to come home," Cab said softly. "Peach had no family. I want to take care of everything."

"Of course." Maggie added after a pause, "Regardless of what happens to Dean Casperson, the man who actually did this to her is dead. There's justice in that."

Cab finally turned the photograph facedown. He retrieved all the pictures and returned them to the file folder, then closed it and put his hands on top. His blue eyes turned to Maggie, and his jaw hardened in determination. Grief was done. Time to move on.

"What about Peach's notes?" he asked. "Did they give you anything useful?"

"We didn't find any notes," Maggie replied. "John Doe got to her apartment first. He cleaned everything out."

"You found nothing at all?"

"No. The only evidence left in her apartment was the Chinese food receipt that took us to the house where she was spying."

Oddly, Cab didn't look unhappy at this news. In fact, a smile crept over his face, and Maggie didn't understand it.

"What is it?" she asked.

"Peach was one of the most secretive people you'll ever meet," Cab explained. "Her nickname was Peach Paranoid. She hid everything. She had backups of everything. Trust me, I know that girl. Peach left something behind. We just need to find it."

# 31

Serena twisted the knob and opened the front door at Aimee Bowe's rental house. She knelt in the doorway and checked the lock to make sure there were no signs of tampering, but the latch was old and no longer clicked securely into place.

Inside, she took off her boots on the mat and explored the house in her stocking feet. There was dried mud on the floor, but she and Guppo had brought that in. She retraced their search from the previous night in her head and realized that they'd looked for Aimee only in the obvious places. The bedrooms. The bathrooms. The porch. There were plenty of hiding places for someone who didn't want to be found.

Serena didn't know whether to believe Aimee's story about someone hiding inside. The actress had been drugged and nearly delusional the previous night, so she could have imagined the whole thing. However, Serena had seen footprints in the snow outside when she'd responded to Aimee's first call. Someone had been there. It wasn't a stretch to believe that whoever it was had come back.

The trouble was everything else that Aimee had said.

*I knew they were going to be put me in the box.*

*They've been watching me for weeks.*

*Sometimes I channel other people.*

None of it made sense.

She made sure that the house was really empty. She checked the places she'd overlooked the night before. The closets. The basement. The garage. She even brought in a ladder and pointed her flashlight around the attic. She found nothing up there but dust and spiderwebs.

As she stood on tiptoe on the ladder steps, however, she heard something unusual in the house. She swung around quickly and nearly lost her balance. Her flashlight lit up the shadows of the hallway.

"Hello? Who's there?"

Serena climbed down the ladder and returned to the living room. Through the porch windows, the bed of snow stretched down the hillside. The dark lake merged with the dark clouds. She flipped on a light switch, but the light was broken. The house felt cold. She spotted the thermostat on the wall and found that the inside temperature was fifty-nine degrees. Aimee hadn't set it that low. Not a Los Angeles girl.

There was a bitter draft from somewhere.

She checked the porch and found the back door was open. Raw air chilled the space. When she tried to shut the door, the wind nudged it open again. There was no mystery about it. She did a tug-of-war with the breeze as she tried to secure the latch, and finally she grabbed a chair and wedged it under the doorknob. The chair rattled, but the door stayed closed.

Then she heard a noise again.

It was almost right behind her. She spun and saw nothing as she peered into the living-room shadows. She didn't move, and her hand edged closer to the butt of her gun as a precaution. As she stood there, the same noise beckoned her into the other room. It was a whistle, like someone softly alerting her that she wasn't alone. It happened twice. *Hey there, hey there.*

"Is someone in the house?" she called loudly. "This is the police."

But the living room was empty. She wondered if her mind was playing tricks on her. There was no way anyone could have gotten inside without her hearing him, and she was certain that she'd searched the entire house.

*Hey there.*

The low whistle taunted her again. This time it came from the master bedroom at the end of the hallway, as if whoever it was had traveled invisibly from one end of the house to the other. She'd already been in the bedroom, and she knew it was empty, but she retraced her steps and assessed the gloomy interior from the doorway.

*Hey there.*

Serena smiled in relief. A black-and-white chickadee had perched atop the curtain rod by the bedroom window.

"Well, hi," she said to the bird. "Did you come in through the back door?"

*Hey there, hey there*, the bird replied.

"And I bet you want to get out again, don't you?" Serena asked. She went to the casement window, which had no screen, and cranked the metal handle to open the window toward the winter air. As if the bird could smell freedom, it vanished quickly through the opening with a flutter of wings. Serena shut the window and locked it. It was one of the few locks in the house that seemed to work.

She laughed at her own anxiety. The dark house. The open door. The whistle of the bird. In the end, it had all proved to be nothing. Yet her unease refused to let go, and she wasn't sure why.

Then she remembered.

It was something Lori Fulkerson had said.

*There was a bird inside the box. Did they tell you that? A chickadee. You can't see it, but it flies around, and it sings to you. It's like this one beautiful thing that keeps you alive and reminds you of the outside world.*

Aimee's drugged delusion was that someone was going to kidnap her and put her in the box just like Art Leipold's other victims. And now here was a chickadee trapped inside her house.

Serena knew it was a coincidence. Tiny little chickadees were one of the few songbirds tough enough for Minnesota winters, and they were common even in January. The lock on the back door didn't work. The wind pushed it open. The bird flew inside. That was all it was.

Unless someone was playing a very strange game.

*

Stride found the small self-storage complex on a dirt road north of the city. It had been built on cheap land surrounded by acres of forest. There were three long, low buildings with rows of red garage doors. Piles of dirty snow had been plowed up to the edge of the trees, but the gravel driveways were slick with ice. He saw a gray Mercedes parked halfway down the third building, and he drove up next to it in his Expedition. He opened his window.

Chris Leipold was inside the Mercedes. He could see in Chris's face that the stress and long hours of the movie production were taking their toll. Behind the man's small wire-rimmed glasses, his eyes were watery. His skin was pale, and his thinning blond hair was greasy and unwashed. Chris opened the Mercedes window, and when the cold air hit his lungs, he unleashed a rattling cough.

"You okay there, Chris?" Stride asked.

"Flu. A little welcome home present from Minnesota."

"Yeah, it's going around. You should get some rest."

"I'll rest when we're done filming," Chris said.

"Is that going to be soon?"

Chris shrugged. "Depends on Aimee Bowe. We weren't counting on losing her today, so we have to rearrange the shooting schedules. Hopefully, she'll be back on the set tomorrow."

"I wouldn't count on that. She almost died."

"Death's a pretty good excuse, but short of that, actors have contracts."

"Does Aimee have any scenes left with Dean Casperson?" Stride asked.

"One," Chris replied. "Why?"

"I just thought it might be difficult for her."

Chris shook his head. "I don't know what you mean."

"Come on, Chris. It's just the two of us out here. Off the record. No notes, no reports. You can't tell me it's not all over the set that Aimee was drugged."

"I talked to Dean. He says Aimee was clearly high on something when she arrived at his place last night. He asked me to try to keep it under wraps as best as I can. The last thing Aimee needs is to have people start saying she's unstable. If that gets around, no one will hire her again."

"So Casperson already has his knives out," Stride said. "Discrediting her. Making sure she doesn't talk."

"He's protecting her," Chris replied.

Stride sighed in frustration. Everyone around Dean Casperson did his dirty work for him. Chris Leipold was essentially a good man, but in Hollywood, even good men made compromises. Everything was a trade-off. Sometimes talent came with perversions and secrets, and you had to live with it. If you wanted to get a film made, you couldn't risk being blackballed, so you kept your mouth shut.

"Why did you want me out here?" Stride asked Chris, gesturing at the self-storage units.

"I got a call from the owner this morning. He came over here and saw one of the units with an open door. Somebody broke in overnight. It was my unit, so he wanted me to know about it."

"You still keep a storage unit here in Duluth?" Stride asked.

Chris coughed phlegm into a tissue. The effort wore him out, and he laid his head back against the seat. "I keep all of Art's crap here. That's his whole life, crammed inside that little box. Appropriate, huh?"

Stride said nothing.

"I should have burned it long ago," Chris went on. "Instead, I put all of it in here after the trial, and I've never wanted to deal with it since then. I just pay the bill month after month."

"And now someone broke in?"

"Looks that way."

"Is anything missing?" Stride asked.

"I haven't gone inside. I probably didn't need to call you, but if it involved Art, I figured you'd want to see it first. Old habits die hard."

"Who knows you rent this unit?"

"Other than the guy who owns the complex? Nobody. That's what makes it a little weird. The thing is, I came out here last week and spent some time going through everything. It was the same day I visited the hunting land. I don't know, I guess I needed to face Art again."

"Do you think someone followed you?" Stride asked.

"I can't think of anything else."

"Well, let's take a look," Stride said.

They both got out of their vehicles. Chris was slightly hunched from the flu and looked even smaller than he was. Stride checked the door to the storage unit and saw a padlock sitting in the snow, its shackle cut open. He bent down and slid up the garage door. Inside, the unit was crammed with furniture and boxes stacked on gray steel shelves. There wasn't much room to walk. He saw paintings and framed photographs leaning against the walls on either side, and he recognized some of them from inside Art's house.

Several of the boxes had been pulled off the shelves. They lay on the concrete floor, their lids open. A square nineteen-inch Panasonic television sat next to the boxes, its cord plugged into a power outlet on the wall. There was an old VHS player connected to the television, and its green light was on. He pushed the eject button, but the machine was empty.

"Did you leave it this way?" Stride asked.

"No, the boxes were on the shelves, and the TV wasn't plugged in."

"Somebody was watching something," Stride said.

Stride squatted and pawed through the boxes on the floor. It was like an encyclopedia of Art's career. He saw newspaper clippings of Art getting journalism awards and Art emceeing outdoor city events. There were plaques from charities and reading lists from the classes he'd taught. Stride also saw dozens of videotapes. They were archives of stories Art had done over the years. Each was neatly labeled, and Stride recognized Art's handwriting. He took them out of the box one after another, and he remembered each of the stories from years earlier. It was like a history of his own life.

Murder-Suicide at Antenna Farm
Kerry McGrath Lakeside Disappearance
Mort Greeley / Child Abduction at the Zoo
Wallace Corruption Investigation

"Is anything missing?" Stride asked in a flat voice.

Chris sat silently on the cold concrete six feet away. He had another box between his legs, and he'd removed some of the contents. Stride could see gruesome memorabilia from Art's other job as a serial killer. Newspapers with headlines about the trial. An old pair of boots that Stride knew had been found with traces of DNA from one of the victims in the box. Even a long ribbon of fabric that had been torn from a prison bedsheet. Stride was surprised Chris had kept it. It was the cell-made rope Art had used to hang himself.

"Anything missing?" he asked again.

"Only one thing that I see," Chris replied finally. "The tape recorder."

"What?"

"The old cassette recorder that Art used to make the victims tape their messages to you. I kept it in this box. Now it's gone."

# 32

"So who's Troy?" Cab asked Maggie as they drove to the Central Hill-side apartment that Peach Piper had rented. "I heard Serena mention him to you after the meeting."

"Troy is my Mosquito," Maggie explained.

"Ah. Recent breakup?"

"Christmas," she said.

"Very recent. So what happened?"

She wiggled the fingers of her left hand. "He wanted to put a ring on that."

"And you don't want anything on your finger?"

"Nope."

With only one hand on the wheel, Maggie nearly lost control of the Avalanche. The truck bumped halfway onto the sidewalk before she steered it back into the street. In the process, she breezed through a stop sign and nearly collided with a panel van coming down the steep hillside toward the lake. The back of the Avalanche fishtailed, and the van's angry horn blared in their ears.

"I think I just saw my dead grandmother," Cab remarked.

"You and Stride. Always with the crap about my driving."

"Not at all. Next time I rob a bank, you're my getaway driver. Utterly fearless. So what's the deal with Troy? Is he a tall suave blond like yours truly?"

Maggie chuckled. "Troy's not much taller than me and not much smaller than Guppo. He could also bench-press the two of us put together. He's a widower with two daughters and a heart the size of Alaska. So in other words, he is nicer and sweeter than me in every possible way."

Cab was silent for a long time. "If you hadn't sworn to me that you wanted nothing but casual relationships, I would almost think that you were still in love with him."

"That is not a good way to get laid tonight, Bolton," Maggie replied sharply. "Can we drop it?"

Cab grinned. "Consider it dropped."

Maggie spotted the apartment building ahead of them and pointed the Avalanche at it like a torpedo. She parked at a forty-five-degree angle on the street with one wheel over the curb and then swiveled her head to stare at Cab, as if daring him to say something. He was smart enough simply to smirk and keep his mouth shut.

She let them into Peach's ground-floor apartment.

"Stride and I searched the place after she went missing," Maggie told him. "Then Guppo did another search after we found the body. If Guppo didn't find anything, there's nothing to be found."

"Well, I know how Peach thinks."

"I get that, but John Doe got here ahead of us. He took everything."

Cab didn't look discouraged. He wandered around the apartment, picking things up and putting them down, as if they would give him inspiration. Peach hadn't left behind many personal items. Near the sofa was a pair of red Crocs, and Cab turned them over with the toe of his shoe and examined the bottoms. Then he kicked them away. He saw a rubber band on the carpet and picked it up and stretched it between his hands. He went into the kitchen and opened the freezer, which contained nothing but a pint of mocha chip ice cream, a Heggies pizza, two Lean Cuisine dinners, and a package of frozen spinach. Cab opened the ice cream container and dug around inside with one of his fingers.

"You think she hid something in there?" Maggie asked.

"No, I just like mocha chip," Cab said.

He licked away the ice cream and then took the package of spinach and popped it in the microwave and zapped it on high.

"You want some spinach, too?" Maggie asked dubiously.

"I love spinach," he said with a little smile, "but more importantly, Peach hates it. When I first met her, I watched her pick it off a pizza at a motel in Lake Wales, Florida."

Maggie cocked her head and did a double take. "I'll be damned."

She waited next to Cab while the little brick of spinach went around and around in the microwave. A few minutes later, the timer dinged, and Cab retrieved the mushy package and put it on the counter. He carefully unsealed the wrapper and opened the white plastic carton inside. Then, using the tines of two forks, he carefully picked through the green wad of spinach.

"*Et voilà,*" he said.

"What the hell is that?" Maggie asked.

It was a small package of plastic wrap, no more than two inches by two inches, that Peach had secreted inside the spinach and then resealed. Still using the forks, Cab carefully peeled back the folds of the plastic until it was open on the counter. Inside was a rhinestone button shaped like a crystal flower, the kind that might appear on a woman's dress.

Maggie began to feel sorry that she'd never had a chance to meet Peach Piper. The girl was clever.

"A button," she said. "I wonder where she got it. And who it belonged to."

"I have no idea, but Peach obviously thought it was important."

"Do you think there's anything else in the apartment?" Maggie asked.

"Yes, I do," Cab said.

They left the kitchen and went into the bedroom, and this time Cab didn't even hesitate or look anywhere else. He went straight to the white mannequin standing behind the door with her arm cocked seductively behind her head.

"Sexpot," he said, as if talking directly to the mannequin. "What are you doing here?"

"I'm sorry, what?" Maggie asked.

"Peach had a collection of mannequins," Cab explained. "It was a little weird, and she'd be the first to say so. She had six of them in her bedroom in Florida. Ditty, Petunia, Harley, Bon Bon, Rickles, and Sexpot. I don't know how the hell she got Sexpot up here with her, but there was very little that Peach couldn't do."

He put his hands on his hips and studied the mannequin, which was made of fiberglass and was connected to a heavy glass stand by a jointed metal rod. He began to undress it.

"Something you want to tell me about your fetishes?" Maggie asked.

Cab winked at her.

When Sexpot was naked, he carefully detached the mannequin's cocked arm from the rest of the body. He studied the metal plates on both sides, then reattached the arm and did the same thing on the other side. Then he removed the head and segmented the torso from the legs. When he found nothing, he lifted the entire mannequin off the metal rod that secured it on the glass base. Two screws with plastic caps held the rod in place on a metal pole that jutted out of the base, and Cab loosened both screws and separated the rod from the base. It was hollow.

He peered inside the small square tube.

"Can you grab me a wire coat hanger from the closet?" he asked.

Maggie found one and handed it to Cab, who straightened the hook end and stretched the rest of the hanger until it was no wider than the mouth of the rod. He shoved the hook end inside the rod and wiggled it around. Then he yanked. The coat hanger slid out of the rod, and so did a wad of gum. After that, a small piece of plastic and metal dropped into Cab's hand.

A flash drive.

Maggie smiled. "I like this girl."

"So did I," Cab replied. "Do you have a laptop in your car?"

"I do."

Maggie left the apartment and jogged back to her Avalanche and retrieved a laptop from underneath the backseat. She came back and found Cab sitting at the weathered oak desk near the window. She dragged another chair next to him, and together they booted up the laptop. The wallpaper on Maggie's computer screen showed a photo of Troy Grange with his bulging squirrel cheeks and shaved head in the cockpit of his time-share Cessna, wearing pale green headphones. He grinned at her from the computer, and Maggie winced.

"Guess I better change that," she said.

Cab said nothing. He inserted the flash drive into one of the USB ports. A few seconds later, the drive opened and spilled a list of dozens of JPEG photos down the screen across Troy's face. He switched the view to thumbnails, and when he opened the first of the photographs, he saw the double front doors of a house. The picture had been taken at night, with the faces of two women dimly illuminated by a porch light.

"Do you recognize this place?" Cab asked.

Maggie squinted. "Looks like the house Casperson is renting."

"What about the women?"

"I don't know them."

Cab clicked to the next picture, which showed the same angle on the house, with a man on the porch with his back to the camera. Each of the next several photographs showed different people entering the house. Maggie spotted a couple of individuals she recognized from the film set, but most were strangers or their faces weren't visible in the pictures.

"Looks like she's documenting a party," Maggie said. "What's the date on the files?"

Cab checked. "A week ago Saturday."

He went slowly through the photographs one by one. Maggie studied the faces where she could see them, but they told her nothing. After fifty nearly identical pictures, the people began to blur. Then, as Cab clicked to the next picture, her mind caught up with her eyes.

"Hang on, go back one," she said.

Cab used the touch pad to return to the earlier photograph, which showed a man just inside the open door, slipping off a coat to reveal the shoulders of a red dress shirt. He was partly blocking a tall young woman next to him, who was in profile. She caught a glimpse of long reddish hair covering most of her face, but she could also barely make out a hint of her glasses. They were turquoise blue.

"I think that's Rochelle Wahl," Maggie said. "She was there, just like Serena thought."

"Who's that with her?"

"I can't be sure from the back, but it looks like Jungle Jack to me."

Cab enlarged the photo and studied the man. "I think you're right."

"Skip ahead. Is there anything with Casperson?"

Cab scrolled through the array of photographs. He opened up several with different angles, but they were mostly dark exterior shots of the house. Peach had zoomed in on a second-floor room where the lights were on, but it was impossible to make out any details behind the curtains.

"That's Casperson's bedroom, but we can't see inside," Maggie said. "What about photos of people leaving? If the girl Curt Dickes saw was really Rochelle Wahl, she had to be helped out of the party."

"They wouldn't have taken her out the front door," Cab said.

Maggie nodded. "You're right. Are there any photographs that focus on the side of the house?"

He enlarged the window and leaned forward to get a better look at the thumbnails. At some point during the evening, the photographs shifted, showing people heading out the house's front door. Peach had shot all of them one by one, but Maggie didn't see Rochelle Wahl, and she didn't see a man wearing a burgundy shirt. Then, near the end of the array, the camera switched to a different angle.

"There," she said.

The photograph showed a sedan parked in the driveway beyond the main entrance, in the shadows of the north wing. There was only low light glowing through the house windows, making the details hard to distinguish as Cab enlarged the picture.

"I'm pretty sure that's John Doe's Impala," Maggie said.

The next picture confirmed it. The driver's door and a rear door were both open, lighting up the car and two people around it. She saw John Doe loading an unconscious woman into the back of the Impala. Peach had taken several photographs one after another, catching the action in progress; she knew she was witnessing something important. Most were out of focus. One photograph, however, caught the girl's face turned toward the camera, eyes closed, hair spilling across her face, blue glasses dangling off one ear.

"That's definitely Rochelle," Maggie said. She added in a subdued voice, "She doesn't look fifteen, does she?"

"No."

"I wonder if they found her school ID in her purse and panicked," she said.

"Look at her dress, too," Cab added, zooming in as far as the resolution of the photograph would take him.

The dress was hard to make out in the enlargement, but it was either navy or black. At first, Maggie didn't understand what she was looking for, but then she spotted tiny silver glints running in two rows down the front of the dress.

"Are those buttons?" she asked.

"I think so."

"Is that what Peach hid in the freezer?"

"Could be," Cab said.

Maggie rocked back in the chair, lifting the front legs off the carpet. "Where did she find it?"

Cab kept scrolling. He saw a shift in the character of the thumbnails on the screen. Night changed to day. The location was different, too. Peach had staked out a location across a rural highway from a small complex of rental cottages.

"That's where John Doe was staying," Maggie said. "What day were these pictures taken?"

"Monday."

"So that's the day after Rochelle's death hit the evening news and one day before Peach disappeared."

"Except how did she know where to find John Doe?" Cab asked. "I can't believe he was hanging around the movie set. Casperson would have wanted to keep him under wraps."

He opened more photographs. It was obvious that Peach had staked out the apartment complex for hours, taking photographs of every vehicle coming and going from the highway. The pictures stretched through the afternoon hours and into the evening. The darkness made the details harder to distinguish, but Peach stayed there as if waiting for someone.

"Look at that," Maggie said, pointing at one of the pictures, which showed a familiar face outside the cottages. "She wasn't staking out John Doe; she was staking out Jungle Jack. She saw Jack arrive with Rochelle and saw her getting helped out to the car. And the next day, Rochelle's death was all over the news. Peach knew that girl didn't freeze to death in her PJs. She was at Casperson's party."

Cab clicked a few more pictures forward. "Look who's talking to Jack," he said.

"John Doe. They're together. We've got Rochelle at the party with Jack, John Doe driving her away, and then Jack and John Doe together at the apartment complex two days later. And in between, Rochelle's death was staged to look like an accident instead of murder."

"Is that enough to bring Jack in?"

Maggie reached over and put her hand over Cab's and moved the touch pad down to reach the last file on the flash drive. It was a video, time-stamped the same evening.

She played it.

Peach was on the move, obviously wearing a video camera clipped to her coat. She was in the parking lot of the complex, outside John Doe's car. In the audio background, Maggie could hear Peach breathing. The interior of the car was too dark to make out any details, but as they watched, Peach used a slim jim to dig into the driver's side window and unlock the vehicle.

She opened the door. The dome light went on. They could see Peach turn nervously back to watch John Doe's rental cottage, which was only a few feet away. The lights in the cottage were off.

"Aw, hell, Peach, what were you doing?" Cab murmured.

Peach opened the car's back door, and the video followed her as she began searching the interior of the car, where Rochelle Wahl had been stretched out unconscious after the party. She dug her fingers into the seats, and they could hear her frustration at finding nothing. Then she began peering under the seats, and she pulled out a penlight and shone it along the car's floor.

They heard a tiny squeal of excitement, and Peach's hand disappeared under the seat. When it came out, there was a rhinestone button pinched between her fingertips. They could hear her voice on the video, just a whisper.

Maggie realized it was the only time she'd ever have a chance to hear Peach Piper speak.

"Gotcha," Peach said.

# 33

"I suppose you can't smoke in here," Jungle Jack said as he sat across from Stride in the police interview room. He pulled a crumpled pack of cigarettes out of the pocket of his burgundy shirt.

"No," Stride replied.

"Oh, well." Jack shoved the cigarettes back in his pocket. "I bet you used to be a smoker. Am I right?"

"In fact, you are."

Jack grinned. "I can always tell. Doesn't matter how long since somebody's quit, I can see it in their face when they look at a pack. There's still that longing, you know? It never goes away."

Stride ignored the comment, although Jack was right. "Before I ask you any questions, I'm going to read you your rights."

He rattled off the Miranda warning, and Jack listened with amused disinterest. The man didn't seem intimidated or concerned. "Are you willing to talk to me without a lawyer present?" Stride asked.

"I can't imagine why I'd need one."

"Okay, good." Then he added, "I like your shirt, Jack."

A little furrow of confusion crossed the man's brow. "Thanks."

Stride took a photograph out of a folder and put it in front of Jack. It was the photograph Peach Piper had taken of the front door of

Casperson's house, with Rochelle Wahl standing next to a man who looked a lot like Jack Jensen. "Same shirt, right?" he asked, pointing at the picture.

"Could be."

"That's you, isn't it?"

"It looks like me," Jack allowed. "From the back, it's hard to tell."

"This was taken last Saturday night."

"Right. The party."

"Who's the girl with you?" Stride asked.

"I have no idea."

"You didn't bring her to the party?"

"No."

"She's standing right there with you," Stride pointed out.

"She must have arrived at the same time."

"You've never seen her before?"

"No, not that I recall."

"She's not connected to the movie. How would she have gotten into a party at Dean's house?"

"Pretty girls hang around the set all the time," Jack said. "They hear about a party. They show up. Nobody says no."

"Did you sleep with her?" Stride asked.

"No."

"Did you sleep with anyone at the party?"

"The night's a bit of a blur, but I usually do."

"Who?"

"They all blend together, Lieutenant."

"Did Dean sleep with this girl?" Stride asked.

Jack's eyes narrowed in suspicion at the shift in questions. "Dean? Absolutely not."

"How do you know? It sounds like you were pretty busy that evening."

"I know Dean."

"So you don't actually *know* whether he did or didn't?"

"I guess you'll have to ask him," Jack replied.

Stride took another photograph out of the folder. "Here's a picture of the same girl leaving the party."

Jack leaned forward. "Looks like she had a little too much to drink."

"In the morning, she was found dead. Her name was Rochelle Wahl." Stride waited a beat. "She was fifteen."

Jack took a long time before he said anything. "Really. I'm sorry to hear it."

"What was a fifteen-year-old doing at Dean Casperson's party?"

"Lying about her age, I imagine," Jack replied. "It happens."

"If it came out that an underage girl had sex at one of Dean's parties, there would be serious consequences. For the movie. For him and his reputation."

"Yes, I suppose so."

"It makes me think Dean would be willing to do just about anything to get that girl out of the house and make sure no one knew she was there," Stride said.

"It sounds to me like you've been watching too many of Dean's thrillers."

Stride tapped the photograph. "We think this other man took Rochelle back to her house and changed her clothes and then knocked her unconscious and left her out in the snow to freeze to death."

"Or maybe she went home and had an accident. If you're a kid and you drink too much, bad things can happen."

"Except when a girl leaves a party with a hired killer, it's usually murder, not an accident."

"Hired killer?" Jack asked. He made a show of looking at the photograph again. "Oh, this guy. You asked me about him before. He was staying at the same apartments as me. Hey, I wish I could tell you more about him, but like I said, I only bumped into him a couple times. That's all."

Stride showed him one of Peach's photographs that showed John Doe and Jack Jensen talking outside John Doe's rental cottage. "Was this one of the times you bumped into him?"

Jack smiled. "You have a lot of pictures, Lieutenant."

"What were you two talking about?" Stride asked.

"I have no idea. He was probably asking me for a restaurant recommendation in town. I like that place by the water. Grandma's."

"Who called this man to pick up Rochelle Wahl at the party?"

"I have no idea about that, either. For all I know, he was at the party himself. Maybe he and this girl came together. Or maybe he's an Uber driver. I don't know anything about this, Lieutenant. You're talking to the wrong guy."

"We have his cell phone records," Stride said. "Half an hour before this photograph was taken of him putting the girl in his car, he got a call from a burner phone. Do you know anything about that?"

"Not a thing."

"Did you make that call? Was it your phone?"

"Nope."

"Could Dean Casperson have made the call?" Stride asked.

"Dean? He can barely operate a flip phone."

"Someone called this man to the party, he picked up Rochelle Wahl, he killed her."

"I can't believe that's true," Jack replied, "but I don't know anything about it."

Stride leaned across the interview table. "Do I need to lay it all out for you, Mr. Jensen? We have a picture of you arriving at the party with Rochelle Wahl. We have a picture of John Doe loading her unconscious body into his car two hours later. We have a picture of you and John Doe together two days after that. These pictures were all taken by the young woman who called herself Haley Adams. She was really a private detective from Florida named Peach Piper. The day after Peach took these photos of you and this man together, Peach disappeared. We found her body. She'd been shot by the gun that was found in this man's car. By the way, that same gun was used to shoot a waitress in Florida on the same day *you* ate at her restaurant. Would you like to explain all of that for me, Mr. Jensen?"

Jungle Jack chuckled and shook his head. "So you really can't smoke in here, huh?"

Stride said nothing.

"Well, look, I'd love to explain it for you, but none of it makes any sense to me. You'd have to ask this John Doe character, but I guess you can't, because he's dead, right? Too bad. If I'm hearing you right, he's the one that killed all these people. Me, I had lunch in Florida, I went to a party at Dean's place, and I said 'Hey' to a man who happened to be renting a cottage near mine. That's what this all boils down to, isn't it? The only contact I had with this so-called assassin was telling him where he could get a burger. Now you're the cop and I'm not, but that sure sounds like *squat* to me. So if you want to put the cuffs on me, go ahead. Otherwise, I've got to be on the set in twenty minutes."

Jack got out of the chair. He hesitated for a second to see what Stride did, and when Stride did nothing, Jack laughed and strolled out of the interview room. Stride sat there alone and waited. Not long afterward, Maggie and Cab joined him. They'd been watching the interview from the other side of the one-way window.

"He's right," Stride said as they sat down. "We've still got squat. We can pin everything on John Doe, but we can't connect Doe to Jack or Casperson. All we've got is a burner phone that doesn't lead anywhere. We need more."

"Jack didn't even bother lawyering up," Cab said. "He knows we can't touch him. This isn't his first rodeo."

"So what do we do?" Maggie asked.

"The strategy hasn't changed," Stride said. "We need to tie Jungle Jack to John Doe and not just with a meeting in the parking lot. If we do that, we can get Jack to flip on Casperson."

Maggie shook her head. "Those two are thick as thieves. Jack owes everything to Casperson. He's never going to rat him out."

"He will if it means getting a deal on a murder charge."

"Except like you said, it's still all smoke," Maggie pointed out. "With John Doe dead, Jack's in the clear. We can't tie them together."

There was a long silence in the room. Then Cab Bolton spoke.

"No, Stride's right," he said. "We're forgetting something."

"What?" Maggie asked.

"We think Jack was John Doe's local contact, right?" Cab said. "He had to be the go-between who was using the burner phone. Well, we know the go-between made one mistake."

Stride thought about it, and so did Maggie, and they both blurted it out at the same moment.

"He ordered a pizza."

# 34

Aimee Bowe was quiet as Serena drove her back to the rental house from the hospital. She looked better and stronger, but Serena could see her anxiety as they neared the house overlooking the lake. When they got there, Aimee made no effort to open the car door.

"You know, you're welcome to stay with me and Stride," Serena told her. "You can pick up a few things and come home with me."

"Thanks, but I don't do well with other people. I'm better on my own. It's not for much longer. Chris thinks we should be able to wrap up the filming tomorrow, and then I'll be out of here and back to Los Angeles. No offense, but I'm not going to miss Duluth."

"I'll walk you inside and check the house again," Serena said.

She got out of the Mustang and came around to the passenger door. She made sure Aimee was secure walking in the snow that led to the house. There had been flurries throughout the afternoon, giving the yard a fresh look and brushing it clean of footprints. No one had been there.

Serena stopped and looked up at the sky, which was dark and starless under a low swath of clouds. She'd lived in Minnesota long enough that she could taste snow in the air. They'd be buried tomorrow. The wind was still, as if holding its breath in anticipation of a storm.

"Everything okay?" Aimee asked.

"Fine."

The actress studied the open yard and the surrounding trees. "Where did you find me?"

Serena pointed. "Down there, near the band of spruces."

Aimee looked as if she wanted to remember, but she didn't.

They reached the house, and Serena went in first. Aimee came in behind her and took off her coat as Serena checked each of the rooms again, making sure the place was empty. Nothing had changed since her earlier visit. The back door was still blocked with a chair wedged against the doorknob. Aimee wandered around the living room, studying the photographs of the family who owned the house. She picked up one picture frame and dusted the top with her fingers.

"Do you know the people who live here?" she asked Serena.

"No."

"I suppose not; why would you? They look nice. Cute couple, cute kids. I have a sister with that kind of life. She lives in the suburbs of Cleveland. Three kids, two, four, and seven. All boys. It's funny. As things started taking off for me, I felt a little bad for her. There I was jetting around the world, making more money than she'd ever see in her lifetime. I wondered if she was jealous. And then last year, out of nowhere, she told me how much she hated the kind of life I led. No roots, no husband, no kids. She said she would never want that for herself in a million years, and she couldn't believe I *chose* it."

"We all want different things," Serena said.

"Well, it was an eye-opener for me. It made me more humble." Aimee sank down into a sofa opposite the brick fireplace. "I don't suppose you know how to light a fire, do you? I've been staring at this thing every evening, and I have no idea how to get it going."

Serena smiled. "Jonny gave me lessons."

She opened the flue and stacked several of the wood logs piled near the hearth in a rough pyramid in the grate. As she did, she disturbed a black spider that skittered away across the old ashes. She crumpled several sheets of newspaper and wedged them under the logs, and then she found a book of long matches that she used to start the fire. Everything was dry. The logs caught quickly, warming the room. Serena took a seat next to Aimee. The crackling, dancing fire had a hypnotic quality that entranced them both.

"Do you want a drink?" Aimee asked after they had sat in silence for several minutes. "I need some wine."

"No, thanks."

Aimee got up and then looked down at Serena. "You can't drink, can you? You have a problem with it."

Serena shook her head in puzzlement. "How do you know these things?"

"I wish I knew, Serena. I dated a scientist in college who said I picked up on things without consciously spotting the clues. You weren't drinking at the party when I first met you. And there was something in your tone of voice just now."

"I guess I can believe that," Serena replied.

Aimee went to the refrigerator and uncorked an open bottle of Pinot Grigio. She poured herself half a glass and returned to the sofa and sat down. "It's not just you. My thing scares a lot of people."

"I'm not scared. Just skeptical."

"Have you ever used a psychic on any of your cases? It happens more than you think. The CIA had a whole program for it."

"I'd like to see Jonny's face if I suggested that," Serena said, smiling.

"Well, most are charlatans, but if even a handful produce results that are impossible to explain, doesn't that make you wonder?"

"I don't really think about it."

Aimee sipped her wine. She hesitated, as if she had things to say and didn't want to say them. "You probably don't want me to tell you this. I think your husband is wrong about the Art Leipold case."

Serena stared at her. "What?"

"Someone else put those women in the box."

"What are you talking about? The evidence against Art Leipold was overwhelming. Fingerprints, DNA, soil samples, connections to the victims. The jury took less than an hour to convict him. It was an open-and-shut case, and there aren't many of those."

"I know. I read all about the case when I was preparing for the role."

"I'm sorry, Aimee. Jonny doesn't make mistakes about that kind of thing."

"Everybody makes mistakes."

"Not like that. What do you base this on other than intuition?"

"It's not intuition," Aimee said.

"Then what is it?"

"I told you, I don't know. But it's real. Look, you don't have to listen to me and you don't have to believe it. All I'm telling you is what I feel."

Serena didn't say anything for a while. She remembered what Aimee had told her the first time they'd met. Don't trust anyone.

"Forgive me for saying so, but I hope this isn't some kind of weird game to drive publicity for the movie. That would be a horrible thing to do to the families of the victims."

Aimee put her wineglass down and brushed her hair from her face. "I'm hurt that you would even think that."

"I'm sorry, but you've lied to me before," Serena said.

"What do you mean?"

"You know exactly what I mean."

Aimee studied the fire and pushed her lips together into a frown. "You don't understand my situation, Serena."

"Yes, I do. You're protecting yourself and your career. The trouble is, you're protecting *him*, too."

"I have no choice. You may think I'm a star, but in this industry I'm a nobody. Nobodies don't go up against Dean Casperson, not if they ever want to work again. Don't believe the hype that Hollywood has changed. If you think that, you're kidding yourself."

"If you talk, others will, too."

"Or I'll be hung out to dry," Aimee said. "Either way, my career will be over. In public, people may talk about how brave you are, but behind the scenes, they'll label you a troublemaker and a bitch. Those women don't get parts."

Serena held her stare in the firelight. "Tell me the truth. Did you take the Xanax yourself?"

Tears filled Aimee's eyes. "No. Of course I didn't."

"Did he assault you once before? When you did the first movie together?"

She nodded silently. "It was awful."

"Then why go to his house? Why be alone with him again?"

"When Dean Casperson calls, you don't say no," Aimee replied.

"Will you come in and make a statement?"

"No. If you repeat what I've said to anyone, I'll deny it. This is between you and me and no one else."

"There has to be a first domino," Serena said. "Someone has to talk."

"Not me." Aimee wiped her face. "You should probably go. I have an early call for makeup on the set."

Serena stood up. The fire was hot on her back. Knowing the truth and not being able to do anything about it was more frustrating than the lie. "Okay. Fine."

"I wish I could help you."

"I wish you could, too." She headed for the front door. "I'll have an officer do a drive-by overnight. Just to make sure the area is secure. If you have any kind of problem, call me."

Serena left the house and pulled the door shut behind her. She stood on the porch under the dark sky, anticipating the snow. She studied the yard again, making sure there were no fresh footprints around the house. She was about to leave when she heard a voice in the house behind her. It was Aimee, talking to someone. Serena immediately turned back and shoved the front door open again.

"Aimee? Are you okay?"

The actress was standing in the living room with her wineglass in her hand. She pointed at the mantle over the fireplace. "I'm fine. I have a little visitor. I don't know where he came from."

Serena stared across the shadows and saw a tiny flutter of movement in black and white.

It was a chickadee.

*

Cat was already in bed at midevening, but she couldn't sleep.

She'd been playing Words With Friends with a boy in Idaho, but when she got 112 points for "quiz," he became irritated with her and signed off. She checked Facebook, but it was late and none of her friends was streaming live. She pulled the Rubik's Cube from Curt off her nightstand, but she'd solved it a dozen times and was bored with it.

Her phone had a Netflix app. She opened it up and ran a search with the words "Dean Casperson." Dozens of movies came up, going back years. She'd seen most of them. She picked a romantic comedy and then fast-forwarded through the movie until she reached Dean's first scene. She froze the image with his face on the screen.

The movie was only a few years old. He looked exactly as he had at the party on the North Shore when she'd met him in person. She was ashamed of what a fool she'd been for him that night. *You are so amazing. I just love you.*

And then to hear him flirting back, knowing full well that she was melting for him. *Cat, as in meow?*

Now she knew the truth about him. It made her sick.

She got out of bed and pushed her tiny feet into boots and retrieved her heavy coat from the closet. She went over to the bedroom window and did what she always did when she couldn't sleep. She climbed out onto the cottage's front porch. She pulled one of the Adirondack chairs close to the white railing and sat down and propped her feet.

Minnesota Avenue was hushed. She heard nothing but a low murmur as the snow started. A tiny advance guard fell through the streetlight ahead of the army behind it. The windshield of her Civic already had turned white. She thought about driving to the end of the Point to hang out on the green bench by the harbor. It was like an oasis. Stride went there to deal with crossroads in his life, and she'd picked up the same habit. But she didn't want Stride to worry if he looked in on her bedroom and she was gone. She knew he checked on her sometimes.

Her phone vibrated in her pocket. Curt was inviting her to a video chat. She accepted the call and saw a shadowy close-up of Curt's face and his happy, cocky smile. He was in his car, driving one-handed. His long black hair was loose. Snow made sticky streaks on the side window behind him.

"Kitty cat!"

"Hey, Curt. Where are you?"

"I'm on 35. I just left the casino at Black Bear. I think the sky's falling."

"Looks that way."

"You want me to come over there? We could hang."

"Nah, Stride would freak," Cat said.

"Come on, Stride loves me. I'm the hero. I rescued you. That should count for something."

"I know, but I think he's pissed at both of us. I'm just sitting out here by myself for a couple minutes. I'm heading to bed soon."

"It's early."

"Yeah, but I'm bored," Cat said.

"You're sounding all down again."

"I know."

"So talk to me," Curt told her. "What's with the frown?"

"Stride won't let me tell anyone what I saw at Dean Casperson's house. It's stupid. I want to help."

"Well, you didn't see anything really juicy, right?"

"Maybe not, but I *know* what was going to happen."

She saw a truck pass Curt on the freeway with a blare of its horn and a flash of its high beams. The snow got heavier.

"You should probably hang up," she said. "It's not safe driving like that."

"I'm not hanging up until I see you turn the world on with that smile of yours."

"Well, that's not going to happen tonight."

Curt gave an exaggerated sigh. "Look, I know you don't want to hear this, but I'm with Stride on this one. If you try to make people think Casperson is a sleazebag, the only one who gets hurt is you. It's not worth it."

"Everybody wants to protect me like I'm still a kid. I'm sick of it."

"I'm just saying, when it's your word against Dean Casperson, who do you think the world is going to believe? Sorry, kitty cat, it ain't you. It ain't me either, or Stride, or Serena, or anybody else. People love this guy. They don't want to believe he's a dick. If they don't see it with their own eyes, trust me, it doesn't matter what you say. They'll just call you a liar and plunk down their money for his next flick."

"Yeah. I know." Curt was right. So was Stride. No one would believe her.

"Besides, it'll all be over soon," he went on. "No use sweating it now."

"What do you mean? Why?"

"Word is, the film's wrapping soon. There's a big party tomorrow night."

"Another party? At Casperson's place?"

"Nah, they rented out one of the ritzy resorts on the North Shore. I guess Dean figures there's too much heat at his place. It's supposed to be hush-hush to fool the tabloids."

"Do you know where it's happening? Will you be there?"

"I'm everywhere. You know that. Nothing happens in this town that I don't know about."

She bit her lip and thought. Her knee bounced. Her eyes narrowed. She didn't say anything for a long time. Curt whistled on the other end of the phone as he stared at her.

"I don't like that look, kitty cat. You're up to something."

Cat lowered her voice and looked over her shoulder on the porch to make sure Stride and Serena weren't watching from inside the house. Then she pushed her face close to the phone.

"You're right. I've got an idea," she whispered, "but I need your help."

# 35

Maggie opened the shower door and stepped onto the plush mat. Steam clouded the mirror and made the bathroom feel like Florida. She grinned as Cab followed her out of the oversized marble shower stall, then wrapped his arms around her wet waist. He lifted her off the ground until they were face to face. Water from their hair dripped down their cheeks, and their slippery skins squeezed together.

"I'm starting to like Minnesota," he said as he nibbled her ear.

She reached down. "I can tell."

They both toweled off and got partly dressed. Barefoot, Cab wandered back into the living room of Maggie's condo, which was situated above the downtown Sheraton hotel. He went to the floor-to-ceiling windows, and she joined him there. Snow poured down through the glowing lights of Superior Street below them. The lake was a black shroud immediately behind the buildings.

"Nice place," he told her.

"It's not the Gulf," she replied, "but it's not bad."

"You like things modern?" he asked, noting the sleek Scandinavian design of the furniture, which was heavy on metal, glass, and blond wood.

"Yeah, when I was married, I lived in a *Dark Shadows* house. This is more me."

"What about Troy? Is he modern like you?"

Maggie thought about being annoyed that Cab had brought up Troy again, but she was mellow enough from sex and wine not to worry about it. "Troy? No, he says coming here is like walking into a Woody Allen movie. That's not a compliment. He's a Minnesota dude. Fisherman, pilot, hunter."

"And father?"

"Yeah, his girls are sweet. I suppose I don't seem like the type for kids."

"Oh, I don't know," Cab said. "I think you'd be a cool mother."

Maggie turned away from the lake and sat down on one end of her black-and-white sofa and stretched out her feet. "I tried to adopt, but being a single cop whose husband was murdered is apparently not the ideal background for stable parenting. At least that's what the adoption agencies told me."

Cab sat down across from her on the other end of the sofa. His feet played with her toes.

"What about you?" Maggie asked him. "Do you want kids?"

"I'm still too busy trying to figure out my mother. Lala wants kids. I imagine she'll be married and pregnant soon enough."

"I've thought about getting a dog," Maggie said. "Or maybe a cat. Or a fish. Except I'm never home. I sleep here and that's about it. Lately, I haven't even done much of that."

"Dogs are too clingy, cats are too judgmental, and fish are too slimy."

"Don't you get lonely?" she asked. "Your house is in the middle of nowhere. I'm not sure I like myself enough to spend that much time alone."

"Ah, well, that's the difference between us," Cab said. "There's no one I like more than myself."

Maggie chuckled and shook her head. "You really are a piece of work."

"Thank you." Cab craned his long neck to stare at her stainless steel refrigerator. "Sex makes me hungry. Are you hungry?"

"I think I have some cold Sammy's pizza from a couple days ago."

"Sold," he said.

He hopped off the sofa and made his way to the kitchen. When he opened the door, he peered around at the mostly empty shelves. "Not much of a chef, are we?"

"Not much."

"There's a pizza box in here, but it's empty," Cab said.

"Oh, sorry. I guess I finished it. Or maybe the fish ate it."

Cab took out the empty box and dropped it in the wastebasket. He returned to the sofa and staked out the same spot he'd been in before. "So tell me again about the burner phone."

Maggie sighed. "We've been down that road and haven't gotten anywhere."

"Yes, but this is how my brain works. One layer at a time. Think of it as adding pizza toppings."

"Okay, now you're talking my language. Here's what we know. About a week before Rochelle Wahl died, there was a call between the burner phone and John Doe's cell phone just after nine o'clock in the evening. The call lasted four minutes. It was the day John Doe arrived in town, so we figure it was a confirmation that he was around and available. Almost immediately after that call, the burner phone made a one-minute call to the downtown Sammy's Pizza. That's the only call in the phone's records that was *not* to John Doe."

"Got it. So first of all, what does that tell us about John Doe?"

"He was on call," Maggie said. "They didn't bring him to town just for Rochelle. They had him around in case a Rochelle situation arose. Which tells me that this wasn't the first time a problem like this came up."

"Agreed. I'd be willing to bet we'd find John Doe staying somewhere in the area when most of Casperson's movies were being filmed."

"But probably with a different identity each time."

"Yes, unfortunately."

"As far as the pizza order goes," Maggie went on, "the restaurant doesn't have trackable records that we could link back to a delivery address. We also don't know if it was a delivery or pickup order."

"And the delivery drivers?"

"Guppo interviewed all the drivers who were working that night. None of them remembered anything useful. These guys do dozens of delivery runs every single evening."

"So nobody remembered a drop-off at Casperson's rental house?"

Maggie shook her head. "No."

"Well, that's not very helpful, is it?" Cab asked.

"No."

"I'm still hungry," Cab said. "All this talk about pizza is putting me in the mood for some."

"So order us a Sammy's," Maggie told him.

"What do you like on your pizza?"

"Sausage. I'm a purist."

Cab rolled his eyes, as if she were a savage for not wanting kale and goat cheese. He took out his phone, ran a quick web search, and then tapped the button to make a call. "I'd like to place an order for delivery," he said into the phone when the store answered. "Can you do a *quattro stagioni*?"

There was a long pause, and then he covered the phone with his hand. "They don't know what that is."

"Shocking," Maggie said.

"Just make it an extra large sausage," Cab said into the phone with pain in his voice. Then to Maggie: "What's the address?"

She rattled it off, and Cab repeated it into the phone. He said it twice and then hung up. "They won't deliver to you," he told her.

"What are you talking about? I order from there like twice a week."

"They said I should try the location on First Street," Cab said.

"Why, which location did you call?"

"Duluth Lakeside."

"Nope, wrong one," Maggie said.

"I'm sorry, isn't that the lake right outside? As in Lakeside?"

"You'd think so, but no." She grabbed the phone from him and dialed the number of the downtown Sammy's, which she'd memorized long before. She ordered an extra large sausage pizza and then hung up the phone. "Thirty minutes. See how easy that was?"

"I guess I'm not familiar with the intricacies of Duluth pizza ordering," Cab said.

Maggie grinned at him. "You're pretty good at other intricacies."

She hopped off the sofa and headed for the bedroom. "I suppose I ought to be wearing something more than a bra and panties for the driver."

"I don't know. Sounds like the making of an adult movie."

She went to her dresser and pulled out a T-shirt and shorts from the middle drawer and threw them over the rumpled sheets of her bed. Then she stopped. Without putting them on, she went back to the doorway and stood with her hands on the frame. "Cab," she said.

"Yeah?"

"What if our guy with the burner phone did the same thing?"

Cab turned his phone over in his hands. "You mean, what if he called the wrong delivery location?"

"Exactly."

"There was only one call in the phone's records," Cab pointed out.

Maggie came back and sat down on the sofa. "Yeah, I know. Think about it. He's talking to John Doe. When he's done, he decides to order a pizza, and he accidentally uses the same phone and calls the downtown restaurant. Except if it's Jungle Jack and he's up in Hermantown, they don't deliver up there. He hangs up and then realizes he used the wrong phone to make the call."

"So he calls back to the right location with a different phone."

"Exactly," Maggie said. "That's why Guppo couldn't find anything. He was talking to the wrong delivery drivers."

*

Stride carried his travel mug of black coffee out to his Expedition in the driveway of the cottage. The sun wasn't up yet at seven in the morning. Four inches of snow had fallen already, and it was still coming down like a dense curtain across the Point. He used a brush to clear the truck. By the time he was done, the windshield was partly covered again by heavy wet flakes.

He drove into the storm. Josh Turner sang on his radio. He followed a snowplow up the hill, but his twenty-minute drive to police headquarters still took forty-five minutes through the slippery streets. By the time he arrived, he was out of coffee. He headed for the building through the parking lot and got more coffee before making his way to his office. When he sat down, he swung the chair around and stared out at the streaks of snow landing on the glass.

His phone rang before he had a chance to do anything else. It was Chris Leipold.

"Good morning," Stride said when he answered. "Looks like Duluth is giving your film crew a January send-off."

"It is."

"If you're calling about the storage unit, I don't have any information for you. There aren't any security cameras out there to figure out who broke in."

"I'm not calling about that," Chris said. His voice was still raspy from the flu.

"What's up?"

"I was wondering if Serena had talked to Aimee Bowe this morning."

"She took Aimee back to her house from the hospital last night," Stride replied. "I don't think they've connected since then. Why?"

"We can't find Aimee. She was due on the set early, but she didn't show."

"It's probably the storm slowing everything down," Stride said. "It took me twice as long to get to work."

"No, she wasn't at her house. We sent a car to pick her up. The driver got there at five-thirty in the morning and knocked on the door, but there was no answer. Given what happened to her, I told him to try the door. It was unlocked. He went in and said the house was empty."

"Aimee was gone?"

"Yeah. He said the bed didn't even look slept in."

Stride frowned. "Okay. We'll check it out. Thanks for letting me know."

"Keep me posted," Chris said.

Stride hung up the phone and immediately dialed Serena, who was still back at the cottage. She'd slept late, and her voice sounded sleepy. "It's me," he said. "We may have a problem. Aimee Bowe is missing."

Serena took a long time to reply. Even in the silence, he could feel her concern.

"Can you meet me over at her house?" she asked.

"I'm on my way."

Stride got up and grabbed his leather jacket from the hook behind the door. The coat was still wet. He alerted Guppo and then made his way back out to the parking lot. The snow continued to fall, but the engine of the Expedition was warm enough that the snow still melted as it hit the metal. He unlocked the door, but before he got inside, he stopped.

Something was wedged under his driver's side windshield wiper.

A small padded envelope.

Stride looked around. He hadn't been away from the truck for more than fifteen minutes. He saw footprints near the front of his truck, but whoever had left the package had kicked his way back through the snow to erase his tracks. None of the imprints of tread was left. He followed the prints until they got lost in the jumble of others coming and going from the building.

Someone had been waiting for him in the parking lot.

He removed the padded envelope from his windshield with his gloved hands. There were no markings on the outside. The flap was self-adhering; they wouldn't find DNA on the gum. He stood in the darkness and snow, weighing the envelope in his palm. It was light but not empty. When his fingers traced the contents, he could feel something hard, small, and rectangular inside.

Somehow he knew. He just knew.

Stride took a small Swiss Army knife from his pocket and cut a slit in the narrow bottom of the envelope. He separated the two flaps and looked inside. It wasn't easy to see the contents, but he recognized what it was. He'd received a package just like this four times before. The envelopes had all been left on his truck in different places around the city.

They were messages from the women locked in the box. Messages to him.

Stride felt an ugly sense of déjà vu. He thought about the break-in at Chris Leipold's storage unit, where only one item had been stolen.

Art's old cassette recorder. It took on a whole new significance now. What he was thinking was impossible, yet here it was in front of him.

He reached into the envelope and pinched the corner of the contents with his gloves. He pulled it out and covered it with his hand to protect it from the snow. It was just what he feared. A Maxell-brand cassette tape.

Someone had scrawled a message on the label.

Save me, Jonathan Stride.

# 36

Outside Aimee Bowe's house, Max Guppo looked like a snowman, completely encrusted in white.

"We've checked with all the neighbors," he told Stride. "No one saw or heard anything last night. Serena had an officer cruise by three times between midnight and five in the morning. He didn't see anything. No lights. No cars on the street."

"Where do we stand with the cassette tape?" Stride asked.

"It's not that easy to find a cassette player these days. I sent somebody over to my grandmother's place to see if she has one in her attic. Unless you still use one at home, boss."

"Nothing but eight-tracks for me, Max."

Guppo chuckled.

The two of them pushed through the snow to the front door of Aimee's house. Serena was visible at the fringe of the yard, looking like an apparition in the storm as she searched the grounds. Stride and Guppo took off their boots and replaced them with plastic booties as they went inside the house.

"What do we know so far?" Stride asked.

"Serena already mentioned that several of the windows and doors don't have working locks. If someone wanted to get inside and surprise Ms. Bowe, it wouldn't have been hard."

"But?"

"But the bed doesn't look slept in, and there are no signs of a struggle. If it was a stranger abduction, I'd expect to find evidence of violence. Even so, she didn't leave voluntarily. Look at this." Guppo squatted with difficulty and pointed at the leg of an oak end table in the living room. "Right here, where the leg connects to the table, we found hair caught in the seam."

"So she was dragged along the floor?" Stride asked.

"That's what it looks like."

"Which means she was already unconscious," he added.

Guppo frowned. "Or dead."

"Any evidence of blood?"

"No."

Stride wandered over to the fireplace and stared at the cold ashes. Wind whistled down through the open flu. "What else?"

"There was a wooden coaster on the coffee table. We identified minute traces of powder in the ridges. We'll be having it tested."

"What's your theory?"

"According to Serena, Aimee was using the coaster where we found the powder to hold her wineglass. Serena said the open wine bottle in the refrigerator was mostly full when Aimee poured a glass. Now there's barely two inches of wine left in that bottle."

"So either she kept drinking a lot after Serena left," Stride said, "or she had company."

"Right."

"She knew whoever abducted her."

"I think so," Guppo replied. "And my bet is that when the results come back on the powder we found, it will probably be some kind of sedative drug. Whoever was here drugged her wine."

"Well, that sounds familiar, doesn't it?"

"Yes, it does."

"Make sure we test the sofa for any hair or bodily fluids. I want to make sure Aimee wasn't sexually assaulted before she was dragged out of here."

"On it," Guppo said.

Stride went back to the front door. He reclaimed his boots and headed outside, where the snow stung his face. He crammed his hat down on his head and squinted into the wind. The morning was gray, buried under clouds. He felt the cold with each breath, and it was one of those days when he missed having cigarette smoke in his lungs. Jungle Jack was right. The craving never went away.

At the street, Serena waited for him at his Expedition. Her long black hair was wet. Her hands were shoved into the pockets of her black jeans. She stared upward at the electrical wires strung along the street. She looked tall and strong, the way she always did, but her expression was troubled.

He came up beside her. "Did you find anything in the yard?"

"No."

"Not finding a body is a good thing," Stride told her.

"I know that."

"This isn't your fault."

"It *is* my fault," she snapped back at him. "I never should have left her alone. I should have trusted my instincts. I was so busy trying to convince myself that Aimee's mystical talk was all crap that I stopped listening to my own gut."

"What did it tell you?" Stride asked.

"That she was in danger."

"There's no way you could have predicted something like this. And we have no idea what's really going on. Guppo doesn't think it was a break-in. He's guessing she was drugged."

Serena frowned in confusion. "Do you think this could be Casperson?"

"Maybe, but I don't know what he would gain by staging a copycat of Art Leipold. He tries to stay out of the headlines."

He felt his phone vibrating inside his pocket. He checked it and saw that Guppo was calling from inside the house. It was a quick call, and then Stride shoved his phone back in his jeans.

"Max says they were able to find a cassette player," Stride said. "We can listen to the tape. Let's get back to headquarters."

Stride turned away, but Serena reached out and grabbed his arm. "Jonny? What if this *isn't* a copycat?"

He stared at her face, which was flushed with cold. Snow gathered on her eyelids and melted into water on her cheeks. "What do you mean?"

"Last night, Aimee told me she thought Art Leipold was innocent. She said somebody else put all those women in the box. I didn't believe her when she said it, but now? I don't know."

"Did she say why she thought so?"

"This is Aimee. I think she just sensed it."

Stride shook his head. "Come on, Serena."

"It sounds crazy to me, too, but look what's going on."

"It's been eleven years. If Art was innocent, why would the killer have gone dark all that time?"

"I don't know."

"Every shred of evidence pointed to Art. He did it."

"I hope you're right, Jonny," Serena told him. "I do. But even with Art dead, we both know what's waiting for us at headquarters, don't we? We're about to listen to a tape from a woman who's locked in a cage somewhere. And if we don't find her soon, she's going to die."

*

*"Save me."*

That was the first whisper Stride heard.

He looked at Serena, who nodded at him. There was no doubt. It was Aimee Bowe's voice. The tape crackled as if time had rewound. It might as well have been eleven years earlier, when Stride stood under a water-stained ceiling in the basement of City Hall. Back then, he'd listened to the first victim, Kristal Beech, saying the same words to him. Maggie had been there. So had Guppo. He'd gone home to his wife, Cindy, and told her about the horror he felt as he listened to the tape.

They'd all been much younger.

*"It's cold. Oh, my God, it's so cold. And dark. I can't see anything. I can't even see my hand when I put it in front of my eyes. Where am I? Tell me where I am. Who are you? Why are you doing this to me? I know, I know, I'm supposed to say it. Save me. Save me."*

He heard static in the silence. He listened for something in the background, some clue, some noise, that would tell them where she was. But the cage was virtually soundproof. Just as it had been back then. The only sound was the ragged in-and-out gasp of Aimee's breathing.

When she spoke again, her voice was louder.

*"I don't know how much time I have. There's no water in here. No food. And the cold is like a knife. You have to find me. Quickly. I know about the others. I know they died because you failed. Yes, you. Jonathan Stride. I'm here because of you. I'm paying for your mistakes."*

Stride pushed the plastic button on the tape recorder to pause the playback.

"Is this real?" he asked Serena.

She didn't say anything.

"What do you think?" he asked again. "Is this real? Or is something else going on here?"

"I don't know."

He started the tape again.

*"My name is Aimee Bowe. I don't know where I am, but you know all you need to know to find me. My life is in your hands. I need you to save me if you can. Save me, Jonathan Stride."*

The tape rolled on, but the recording was over. Stride let it play for several more minutes to see if anything else was on the tape. It was empty.

"I didn't hear any clues," he said. "Nothing that would tell us where she is."

"'You know all you need to know to find me,'" Serena quoted. "Did the others say anything like that?"

"Yes."

"What about the tape itself?" she asked.

"There are no fingerprints on it. Apparently, Maxell cassettes are still surprisingly easy to find. Whoever did this could have gotten the tape just about anywhere. The forensic team thinks it's new."

"But why steal Art Leipold's tape recorder? You can still buy tape recorders in various places, can't you?"

"Maybe because it belonged to Art. If a copycat wanted to follow in Art's footsteps, that's one way to do it." He noted Serena's dubious expression, and he continued. "We found the tape recorder next to the box in the hunting lodge. Art's fingerprints were all over it."

"You worked that case, Jonny. I didn't. I'm not doubting you."

But he could see that she was, and it bothered him.

"Why did you ask me if the tape wasn't real?" Serena said. "Did you hear something?"

Stride didn't answer immediately. He rewound the tape and played it over from start to finish without stopping. When he heard the final words—*Save me, Jonathan Stride*—he clicked it off. He watched Serena's face.

"You hear it, too, don't you?" he asked. "It's too perfect. The original tapes from the victims were rough. They stuttered. They made mistakes. They started and stopped. Aimee sounds rehearsed, like an actress, not a victim. She sounds as if she's reading from a script."

"She is," Serena said.

"What do you mean?"

"Everything she said is from the script of the movie. I heard the first take she did in the warehouse when she was doing her scene in the box. The words match. I'm pretty sure they match *exactly*. The only thing she changed was to take out the fictional character, Evan Grave, and put in your real name."

"So it's fake?" Stride said.

"I'm not sure about that, Jonny."

"You said yourself she's an actress reading lines. What else could it be?"

Serena played the tape one more time. Then she said, "No, I don't think it's fake. Aimee's in danger. But she knows I was there to watch her in that scene, so she knows I'd realize what she was doing. Somehow, she's trying to send me a message."

# 37

Stride met Chris Leipold at the dead end spur off Highway 44 near Art Leipold's hunting land. When Chris got out of the car, Stride could feel the blast of warm air from inside. It was desolate out there. They were the only two people around for miles. He watched Chris shiver as the cold penetrated his skin. The man still looked dragged down by the flu virus. Or maybe he felt the ghost of his father in this place.

"Sorry to pull you away from the movie," Stride said.

"I've got assistants to keep it rolling. Dean's done. Really, all we need is Aimee, but we don't have her." A gust of wind made a mournful cry in the trees, and he added in the quiet aftermath, "I don't understand what happened."

"Neither do I."

"You said you got an audiotape. A message. Like all those years ago?"

"Yes."

"Why did you want to meet me here?" Chris asked.

"Because someone is playing Art's game. And this is where we found Art's victims."

Together, they took the bridge over the Cloquet River. Several more inches of snow had fallen overnight, covering up the evidence of anyone who had trespassed there in the interim. He noticed that Chris didn't say much and looked uncomfortable being there at all. The cold air made the man cough repeatedly as he inhaled.

They followed the trail inside the trees, where the snow had trouble penetrating the branches overhead.

"Why did you never sell this land?" Stride asked him.

"I tried. No one wanted it. Can you blame them? The hunters come out here anyway. They don't care who owns the land. And it wasn't worth the money to keep curiosity seekers away from the cabin. So I just let it rot."

Where the trail narrowed, Stride took the lead. Chris kept pace behind him. The remnants of footprints lingered where the snow was shallower, but there were too many to isolate fresh tracks. Even so, he noticed a few places where the prints had been scrubbed away down to the mud, and it made him wonder if someone had been trying to make sure that nothing was left behind. He kept an eye on the dense woods ahead of him, looking for movement.

"What did Art say to you when he was first arrested?" Stride asked.

"That he didn't do it."

"Did you believe him?"

"Sure. He was a son of a bitch, but he was my dad. I didn't want to think that he could be such a monster."

"After the trial was over, did you ever wonder?" Stride asked.

"Wonder what?"

"Whether Art really did it."

There was no answer behind him. Stride took a few more steps, then turned around. Chris had stopped where he was. It was hard to interpret the look on his face. Anger. Disbelief. Confusion.

"What the hell are you saying?" Chris asked.

"I'm not saying anything."

"Art killed those women. You said so. The county attorney said so. The jury said so."

"I know."

"How could he be innocent? The women died here. They were all connected to Art. You found evidence in our house. You *told me* it didn't point any other way."

"That's all true."

Stride started walking again. Eventually, he heard the slushy footsteps of Chris catching up with him. They didn't talk more as he pushed through the trees that grew across the trail. He stopped at the fringe of the clearing as the ruined cabin came into view. Chris stood beside him, and they both stared at it like it was a monument to bad history. Stride watched and listened. The cabin was deserted.

"Did you come out here much as a kid?" Stride asked.

"To the cabin? Not very often. It was pretty rustic. I remember the spiders and the wasp nests. It scared me to sleep here, so I didn't like it. Art was a hunter. Me, not so much. I didn't really see the point."

Stride knew Chris was cold and wanted to leave. The man danced on his feet impatiently, and his nose ran.

"How did you write the script for Aimee's scenes?" Stride asked in a low voice.

"What do you mean?"

"How did you make it convincing? We didn't release much information to the public."

"You released transcripts of the audiotapes," Chris said.

"But that's all we did. Nothing else. What the women said on the tapes was coached. It wasn't really them talking. I was just wondering how you got inside their heads for the movie."

"Well, that's what writers do. We put ourselves inside someone else's life."

Stride nodded. "There was something strange in Aimee's message on the tape. She used your words."

"My words?"

"She took it straight from the film script. Do you have any idea why she would do that?"

"No."

"Serena thinks she was sending us some kind of message," Stride said.

"I don't know what it could be. Aimee's an actor. Actors memorize lines. If she was under pressure, maybe that's all she could think to say."

"You said Aimee liked to improvise. After the first take, she almost never stuck to the script."

"That's true."

"So I wonder why she would go back to your original words right now."

"I can't explain it, Lieutenant."

Stride nodded. "Okay. That's fine. You can leave now if you want, Chris. You look like you're freezing."

"I am."

Chris turned around and hiked at a fast pace back into the woods, which swallowed him up quickly and left Stride alone. He waited until he couldn't hear or see Chris at all, then made his way into the small clearing. The evidence of trespassers was everywhere. In the daylight, he could see the black scorch marks where the walls had burned and the open mouth of the caved-in roof. He walked all the way up to the front of the cabin, where he could see inside.

There had been a cage there eleven years ago. A box.

Not now. Now it was empty. He was in the wrong place.

But whoever took Aimee had expected him to come here. There was a fallen beam from the roof immediately inside the cabin, and someone had spray-painted a message in red across the timber.

It was the same message that had come with each dead body.

## BETTER LUCK NEXT TIME.

*

Serena arrived at Lori Fulkerson's house while Lori was turning her Yaris off the gravel road into her yard. Both women got out into the cascading snow. Serena met Lori at the sagging wooden steps that led up to the storm door. Inside the house, her Yorkshire terrier jumped and pawed at the glass.

"Ms. Fulkerson, do you have a minute?" Serena asked.

"I have all day," she replied. "The store closed because of the storm."

Lori opened the door and scooped her dog off the floor. Serena followed the woman into the tiny, cluttered living room and had to sit on top of newspapers again. Lori sank into her recliner with the dog in her lap. The house was cold. Snow plastered over the windows made the interior dark and gloomy.

"What's going on?" Lori asked.

"I don't know if you've seen the news reports, but Aimee Bowe is missing."

"Missing? What do you mean?"

"Her disappearance seems to be a replay of what happened to Art's victims."

"Art's dead," Lori said. "How could that be?"

"That's what we're trying to figure out. I was wondering if you'd noticed any unusual activity around your house or in the neighborhood."

"Do you think *I'm* in danger?" Lori asked.

"I don't know. I hope not, but we're not taking any chances. You're one of only a handful of people with a direct connection to what happened back then. I'm going to ask a police officer to stay on the road outside and keep an eye on your house while we're investigating. There's probably no danger to you, but until we understand the threat, I'd rather be safe."

"I have a dog," Lori said.

Serena smiled. The Yorkie in Lori's lap wasn't two feet long from nose to tail. "And he does look ferocious, but I'd still like to have an officer close by."

Lori shrugged. "Okay."

"I know this is difficult, and I'm sure you went through it many times eleven years ago, but I was hoping you could tell me a little more about what you remember from your experience."

"Inside the box? I already told Aimee more than I've ever told anyone else."

"I meant the abduction itself. Were you conscious? Did you see or hear anything?"

"No. I was sleeping when he hit me in the head. I woke up in the box."

"So you never actually saw Art Leipold?"

Lori's eyes narrowed with suspicion. "What are you saying?"

"It's just a question."

"No, I didn't see him," she replied.

"When you made the audiotape, how did you know what to say?" Serena asked.

"There was a voice. He said if I wanted to be rescued, I had to beg for it. I had to ask to be saved. He told me the name I had to use. Jonathan Stride. He said he was the only man who could rescue me."

"Did you recognize the voice? Did it sound familiar? Art was on television. His voice must have been pretty distinctive."

"The voice was disguised," Lori said. "Muffled. Whiny. He didn't want me to recognize it."

"Did you have some kind of connection with Art? The three earlier victims had all intersected with him at one point or another. I was wondering if that was true of you, too."

Lori nodded. "I helped him on special orders for parts. He was a car collector. He was in the store a lot."

"Did he pay any special attention to you?"

"I didn't think so at the time, but I guess I was wrong. I'd only been back in town for a few months at that point. He used to ask me a lot of questions about growing up here and what it was like to move away and come back. I just figured he was making small talk."

"What about Art's son, Chris? Did you ever meet him?"

Lori looked at her strangely. "You mean before the movie?"

"Yes."

"Yeah, he came into the store with Art once. I only remember because they were having a big argument."

"Do you remember what the argument was about?"

"No. Why do you care?"

"I wasn't in Duluth during that investigation," Serena said. "I'm just trying to understand whether anything from the past could be connected to Aimee's disappearance."

"I don't see how," Lori said.

"Have you talked to Aimee recently?"

"I went to her house the other night. I saw you there. That's all."

Serena stood up. "Well, thank you for your time, Ms. Fulkerson. You should see a squad car outside your house very soon. Regardless, if you see anything unusual, please call me right away."

Lori nodded but didn't say anything.

"I do have one more question," Serena said, "and I know this will sound strange."

"What is it?"

"When I talked to you at Aimee's house, you said you felt connected to her. Like she was inside your head."

"So?"

Serena took a breath. This wasn't the kind of question she'd ever imagined herself asking. "So I was wondering if you still felt that way."

Lori stroked the head of her dog and didn't look up at Serena. "I do feel something. Until you showed up, I thought I was crazy. I figured the movie was getting into my head. You know, seeing Aimee pretend to be me."

"What do you feel? What do you think happened to her?"

"She's in the box," Lori said.

# 38

Maggie drove toward the campus of the College of St. Scholastica. Her windshield wipers struggled against the snow, and the lanes in the street were no more than ruts tamped down by the other cars. Her route down the street was a serpentine path as her tires slipped and skidded. Ahead of them, the twin gray towers of the administration building loomed atop the campus hill.

It was already late afternoon. They weren't any closer to tying Jungle Jack and John Doe together.

"Maybe we were wrong about the second phone call," Cab suggested. "If Jack realized that he used the burner phone to make the first call, he might have freaked out and not wanted to leave a trail. So instead of ordering a pizza, he went out and got a Big Mac or something."

"True."

"Even if we find a driver who remembers him, it will be tough proving he made the first call," Cab added.

"Also true," Maggie said.

Even so, she wasn't ready to give up. They had two more delivery drivers to track down from the Hermantown Sammy's. One was a St. Scholastica freshman named Ginny Hoeppner. Maggie drove onto the college campus and wound around to the parking lot near Tower Hall. The two of them got out, but neither bothered putting on a coat despite the snow. Maggie wore furry calf-high boots, but Cab was in a suit with leather dress shoes. He walked gingerly on the icy pavement.

The receptionist in the housing office directed them to Somers Hall to find Ginny Hoeppner. One wing of the residence hall butted up to the same parking lot, so they didn't have to go far. Inside, they found themselves surrounded by fresh-faced young college students, and Maggie noticed that most of the girls took long looks at Cab as they made their way down the hall. When they found the room they were looking for, Cab drummed his fingers on the door as if he were playing the piano.

A slim raven-haired girl answered the door. She wore an untucked flannel shirt over tattered jeans. As with the other students they'd met, her eyes immediately went to Cab's face.

"Ginny Hoeppner?" Maggie asked.

"Yeah, that's me."

"My name is Maggie Bei with the Duluth Police. This is Cab Bolton. Do you mind if we ask you a couple questions?"

"Um, okay, yeah. Is there a problem?"

"No problem at all," Cab assured her with a charming smile.

Ginny shrugged and invited them inside. She lived in a typical utilitarian dorm room with bunk beds near the window and desks on opposite walls. Maggie saw open boxes on the floor. The new semester had just begun, and the roommates hadn't unpacked fully. A textbook on religion lay on the pillow of the lower bunk bed, and Ginny sat down on the bed next to it.

"Do you deliver pizzas for the Hermantown Sammy's restaurant?" Maggie asked.

"I do, yeah."

Maggie rattled off the day and date of the night on which someone with a burner phone had called the downtown Sammy's. "Do you remember if you were working on that particular evening?"

"I'm sure I was. I worked pretty much every night after Christmas."

"Do you keep records of your deliveries?" Cab asked.

"No, I just drive. Go out, come back, go out, come back. One night's the same as every other."

"Has it been busier with the film crew in town?" Maggie asked.

"Oh, yeah. The pizza in L.A. must suck, because we've been delivering to them all the time."

"It must be pretty cool meeting a lot of movie people," Cab said.

Ginny's face lit up. "It is! I've been thinking about a film studies major, so this is great. I love having it happen right here in Duluth."

"Have you met anybody famous?" he asked.

She shook her head in disappointment. "No, the actors don't usually order anything themselves. They've got assistants for that, you know? But I've met a bunch of folks who work on the crew."

"Do you remember making deliveries to any film people on that evening?" Maggie asked.

"I don't know. Like I said, the nights all blend together."

"Have you ever made a delivery to a man named Jack Jensen? He's a stunt double for Dean Casperson. He goes by the nickname Jungle Jack."

"I'm not sure. Most of the time, I don't get anything more than a last name on an order. Unless it's something really weird, I don't remember it. Plus, unless they're wearing a T-shirt or something that gives it away, I don't usually know if they're part of the film crew. Sometimes I ask if they've got that Hollywood look, know what I mean? Most of them are pretty cool about it. They'll take selfies with me even if their pizza's getting cold."

Maggie shot a quick look at Cab.

"Selfies?" he asked.

Ginny looked embarrassed. "Yeah, I know it's lame, but I do it anyway."

"Do you mind if we take a look at the photos on your phone?" Cab asked.

"Um." She hesitated as if trying to make a quick mental calculation about whether there was anything embarrassing on the phone.

"It would really help us out," Cab added.

"Yeah, sure, if you want." Ginny got off the bed and went over to her desk. She unlocked the screen on the phone and handed it to Cab.

"I got a new iPhone 8 Plus for Christmas, so I've been taking a lot of pictures."

Cab held the phone so that Maggie could see the screen and scrolled backward through the camera roll of thumbnails. Ginny was right. She'd taken a lot of pictures. They saw dozens of Instagram-ready photos taken of friends in the dorm and artistic photos of snow-covered landmarks shot around campus. Then they spotted a selfie of Ginny wearing a Sammy's baseball cap, posing next to a middle-aged Asian woman in a California sweatshirt. Maggie didn't recognize her, but she was obviously part of the film crew. They were both making a thumbs-up gesture for the camera.

Cab kept scrolling and found other nighttime selfies with pizza customers. Ginny wasn't shy about asking for pictures. Maggie spotted a couple of faces she'd seen on movie sets around the city.

And then there he was.

Jungle Jack.

He was bent down next to Ginny with his cheek against her face and his arm casually slung around her shoulders. He wore his usual self-satisfied grin, the look that said he knew exactly how handsome he was. There was an exterior door cracked open behind him, and Maggie recognized the architectural style of the Hermantown rental cottages.

"Jack just can't say no," Maggie said. "You have to love that. When was this taken?"

Cab checked the details of the photograph. "Forty-two minutes after the call on the burner phone. Just enough time for a delivery."

He turned the phone around and showed the picture to Ginny. "Do you remember anything about this man?"

The girl took a look at the photograph. "Just that he was really cute. I figured he was too good-looking to be from Duluth, so I asked if he was part of the movie. He said he was."

Cab chuckled. "Did he say anything else to you? Or did you see anything inside his apartment?"

"Not that I recall. I'm usually only at the door for a few seconds and then I'm gone."

Cab checked the picture files again. He scrolled backward and found additional photos of Ginny and Jack together. The girl obviously had struggled to get the camera angle right to get them both in the frame. Maggie leaned in as they reviewed each picture. She noticed that one of the selfies was pointed wildly wrong, as if Ginny had accidentally pushed the button while positioning the camera. The photograph showed nothing but Jack's shoulder on the side of the picture. Behind him was a clear shot of the interior of the apartment.

"Holy crap, is that what I think it is?" Maggie asked. "Zoom in."

Cab did. In the photo, they could see something hung on the back of a wooden chair near the kitchenette.

"Does that mean something to you?" he asked.

"Oh, yeah," she replied. "That's our smoking gun. We've got him."

*

Cat studied herself in the mirror of the bathroom in the cottage.

She wore a black cocktail dress that was the sexiest thing she owned. She'd worn it only once before, at the party after Stride and Serena's wedding, and she'd had a big fight with Stride about wearing it in public. It hugged her curves and clung tightly to her legs, where it ended at midthigh. The sleeves were lace, adorned with black flowers, and a lace panel stretched below her neck. Underneath the lace, an oval cutout showcased her cleavage. When she turned sideways, she saw black fabric swooping low beneath her shoulders. Another cutout bared the hollow of her back.

Her chestnut hair glistened, long and full. She'd spent an hour on her makeup, getting her blush and eyes perfect. Serena's emerald earrings dangled from her ears. She wore strappy black heels. For all the times Cat struggled with self-confidence, she knew that there wasn't a man with a pulse who would be able to look away from her tonight.

She was beautiful.

She was also scared to death and had to swallow hard to avoid throwing up.

Cat came out of the bathroom, where Curt Dickes was waiting. He had his back to her as he eyed the thrillers on Stride's bookshelf. When he turned around, he whistled loudly in admiration as Cat presented herself with one hand poised on her hip.

"So what do you think?" Cat asked in her best "I'm nowhere near seventeen years old" voice.

"Kitty cat, that dress should be registered as a lethal weapon," Curt said.

Cat dropped her sexy persona and giggled like a teenage girl again. "Thanks. You look pretty good, too, you know."

"Of course. I am always styling."

Curt wore a long-sleeved untucked batik shirt over lavender slacks. His shoes matched his pants, and his hair was tied in a ponytail. His cologne overpowered the room. Cat knew that when Stride and Serena got home, they'd realize that Curt had been there, but it was too late to worry about that.

She went into her bedroom and checked her phone to make sure it was fully charged. Then she slipped it inside her frosted black clutch and slid the gold chain over her shoulder.

"Is there cell signal at the resort?" she asked.

"Probably. If not, there's Wi-Fi."

"How long does it take to get there?"

"Depends on how the roads are. Maybe an hour in the storm. The movie types are taking a bus."

"Okay. We should go."

Cat clicked across the hardwood floor in her heels, and she could feel Curt's eyes on her back. It was going to be that way all evening, with men watching her and hitting on her. She went into the kitchen and found a yellow pad. She pulled off a sheet of paper, grabbed a pen, and thought about what she needed to say to Stride.

She wrote a few words, then crumpled up the paper and threw it away. She tried again and did the same thing. And again. Finally, she pulled another sheet of paper and wrote what was in her heart.

She'd never said those words to him in her life:

You're wrong.

Cat finished the note, folded it, and wrote Stride's name on the outside. When she looked up, Curt was watching her. His face was serious and unsmiling, which was highly unusual for Curt.

"You really sure about this, kitty cat? I'm not much of a fan of this plan. You could get yourself in serious trouble, and this time I won't be able to pull you over a wall or anything."

Cat chewed her lip. She put on a brave front, because she couldn't do anything else, no matter what she really felt inside. She'd made up her mind, and she wasn't turning back. She marched toward Curt and placed the note for Stride on the bookshelf near the front door. Then she took Curt's arm.

"You said people have to see it for themselves to believe the truth," Cat said. "I'm going to make sure they do."

# 39

The owner of the studio apartments in Hermantown wasn't happy to see Maggie and Cab arrive with a forensics team and cordon off the area with crime scene tape. They'd searched John Doe's apartment earlier in the week, and now they were back to do the same thing to Jungle Jack's cottage.

"Having cops in my parking lot ain't exactly good for business," the man told them, shaking the snow out of his gray hair. He was small and slightly bent, in his sixties, dressed in a hooded winter coat and beige corduroys. His name was Stig Swenson.

"Renting to murderers isn't too good for business, either," Maggie replied.

"Well, I'm sorry if I don't have a box for that on the application. Is this going to take long?"

"It will take as long as it takes. Did you print out the phone records for the apartment like I asked?"

"Yeah, yeah, hang on."

Stig dug in the pocket of his pants and came out with a single sheet of computer paper that had been folded multiple times. He handed it over to Maggie, who smoothed it out and held it up so that she and Cab could read it. They squinted at the small type, which had been made on a printer that badly needed toner. Even so, they saw what they wanted to see.

"Two minutes," Maggie said. "Jack called the Hermantown Sammy's two minutes after the call on the burner phone to the downtown restaurant."

"A jury's going to like that," Cab said.

Maggie turned back to the apartment manager. She produced photographs of John Doe and Jungle Jack and held them up side by side. "Let's go over this again. Did you see these two men together?"

"Once they sign the rental agreement, they're not my problem," Stig replied. "People don't need me to pay attention to what they're doing, so I don't."

"You don't keep an eye on who's coming and going in your apartments?" Maggie asked. "Because I'm looking over at your place, and I can see your cat sleeping on top of a La-Z-Boy. You've got a perfect view from there."

"It's not my cat," the man grumbled. "I'm pet sitting while my sister is in Norway."

Maggie rubbed her forehead in frustration. "Do I look like I care whose cat it is, Stig? Come on, we both know you've had your eyes glued to the parking lot while you had a Hollywood stunt man staying here. So tell me what you saw, okay?"

Stig snuffled loudly. "Lots of girls. It's like a parade. Every night a different girl."

Maggie dug in her pocket for a photograph of Rochelle Wahl. "What about this girl? Did you see her?"

"I don't think so."

Cab opened up his phone. "How about her?"

Stig leaned in and studied the photograph of Peach Piper. It was Cab's favorite photograph of Peach. She'd been visiting him at his house south of Naples, and she'd gone out with him to walk on the wet sand. He'd snapped the picture of her before she knew he was taking it, while her freckled face was creased into an innocent smile and the wind was playing with her pageboy blond hair.

The man frowned and didn't answer.

"Stig?" Maggie said. "Do you recognize her?"

"Yeah, I saw her hanging around here," he replied.

"Hanging around? What do you mean?"

"I saw her sneaking through the parking lot. She was heading toward the cottages in the back. I didn't like the look of it, so I went out to see what she was up to. She must have heard me coming and taken off, because I couldn't find her. That was last Sunday night, I think."

"Was that the only time you saw her?" Cab asked.

"No. She was back again a couple nights later."

"Doing what?"

"Looked like she was spying on Jack's place," Stig said. "I figured maybe she was a wife or a girlfriend, you know? With all the action over there, maybe somebody got jealous."

"What did you do when you saw her?" Maggie asked.

"I called Jack. If a guy rents from me, he's got a right to know if somebody's up in his business."

Cab took a deep breath. "What happened after you called Jack?"

"He came out and rousted her. Sounded pretty loud, but I couldn't hear what they were saying. Then he dragged her inside his place."

"What time did this happen?" Maggie asked.

"Somewhere around ten o'clock, I think."

Maggie grabbed a notebook from her back pocket and flipped backward through several pages. She already knew the answer—she remembered details by seeing them in her head—but she wanted to confirm what she'd written down. "There was a call between John Doe's phone and the burner phone at 10:10 last Tuesday night."

"Jack found Peach outside his place," Cab said, "so he called John Doe to figure out what they needed to do about her."

"Did you see the girl and Jack again after they went inside the apartment?" Maggie asked the owner.

Stig nodded. "Yeah. About half an hour later, Jack and the girl left."

"Where did they go?" Maggie asked.

"Back behind the cottage. They were headed for the woods. I couldn't see them after that."

Cab shook his head. "They were headed for the woods?"

"Yeah."

"And you didn't do anything?"

"What was I supposed to do?" the man asked.

Cab stared at the apartment owner with silent rage. Then he spun away and marched across the plowed parking lot toward the lineup of spruce trees towering behind the cottages. The snow made a cloud around him like a white tornado. Maggie chased after him.

"Cab?" she called. "Cab, hang on."

She got in front of him and stopped him with a hand on his chest. "What are you doing?"

"They killed her that night," Cab replied. "Jack met John Doe back here, they took Peach into the woods, and John Doe shot her in the head."

Maggie nodded. "I'm sorry. You're probably right."

"I want to find where he did it."

"Cab, we'll search the woods in the morning. It's dark, and the storm is still dumping snow. We could spend hours in there and not find the crime scene. Guppo will get a team out here as soon as it's light. If that's where Peach was killed, he'll find it."

Cab stared into the black mouth of the forest, his body tall and stiff like a statue. His normally spiky hair was flat and wet on his head. Maggie could see snow landing on his face and couldn't tell whether the melting snow was mixed with tears. He looked oddly elegant, standing there in his suit and tie, yet she knew his heart was broken.

"This is not the way it should have been," he murmured.

"I know."

"She spent her last few seconds right here in this pissant place. She knew what was going to happen to her."

Maggie didn't say anything, but she took hold of his hand.

"This was my case," he went on. "It wasn't hers. If anyone should have faced down that gun in the woods, it was me."

"Come on, Cab. Don't do this to yourself. There's only one thing we can do for Peach, and that's the most important thing."

Cab stared down at her and nodded.

"Let's go get Jungle Jack," he said.

\*

Stride found Serena sitting in her Mustang outside their cottage. She hadn't gone inside yet. He parked his truck and walked across the snow to her car and climbed into the front seat. She looked cold. Her long black hair was mussed. He could barely see her green eyes in the shadows.

"You okay?" he asked softly.

"Aimee's locked up in a cage," Serena replied. "She's probably freezing to death. And I don't know where she is or who did this or how the hell we'll ever find her."

"Believe me, I know what you're going through."

"Is it starting all over again? I mean, is it really possible that you were wrong about Art Leipold?"

Stride allowed doubt to creep into his mind for the first time. "I don't know. Art didn't do this, that's for sure."

"So what can we do?" Serena asked.

"I retrieved the case files from storage. All the notes, evidence, interviews, media reports, everything we gathered. We can go through it again together."

"Looking for what?"

"To see if I made a mistake," Stride said.

They both got out of the Mustang. Stride went up the driveway to the rear door of his Expedition and opened the back panel. He had several boxes inside. He stacked three of them together, then Serena took two more, and they climbed the porch steps to the front door of the cottage.

Inside, he dropped the boxes behind the red leather sofa. He checked his watch. It was nearly ten o'clock.

"Cat?" he called. "We're home."

There was no answer.

Serena went into the girl's bedroom and came back out with a worried look on her face. "She's not there. Did she say anything about going out tonight?"

"No." Stride took a deep breath, and musk cologne filled his nose. His mouth screwed into a frown. "Curt Dickes was here. Cat's car is still outside. She must have gone somewhere with him."

He took out his phone and dialed Cat's number, but the call went straight to voice mail. "Do you still have that tracking app on her phone?" he asked Serena.

"No, I disabled it. I wanted her to feel like we trusted her. I guess that was a mistake."

Stride dialed Maggie's number next. He had a brief conversation and then hung up the phone.

"Maggie and Cab are at Casperson's rental house," he said. "They were going to pick up Jungle Jack, but he's not there. Neither is Casperson. There's some sort of wrap party tonight up on the North Shore. They're trying to find out where."

"Do you think that's where Cat is?" Serena asked.

"Don't you?"

They turned back to the front door, but Stride's glance strayed across the bookshelf near Cat's bedroom door. He saw a yellow piece of paper with his name written across the outside.

"Wait," he said.

Stride retrieved the page and unfolded it, and he and Serena read the note inside together.

You're wrong, Stride. This time you're wrong. I'm sorry, but I can't do nothing if it means other people get hurt.

He crumpled the note in his fist and swore under his breath. "Cat, what the hell are you doing?"

# 40

The atmosphere at the party was subdued, and Cat knew why. Aimee Bowe was still missing. The lights were low, giving the room a romantic glow and making the faces hard to see. The band played soft string music, and a few people did slow dances on the floor. One wall of the resort ballroom was nothing but floor-to-ceiling windows that acted like mirrors at night. Beyond the glass was the lakeshore and forest trails leading to individual waterfront cottages. The room was warm, but outside the snow kept burying the land.

Cat was a magnet for attention as soon she walked in. Every head turned. She was at a Hollywood-style party with the beautiful people, but she was beautiful, too. Tonight she wasn't seventeen years old. Tonight she was someone else.

A waiter passed them with sparkling water in a champagne glass, and she took one. She wanted to keep her wits about her for what would come next. Curt already had a cocktail.

"Are any of your girls here?" she asked.

"Oh, yeah, I arranged for half a dozen to be on the bus. None of them is a stunner like you, though."

"You know what you have to do, right? If you see Jungle Jack, keep him distracted. Make sure your girls are talking to him. He's the only one who knows who I am. I don't want him seeing me here."

"Hey, I know the plan. Take Jack out of the play. You got it." Curt leaned down and whispered in her ear. "Last chance to back out of this, kitty cat. We can turn around and leave right now."

"No, I can't do that."

"Okay, you're the boss."

Curt drifted into the crowd, sliding an arm around one of the other girls as he looked for Jungle Jack. Cat ignored the queasy feeling in her stomach and let a brilliant smile spill across her face. She fluffed her chestnut hair. She was alone, but she knew it wouldn't be for long. Men began to descend on her as she navigated the room. They dropped whoever they were with, and the women who were left behind shot Cat icy glares. She didn't care.

She wasn't seventeen. She was someone else.

With each man who approached her, she made small talk about Duluth, about the weather, about the movie. When a man's eyes wandered, she gently nudged his chin with her finger and moved his gaze back to her eyes. She teased the men, but when they tried to move in closer, she moved on. No one got more than five minutes of her time, but it still took her nearly an hour to cross the room. She had only one target tonight, and she wanted him to realize that she was the most in-demand, most wanted, most available woman at the party.

Cat kept flirting, but she was aware of everyone around her. Her plan was simple. Avoid Jungle Jack. Hunt for Dean Casperson.

Finally, she spotted him.

He stood by the tall windows, framed by the darkness around him. Even among the Los Angeles crowd, the party people gave him space, because he was special. He was the star. Casperson swirled a drink in his hand, and his black tuxedo made him look like James Bond. His hair had been colored to its usual black luster. Three other men—probably rich and powerful, too—talked and laughed with him, but his eyes moved around the room, missing nothing. It was only a matter of time until he saw her.

Cat chatted with a young man who told her that he was a rigging gaffer. She didn't know what that was and only half paid attention to what he was saying. Her eyes went back and forth between the gaffer and Dean Casperson, who was standing just a few feet away from her. She angled her body toward him. She laughed at something the gaffer said, but the laugh was for Casperson. She baited the hook, then cast the line.

The next time she looked Casperson's way, he was staring back at her. She felt his eyes all the way inside her body. Her reaction was raw and physical, and she had to remind herself who he was and what he'd done and why she was there. His gaze didn't let go of her. The gaffer felt it, and he melted away like a cub making way for a lion. Casperson came toward her, leaving the men to watch him go. People saw them nearing each other. She was aware of smirks and whispers around her. They all knew she was the chosen one. She knew it, too.

"I remember you," he said with a slight question mark in his voice. He took her hand and cupped it in his. His palm was warm.

"Cat, as in meow," she replied. She hoped he'd forgotten how immature and foolish she'd been at the earlier party, when she'd fallen all over him. She didn't want him thinking about her as young. She wanted him to think of her as prey.

"Of course. I saw you the other night. I didn't think it was possible for you to be more gorgeous than you were then, but you've done it."

"Thank you."

He didn't ask for a compliment in return. Dean Casperson didn't need to be reminded how attractive he was.

"I don't believe you told me who you are and what you do," he went on.

"I write for a local magazine in Duluth," she lied.

"And how is it that you're here at the party?"

"I met someone from the crew at a local bar. He called himself a best boy, whatever that is. Between you and me, he was really only a so-so boy, if you know what I mean."

Casperson's mouth formed a grin. "Well, that's what distinguishes the men from the boys."

"You are so right."

"Would you like to dance, Cat?" Casperson asked. "I feel like dancing."

She hesitated, wondering if her inexperience and high heels would betray her. "I'm not much of a dancer."

"Not to worry. I'm good enough for both of us."

He led her onto the small dance floor, where the others gave them room. More knowing glances and whispers passed through the crowd. Casperson shot a look at the guitarist in the band, and as if they'd used a secret code, the band switched songs. They played "What a Wonderful World." The music had a sad, mournful quality, as if this were the last day on earth. Maybe that was the way Casperson wanted her to feel.

He was right about his dancing. He made it easy to follow him. Without knowing any steps, she found herself turning in his arms, going where he nudged her to go. Everyone was watching them. She hoped that Curt had kept Jungle Jack far away, where he wouldn't see Cat and Casperson together.

"You move very well," Casperson told her.

"That's all you."

He knew that was true, but he smiled anyway. She felt small and light in his arms, and he made her a little dizzy. She tried not to think about where she was and what she was doing. The only thing she knew was that his fingers were pressed firmly on the bare skin at the small of her back.

"So you write," he said.

"Yes."

"What do you write?"

"It's not exciting. New restaurants, upcoming events, that kind of thing."

"Have you thought about acting? You have the looks for it."

"I don't think I could ever do that," Cat said. "I'm sure it's way too hard."

"I'll let you in on a secret. It's really not."

"I'm sure it's impossible to break in."

"Not when you know the right people," Casperson said.

They kept dancing. The slow song ended and blended without a pause into something with a salsa beat. Casperson switched his movements effortlessly, and Cat tried to keep up, but she felt awkward on the dance floor. Casperson seemed amused by her lack of grace. He let half the song go by, then took her hand and guided her away. Others in the crowd filled the space they'd left behind.

Everyone stayed away from them. The crew. The money men. The staff. Security. They all knew what was going on.

Cat fanned herself. "It's warm."

"Too many people here," Casperson said.

"That's true."

"Would you like to get some air?"

"It's cold, and it's snowing," Cat replied, smiling.

"Well, I have a waterfront cottage a few steps away. There's wine, fresh air, and a fireplace."

"That sounds lovely."

"Come on, then."

He guided her to the glass door that led outside. Cat found herself on the balcony, looking down at the trees and the lakeshore. Someone had built a campfire in the snow that looked oddly appropriate and inviting in the winter. There were a handful of people in silhouette around it, laughing and drinking. The wind sang an ominous song, and the snow refused to let up. It landed on her skin like little needles. She heard the rhythmic thump of the waves.

"I don't think I can walk in these heels," Cat said.

"Do you trust me?"

She blinked. "Of course. You're Dean Casperson."

He literally swept her off her feet. One moment she was standing on the balcony, the next she was in his arms. He carried her as if she weighed nothing. He made his way effortlessly to the path and through the trees to a two-story cottage not far away. With a tap of his foot, he kicked open the door and carried her over the threshold and set her down.

"How's that?" he asked.

"Wow," she said.

Music already played from hidden speakers, a low piano solo so clear and perfect that she thought he must have a pianist in the cottage. The gas fireplace was already lit. That was the only light in the room. The white wine was in an ice bucket with two crystal glasses next to it on a wet bar. This had all been planned. A girl was going to come here with him this evening, and whatever was going to happen was going to happen. If not to her, then to someone else.

She didn't have much time to think. Her gaze explored the room quickly. The fireplace was surrounded by flagstone that took up the entire wall. Among the stone shelves near the glow of the fire was a large flat-screen television. The picture window had no ledge and looked out on the lake. There were two leather chairs and a table with a lamp, but the lamp was turned off. A plush red sofa waited for them with multicolored pillows and a chaise. It had plenty of room for two. Beyond the sofa, a doorway led into the full kitchen. The bedrooms were upstairs, but she didn't think they'd make it that far.

She thought: *Where?*

She had only seconds to decide. She sat down on the sofa and kept looking around the room.

"Would you like a drink, Cat?" Casperson asked. "Trust me, the wine is superb. It's one of my favorites from a little winery outside Lyon."

"Actually, could you get me some water first? I'm really dry."

He smiled at her. "Of course."

Casperson turned around and disappeared into the kitchen. Cat moved fast. She grabbed her purse and took out her phone and tapped out a quick text to Serena. Then she leaped off the sofa and endured five seconds of interminable hesitation as she tried to decide the best place in the room. Not the floor. Not the windows. Not the table. She ran to the television and propped her phone against it, with the black case covering up everything except the camera. She didn't have time to go back and check the angle; she had to hope that it was right and that there was enough light from the fire. She already could hear the refrigerator door closing. She ran back and settled down on the sofa just as Casperson loomed in the doorway again. He handed her a small open bottle of Fiji water.

"Here you go," he said.

"Thank you, Dean."

She held the bottle, which was almost impossible because her fingers were shaking so hard. The reality of everything, of where she was, of what she was doing, of what was about to happen, crashed down on her. She'd planned it all out, but now she didn't know if she could do it. She wanted to run. Her throat felt tight. She drank half the water with one thirsty swallow and gave him a nervous little smile. Then, trying to hide her fear, she finished the bottle and put it on the floor.

"How about that wine now?" he asked.

"Sure. That sounds great."

He went over to the wet bar, and she watched him carefully. The wine was already uncorked, bathing in the ice bucket. She heard the slosh of water and ice. He glanced back at her with a confident, seductive smile. He was going to do it now. Definitely. Absolutely. He was so smooth as he poured that she didn't even see it happen. She didn't spot his hand dipping into his pocket for the vial. No one would know he'd done it. No one who didn't realize it was about to happen.

"So what's it like being Dean Casperson?" she asked him.

Casperson turned around with two wineglasses in his hand.

*Don't look at the television*, she thought, staring at him, holding on to his gaze with her smoky eyes.

"Honestly? It's an amazing life."

He came and sat down next to her and handed her a wineglass. If you knew what to look for, you could see the predatory anticipation in his face. This was more than romantic seduction. Most of the women who came here would have slept with him anyway, but it wasn't about that. She'd been with men who needed to dominate. Who needed to win. Who needed to abuse. She'd seen that sickness, and there was no cure.

"To the most beautiful girl I've met in Minnesota," he toasted her, clinking their glasses together.

This was the moment. It was now or never.

Cat stared down into the golden pool of wine and tried to will herself to drink. He watched with a hawk's eyes and waited for her to take a sip. She didn't know what he'd put in her glass. Xanax. Ecstasy.

Rohypnol. Ketamine. She only knew she was about to be drugged. And then much, much worse.

"You're being very sweet to me," she said, forcing a smile and twisting the glass in her hand. Her fingers on the stem were slippery with sweat. *You have to drink.*

"Naturally," he said. "That's what you deserve."

The fire sparkled in the wine. Cat brought the glass to her mouth, but her hand quivered.

"I don't want to lead you on," she said, playing for time. "It's fun to talk and this is very flattering, but we're *not* going to have sex. I don't do that with men I've just met. Even if you are Dean Casperson. Are we clear about that?"

"I would never make you do something you don't want to do," he told her.

Cat tried to make her expression sincere. "Well, good. As long as we understand each other."

"Try the wine," he urged her. "I think you'll love it."

*You have to drink.*

She tilted the glass, fully intending to taste it, to let it happen. The wine splashed against her lips, but she kept her mouth closed. She couldn't even run her tongue over her damp lips. She couldn't do it. Everything about her past began to flash in her mind. Every man she'd been with, every man she'd hated, was there in the room with her. They knew she would drink. She'd done it before. She'd taken drugs. She'd been with men who did what Dean was going to do to her. What did it matter if she did it one more time?

This was no big deal. This was who she was.

Let it happen.

But she couldn't. She stared at the wine, which began to float in front of her eyes like an amber lake, and she kept screaming at herself in the cavern of her head. *Drink. Do it. You have to drink.*

No.

No, no, no, this was not her anymore. This was everything she'd run away from, everything she'd left behind. If she did this, she could never look at herself again. The men in the room would laugh at her.

They'd know that nothing had changed. She was still the girl on the street. The whore.

It didn't matter how evil the man in front of her was. She couldn't do it.

"I—I—think," Cat began.

It was hard to form words. She tried to grab the words and put them on her tongue, but they skittered away from her. Why was it so hard? Just say it. *I need to go. I can't stay here. I can't let you do this to me, you son of a bitch.*

"Relax, Cat. Drink the wine."

"I—I—can't. I need—"

"What do you need, Cat?" he asked her in a voice that lilted up and down like the notes on the piano. "Tell me what you need."

"To go."

"Oh, you don't want to do that," he told her. "The party's just starting."

"Feel strange," Cat murmured.

She labored through quicksand, unable to understand what was happening to her. She hadn't tasted the wine. She was still free. All she had to do was get up and leave. Push him away. Run.

Why couldn't she run?

The glass swayed like a tree in the wind, still full, still untouched. Some of the wine spilled over the rim onto her fingers. She couldn't hold the stem upright anymore. It was going to topple and spill. He reached over and took the wineglass from her hand. She squinted at him and watched him put the glass to his mouth.

He drank it. He finished the whole glass.

*Oh, no.*

Somewhere in the fog, Cat understood. She knew what he'd done to her. She knew it was too late to go back now, too late to stop, too late to escape. She felt herself falling off a cliff into air, going down and down and down.

He hadn't put the drug in the wine.

He'd put it in the water. The empty bottle of water on the floor. It was already in her blood.

\*

Stride drove north through the snow that streamed across the scenic highway. He drove faster than he should. His truck led the way, and Maggie's Avalanche followed. There were two more police cars after that, like a caravan on the North Shore road.

"Did you try calling her again?" he asked Serena.

"I did. She must have her phone on mute."

He kept his eyes on the road. His headlights were the only light around him, and otherwise the night was black. "It'll be okay. There's probably a hundred people at the party. We'll get Cat out of there."

"I know."

But they had miles to go, and the resort seemed far away. Stride kept the radio off. The truck was silent except for the patter of snow. Then, strangely, he heard the toot-toot of an old-fashioned car horn.

Serena grabbed her phone from the seat.

"That's Cat's text tone," she said with relief. "Thank God."

"What does it say?"

He glanced over and saw Serena's face cloud with confusion. "I don't get it. It says, 'Check Facebook.'"

"What does that mean?"

Serena pushed a few more buttons on her phone. Stride's eyes shifted back and forth from the road to his wife's face. Her expression was calm and curious. He watched her scroll to Cat's profile, and then, out of nowhere, she slapped a hand over her mouth. A cry broke out of her throat. She choked; she gagged. She threw the phone down as if it were on fire. She was instantly sobbing, disintegrating into panic next to him.

"Jonny, drive, drive, speed up; we have to get up there right now!"

"What's going on?"

"Cat's with Dean Casperson. It's just him and her alone. He's going to rape her, Jonny, *and she's streaming it live for the whole world to see.*"

# 41

It felt like a dream.

A gauzy curtain draped over Cat's mind. Shapes in the fire-lit room grew larger and smaller as if she were seeing them in a fun house mirror. Her limbs were leaden. She willed her arms and legs to move, but they only stared sullenly back at her. She had trouble keeping her head up; it kept lolling onto the sofa cushion. She was vaguely aware of Casperson slipping off his tuxedo coat, undoing his tie, and unbuttoning a couple of buttons on his shirt. His face had the intense, curious look of a scientist studying the reactions of a new specimen.

"It's a little different every time," he told her. "Most women would be unconscious by now, but you're still awake. That's interesting. I like it better that way."

He sat down next to her. Their legs were touching. He put an index finger on her cheek and slowly slid it down her face, along the line of her chin, and into the hollow of her neck. She wanted to slap his hand away, but she didn't know how. She was watching his face as if through a kaleidoscope, broken into pieces and moving in circles.

"I wasn't lying about how beautiful you are. That wasn't just a line. You really are unique."

He stroked her chestnut hair. He pulled his fingers through it and let the strands fall in a messy pile across her eyes. He traced the outline of her full lips, but his touch made it feel like he was caressing the marble of a statue. She was trapped inside, and she couldn't feel what he was doing. She was a girl in a box, unable to escape or resist. She was a thing to him. A robot. A doll. Something over which he exerted complete control.

Her mouth formed a word, but her tongue felt thick. She wasn't even sure if she'd said it aloud. *Stop.*

"Stop? I wish I could. Truly. I don't like this part of myself. In the early years, I tried to resist, but the strange thing is, my acting suffered when I didn't have an outlet. I finally realized that I had to accept myself as a whole package. The good and the bad. I'm not proud of it, but every life requires a balancing of the scales."

She tried to curse. Two short words. It made him laugh.

"You're brave. I like that about you. The fact is, you won't remember anything about tonight. Or if you do, you'll never really be sure exactly what happened. No one will believe you if you tell anyone, because you're nobody and I'm me. That's just the way it is, Cat."

She wanted to scream. Inside her head, she screamed at him. The effort made her dizzy. She could feel unconsciousness closing over her like an eclipse, blocking out her thoughts like the moon did to the light of the sun, but she fought back. She wouldn't give in. She wouldn't forget.

Yet she was helpless.

"It's the unwrapping I love," he said. "Seeing the secrets each woman hides."

He placed his fingers lightly on the bare skin where her breasts began to swell and gave her the slightest nudge. She found herself toppling backward, slowly, sinking as the room spun. She lay sprawled on the sofa. She blinked as she stared at the ceiling, and each blink took forever. Her arms lay next to her, useless appendages covered in black lace.

She knew what it would be like.

She'd been on this ride before.

The other men from her past were still here with her. She could see them. Every man she'd been with in the bad days leered at her in the hot room. She saw their faces, smelled their breath, heard their panting, felt them between her legs, winced at the pain. She wanted to close her eyes so that she couldn't see, wanted it to be over, wanted to wake up from a nightmare and be home and safe. But this was real.

His fingers touched her everywhere, and she couldn't stop him.

His hand followed the skin of her leg until it was under her dress, and she couldn't stop him.

Her eyes were glazed little slits on her face. In her head, she beat her fists against the bars of her cage, but she was powerless. She wondered if anyone was watching this happen. She wanted to know if people could see her and what they were saying and whether the secret was passing from one person to another. It didn't matter. Wherever the voyeurs were, they weren't here, and they didn't know where she was. For now, she was absolutely alone.

"This doesn't have to be unpleasant," he said as he began to peel off her clothes.

She heard that single word over and over, like an echo. *Unpleasant.* Like an airport delay. Like an overcooked meal.

The eclipse deepened and headed toward totality. The shadow crossed her brain; time stood still; consciousness drifted in and out. She was aware of her bare skin, her body open to him, exposed, making her feel small. She smelled his scent, which reeked of his hunger. He began to shed his clothes, but she looked away so that she didn't have to see. She heard, oddly, the tearing of foil. He showed her a moist, rolled condom between his fingers with a bizarre pride, as if somehow that would make everything better.

"See? I take precautions."

Cat lay on her back, paralyzed. She couldn't even cry.

She thought: *Save me.*

But no one was coming to save her.

*

*"Where the hell is Dean Casperson?"* Stride shouted, shocking the party into silence.

Serena pushed into the ballroom of the resort behind him. Seconds later, so did Maggie, Cab, and half a dozen uniformed police officers. The strangers in the room were frozen, as if they didn't dare open their mouths.

Saying anything meant going against Casperson.

He spotted a man sauntering toward them with a young woman on his arm and a drink in his other hand. Next to Stride, Cab Bolton tensed like a tiger about to strike. It was Jungle Jack. Stride felt Cab take an ominous step in Jack's direction, so he shot out his hand to hold the detective back.

"Jack, where did Casperson take the girl?" Stride asked.

Jungle Jack looked unimpressed by the sight of the police. He handed his drink to the woman with him and wandered up to Stride as if he had nothing to fear. "What girl are you talking about? The last time I saw Dean, he was shooting pool with some of the producers."

"I don't have time for this," Stride replied. He gestured to Maggie. "Arrest this son of a bitch."

Jack's calm faltered. "*Arrest* me? For what?"

"For murder," Stride snapped.

The cuffs appeared in Maggie's hands like a rabbit out of a magician's hat, and before Jack could protest, he'd been spun around with the cuffs snapped onto his wrists, and the police were shoving him out of the resort.

The ballroom was still in a state of suspended animation, and Stride woke them up with another shout.

"In five more seconds, I start arresting everybody here," he called. *"Now where did Casperson take the girl?"*

No one wanted to be the first to talk. No one had any courage. Then, finally, an attractive young woman in a magenta dress stepped forward from the silent crowd and pointed at the glass doors to the patio. She called to him in a loud voice, as if she were freeing herself from prison. "They left through there. Dean rented the first waterfront cottage down the path."

Her phone was in her hand. She'd been watching. She knew.

"You better hurry," she added.

Stride ran. So did Serena. The crowd parted to let them through, and Stride reached the windows at the back of the room and slammed through the outer doors onto the balcony. Gales and snow surged into his face. He saw the darkness of the lake and the dragon flames of the fire pit on the beach. Looking left, he saw the dark outline of a two-story cottage facing the water. Its lights were off, but he saw footprints on the path leading that way that were being erased quickly as the wind blew.

In a second, he was down the balcony steps. He sprinted along the snow-covered trail, where the trees clawed at him. The ground was slick underfoot, slowing him down. He ran for the cottage door and didn't pause as he reached it. His shoulder hit the wooden door and crashed it inward, slamming it off its hinges with a splintering crack of wood. He wasn't aware of the pain. He took two steps into the room, and there they were.

Dean Casperson.

And Cat.

The firelight licked at both of them. Cat lay on the sofa, stripped naked, her eyes unfocused and half closed. Casperson knelt between her legs. His shirt was unbuttoned, his pants and underwear pooled at his ankles. He looked over at Stride as the door crashed in, and in that one split second, he knew he was done. He put up his hands in defense as Stride closed the distance between them. With adrenaline storming through his blood, Stride lifted Casperson bodily into the air and threw him like a toy across the room. Casperson's head slammed into the stone wall, and he sank to the floor. Blood trickled from his hairline across his face and onto his neck.

Behind Stride, Serena was already at Cat's side. She gathered the girl up in her arms and covered her with a blanket from a wicker basket on the floor. She hugged her with a fierce protectiveness.

"Cat, are you okay? We're here, it's over."

But for Stride, it wasn't over. It wasn't over at all.

He didn't even know how it happened, but his gun left his pocket and found its way to his hand.

His fist tightened on the grip.

The safety came off.

His index finger moved onto the trigger.

He bent down and yanked Casperson off the floor with a hand clenched around the man's throat. His other hand shoved the gun into Casperson's forehead. The actor choked, and his eyes bulged; he couldn't breathe. Stride's rage was so deep that he couldn't even form words. His hatred burned like the heat of the fire on his back. It wasn't enough to see terror in Casperson's face, or surrender, or humiliation, or defeat. He wanted this man dead on the floor, with blood and brains sprayed on the wall behind him. He wanted to kill him, to erase him, to murder him, to send him to hell.

All he had to do was squeeze the trigger.

"*Jonny!*"

It was Serena, screaming over and over.

"*Jonny!* Put it down! Don't do it!"

Her voice was frantic, but he barely heard her. His fury boiled. He had never felt anything so primal toward another human being. He didn't care about the consequences, or the rest of his life, or anything except destroying this man. Pull the trigger. Watch the wretched life vanish from Casperson's eyes.

Then another, tremulous voice called to him.

"Stride."

It was Cat.

Her drugged, dreamy voice reached out to him and cut through his anger. "Stride, please don't. Please."

He took a breath. His fever broke. He let go of Casperson's throat, and he could see the red imprint of his fingers on the man's neck. Casperson gasped for air and fell backward, coughing. Stride slid his finger off the trigger, secured his weapon, and returned it to his holster. His fingers curled into a fist, but this man wasn't even worth the broken bones. Instead, he grabbed Casperson's collar and shoved him facedown on the floor, where his ass was still obscenely displayed. He cuffed him, then went to Cat on the sofa and put his arms around her.

This girl was always saving him. Again and again.

She had no strength to hug him back, but a tiny smile flitted across her face and melted his heart. She mumbled something he didn't understand. "How many?"

"What?"

"How many watching? A hundred?"

That was when he remembered that Cat's phone was still broadcasting the entire scene to the world on Facebook Live.

He glanced at Serena, who retrieved the phone from beside the television. Before she disconnected it, she checked the stats on the video and shook her head in disbelief.

"More than a hundred, Catalina," she said.

"How many?"

Serena went over to Casperson, took him by the hair, and shoved the phone screen in the man's face. "Let's tell Dean how popular he is. Congratulations, dirtbag. *Four and a half million people* just watched your latest film, and they all saw the disgusting pig you really are."

# 42

"I'm going to sue you," Dean Casperson told Stride. He leaned angrily across the interview table, but his hands were cuffed to a metal bar and he couldn't stand up. Blood had dried on his face and made a red stain on the collar of his white tuxedo shirt. "That was police brutality. You shoved a gun in my face. You nearly choked me to death."

Stride shrugged and showed no concern. "I'll take my chances. Meanwhile, Mr. Casperson, you've been charged with second-degree criminal sexual conduct. The sentence on that charge is at least seven and a half years, and we're just getting started with you. You've been advised of your rights, and you know that you don't need to talk with us if you choose not to. Are you willing to answer our questions?"

A smart man wouldn't talk. An arrogant man couldn't stop himself. Casperson was both, but Stride didn't have any trouble guessing which side of the man would have the upper hand.

"File all the charges you want," Casperson snapped. "Nothing will stick. This was entrapment. You sent that girl to the party to seduce me. Everything that went on in there was consensual."

"*That girl* got the whole encounter with you on video."

Serena sat next to Stride. She calmly checked her phone and said to Casperson, "It's still going viral, Dean. You're past 10 million views now. You should see the comments, too. It's not pretty when heroes fall."

"You don't think my lawyers will get that video thrown out?" Casperson asked. "No jury's ever going to see a minute of it. Face it, you have no idea of the shit storm you just brought on yourselves. When I'm done with you, you won't have a house, a job, or a nickel in the bank. You'll be lucky if a nightclub hires you as a bouncer."

Stride waited as Casperson rocked back in the chair in frustration, only to have the cuffs jerk him forward again.

"You might want to save your money, Dean," Stride told him, "because you're going to need it for all the lawsuits that are about to be filed. I don't think you fully understand what's happening to you right now. My voice mail is already full with messages from news media, national magazines, and journalists around the world. You are done, Dean. You're finished."

Casperson was having a hard time grasping the reality of his situation, but Stride had said the magic word. *Media.* The actor who valued his reputation more than anything knew what was coming next. He could write the headlines on TMZ. He could see the video stills reprinted in *Entertainment Weekly.* Another sex scandal was like a feeding frenzy these days, and the sharks could all smell blood in the water.

"This isn't just about Cat," Stride went on. "She started the ball rolling, but there's no stopping it now. In the last three hours, twenty-three other women have already come forward on social media to tell their own stories of abuse and rape by you. Do you want Serena to read some of them? They're very detailed and very graphic. Several of the incidents are well within the statute of limitations in the various jurisdictions you were in, so plenty of other prosecutors will want a shot at you when we're done. And regardless, all the women are going to be suing you. Your career is over. You're radioactive. Your fortune will be gone soon enough. The only real question is how much of the rest of your life you spend behind bars. The best thing you can do right now is give us a full and complete accounting of what you've done."

Casperson sat in silence, as if he were looking for a way out in a room with no doors or windows.

Serena shook her head. "Don't you get it, Dean? Being a celebrity protected you for decades, but all that evil finally caught up with you. All thanks to a seventeen-year-old girl."

"You'll never prove I did anything wrong," he retorted, but the bravado was gone from his voice.

"Keep telling yourself that if you want," Stride said. "The fact is, the sexual assault charge is going to be open and shut. That's the minimum, but you know where it goes from here. We've got Jungle Jack in the interview room next door. He knows the rest. He knows *everything*. We have enough hard evidence on Jack to put him behind bars for the rest of his life. You don't think he's going to jump at the chance to give you up in exchange for a deal?"

"And when he does, you're the one who's looking at life behind bars," Serena added. "I hope you enjoyed your time in Minnesota, because you're never going to leave the state again."

"Life in prison? Are you kidding me?"

"That's the penalty for first-degree murder," Stride told him.

Casperson looked genuinely shocked. His gaze zigzagged between them, and for the first time his face showed fear. "*Murder?* What the hell are you talking about? I don't know anything about murder."

*

Jungle Jack was the opposite of Dean Casperson. He refused to say a word. He sat in the interview room, cuffed, and stared back at Maggie with a permanent smirk tattooed on his mouth. His dark eyes were hooded with contempt. He didn't ask for a lawyer, and he listened to Maggie lay out the evidence against him without any reaction at all. The only words out of his mouth were to ask for a cigarette, and when Maggie said no, he shrugged and went back to his stony silence.

"I know you and Lieutenant Stride talked about this man," Maggie told him, laying a photograph of John Doe's body in front of him. "He's dead, so he won't be testifying any time soon. But this man is—was—a killer. Anyone who helped him commit premeditated murder is a killer, too. That means being a guest at the state correctional facility in Oak Park Heights for as long as you're alive. By the way, Oak Park Heights is where we house the guys who don't know the meaning of 'Minnesota nice.' I've seen it. Trust me, Jack, you're going to spend a lot of years behind bars. You don't want to spend them there."

Jack used his thumb to dig dirt from under his manicured fingernails and didn't even bother looking up.

"We know that our friend John Doe—say, do you know his actual name, Jack? That would really help us out."

This time, Jack looked up and gave her a smile.

"No?" Maggie went on. "Well, suit yourself. We know John Doe murdered a young woman named Peach Piper here in Minnesota and a woman in Florida named Haley Adams. The gun found in his car was used to murder both women. End of story; that's the easy part. By the way, do you know what else we found in John Doe's car? This cowboy hat."

She laid a photo of a black cowboy hat in front of Jack, who glanced at it with only the slightest puzzlement.

"Nice hat, isn't it?" Maggie said. "The feather is cool, too. What is that, a red-tailed hawk? I think I'd look pretty good in a cowboy hat like that. I may have to get one. Anyway, I'll come back to the hat. The thing is, we know John Doe killed Peach Piper, and we're pretty sure he killed Rochelle Wahl, too. Rochelle was a fifteen-year-old girl. We're still gathering evidence to link him to that murder, but we already know he left a party at Dean Casperson's house with Rochelle, and she was found dead a few hours later. Remember that? It was the party where we have a picture of *you* arriving with Rochelle. That's a pretty interesting coincidence for anybody sitting on a jury."

She hadn't broken through Jack's silence yet, because he didn't see any threat. She hadn't shown him anything that he didn't already know. But he was curious. She could see the wheels turning, wondering what the police had and why they'd felt confident enough to charge him with murder this time.

"We know John Doe had an accomplice," she went on, "and we know that accomplice is you."

Jack waited. His shoulders gave the smallest shrug.

I get it; you think I'm blowing smoke," Maggie said. She turned around and waved at the interrogation window. "Cab, what do you think? Am I blowing smoke in here?"

Cab's voice crackled through the intercom. "No, you're not."

Maggie smiled at Jack. "No, I'm really not. See, we found John Doe's phone in his car, along with the gun and the cowboy hat. The phone records show that he was in communication with somebody in town. Namely, you. And yeah, as soon as you heard John Doe was dead, I'm sure you ditched the phone. That's okay. We got the call records on the burner phone anyway. You remember the mistake you made, right, Jack?"

Jack stared back at her, but this time, he sucked his lower lip nervously between his teeth. Maggie grinned.

"Yeah, that's right, the pizza," she said. "Look, I don't blame you. When I'm jonesing for a Sammy's, nothing else will do. But using the burner phone to call for delivery? Not smart. Of course, you called the wrong location, didn't you? They told you they wouldn't deliver up to Hermantown. So you hung up and looked at the phone in your hand, and you thought—shit. Lucky break that you didn't actually place an order, huh?"

She put a copy of the sheet with the apartment phone records on the interview table in front of Jack.

"Except then you used the phone in your apartment to call the Sammy's restaurant in Hermantown. Two minutes later. That doesn't look good, Jack. You think anyone is going to believe that's a coincidence?"

She took out another sheet of paper from her folder and put it facedown on the table. She could see Jack look at it; she could see him wondering what it was. The anticipation was always the worst part. That was what ate into a suspect's confidence. The not knowing.

"I got the phone records from the apartment owner," Maggie said. "He's a nosy guy, that Stig. Likes to keep an eye on things. We have a statement from him, Jack. He saw Peach Piper hanging out near your apartment. In fact, he called to tell you that some girl was spying on you, and you went out and confronted her. Then you walked her toward the back of the complex. John Doe was staying in one of the cottages back there. So we figure the two of you took Peach into the woods and John Doe shot her. Did you watch him do it, Jack? Have you seen people killed before? It's not pretty. I hope you didn't throw up or anything. Because we'll be searching the woods tomorrow. We're going to find the crime scene."

She still hadn't turned over the sheet of paper in front of Jack.

"The fact is, the game's over," she went on. "First-degree murder, Jack. Life in prison. You don't have anybody to blame but yourself, you know. It's that ego of yours. The girl who delivered your pizza asked if you were part of the movie crew, and you couldn't stop yourself, could you? You had to say yes. You had to let her take a selfie with you. Except the thing is, she clicked a few shots before you closed the apartment door, Jack."

Maggie reached out and turned over the paper on the table. It was an enlarged photograph taken from Ginny Hoeppner's phone. Maggie took a red Sharpie and drew a circle on the picture.

"This is inside the apartment, Jack. See where I drew the circle? Look closely. It's easy to make out if you squint."

Jack did. Then he sighed and closed his eyes.

"Yeah. It's a black cowboy hat with a red-tailed hawk's feather. It's John Doe's hat. And I might not even have noticed it without the hat, but the fact is, that's not even your apartment. The furniture isn't right. You had the pizza delivered to *John Doe's* apartment. That's why you're here, Jack. That's why you're going to spend the rest of your life in prison. If you want, you can wait and talk to the lawyer that Dean Casperson gets for you. But if Dean's paying for it, who do you think that lawyer is really going to represent? Little tip: it's not you. My advice is, you cut a deal right now and tell us about Casperson's involvement in the murder of Peach Piper, the murder of Rochelle Wahl, the murder of Haley Adams, and the murders of anyone else you scumbags have been involved with in the last twenty years."

Jack stared at the ceiling. He exhaled slowly, and the stale aroma of cigarette smoke breathed from his mouth. He took another look at the photographs spread out across the table. Finally, he spoke.

"Dean's not the one you want," he said.

"Excuse me?"

"Dean's a pervert and a predator," Jack continued, "and you can put him away for that, but he doesn't know anything about the murders. He just thinks we paid the girls off."

"Then who's behind it?" Maggie asked.

"Mo," Jack replied. "It's always been Mo. Let me tell you, bring a whole squadron when you arrest her, because you've never met a steelier character than Dean's wife. She will do *anything* to protect his reputation. She made all the calls about who we needed to get rid of. She decided who lived and died. Give me a deal, and I can give you names, dates, places, everything you need. Mo's the one who hired John Doe. Mo's the scorpion."

# 43

"Do you believe him?" Stride asked Cab. "You and your mother know Mo Casperson better than any of us."

Cab sipped his three-in-the-morning coffee and made a sour face. "Jack knows you have a rock-solid case against him. If he had evidence against Dean, I think he'd give it to us. If he's pointing the finger at Mo instead, she's probably been his contact all along."

"I met Mo," Maggie added. "I have no trouble imagining her as ruthless enough to hire a killer. I watched her tear into Tarla's reputation at just a hint that she might go public about what Dean did to her. I think Mo would do whatever it takes to keep Dean propped up."

Stride got up from the conference table and went to the vending machine, where he bought himself a can of Coke. It was his third since midnight. "Even if Mo was the one behind the murders, I have a hard time picturing Dean as completely out of the loop. He had to know what was going on."

"I agree," Cab replied, "although I'm not sure if you'll be able to prove it."

"Mo may have tried to compartmentalize him," Maggie said, "so she'd be the one to take the fall if things went south. Or maybe she just didn't think Dean had the stones to make the tough calls."

"We won't know until we talk to her," Stride said.

Cab smiled. "Well, Lala and the Naples Police are on their way to Captiva to give Mo a little wake-up call."

Stride focused on Serena, who was pacing back and forth in the conference room. She hadn't joined the discussion. She still had restless energy driving her forward despite the late hour. One part of the investigation was done, but one part was still open, and the clock was ticking. Aimee Bowe was still missing.

"Serena, how's Cat?" Maggie called.

Serena stopped in the middle of the room. "She's spending the night at St. Mary's for observation. Physically, she's okay. The drugs just need to get out of her system."

Cab spoke in a quiet voice. No one had wanted to bring up what really had happened between Dean and Cat. "Forgive me for asking, but was she actually—?"

"No. We got there in time." Serena shook her head and glanced across the room at Stride. "Another thirty seconds and I think our lives as we know them would have been over."

Stride said nothing. He knew what she meant. If they hadn't arrived in time—if Dean Casperson had gone through with the rape and Stride had found them afterward—he wasn't sure he would have been able to stop himself from pulling the trigger when he put his gun to Casperson's head. As it was, it had been a close call. He could still feel the violence in his veins.

"I'm worried about what comes next for Cat," Stride said. "The media focus on her is going to be ferocious. I don't know if she's ready for this. The whole world is going to know who she is. Her past will be in every magazine. Then there's the trial, too. If the county attorney can't do a plea bargain, Casperson's attorneys will try to shred her on the stand."

"Cat's tough," Maggie reminded him.

"What she did took guts," Cab added. "She succeeded where everyone else failed. She took Dean Casperson down all by herself."

Stride caught Serena's eye. That was Cat, full of contradictions. He wanted to lock her in her room and keep her safe, he wanted to scream at her for being so stupid, and he wanted to tell her how proud he was that she would sacrifice herself to right a wrong that had been going on for decades.

Serena sat down at the conference table. "Meanwhile, we still don't know where Aimee Bowe is."

"I don't think Jungle Jack was involved," Maggie told her. "We asked him about Aimee after he started talking, and he said he and Mo didn't have anything to do with it. I think he's telling the truth on this one."

"I agree," Serena replied. "I don't see what Dean, Mo, or Jack would gain by staging a sick copycat of what happened eleven years ago."

"Except Aimee echoed the movie script when she made the audiotape," Stride pointed out. "Why do that if whoever took her had nothing to do with the movie? What's the message?"

Serena shook her head. "Aimee told me Art didn't do it. Maybe she's giving us a clue about who did."

The room was silent for a while. Then Maggie spoke carefully, as if she knew she was on shaky ground. "Serena, you weren't around here back then. You didn't know Art. We dotted every 'i' and crossed every 't' on that investigation."

"I'm not saying you didn't. You still could have missed something. It happens." She got out of the chair and slipped on her winter coat. "I'm going to the hospital to check on Cat. Then I'm heading home to go over the Leipold case files."

Stride nodded. "I'll be there soon, too."

Serena left the room, her face grim.

Cab's phone started ringing, and he left the room to take the call. Stride and Maggie were alone, but the past was in the room with them. They'd spent hours in a room like this eleven years earlier, when they were tying Art Leipold to the murders. They stared at each across the table.

"Do you think Serena could be right?" Stride asked.

"About Art? No. Either it's a stalker or it's a copycat."

"I wonder," he mused. "I don't like to think about it, but is it possible we were played back then? Did someone hate Art Leipold enough to set him up?"

"Do you have someone in mind?"

Stride frowned. He did have someone in mind, and he didn't like where his thoughts were taking him. There was only one man who was linked to both Art Leipold and the movie.

Before he could say anything more, Cab came back into the room.

"Mo knew we were coming," he told them. "Someone tipped her off about Cat's video and Jack's arrest."

"What do you mean?" Maggie asked.

"That was Lala on the phone. When they got to Casperson's estate in Captiva, Mo was already gone. The staff doesn't know when she's coming back. If she knows we've got Jack in custody, she knows we're coming after her, too. And she's got the resources to hide anywhere in the world."

# 44

When Stride finally got home, the man he was looking for was already there. Chris Leipold was huddled in one of the Adirondack chairs on his porch. The writer was as white as the snow, and he'd obviously been drinking. A half-empty bottle of brandy was still in his hand. He stared at Stride through bloodshot eyes. His speech was slurred by the numbing cold, the lingering effects of his virus, and the dulling effects of the alcohol.

"It's over," Chris said. "It's done."

Stride sat down in a chair next to him. He glanced over his shoulder through the cottage windows. Inside, the lights were on. Serena was already home.

"What are you doing here, Chris?" Stride asked.

"It's over," Chris said again.

"What is?"

"The studio's pulling out of *The Caged Girl*. The movie's dead."

"Ah. I'm sorry."

"Five years of work up in smoke in five hours. Now I'm the guy who wasted tens of millions of dollars and got nothing to show for it."

"It's not your fault that Dean Casperson is a sexual predator."

Chris shook his head. "You don't know Hollywood."

Stride tried to feel bad, but he'd hated the idea of this movie from the beginning. There was no value in celebrating evil. "Be honest with me, Chris. Did you know what was going on?"

The writer turned his head slowly. "About Dean?"

"Yes."

"Of course. Everyone knew. Do you think it's only him? Every actress has a story about someone in this business. They swallow it down and smile and pretend it never happened. It's what women everywhere do with powerful men."

Stride wished that Chris was wrong. But he wasn't.

"I've asked you this question a hundred times," Stride said, "but I've never really gotten an answer. Why did you want to do this movie, anyway? Why did you write a script about what Art did?"

"I already told you; the movie was never about Art."

"Except it is," Stride said. "We both know that."

"I cast a nobody to play Art. I cast *Dean Casperson* to play you."

"Yes, thanks for that," Stride replied drily. "Tell me the truth. How did you really feel about your father?"

Chris took a long time to reply. Then he said, "I loathed him."

"Even before the murders?"

"Yes. He was a son of a bitch. All my life, he made sure I knew that he was *Art Leipold* and I was just a mediocre reproduction. A genetic copy made on bad carbon paper. I was never going to accomplish a fraction of what he did. He was a news anchor. I was a nobody."

"That must have hurt," Stride said.

"Oh, yeah. I've paid a lot of shrinks a lot of money over the years to deal with that. And yes, you're right, that's why I did the movie. Sure it is. I wanted to show him up once and for all. I wanted the world to see who he was. A nobody. A cruel, sadistic nobody. Now look what's happened. Art gets the last laugh. I tried to destroy him, and he destroys me instead."

Stride stood up and extended a hand. "Come on, Chris, let's go inside."

"I should go."

"You're in no condition to drive. You can sleep it off on our sofa."

He helped Chris out of the chair and opened the cottage door. The house was drafty, the way it always was. The lights in the living room were low, and he could hear Serena working in the dining room beyond the great space. He guided Chris to the red leather sofa and draped him across it. He covered him with an afghan. Chris was asleep almost immediately.

Stride joined Serena in the dining room, where the lights were brighter. He kissed her, then went to the kitchen to get another Coke, but the caffeine was losing its punch. He was tired. He took a seat next to Serena and scanned the research she'd been doing. The dining room table was covered with his files and notes from the Art Leipold murders. She'd pulled their television into the room, too, and set it up near the windows. Frozen on the screen was a still of Aimee Bowe from one of her scenes in the movie.

"Any luck?" he asked.

"No."

"This is months of work. You've only been at it a couple hours."

"I don't know how much time Aimee has," Serena said.

Stride jerked his thumb at the living room. "Chris is drunk. I put him on the sofa."

"He was waiting for me when I got here," Serena said. "I asked him to pull Aimee's takes in the movie and put them on a disk for me. I thought he went back to his hotel."

"Did he tell you? The movie is dead. They're shutting it down."

Serena didn't look surprised. "So you're not going to be a star after all?"

"I guess not."

"Well, you're a star to me," she told him, leaning over to kiss him again. "And to Cat. I was worried about you tonight, Jonny. I really thought you were going to shoot Casperson."

"I thought so, too. Did you make it to the hospital? How is she?"

"Sleeping."

"You should probably get a couple hours of sleep yourself."

"I can't," Serena said. "I have to keep at this. I have to find Aimee."

"Okay, we'll do it together." Stride stretched his arms over his head and leaned back in the chair far enough that he could see Chris Leipold in the living room. He made sure Chris was out cold before he spoke.

"To be honest, I was starting to wonder if Chris was the one who took Aimee. I was beginning to think he might have framed Art for the murders back then."

"Why would he do that?" Serena asked.

"To get revenge against Art for making him feel worthless for most of his life. Except now I can see that the movie was really his revenge. He didn't commit murder over it."

"So where does that leave us?"

"Nowhere," Stride said. He gestured at the television. "Why did you want the videos from the movie?"

"I've been going over every take Aimee did to see if there was anything that would give us a clue."

"And?"

"There's nothing that I can see," Serena said.

Stride took the remote control and started the video again. The scene looked familiar to him, and he realized that he'd been on the set while it was being filmed. Dean Casperson was rescuing Aimee Bowe from the cage where she'd been held. It was unsettling to him seeing Casperson in the movie when he'd pointed a gun at the man's head only a few hours earlier in real life. On the screen, they'd traded places. Dean Casperson was him. Casperson was the one with the gun.

He watched the dialogue between the two actors:

*"Who did this—"*
*"It doesn't matter now. We have him. He's not going to hurt anyone else."*
*"I can't move. What's wrong with me?"*
*"Give it time."*
*"I'm so cold."*
*"You'll be out of here soon."*
*"I killed it. I killed it. I killed the little girl."*

Stride stopped the playback. "I know Aimee improvises, but I still don't understand that line. 'I killed the little girl.' What does that mean? Did she say anything to you about where it came from?"

Serena smiled. "You're as bad at movie lines as you are with song lyrics."

"What are you talking about?"

"It's not 'little girl,' Jonny. It's 'little *bird.*' She's saying she killed the little bird. She's talking about the chickadee that was inside the cage with each victim. That was an awful thing. I can't believe you never told me about it."

Stride rewound the video and played it again. He listened carefully and realized that Serena was right.

*I killed the little bird.*

And again and again and again.

*I killed the little bird. I killed the little bird. I killed the little bird.*

Serena stared at him as he kept replaying the scene. "Jonny, what's wrong?"

He thought about all the possibilities, but none of them led him where he needed to go. None of them had an innocent explanation. Something wasn't right.

"How did Aimee know about that?" Stride asked.

"What do you mean?"

"How did she know about the chickadees? We never released that information publicly. We didn't want any of the families to know about it. It was too disturbing."

Serena shrugged. "Lori Fulkerson told her about it."

"No, that's impossible."

"Jonny, I was there when Lori said it," Serena insisted.

"Lori didn't know," Stride replied. "There was no chickadee in the cage with her. The others, yes, but not her. We assumed Art wasn't able to trap one during the winter."

"How can you be sure about that?"

"*Feathers.* There were no feathers in the box with her. When we dug up the bodies of the other women buried behind the cabin, we found feathers trapped in their clothes. And then when we did the autopsies and got the analysis of their stomach contents, we figured out what had happened. It was grotesque. No one needed to know about that. We made a conscious decision to keep it private out of

respect for the victims. The county attorney didn't use that information at the trial."

"Well, Lori found out somehow," Serena said. "Somebody must
have told her."

"No. Nobody told her. There are no more than ten people in Duluth
who know about the chickadees. They're cops and attorneys, and that's
all. I can give you their names. There is no way Lori Fulkerson could
have known about it."

Serena thought about it. Then she shook her head.

"There is one way, Jonny. What if Lori put those women in the
box herself?"

# 45

Gray dawn broke through the snow as Craig Dawson completed his overnight maintenance shift at the Duluth Airport. Stormy nights always made for hard, backbreaking work inside and outside the terminal building. He'd been on the job for sixteen hours straight when his boss finally told him to go home. He was ready for a hot shower, a hot breakfast, and a cold beer.

Craig trudged across the skyway that led from the terminal to the parking garage. He wore his heavy coat, unzipped, his overalls, and his dirty work boots. An empty coffee thermos dangled from his hand. Snow had crusted on the skyway windows, but below him he could see the parking lot, which was mostly empty of cars. Flights had largely been canceled throughout the previous evening, and no one was here to make drop-offs and pickups. The handful of cars in long-term parking wore deep caps of snow.

He reached the covered ramp and made his way to his white F-150 pickup truck. As he turned on the engine, Maroon 5 blared from the radio. He dug in his coat pocket for a bottle of Advil and swallowed two pills. He wiped his brow, which was damp with sweat despite the cold.

No one else was leaving at the same time he was. He drove through the garage and used his key card to exit onto the one-way access road.

He was distracted, thinking about what the driveway would look like at his farmhouse. He kept a plow attachment on his pickup at this time of year, and he knew he'd have to push through a quarter mile of eighteen-inch snow to make it to his garage.

He tapped the wheel to the music as he neared the four-way stop at Haines Road. He wasn't looking for other traffic on the lonely highway, so he had to slam on his brakes to avoid a sleek black limousine that breezed through the intersection without stopping. Craig leaned on his horn, but the limo driver didn't even slow down as he cruised toward the airport terminal.

Annoyed, Craig rolled down the window and shoved his hand into the cold air with his middle finger extended. He shouted a curse, which no one could hear. It made him feel better.

He continued eastward through the four-way stop on his way home.

But he kept thinking about the limousine.

He also remembered the business card tucked into his wallet and the name of the woman who'd given him the card. JoLynn Fields.

He'd met her at Sir Benedict's the previous Thursday, when he'd gone to listen to the weekly Celtic Jam over a pint of Boddington's. JoLynn, with her red-and-blue hair, was obviously an out-of-towner. The two of them were both around thirty, and when JoLynn had started chatting him up at the bar, he'd thought at first that she was hitting on him. Then he realized she was talking to all the men, asking questions about who they were and what they did and dropping off business cards.

She was a reporter looking for spies.

When she found out that Craig worked at the airport, she'd bought him two more drinks and let him put a hand on her leg. As she left, she told him, "If you see anybody famous coming or going or if something looks weird to you, give me a call. There's a hundred bucks in it for every solid tip and five hundred more if it turns out to be something that gets in the paper."

Craig thought an early-morning limousine was just the kind of thing that might be worth a hundred bucks.

He turned his pickup around and headed back toward the airport. At the four-way stop, he turned into the airport complex and was surprised to find the limousine stopped in the small cell phone lot just east of the terminal building. It wasn't dropping off; it was picking up. Craig pulled into the same lot and parked a few empty spaces from the black limo.

He waited. Five minutes passed. Then ten. He was about to give up and go home when he saw lights in the sky. A private jet dropped below the blanket of dark clouds and zeroed in on the main runway. As Craig watched, it touched down, slipped a little, and decelerated all the way to the fence on the other side of the grassy field in front of him.

Craig knew his planes. He recognized it as a Gulfstream G280. It was very sleek and very expensive. He grabbed a pen and notepad from his glove compartment, and while the plane was turning around on the tarmac, he jotted down the tail number.

The limousine headed out of the cell phone lot toward the terminal building. Craig watched it go, and then he followed. The limo didn't stop at the terminal doors; instead, it continued past the main building and turned into the driveway of the rental car parking lot. Craig waited outside the lot and watched with the engine running and his phone in his hands. The limo headed up to the locked gate that led onto the taxiway, and a few seconds later, the Gulfstream taxied into view on the other side of the fence. A guard met the limo and opened the gate, and the car drove up beside the private jet. The driver got out, ready to open the rear door.

The door of the plane swung outward. Metal stairs unfurled to the pavement. One passenger got out of the plane and carefully descended the steps in the light snow. Craig couldn't see who it was. He zoomed in as far as he could and snapped several shots, but he knew the images were out of focus. He didn't have time to do anything else. When the lone passenger had deplaned and climbed into the rear of the limousine, the steps went back up inside the jet and the door closed.

The limo headed for the gate.

Craig shot off in his pickup truck before anyone started asking questions. He'd text the photos to JoLynn Fields as soon as he got home.

This was definitely worth a hundred bucks.

Maybe more.

# 46

Lori Fulkerson was gone.

Serena and Stride arrived at her house, which was steps from the overpass of the I-35 freeway, in the semidarkness of the early morning. There was still a police officer parked outside to watch the house. Lori's red Yaris was parked in the yard on the matted-down snow. Even so, when they pounded on the door, the only answer was frenzied barking from Lori's terrier. They looked through the front windows and didn't see anyone inside.

"Did anything happen overnight?" Serena asked the cop. "Did you see anyone?"

"Negative," the officer replied. "There were no cars on the road during the storm. Nobody came or went. If she left the house, she left on foot, and she didn't use the front door."

"She can't have gone far," Stride said. "I'll check inside and make sure the house is empty."

Serena nodded. "I'll go around back."

She climbed down the steps to the front yard. Ahead of her, on the other side of the narrow dirt road, was a mass of trees and brush marking the fringe of Keene Creek. She couldn't see the freeway beyond the trees, but she could hear the roar of the car engines. She struggled

through the snow to the back of the house, where a wooden deck led
down from the rear door into the grass.

There were footprints in the fresh snow. Lori Fulkerson had left a
trail for them.

Serena grabbed her phone. "Jonny, I've got her. She left tracks leading toward the freeway. I'm going to follow her as far as I can."

"I'll get Guppo to send backup your way. Be careful."

"Understood."

Serena watched the footprints heading away from the house.
The plows hadn't reached the back roads, so there was no difference
between the snow in the streets and the snow in the woods. Wherever
Lori had gone, she didn't seem to be hiding her route, as if she knew
that sooner or later the police would follow her.

The footprints went from the house to the dirt road, then veered
into the trees toward a bridge leading over the frozen creek. Serena
followed, pushing through the deep snow. She crossed the bridge, and
where the woods ended, she found herself adjacent to the I-35 overpass. Matching sets of concrete pillars, like football goalposts, stretched
below the highway decks. Ahead of her was a children's playground
and a small parking lot.

She remembered the photographs in Lori Fulkerson's living room.

*Is that your father?*

*Yeah. Those were taken at the playground near the freeway when I
was six.*

The footsteps led to the climbing equipment. Serena could see that
Lori had stopped for a while and sat down at the base of the kiddy
slide. The snow had been brushed away there.

Why?

What was this all about?

Beyond the playground, the footprints continued under the overpass to Sixty-Third Avenue. The plows already had come through,
erasing any evidence of where Lori had gone next. Serena walked into
the middle of the street. The road was empty, and the morning was still
mostly dark. The freeway overpass ended at a wall built into the side
of a sharp hill. The parallel concrete beams overhead were like railroad

ties. She turned completely around, looking for more footprints, but Lori's trail seemed to stop.

Serena listened as the snow hushed every sound. Every few seconds, car lights passed on the freeway overhead with a thunder of tires. Otherwise, it was desolate here. There was no one else around. She could hear herself breathe, and she could see the steam clouding in front of her face. She felt the cold. The lingering flurries brushed like fingers against her cheek.

She put a question into her mind: *Where are you, Aimee?*

She didn't expect an answer. That wasn't how life worked.

Then, in the silent aftermath, she had the strangest experience of her life. It was as if a voice had whispered in her head. She was utterly alone, but she heard it as vividly as if Aimee had been standing next to her and murmuring in her ear.

*Save me.*

\*

The Yorkshire terrier barked madly as Stride broke into the house. It quivered on its tiny legs with a combination of terror and bravado, making little yips that sounded like an elf coughing. He squatted down, and the Yorkie continued its ferocious din until Stride extended the back of his hand. The dog gave it a quick sniff, decided he was friendly, and began licking his fingers.

"Heck of a watchdog there, buddy," Stride said.

He climbed the staircase, which was barely wider than his torso, to the second floor. A dark hallway led to the rear of the house. He was there when Serena called to let him know that she'd found footprints in the backyard, and he dialed Guppo to request backup. Then he searched the upstairs rooms. Lori Fulkerson might as well have been a ghost. If she'd ever had furniture upstairs, most of it had been moved out. The rooms were empty, just old paint, worn carpet, and occasional wires poking out of holes in the walls.

There was nothing to tell him who she really was.

According to the city and state records they'd found, Lori Fulkerson had arrived in Duluth eleven years earlier, only weeks before Kristal

Beech had been abducted. Before that, she'd been a mystery. She didn't seem to exist. She had no past, no credit, no previous address. If she'd grown up in Duluth as she claimed, she'd grown up as a completely different person.

He took the stairs back down to the ground floor. The dog followed him.

He went into the kitchen, where mail was stacked up on the table in piles. There were weeks of mail that looked as if she'd never gone through it. Everything was addressed to Lori Fulkerson, but most of it was junk. None of it was personal, from friends or family. He didn't see a computer or a smart phone anywhere in the house. There was a calendar thumbtacked to the kitchen wall, but she'd written nothing on any of the dates.

The Yorkie ran for its food bowl in the corner. Stride saw that the food bag had been tipped over, spilling its contents onto a plastic tray. The dog had enough food to last for days. Its water dish was a large bucket filled almost to the rim. Lori Fulkerson wasn't planning on coming back.

She knew the end was near.

Serena was right. There was only one explanation for Lori knowing secrets about the other three women in the cage. She'd put them there herself. She'd murdered Kristal Beech, Tanya Carter, and Sally Wills, and she'd left a trail of bread crumbs leading the police to Art Leipold. She'd manufactured the ultimate alibi by making herself the fourth victim. And then she'd waited for Stride to find her.

The question was why.

Stride went into the living room, which was a sea of old newspapers, dog toys, and CD jewel cases stacked like skyscrapers. Lori had cleared one little spot at a table where she ate her meals. She was a gatherer, someone who was afraid to let anything go or throw anything away. Those were typically people who'd had things taken away from them as a child.

He glanced at the pale yellow living room wall. Three photographs were hung there, all of them from decades earlier. They'd been taken in a children's park near the house and showed a father and daughter together. Stride took one of the photographs off the wall and held it in his hand and stared at it. He had a hard time recognizing Lori Fulkerson's face in the young girl in the picture. This ten-year-old looked innocent and happy, nothing like the angry woman she'd become later in life. She stood on the base of a kiddy slide, with her father standing next to her, his arm around her waist.

Her father.

Seeing the man beside Lori Fulkerson was a sucker punch to Stride's gut.

He knew him. He recognized him all these years later. It was a face he would never forget.

Stride understood. He saw where the stone had gone into the lake and how the ripples had spread. The daughter lost her father, the daughter grew up nursing her rage, and eventually that rage led to revenge and murder. There were plenty of people to blame. Most of all he blamed himself.

He'd let it happen. Years ago he could have stopped it, and he'd done nothing.

Stride took his phone and dialed Serena.

"I know who Lori Fulkerson is," he told her. "I know what this is about. She's Mort Greeley's daughter. Mort lived in a house on a spur road about two blocks from here. I'm betting that's where she's keeping Aimee Bowe."

"I'm already there," Serena replied, "and I'm going in."

# 47

The footprints reappeared a hundred yards down the spur road, where Lori Fulkerson had emerged from the trees.

Nothing had led Serena to search the road except the feeling that Aimee was there. She walked through the deep virgin snow, seeing no sign of Lori's trail until she reached the crest of a shallow hill. There she saw the footprints again, leading out of the woods. Lori didn't try to hide her path. The footprints led to a turnaround at the end of the dead-end road. A two-story 1950s-era house was nestled inside a grove of trees below the slope of the I-35 freeway. Two huge electrical towers guarded the house like soldiers. So did a stand of snow-white fir trees that were twice as tall as the roof.

There were no vehicles parked outside. The only sign of life was Lori's footprints, walking up to the front door.

She had a sense of Aimee's voice in her head, stronger than ever. *Save me. Hurry.*

Serena listened for the sirens of backup, but the morning was dead quiet. Even running, Jonny was five minutes away. She didn't know how much time Aimee had left, huddled in a cage in the cold. All she knew was that Aimee was inside, and so was Lori Fulkerson.

She'd already guessed the truth before Jonny called. She didn't believe in coincidences. When she reached the summit of the spur road, she'd recognized where she was. Jonny had taken her here once before, when he'd told her the story of Mort Greeley. That was how he confessed his mistakes, by going back to the places where they'd happened, as if the locations were sacred. Not even fifty yards away from Mort Greeley's old house, Serena could see another fenced gray house with two cars out front and smoke rising from a chimney against the cloudy sky. Those were the only two homes on the wooded road.

More than twenty years earlier, that house had been the home of an eight-year-old boy who'd been abducted at the Duluth zoo. Eventually, all the suspicion in the crime had landed—falsely—on the man who lived next door.

Mort Greeley.

Lori's father.

With Art Leipold leading the way, the police and media had crucified and ostracized Mort Greeley until he took his own life.

Serena closed on the house. The curtains were shut on every window. Sprays of snow blew off the peaked roof. She followed the footprints to the front door, and she slid her pistol into her hand. The butt was warm against her cold fingers. She tried the knob of the door; it was open. She pushed it ajar and shouted into the house.

"Lori Fulkerson! It's Serena Stride from the Duluth Police. We know about your father. We know everything. It's time to give up. It's time to put an end to this."

There was no answer from inside. She swung the door open with her boot, and the light from the gray day was the only light in the house. With her gun in front of her, she crept inside. The icy air couldn't be more than a few degrees above freezing. The light switches didn't work, and she took a small flashlight from her pocket, throwing a dim beam into the foyer. She listened. No one moved, and no one spoke.

"Lori Fulkerson!" she shouted again.

The house was quiet except for her footsteps on the loose panels of the hardwood floor. She made her way into the living room, shining her light into every corner. Dust floated like summer gnats in the beam of the flashlight. The room was furnished, but all the furniture was covered in white sheets. Flowered red wallpaper peeled from the ceiling in strips. The house had a musty, shut-up smell. She next went to the dining room, which looked like a room for a family of ghosts in a haunted house. The oak chairs were neatly positioned around the dining-room table, which was arranged with white linen place mats, as if dinner would be served soon. There was a bureau on the east wall, still stocked with wedding crystal and china.

In here, time had stood still. In here, Mort Greeley had never been accused, never lost his family and his job, and never shot himself in an upstairs bedroom.

The deeper she went into the house, the darker it got. The kitchen was empty. So was the main-floor bedroom. Serena kept searching, making her way into a long hallway. Her flashlight lit up a wooden floor, beige-painted walls, and a back staircase leading to the second story. She headed that way, swinging the light back and forth. A mouse scurried.

At the base of the stairs, she pointed the light upward.

It landed on the face of Lori Fulkerson.

Lori's face was pale and expressionless in the glow of the flashlight. Her curly hair looked flat. She sat on the top step in a sweatshirt and khakis. Her arms were at her sides, and her right hand was curled tightly around a gun. Serena swung her own pistol to point at Lori's chest.

"Place your weapon on the step, Lori, and then put your hands on top of your head."

Lori paid no attention to her.

"I used to live here," she said.

"Lori, I need you to put the gun down right now."

"It's been like this for years. Abandoned. My mother owned it, but she couldn't sell it. No one wanted it."

"The *gun*, Lori. Put it on the step."

"Aimee's up here," Lori said, gesturing behind her. "I know that's what you want. She's in the box."

"Lori, it's time to end this," Serena told her. "Too many people died for nothing. Including your father. Put down the gun. Let me come up there and help Aimee."

"I said too much," Lori went on, as if Serena hadn't even spoken. "I heard the things she was saying on camera. I knew everyone would realize what I'd done. I knew the truth would come out. But it was more than that. It was like she already *knew*. I could feel her inside my head. She could see everything I remembered. I needed to stop her, to shut her out."

"It's over, Lori."

"I know. Secrets always come out eventually, don't they? You can't run away from them forever. But I can still feel her watching me. It's driving me crazy. I need to get her out of my head."

Serena heard noise behind her as someone else entered the house. Then a voice shouted her name. It was Jonny.

"Lori's armed," she called back to him. "Stay back; don't come any closer."

But he didn't listen. He came even faster. She heard footsteps, and a few seconds later he was there with her in the hallway. He was directly at her side, the two of them shoulder to shoulder. Above them, Lori tensed at the top of the stairs, with two flashlights trained on her now. Her eyes glistened with tears and lonely fury.

*"Save me, Jonathan Stride,"* she whispered with bitter irony.

Serena kept her eyes on the gun. If it moved, she was ready to fire.

"Lori, I know you blame me for what happened to your father," Jonny told her. "That's okay. I was a young cop, but I should have done more to help Mort. I knew what Art and my boss were doing was wrong. I thought your father was guilty—I was convinced he took that boy at the zoo—but he didn't deserve to be lynched the way he was. It ruined his life, and it was all a terrible mistake. I'm sorry. I really am."

"My mother took me away from him," Lori murmured. "She took me away from my father and didn't even leave a note. She left him alone. I found out later he sent me letters, but I never got to see them. I wrote him letters, but she never mailed them. My father thought I hated him, like everyone else. He thought I'd abandoned him. My bedroom was upstairs, you know. Just down the hallway. That's where he shot himself. In *my* bedroom."

Jonny nodded. "I know."

"All he did was go to work that day," Lori went on. "He went to the zoo. He never even saw that boy. And you made everyone in the city think he was guilty. That he was a murderer and a pedophile."

Jonny spoke softly, trying to reach her. "You hate me. I understand that. I deserve what you feel toward me. But those women didn't do anything to you or your father. Aimee didn't do anything. She's innocent."

Lori didn't seem to hear him. She glanced down the hallway, as if she could see inside the box that was down there and see all the women she'd imprisoned in the past.

"I went to work with my father at the zoo sometimes," Lori recalled. "He had to clean out the cages for the animals. I kept thinking how horrible it was to be trapped like that. I thought there was nothing you could do to anyone that was worse than that. To put them in a cage. I remember there was this little bird that used to hang out with one of the tigers. It flew around in the cage for days. It would land on the tiger's head, like they were friends. My dad took me to see it, and I thought it was so cute. And then one day, as I was watching, the tiger simply killed the bird with one swipe of its paw and ate it. I couldn't stop crying. But my dad told me that's just what tigers do."

"Lori," Serena murmured. "Please stop this. You don't have to hurt anyone else."

"So you see, *Jonathan Stride*," Lori continued, her voice rising into a shout, "it doesn't matter whether those women were innocent. *That's just what tigers do.* I came back to Duluth to destroy the people who destroyed my father. Art Leipold. And you. I wanted Art to know just what it felt like to be wrongly accused, to be set up for something you didn't do, to have everyone turn on you, to be hated by every person who looks at you. I wanted him to suffer the way my father did. And I wanted you to be the one to do it to him. I wanted you to feel absolutely helpless, like I did. To know that people died and you couldn't stop it. I wanted you to carry that with you for the rest of your life."

"I do."

"I didn't want you to rescue me in the box," Lori said. "I was supposed to die, too. That was supposed to be the end. I was supposed to be with my father when it was all over."

The gun quivered in Lori's grip. She looked down the hallway again toward the bedroom and the cage. All Serena could see in the shadows was one eye, fierce and red, like the eye of a monster.

"No one else needs to die, Lori," Serena told her. "Not Aimee. Not you. Put down the gun. Put your hands on your head and let me come upstairs."

Instead, Lori stood up.

*"Stop stop stop!"* they both shouted at her, their voices overlapping.

"I can still feel her," Lori said. "She's still inside my head. I have to get her *out.*"

In one sudden motion, Lori spun away and disappeared into the darkness. They heard footsteps overhead and the slamming of a door. Serena didn't have time to fire. She thundered up the stairs two at a time, with Jonny immediately behind her. There was no light on the second story, and the flashlight beam showed a maze of closed doors. Then, from the end of the upstairs hallway, came an explosion.

A gunshot.

"Aimee!" Serena shouted.

A second shot followed the first. Then a third.

Serena sprinted for the end of the hallway and slammed through the closed door into the gloom of a small child's bedroom. The beam of her flashlight bounced crazily. All she caught were horrible, disconnected images of cartoon animals on the old wallpaper, colored butterflies hanging on ribbons from the ceiling, and an eight-foot by eight-foot padded cage taking up most of the bedroom floor. Lori Fulkerson fired her gun over and over into the soundproof foam, kicking up a cloud of synthetic white snow.

Serena jumped across the bedroom and hit her from behind, crushing the woman's body against the metal bars of the cage. The gun fell. Serena knocked it away with her heel. Behind her, she was aware of Jonny scooping it up. She threw Lori bodily to the ground and landed on top of her with her knee in the small of her back, and as Lori struggled, Serena grabbed her handcuffs and pinned her wrist in the metal grips.

There were other noises in the house now. More shouts. The thunder of heavy footfalls.

She heard Jonny shouting. "All clear, all clear, all clear!"

*"The key!"* Serena screamed at Lori Fulkerson. She grabbed Lori's shoulder and shoved her over onto her back and bellowed into her face. *"Where's the key?"*

The pause was only a second, but it felt like forever. Then Lori murmured, as if in surrender, "My pocket."

Serena squeezed her hand inside the right front pocket of Lori's pants until her fingers closed around a tiny piece of metal. She pulled it out and crawled to the cage, where she fumbled in the darkness, trying to fit the key into the lock that held the door in place. She tried it again and again, dropped the key, and picked it up. She cursed loudly. Then Jonny was behind her with a firm hand on her shoulder, shining a flashlight onto the lock.

She picked up the key. She put it in the lock.

She opened the box.

The light inside showed Aimee Bowe on her back on the straw floor of the cage. Serena gasped in horror. Blood was everywhere. One of the bullets had hit her thigh. Another had gone through her shoulder. Another had hit her neck. Her breathing was ragged. Serena bent over her, and Aimee's skin was bone white and frigid to the touch. Her eyes were closed.

She heard Jonny calling for an ambulance.

"Hang on, you'll be fine," Serena murmured. She took off her coat and draped it over Aimee's body, trying to keep her warm. "Help's on the way."

Aimee's eyes opened and tried to focus. The pain caught up with her and overwhelmed the numbness. Her lips murmured something, but Serena couldn't hear it. She bent down near Aimee's mouth and listened to what she was saying.

"I felt you coming," Aimee said.

Serena smiled and held her hand. She stayed there, holding on, as Stride and Guppo applied pressure to Aimee's wounds and tried to stop the bleeding. She felt too much time ticking away, too much blood pooling around them and soaking her clothes. The box was wet and cold and awful and evil.

And then, cutting through all of that, she heard a tiny flutter of wings and a greeting from the darkness of the cage.

*Hey there.*

Like a good angel, a chickadee landed on the bars next to Aimee's face and began to sing.

# 48

"You don't have to drive me all this way," Cab said to Maggie. "I can afford a cab, you know. Catch-a-Cab Bolton, that's me."

Maggie shrugged behind the wheel of her Avalanche. It was late afternoon, and the sun already had set. They were on I-35 heading south out of Duluth toward the Minneapolis airport. Cab's flight to Fort Myers was in four hours. She glanced in her rearview mirror at the highway behind her, which she shared with only one other vehicle. The storm had loosened its grip, but the roads were quiet.

"Admit it," she said. "You're afraid of my driving."

"Terrified."

"Well, buckle up, buttercup," she replied with a grin.

Maggie passed the Grand Avenue exit. Not long afterward, she could see Mort Greeley's house in the valley on the left side of the freeway. There were still police cars outside. She continued up the hill. Spirit Mountain loomed ahead of them; it was perfect skiing weather. Cab stared through the windows, and neither of them knew what to say. They had two hours alone in the car together, but she figured they would need all of it to figure out what came next between them. That was mostly because she was certain they would avoid the subject altogether until she was dropping him off at the curb at Terminal 1. Neither she nor Cab was an expert at emotions.

="2"

"So your mother released a statement?" Maggie asked.

"Yes, Tarla said she regretted not having come forward sooner to tell everyone about Dean Casperson. She wished she would have saved other women the trauma she'd gone through."

"Except it wouldn't have done that," Maggie said. "Dean would have destroyed her career and gone on abusing other women just the way he did."

"You're right, but I was pleased to see Tarla say it."

Maggie tried to keep the truck inside the lane, but the white line went in and out of view as she steered with one hand and snaked her other hand onto Cab's knee. She glanced in the rearview mirror again.

"I really am sorry about Peach," she told him.

"Thanks."

"She didn't suffer. That's something."

"I know."

They'd found the scene of the crime in the daylight. Guppo had led the search behind the Hermantown apartments. They'd located a spruce tree thirty feet inside the dense woods that bore the red-black sheen of frozen blood. That was where John Doe had killed her.

"You'll probably have to come back here for the trial," Maggie said.

"Assuming there is one. I think Jack will make a deal."

"Maybe so."

That took them through another mile. They were nearly to the exit for the town of Proctor.

"Have you ever thought about moving?" Cab asked with a suddenness that shocked her. She hadn't expected him to be so blunt.

"What do you mean?"

"To Florida. I need another investigator. Obviously, you're very good at what you do, and it goes without saying that you and I have chemistry."

"Leave Duluth? I've never even thought about it."

"Maybe you should."

Maggie did.

She thought about her life in Duluth, which had occupied all of her memories for twenty years. She thought about Stride, Guppo, and

Serena. And about Stride again. She thought about the heat of Florida and the Gulf waters and being in bed with Cab. She thought about all of that in five seconds, and then she said, "No. Sorry."

"I figured you'd say that," Cab told her, "but it never hurts to ask."

"Duluth is my home. Florida's a nice place to visit, though. I like the amenities down there."

"You should come back and see it sometime," Cab said. "Maybe Troy and the girls would enjoy a vacation there. Magic Kingdom. Universal. Gatorland."

Maggie shot him a sideways look. He was teasing her, but he was right. She had unfinished business with Troy. And she was smart enough to know that Cab had unfinished business of his own. What they'd shared was simply the right interlude at the right time for both of them.

"So do you have someone picking you up at the airport tonight?" she asked. "Since you don't have your new Corvette yet."

Cab waited a beat to reply. "Lala's meeting me, actually."

"Ah. Mosquito. She's taking you home?"

"Yes. She wants an update on everything that happened here."

"I bet she does," Maggie said.

"It's not romantic."

"No, of course not."

She winked at Cab because she didn't believe him. Then she glanced in the rearview mirror again.

At first, she'd assumed she was mistaken, but she wasn't. She made a snap decision. The exit for Highway 2 loomed in front of her, and she did a quick lane change to take the exit. Her eyes stayed on the mirror. Almost immediately, she turned left onto the frontage road. Then she made another right turn on a winding trail that took them up the hill.

"Where are we going?" Cab asked with a puzzled look.

"There's a rest stop up here."

"Do you need to rest?"

Maggie looked for the headlights. They were still behind her, right where they'd been since they'd left the city. As they climbed toward the Thompson Hill Information Center, the headlights climbed, too.

It was a black SUV, but the windshield was tinted, and she couldn't see inside.

"Actually, I think we're being followed," Maggie said.

*

Stride was at a stoplight on Superior Street downtown when his phone rang. The number was unfamiliar, and the area code wasn't local. He'd been getting media calls all day. He was tempted to ignore it, but he answered it anyway.

"This is Stride," he said.

"Lieutenant, this is JoLynn Fields with the *National Gazette*." The woman seemed to anticipate his reaction, and she rushed on before he could say anything. "I realize I'm not exactly flavor of the month for you right now."

"If you're looking for another interview, Ms. Fields, you're at the back of the line."

"Well, maybe I can change your mind."

"I don't think so," Stride replied.

"I'm not coming to you empty-handed, Lieutenant. I'm talking about a quid pro quo. Hear me out."

Stride hesitated, letting the dead air stretch out on the call. He headed past the Fond-du-Luth Casino on his right. The turn toward Canal Park and the Point was two blocks away.

"Go on," he said.

"I find spies wherever I go," JoLynn told him. "It's part of how I get the information I need. One of my spies works at the Duluth Airport. He was getting off work this morning and noticed something unusual. A limo did a pickup at a private jet on the tarmac."

"We've had a lot of private jets coming into town today," Stride said.

"Yes, but my spy sent me photos. The woman getting off the plane was Mo Casperson."

The light at Lake Avenue turned green, but Stride stopped dead and waved the traffic around him. "You're telling me that Mo is in Duluth?"

"That's right. I've spent most of the day trying to confirm it and find out where she is."

"And what did you find?"

"She got a limo to the Sheraton downtown, where she rented a suite and then arranged for a black Lexus LX. She's been holed up at the hotel most of the day, but she just left."

"Headed where?" Stride asked.

"South on 35. That's all I know. So how about that interview?"

"I'll get back to you."

Stride hung up as his phone buzzed. It was an incoming text from Maggie. *Thompson Hill. 911.*

He jammed down the accelerator on his Expedition, turned left, and shot onto the I-35 southbound ramp at high speed.

*

Maggie drove to the far end of the Thompson Hill parking lot and spun the Avalanche around so that her headlights faced the entry road. The rest stop was at the top of the hill. The dark Duluth sky stretched overhead, and the view overlooked the city and the lake below them. She saw two other cars parked near the tourist information building, but there were no people nearby.

The Lexus SUV followed them slowly into the parking lot. It parked oddly far away on the other side of the lot. The two vehicles seemed to stare at each other through the gleam of their headlights. Maggie and Cab waited inside the Avalanche to see what would happen next.

The door of the Lexus opened, and a woman got out.

"Mo Casperson," Cab said.

Mo wore a sleek black leather overcoat that hugged her tall, slim body down to her ankles. Her hands were buried in the coat pockets. Her eyes were hidden behind sunglasses even in the gloom of dusk. Her golden hair was long and loose, flying in the hilltop wind. She walked in high heels in front of the Lexus and stood and stared at them from between the headlights.

Maggie tapped out a quick message to Stride.

Then she and Cab got out of the Avalanche. Maggie already had her pistol in her hand, and she leveled it at Mo at the end of her arms. The sight of the gun didn't seem to bother Mo at all. She watched them take slow, careful steps in her direction, but they were separated by most of the parking lot. Maggie and Cab slowly converged from both sides of the Avalanche.

"Hello, Cab," Mo called.

They both stopped where they were. Maggie didn't lower her gun.

"I'm surprised to see you here, Mo," Cab replied. "I figured you'd be hiding out on an island somewhere."

"I never hide."

"No? Well, maybe you don't appreciate the situation you and Dean are in."

"I appreciate it very well. Believe me. You must be proud of yourself. You and Tarla finally got what you wanted. You took down a great man."

Cab shook his head. "He's a serial rapist. You're the murderer who's enabled him all these years. Truly, I don't how you do it. I don't know how you sit on your patio in Captiva and justify it to yourself."

"Dean made the world a better place," Mo shot back. "Everything worth doing has a price."

Maggie still had her gun trained on Mo, who hadn't moved at all from her position in front of the Lexus. "Mrs. Casperson, take your hands out of your pockets very slowly. I want to see your hands right now."

Mo made no effort to comply. She didn't even look at Maggie, as if there were no more than the two of them in the parking lot. Her gaze was trained on Cab. He was the one she wanted.

"Did you think there would be no consequences, Cab?" Mo called. "Did you think I would go down without a fight?"

"*Hands,*" Maggie repeated, but Mo ignored her.

"You're the one facing consequences," Cab said. "It's called jail."

Maggie started walking again, step by step, across the parking lot. She felt the breeze blowing off the hill onto her face, and an American flag snapped and clanged on its pole near the information building. The standoff between them crackled with danger. She tried to guess the plan. The game. She didn't know what it was, but she knew something was about to happen.

"Oh, Cab," Mo retorted with a nasty smile. "So naive. You forget that I'm much, much richer than you and Tarla."

"Meaning what?"

"Meaning I have the resources to do *this*."

Maggie's Avalanche exploded.

A cloud of hot flame billowed out of the truck, and shattered glass sprayed around them like bullets. The concussion wave lifted Maggie off the ground and threw her across the parking lot, where her body slammed into the pavement and rolled. Her gun bounced away. She was facedown. Her ears heard nothing, only silence. She pushed herself onto her elbows and watched red rain drip to the ground from her hair. It was blood. She got to her knees, but the world spun like a roulette wheel. The heat of the fire burned her cheek, and the black asphalt sparkled with diamonds.

She shouted Cab's name, but she couldn't hear her own voice.

Maggie crawled on the ground. The glass cut her hands. She shook her head to clear her brain. Cab was thirty feet away, lying on his back, with his arms and legs spread into an X. She shouted his name again, and she heard herself like an echo on the other side of a wide canyon. He didn't answer. He didn't move.

Untouched by the blast, Mo Casperson marched calmly across the parking lot. Her heels crunched on broken glass. She passed within a few feet of Maggie, and Maggie lurched upward to grab her but fell back as the world spun. Mo kicked Maggie's gun away and headed straight for Cab. Her gloved hands emerged from her pockets. In one hand, she held a phone; in the other, she clutched a small revolver with a pink grip. She stood over Cab on the ground and dialed the phone.

Maggie was too far away to do a thing. She heard Mo speaking, and it sounded no louder than a whisper in her head.

"Tarla?" Mo said into the phone. "My dear, it's Mo calling. Listen carefully. I wanted to congratulate you on destroying me and Dean. Job well done. I hope you'll decide it was worth it, because the next sound you hear will be me putting a bullet into your son's brain."

*

Stride heard the explosion of the car bomb like a boom of thunder on the hillside above him. Black smoke rose in a thick column above the trees. He floored the accelerator, and his truck fishtailed as he sped up the Thompson Hill access road, which curved like the body of a snake.

He wheeled into the parking lot and jammed the brakes. With his gun in his hand, he dived out of the driver's door and ran. His eyes took in the flaming hulk of Maggie's yellow Avalanche turning black, its hood bent in half, its windows open shells with a few fragments of frosted glass. The melted tires gave off a burned rubber smell. The smoke in his face made him squint.

There were three people in the parking lot in front of him.

Maggie crawled, screaming Cab's name. Cab lay motionless on his back, his face and hands streaked with blood. Mo Casperson had her slim arm outstretched with the barrel of a revolver pointed at Cab's head.

"Freeze!" Stride shouted across the parking lot.

He stopped dead, raising his pistol and aiming it at the dead center of Mo's back. He steadied his wrist with his other hand. There was no more than twenty feet between them. "Put the gun down!"

Mo's arm was steady and straight. The hammer of her gun was cocked and ready, her finger on the trigger. Her head swiveled, and her honey hair swished. She stared at Stride with the disinterest of an A-lister bumping into an extra on the set.

"Too late, Lieutenant," she said.

"Mo, put the gun down; you're under arrest!"

"No, I don't think so," she replied.

She focused on Cab again. She was going to fire, so he fired first.

Stride pulled the trigger once, twice, three times, four times, five times, six times. Every bullet hit Mo Casperson. She jerked with each shot; her arm flew up; her finger yanked back and sent a wild shot into the trees. Her knees sagged beneath her, and she slid straight down like a building imploding. She sank into a pile of black leather and golden hair next to Cab on the ground, her gun spilling from her open fingers.

He ran to them and scooped up Mo's gun and checked on Cab. The blond detective was unconscious, but his pulse was strong. Maggie, wobbling, staggered his way. He grabbed his phone to call for an ambulance, but he already could hear sirens below them on the southbound freeway.

Maggie steadied herself by taking hold of Stride's arm.

"You should sit down," he told her.

"I'm all right. How's Cab?"

"He's alive."

She watched her Avalanche burn to a crisp. "I can't believe that bitch blew up my truck."

"Yeah."

He stared down at Mo Casperson, whose eyes were wide open and fixed. Her blood made a lake under her body. She was already dead, but she stared back at him, as arrogant and condescending as ever. In his decades as a cop, he'd never taken a human life until that moment. The quality of the life didn't matter. Neither did the fact that she'd given him no choice. He'd been the one to kill her. He'd been the one to pull the trigger.

Stride didn't have to bother memorizing her face. She was never going to go away. Mo's eyes would be in his dreams for years to come.

# 49

Cab opened his eyes. He was certain he was either dreaming or hallucinating.

"There you are, darling!" Tarla Bolton announced from the other side of the hospital room. "I've been here watching you sleep. I can't tell you how relieved I am that you're all right."

"You and me both," Cab replied. "What are you doing here, Mother?"

Tarla folded her arms across her chest with a look of annoyance. She was wearing skinny jeans and a red Duluth sweatshirt that was several sizes too large for her. Her long blond hair was pulled back and pinned behind her head, but several strands had made a break for freedom and spilled down her face. She looked perfect, as she always did.

"What, you didn't think I would hop on a plane immediately? I will be with you night and day until you are one hundred percent. Plan on my being your constant companion."

"Constant companion?" Cab asked. "Lucky me."

"Yes, don't worry; I have everything planned. The doctors say you should be out of here in another day or two, and then we can fly back to Florida together. I've already made arrangements to move some of my things into your house in Naples."

"Into *my* house?"

Now he really hoped he was dreaming.

"Well, you're not going to stay alone yet, obviously. I have everything I need to be with you for a month. After that, we'll just take things as they come. Wawa offered to stay with you instead, but I told her I had everything under control."

"Lala wanted to stay with me?" Cab asked.

He felt as if all he could do was repeat Tarla's words with an increasing sense of disbelief.

"Yes, she's worried sick about you. It's sweet. I had a hard time convincing her that she didn't need to come up here with me to drag you back to Florida. Winter is a terrible thing. How can people live in this icebox? It's like the whole world is in hibernation. How I miss the palm trees."

Cab sighed and studied the gray sky outside the hospital window. "You know, Mother, I feel guilty imposing on your time. If Lala's willing to stay with me, that's probably best. We have kind of a rhythm together."

Tarla shook her head. She sat down beside the bed and grabbed a Starbucks Frappuccino from the metal tray where his hospital lunch sat untouched. She sucked on the drink through a straw. "Nonsense. I've cleared my calendar for you. Besides, all you and Wawa ever do is argue. That's the last thing you need right now."

"Because you and I never argue?" Cab asked.

"You argue, darling. I rise above it."

Cab looked for the morphine drip, but the nurses had removed it. He had a headache, but he couldn't blame it entirely on the concussion now that Tarla was here. He'd broken his left wrist in the fall after the explosion, and his back was a mass of cuts and bruises. Even so, he was impatient to get out and go home.

Tarla was right about one thing. He didn't belong in Duluth.

"Where's Maggie?" he asked.

"Your little China doll? I told her to go home and get some rest, since I have the situation handled. I promised her I would not leave your side. This is a very nice hospital, by the way. The doctors and nurses all love me. I've signed dozens of autographs."

"Well, they're probably mistaking you for Naomi Watts," Cab said.

Tarla wagged her finger at him. "Wicked, wicked, wicked. I forgive you, but only because you're injured."

"And tired," Cab added pointedly.

"Yes, of course; more sleep is what you need. Never fear, I will be right here when you wake up again."

"I have no doubt."

Cab closed his eyes. It took no time for him to fall sleep again. In his dreams, he was where he usually was, alone on the beach, watching the surf come and go in Naples. The waves were hypnotic. That went on for what felt like forever, but at some point Mo Casperson rose out of the water in front of him like a horrible mermaid. She pointed her gun at his head and said, "Bang."

He started awake from that dream and had no idea what time it was, but he noticed that daylight had given way to night outside the window. Tarla was gone, at least for the moment. Maggie had taken her place in the chair by the bed, and she was digging into a bag for McDonald's French fries.

"Hey," she said. "How are you feeling?"

"Sliced and diced."

"Well, you are still the most handsome car bomb survivor I've ever seen."

"Thank you."

"Your mother said to assure you she would be back momentarily."

"What a relief," Cab replied.

"I hear she's going to be staying with you in Naples," Maggie added with a snicker.

"So it seems."

"She says Lala volunteered, too. You can't go anywhere without attractive women around, can you?"

"That's true. Present company included."

"Very smooth," Maggie replied. She shoved a French fry in his mouth, and he swallowed it.

"How are *you*?" Cab asked.

"Indestructible. Which is more than can be said for my Avalanche. My insurance agent couldn't believe it when I called him. I'm not exactly his favorite customer to begin with."

"Did you find out who made the bomb?"

"We're still following the trail. Mo made several calls to anonymous numbers. Security cams in my parking garage caught a van with stolen Wisconsin plates coming in overnight. That was probably when they planted it."

"I haven't had a chance to thank Stride for saving my life," Cab said.

"Well, don't," she said with a grin. "It'll just feed his ego. By the way, Tarla met Stride and pronounced him 'tasty.'"

Cab shook his head. "That's my mother."

They were quiet for a while, sitting in the hospital room. Outside, it was snowing again, with the flakes landing and melting against the glass. He was beginning to wonder if it ever stopped snowing up here and if winter ever ended.

"My offer still stands," he said. "About Florida. Come with me."

"I'm flattered, but no. I'm a Minnesota girl. Besides, it looks like Lala wants back in your life."

"She and I are always complicated. What about you? Did you tell Troy about the bomb?"

"Yes, and he was very sweet and very concerned. Actually, I had dinner with him and the girls last night. They've been bugging him about getting a dog for months, so I thought they might like to meet Lori Fulkerson's Yorkshire terrier. He needs a new home. It was love at first sight."

"Dinner," Cab said. "That sounds promising."

"It's a start. I'm still not the marrying kind, but Troy says he's okay with that for now."

They heard a chorus of laughter from the hallway outside Cab's room. He looked through the doorway to see Tarla taking a selfie with two of the nurses. "She's back," he said.

"I guess that's my cue," Maggie replied.

She stood up from the chair and looked down at him. They didn't know what to say to each other. He'd always found that good-byes were more awkward when you knew what someone looked like naked.

"Better go get yourself a new Avalanche," he said.

"Better go get yourself a new Corvette."

"I'm not very good with endings. Will I see you again?"

"Oh, I'm pretty hard to get rid of," Maggie assured him. "You never know where I'll turn up."

She bent down over the bed and gave Cab a kiss that smelled of perfume and French fries. It was soft and perfect and lasted a long time. She wiped her mouth with a little bit of embarrassment and then wiggled her fingers at him as she left the room.

*

"Was that *Tarla Bolton*?" Aimee Bowe asked Serena, sounding starstruck. She pushed herself up with a painful effort and tried to see into the hospital corridor.

"Yes, that's her," Serena replied. "Her son is a detective. He was helping us make the case against Dean Casperson."

"I'd love to meet her. She was one of my role models when I was getting started."

"I'm sure that can be arranged," Serena said. "I don't think Tarla is much of a wallflower."

Aimee smiled from the bed, but just the effort of raising herself up had weakened her. The doctors were optimistic about her recovery, but she had a long way to go. She wasn't leaving Duluth anytime soon. She'd undergone two surgeries since they'd rescued her from the cage, and the combination of bullet wounds and hypothermia had left her fragile. Serena also was concerned about emotional damage.

"Lori Fulkerson pled guilty to the assault on you," Serena told her. "She gave a full confession about the earlier murders, too. She'll be behind bars for the rest of her life."

The news didn't seem to give Aimee any comfort. "It sounds strange, but I feel a little sorry for her. No matter what she did."

"A lot of us have bad childhoods," Serena replied. "At some point, you have to decide for yourself who you really are. If you let it make you evil, that's on you."

Aimee nodded. "What about Dean?"

"The prosecutors say if he ever gets out of prison, he'll be an old man. He won't have a dime left from all the lawsuits. I hope you don't feel sorry for *him*."

"No."

Serena nodded. "Me neither."

"The only thing I wish about Dean is that I'd said something when I had the chance. I let him get away with it."

"You weren't the only one. He and Mo intimidated a lot of victims. And they killed others."

Aimee took Serena's hand in a weak grip. "I've only known you a short time, but you've saved my life twice. Thank you."

"I'm relieved you're okay."

"Can I ask you something? You felt me calling to you when I was in the box, didn't you?"

Serena found herself at a loss for words. She didn't know how to explain what she'd felt as she hunted for Aimee.

"It's okay to admit it even if you don't understand it," Aimee went on. "I told you, I don't understand how it works myself. I just knew if there was one person who could rescue me, it was you. So I tried to reach out to you."

"I wish I could say I believe in those things," Serena replied, "but I'm still not sure. It doesn't matter. What matters is that we found you."

She checked her watch and saw that it was getting late.

"I have to meet Stride," she told Aimee. "I'll be back tomorrow."

"Of course."

"I'll send Tarla your way," she added.

"Thanks."

Serena went to the hospital room door, but then she turned back. She returned to the bed and said, "I do have one question, Aimee."

"Sure."

"You told me that you were sure Art Leipold wasn't guilty."

"That's what I felt," Aimee said.

"Did you also know about Lori Fulkerson?"

"What do you mean?"

"Lori kept saying she could feel you inside her head. She kept talking about you being able to see what she'd done. Like you could look inside her and know she was guilty. I was wondering if that was true. Did you get a bad feeling from Lori Fulkerson even before she abducted you?"

"You don't believe that, Serena. That's not who you are. So why ask?"

"Lori believed it," Serena said. "So I was curious."

Aimee looked away at the darkness and shook her head. A smile played across her lips and then went away. "Well, the irony is, whatever Lori felt was all in her own head. She made that happen, not me. Maybe her guilt finally caught up with her, because I didn't suspect a thing. I didn't feel anything from Lori Fulkerson at all."

# 50

Stride sat on the green bench at the end of the Point.

The Christmas lights decorating the homes in the town of Superior still glittered on the other side of the frozen harbor. Fishing shanties and trucks dotted the ice, and music from someone's radio floated across the bay. He didn't notice the cold or the whip of the wind that sent flurries through the night air. He had his arm around Cat, who huddled next to him with her legs pulled up on the bench. Her chin was balanced on her knees.

Days had gone by since the shooting, but Mo Casperson's eyes still followed him. When he slept, he saw her. When he was awake, he remembered. Sometimes a twitch rippled through his muscles as he felt himself pulling the trigger again and again. He could still see each bullet strike her body like a movie scene replaying in his head.

"Was it awful?" Cat murmured as if she could read his mind.

He didn't answer immediately. Then he said, "It wasn't what I expected."

"How so?"

"It was easier."

"And you don't like that?"

He shook his head. "No. I don't like that."

Cat leaned her head against his shoulder. "Would it have been easy to kill Dean Casperson?"

"If he'd hurt you? Yes."

"I don't regret what I did," Cat told him firmly.

"I know."

"Do you think I was wrong?" she asked.

"I'll always think it's wrong if something puts you in jeopardy. That's just the way it is."

Cat had a copy of the new *People* magazine in her hands. She held it up, which she'd done a thousand times already. The night made it hard to see, but they could both make out her face next to Dean Casperson's on the cover. She was famous, just as he'd feared. The media had camped outside their cottage all week. Her story was everywhere. For now, she was a hero in the press, but for every hero, there eventually was a backlash. The reality of all the attention was beginning to sink into her head and scare her.

"This is who I'm going to be forever, isn't it?" she asked. "I'm always going to be the girl who took down Dean Casperson. Look at the headline: 'The Teenager Who Exposed Hollywood's Dirtiest Secret.' When I die, that's the only thing they'll say about me."

He kissed the top of her head. "That's so not true, Catalina."

"Come on. You know it is."

"What I know is that you're seventeen years old. You have your life ahead of you, and you can do whatever you want with it. By the time you're done, nobody will remember Dean Casperson, but I think they'll all remember Cat Mateo."

She shoved him playfully. "You don't believe that."

"Yes, I absolutely do."

"I'm nobody special," Cat said.

Nobody special.

Stride wanted to laugh at the very idea of it. He thought about this girl and the amount of death she'd seen in her life and the amount of heartache she'd experienced since she was a child. He thought about a girl who would have the courage to let herself go into a room with a predator and turn on a camera and put her life and her body at risk.

"Sometimes it takes a while to recognize special," Stride told her. "Especially in yourself."

She didn't say anything for a long, long time. When he felt a quiver in her shoulders, he realized she was crying silently. He knew it was partly out of love, partly out of terror and relief catching up with her. He simply held her close and let her get lost in her tears. She didn't stop until they heard the rumble of a car engine and saw Serena's Mustang plow through the snow and park beside Stride's Expedition.

"I figured I'd find you two here," Serena called to them.

She got out and joined them on the bench. Cat wiped her face and put on a smile, and Serena put her arm around Cat just as Stride had. The three of them sat on the green bench together in spite of the cold, in spite of the snow. Peaceful minutes ticked by, and none of them gave a thought to getting up and going home.

They were a family.

Stride didn't think about the future. He was done with that. And he was done with the past, too. This month had been a reminder of his mistakes, but he couldn't change them. He couldn't go back and undo what had happened to Mort Greeley. He couldn't save Art Leipold. He couldn't rescue the victims of Lori Fulkerson. Every journey had its failures and setbacks, and all he could do was try harder and do better at whatever came next.

The fact was, life had given him more chances at happiness than he deserved. If he'd taken a last breath at that moment, he would have been at peace with his regrets, because his regrets had led him here. He had a wife again and a teenage daughter, two things he never would have believed possible. He decided he wouldn't change a day of his past or correct his mistakes even if he could.

They were part of him. They were who he was.

They were what made him Jonathan Stride.

# FROM THE AUTHOR

Thanks for reading the latest Jonathan Stride novel. (Or is it a Cab Bolton novel? You'll have to decide for yourself!) If you like this book, be sure to check out all my other thrillers, too.

You can write to me with your feedback at brian@bfreemanbooks .com. I love to get e-mails from readers around the world, and yes, I reply personally. Visit my website at www.bfreemanbooks.com to join my mailing list, get book club discussion questions, and find out more about me and my books.

You can "like" my official fan page on Facebook at www.facebook .com/bfreemanfans or follow me on Twitter or Instagram by using the handle @bfreemanbooks. For a look at the fun side of the author's life, you can also "like" my wife, Marcia's, Facebook page at www.facebook .com/theauthorswife.

Finally, if you enjoy my books, please post your reviews online at sites like Goodreads, Amazon, BN.com, and other sites for book lovers—and spread the word to your reader friends. Thanks!

# ABOUT THE TYPE

Typeset in Adobe Garamond at 11.5/15 pt.

Adobe Garamond is named for the famed sixteenth-century French printer Claude Garamond. Robert Slimbach created this serif face for Adobe based on Garamond's designs, as well as the designs of Garamond's assistant, Robert Granjon.

Typeset by Scribe Inc., Philadelphia, Pennsylvania.